DAVID MARCUS

David Marcus was born in Cork, read Law at University College, Cork, and King's Inns, Dublin, and was called to the Irish Bar in 1945. The following year he founded *Irish Writing*. In 1954, shortly after the publication of his first novel, TO NEXT YEAR IN JERUSALEM, he went to live in London, where he spent the next thirteen years. He then returned to Ireland and joined *The Irish Press*, where he was Literary Editor from 1968 to 1986 and in which he founded 'New Irish Writing', a weekly page of short stories and poetry which became a national institution.

David Marcus has had many stories and poems published in Ireland, Britain and the USA. He has translated the 1,000 line, eighteenth-century Gaelic poem *The Midnight Court*, edited several anthologies of Irish stories including STATE OF THE ART, and has published two further novels and a collection of his own short stories.

sceptre

*Also edited by David Marcus
and available from Sceptre Books:*

**IRISH SHORT STORIES
STATE OF THE ART: Short Stories
by the New Irish Writers**

IRISH LOVE STORIES

Edited and Introduced by
David Marcus

To Sarah,

Save all your kisses for me.
Save all your kiss es for me.
Don't know the rest.
          love petexxx.

sceptre

Collection, Introduction and Notes
Copyright © 1994 by David Marcus
For individual copyright in the
stories see page 351

First published in Great Britain in
1994 by Hodder and Stoughton
A division of Hodder Headline PLC

A Sceptre original 1994

British Library C.I.P.

A C.I.P. catalogue record for this
title is available from the British
Library

ISBN 0 340 59777 1

10 9 8 7 6 5 4 3 2 1

Printed and bound in Great Britain
for Hodder Headline PLC, 47 Bed-
ford Square, London WC1B 3DP)
by Cox and Wyman Ltd, Reading,
Berks. Photoset by Rowland Photo-
typesetting Ltd, Bury St Edmunds,
Suffolk.

CONTENTS

IRISH LOVE STORIES

INTRODUCTION

No anthology on the theme of love could possibly reflect all its myriad variations, so this collection of twenty-six love stories by Irish writers makes no claim to be comprehensive. The most it can do is attempt to provide twenty-six glimpses of the ages and stages of the twentieth-century Irish love story.

Not so long ago the predominant ruralism of Irish society dictated that marriage was more often a land contract than a love contract – 'Many an Irish property was increased by the lace of a daughter's petticoat' runs a now defunct old Irish proverb. Separation of the sexes was the norm, company keeping was at worst actively prevented and at best zealously monitored by a vigilant clergy, sex was an iceberg not even the tip of which was allowed to show, and there was a suspicion that love itself was more of a risky, even reckless, foreign game than a fitting occupation for Irish men and women.

The latter half of the twentieth century changed all that. Media tentacles gathered Ireland into an all-embracing missionary-position homogeneity, and even in the Island of Saints and Scholars love was discovered to be a sexually-transmitted disease.

That discovery, and the subsequent rapid erosion of other centuries-old taboos, came at just the right moment for the Irish love story. Young writers – among whom women, previously greatly outnumbered, were beginning at last to find both voice and platform – had shaken themselves free of traditional tenets and were released to record the love experience with a complete absence of inhibition and censoriousness. Love, in and out of marriage, was subjected to an examination far more rigorous, far less romantic, than had been the norm before.

Monk Gibbon, an Irish writer of the first half of the twentieth century, had written, 'Love is the discovery of an unsuspected and exceptional value in a particular individual'. Substitute 'defect' for 'value' and you have the other side of the coin which became the most negotiable currency of the Irish love story, post-World War II. With the undertones and overtones of Yeats' 'But Love has pitched his mansion in/The place of excrement' providing a plangent ground-bass to an era in which the writ of full frontal disclosure could run riot and Irish Siamese-twinned sin and sex were no longer indissolubly joined, it was inevitable that love's adulteries and adulterations would constitute the writers' main environment and material.

Not all, however, was darkness and blight: 'shadows of love, inebriations of love, foretastes of love, trickles of love' – the catalogue is Edna O'Brien's – were still celebrated, splendours that gained an extra effulgence against the angry and anguished hues of the times. The Irish love story was in balance. It had, at last, come of age.

David Marcus
1994

THE CLERK'S QUEST

GEORGE MOORE

GEORGE MOORE

George Moore was born in Co. Mayo in 1852. He lived in London from 1869 to 1873, when he moved to Paris to study painting. Returning to London in 1880 he committed himself to writing, and responded to an appeal from W. B. Yeats and others to come back to Ireland and help launch an Irish drama movement. *The Untilled Field*, from which 'The Clerk's Quest' is taken, was planned as a volume of short stories about Irish life, modelled on Turgenev's stories, and translated into Gaelic to be used as school texts in the revival of the language.

FOR THIRTY YEARS Edward Dempsey had worked low down in the list of clerks in the firm of Quin and Wee. He did his work so well that he seemed born to do it, and it was felt that any change in which Dempsey was concerned would be unlucky. Managers had looked at Dempsey doubtingly and had left him in his habits. New partners had come into the business, but Dempsey showed no sign of interest. He was interested only in his desk. There it was by the dim window – there were his pens, there was his penwiper, there was the ruler, there was the blotting-pad. Dempsey was always the first to arrive and the last to leave. Once in thirty years of service he had accepted a holiday; it had been a topic of conversation all the morning, and the clerks tittered when he came into the bank in the afternoon saying he had been looking into the shop windows, and had come down to the bank to see how they were getting on.

An obscure, clandestine, taciturn little man occupying in life only the space necessary to bend over a desk, and whose conical head leaned to one side as if in token of his humility.

It seemed that Dempsey had no other ambition than to be allowed to stagnate at a desk to the end of his life, and this modest ambition would have been realised had it not been for a slight accident – the single accident that had found its way into Dempsey's well-ordered and closely-guarded life. One summer's day, when the heat of the areas was rising and filling the open window, Dempsey's somnolescent senses were moved by a soft and suave perfume. At first he was puzzled to say whence it came; then he perceived that it had come from the bundle of cheques which he held in his hand; and then that the odoriferous paper was a pale pink cheque in the middle of the bundle. He had hardly seen a flower for thirty years, and could not determine whether the odour was that of mignonette, or honeysuckle, or violet. But at that moment the cheques were called for; he handed them to his superior, and with cool hand and clear brain continued to make entries in the ledger until the bank closed.

But that night, just as he was falling asleep, a remembrance of the insinuating perfume returned to him. He wondered whose cheque it was, and regretted not having looked at the signature, and many times during the succeeding weeks he paused as he was making entries in the ledger to think if the haunting perfume were rose, lavender, or mignonette. It was not the scent of rose, he was sure of that. And a vague swaying of hope began. Dreams that had died or had never been born floated up like things from the depths of the sea, and many old things that he had dreamed about or had never dreamed at all drifted about. Out of the depths of life a hope that he had never known, or that the severe rule of his daily life had checked long ago, began its struggle for life; and when the same sweet odour came again – he knew now it was the scent of heliotrope – his heart was lifted and he was overcome in a sweet, possessive trouble. He sought for the cheque amid the bundle of cheques, and finding it, he pressed the paper to his face. The cheque was written in a thin, feminine handwriting, and was signed 'Henrietta Brown,' and the name and handwriting were pregnant with occult significances in Dempsey's disturbed mind. His hand paused amid the entries, and he grew suddenly aware of some dim, shadowy form, gracile and sweet-smelling as the spring – moist shadow of wandering cloud, emanation of earth, or woman herself? Dempsey pondered, and his absent-mindedness was noticed, and occasioned comment among the clerks.

For the first time in his life he was glad when the office hours were over. He wanted to be alone, he wanted to think, he felt he must abandon himself to the new influence that had so suddenly and unexpectedly entered his life. Henrietta Brown! the name persisted in his mind like a half-forgotten, half-remembered tune; and in his efforts to realise her beauty he stopped before the photographic displays in the shop windows;

but none of the famous or the infamous celebrities there helped him in the least. He could only realise Henrietta Brown by turning his thoughts from without and seeking the intimate sense of her perfumed cheques. The end of every month brought a cheque from Henrietta Brown, and for a few moments the clerk was transported and lived beyond himself.

An idea had fixed itself in his mind. He knew not if Henrietta Brown was young or old, pretty or ugly, married or single; the perfume and the name were sufficient, and could no longer be separated from the idea, now forcing its way through the fissures in the failing brain of this poor little bachelor clerk – that idea of light and love and grace so inherent in man, but which rigorous circumstance had compelled Dempsey to banish from his life.

Dempsey had had a mother to support for many years, and had found it impossible to economise. But since her death he had laid by about a hundred and fifty pounds; he thought of this money with awe, and, awed by his good fortune, he thought how much more he might save before he was forced to leave his employment; and to have touched a penny of his savings would have seemed to him a sin near to sacrilege. Yet he did not hesitate for a single moment to send Henrietta Brown, whose address he had been able to obtain through the bank books, a diamond brooch which had cost twenty pounds. He omitted to say whence it had come, and for days he lived in a warm wonderment, satisfied in the thought that she was wearing something that he had seen and touched.

His idea was now by him and always, and its dominion was so complete that he neglected his duties at the bank, and was censured by the amazed manager. The change of his condition was so obvious that it became the subject for gossip, and jokes were now beginning to pass into serious conjecturing. Dempsey took no notice, and his plans matured amid jokes and theories. The desire to write and reveal himself to his beloved had become imperative; and after some very slight hesitation – for he was moved more by instinct than by reason – he wrote a letter urging the fatality of the circumstances that separated them, and explaining rather than excusing this revelation of his identity. His letter was full of deference, but at the same time it left no doubt as to the nature of his attachments and hopes. The answer to this letter was a polite note begging him not to persist in this correspondence, and warning him that if he did it would become necessary to write to the manager of the bank. But the return of his brooch did not dissuade Dempsey from the pursuit of his ideal; and as time went by it became more and more impossible for him to refrain from writing love-letters and sending occasional presents of jewellery. When the letters and jewellery were returned to him he put them away carelessly, and he bought the first sparkle of diamonds that caught his fancy, and forwarded ring, bracelet, and ear-ring, with whatever words of rapturous love that came up in his mind.

One day he was called into the manager's room, severely reprimanded, and eventually pardoned in consideration of his long and faithful services. But the reprimands of his employers were of no use, and he continued to write to Henrietta Brown, growing more and more careless of his secret, dropping brooches about the office, and letters. At last the story was whispered from desk to desk. Dempsey's dismissal was the only course open to the firm; and it was with much regret that the partners told their old servant that his services were no longer required.

To their surprise Dempsey seemed quite unaffected by his dismissal; he even seemed relieved, and left the bank smiling, thinking of Henrietta, bestowing no thought on his want of means. He did not even think of providing himself with money by the sale of some of the jewellery he had about him, nor of going to his lodging and packing up his clothes, he did not think how he should get to Edinburgh – it was there that she lived. He thought of her even to the exclusion of the simplest means of reaching her, and was content to walk about the fields in happy mood, watching for glimpses of some evanescent phantom at the wood's edge wearing a star on her forehead, or catching sight in the wood's depths of a glistening shoulder and feet flying towards the reeds. Full of happy aspiration he wandered, seeking the country through the many straggling villages that hang like children round the skirts of Dublin, and

passing through one of these at nightfall, and, feeling tired, he
turned into the bar of an inn, and asked for a bit to eat.

'You look as if you'd come a long way, Mister.'

'I have come a good twenty miles, and I'll have to go a good
few more before I reach Edinburgh.'

'And what might you be going to Edinburgh for – if you'll
excuse me asking?'

'I am going to the lady I love, and I am taking her beautiful
presents of jewellery.'

The two rough fellows exchanged glances; and it is easy to
imagine how Dempsey was induced to let them have his diamonds, so that inquiries might be made of a friend round the
corner regarding their value. After waiting a little while, Dempsey paid for his bread and cheese, and went in search of the
thieves. But the face of Henrietta Brown obliterated all remembrance of thieves and diamonds, and he wandered for a few
days, sustained by his dream and the crusts that his appearance
drew from the pitiful. At last he even neglected to ask for a
crust, and, foodless, followed the beckoning vision, from sun-
rise to sundown.

It was a soft, quiet summer's night when Dempsey lay down
to sleep for the last time. He was very tired, he had been
wandering all day, and threw himself on the grass by the roadside. He lay there looking up at the stars, thinking of Henrietta,
knowing that everything was slipping away, and he passing into
a diviner sense. Henrietta seemed to be coming nearer to him
and revealing herself more clearly; and when the word of death
was in his throat, and his eyes opened for the last time, it
seemed to him that one of the stars came down from the sky
and laid its bright face upon his shoulder.

THE WAKE

DONN BYRNE

DONN BYRNE

Donn Byrne was born in New York in 1889 and christened Brian Oswald Donn-Byrne. His parents returned to their South Armagh home when he was a baby, and he was brought up and educated in Ireland, becoming a fluent Irish speaker. In 1911 he emigrated to New York, married an Irish girl, and started to write. His stories were published by the leading New York magazines, and in all he wrote three collections and some dozen novels. During the 1920s he lived in Europe. He was killed in a car crash in West Cork in 1928.

AT TIMES THE muffled conversation in the kitchen resembled the resonant humming of bees, and again, when it became animated, it sounded like the distant cackling of geese. Then there would come a pause; and it would begin again with sibilant whispers, and end in a chorus of dry laughter that somehow suggested the crackling of burning logs.

Occasionally a figure would open the bedroom door, pass the old man as he sat huddled in his chair, never throwing a glance at him, and go and kneel by the side of the bed where the body was. They usually prayed for two or three minutes, then rose and walked on tiptoe to the kitchen, where they joined the company. Sometimes they came in twos, less often in threes, but they did precisely the same thing – prayed for precisely the same time, and left the room on tiptoe with the same creak of shoe and rustle of clothes that sounded so intensely loud throughout the room. They might have been following instructions laid down in a ritual.

The old man wished to heaven they would stay away. He had been sitting in his chair for hours, thinking, until his head was in a whirl. He wanted to concentrate his thoughts, but somehow he felt that the mourners were preventing him.

The five candles at the head of the bed distracted him. He was glad when the figure of one of the mourners shut off the glare for a few minutes. He was also distracted by the five chairs standing around the room like sentries on post, and the little table by the window with its crucifix and holy-water font. He wanted to keep thinking of 'herself', as he called her, lost in the immensity of the oaken bed. He had been looking at the pinched face, with its faint suspicion of blue, since early that morning. He was very much awed by the nun's hood that concealed the back of the head, and the stiffly posed arms and the small hands in their white cotton gloves moved him to a deep pity.

Somebody touched him on the shoulder. 'Michael James.'

It was big Dan Murray, a gaunt, red farmer, who had been best man at his wedding.

'Michael James.'

'What is it?'

'I hear young Kennedy's in the village.'

'What of that?'

'I thought it was best for you to know.'

Murray waited a moment, then he went out, on tiptoe, as everybody did, his movements resembling the stilted gestures of a mechanical toy.

Down the drive Michael heard steps coming. Then a struggle and a shrill giggle. Some young people were coming to the wake, and he knew a boy had tried to kiss a girl in the dark. He felt a dull surge of resentment.

She was nineteen when he married her; he was sixty-three. Because he had over two hundred acres of land and many heads of milch and grazing cattle and a huge house that rambled like a barrack, her father had given her to him; and young Kennedy, who had been her father's steward for years, and had been saving to buy a house for her, was thrown over like a bale of mildewed hay.

Kennedy had made several violent scenes. Michael James remembered the morning of the wedding. Kennedy waylaid the bridal-party coming out of the church. He was drunk.

'Mark me,' he had said, very quietly for a drunken man – 'mark me. If anything ever happens to that girl at your side, Michael James, I'll murder you. I'll murder you in cold blood. Do you understand?'

Michael James could be forgiving that morning. 'Run away and sober up, lad,' he had said, 'and come up to the house and dance.'

Kennedy had gone around the countryside for weeks, drunk every night, making threats against the strong farmer. And then a wily sergeant of the Connaught Rangers had trapped him and taken him off to Aldershot.

Now he was home on furlough, and something had happened to her, and he was coming up to make good his threat.

What had happened to her? Michael James didn't understand. He had given her everything he could. She had taken it all with a demure thanks, but he had never had anything of her but apathy. She had gone around the house apathetically, growing a little thinner every day, and then a few days ago she had lain down, and last night she had died, apathetically.

And young Kennedy was coming up for an accounting to-night. 'Well,' thought Michael James, 'let him come!'

Silence suddenly fell over the company in the kitchen. Then a loud scraping as they stood up, and a harsher grating as chairs were pushed back. The door of the bedroom opened, and the red flare from the fire and lamps of the kitchen blended into the sickly yellow candlelight of the bedroom.

The parish priest walked in. His closely-cropped white hair, strong, ruddy face, and erect back gave him more the appearance of a soldier than a clergyman. He looked at the bed a moment, and then at Michael James.

'Oh, you mustn't take it like that, man,' he said. 'You mustn't take it like that. You must bear up.' He was the only one who spoke in his natural voice.

He turned to a lumbering farmer's wife who had followed him in, and asked about the hour of the funeral. She answered in a hoarse whisper, dropping a curtsy.

'You ought to go and take a walk,' he told Michael James. 'You oughtn't to stay in here all the time.' And he left the room.

Michael James paid no attention. His mind was wandering to strange fantasies he could not keep out of his head. Pictures crept in and out of his brain, joined as by some thin filament. He thought somehow of her soul, and then wondered what a soul was like. And then he thought of a dove, and then of a bat fluttering through the dark, and then of a bird lost at twilight. He thought of it as some lonely, flying thing, with a long journey before it and no place to rest. He could imagine it uttering the

vibrant, plaintive cry of a peewit. And then it struck him with
a great sense of pity that the night was cold.

In the kitchen they were having tea. The rattle of the crock-
ery sounded very distinctly. He could distinguish the sharp,
staccato ring when a cup was laid in a saucer, and the nervous
rattle when cup and saucer were passed from one hand to the
other. Spoons struck china with a faint metallic tinkle. He felt
as if all the sounds were made at the back of his neck, and the
crash seemed to burst in his head.

Dan Murray creaked into the room. 'Michael James,' he whispered, 'you ought to take something. Have a bite to eat. Take
a cup of tea. I'll bring it in to you.'

'Oh, let me alone, Daniel,' he answered. He felt he would
like to kick him and curse him while doing so.

'You must take something.' Murray's voice rose from a
whisper to a low, argumentative singsong. 'You know it's not
natural. You've got to eat.'

'No, thank you, Daniel,' he answered. It was as if he were
talking to a boy who was good-natured but tiresome. 'I don't
feel like eating. Maybe afterwards I will.'

'Michael James,' Murray continued.

'Well, what is it, Daniel?'

'Don't you think I'd better go down and see young Kennedy,
and tell him how foolish it would be of him to come up here and
start fighting? You know it isn't right. Hadn't I better go down?
He's at home now.'

'Let that alone, Daniel, I tell you.' The thought of Murray
breaking into the matter that was between himself and the
young man filled him with a sense of injured delicacy.

'I know he's going to make trouble.'

'Let me handle that, like a good fellow, and leave me by
myself, Daniel, if you don't mind.'

'Ah well, sure. You know best.' And Murray crept out of the
room.

As the door opened Michael could hear someone singing in
a subdued voice and many feet tapping like drums in time with
the music. They had to pass the night outside, and it was the
custom, but the singing irritated him. He could fancy heads

nodding and bodies swaying from side to side with the rhythm. He recognised the tune and it began to run through his head, and he could not put it out of it. The lilt of it captured him, and suddenly he began thinking of the wonderful brain that musicians must have to compose music. And then his thoughts switched to a picture he had seen of a man in a garret with a fiddle beneath his chin.

He straightened himself up a little, for sitting crouched forward as he was put a strain on his back, and he unconsciously sat upright to ease himself. And as he sat up he caught a glimpse of the cotton gloves on the bed, and it burst in on him that the first time he had seen her she was walking along the road with young Kennedy one Sunday afternoon, and they were holding hands. When they saw him they let go suddenly, and grew very red, giggling in a half-hearted way to hide their embarrassment. And he remembered that he had passed them by without saying anything, but with a good-humoured, sly smile on his face, and a mellow feeling within him, and a sage reflection to himself that young folks will be young folks, and what harm was there in courting a little on a Sunday afternoon when the week's work had been done?

And he remembered other days on which he had met her and Kennedy; and then how the conviction had come into his mind that here was a girl for him to marry; and then how, quietly and equably, he had gone about getting her and marrying her, as he would go about buying a team of horses or making arrangements for cutting the hay.

Until the day he married her he felt as a driver feels who has his team under perfect control, and who knows every bend and curve of the road he is taking. But since that day he had been thinking about her and worrying, and wondering exactly where he stood, until everything in the day was just the puzzle of her, and he was like a driver with a restive pair of horses who knows his way no farther than the next bend. And then he knew she was the biggest thing in his life.

All there was left of her now was a pair of white cotton gloves, resting stiffly on a bedspread, with ten cramped, blue fingers inside of them.

The situation as it appeared to him he had worked out with difficulty, for he was not a thinking man. What thinking he did dealt with the price of harvest machinery, and the best time of the year for buying and selling. He worked it out this way: here was this girl dead, whom he had married, and who should have married another man who was coming tonight to kill him. Tonight sometime the world would stop for him. He felt no longer a personal entity – he was merely part of a situation. It was as if he were a piece in a chess problem – any moment the player might move and solve the play by taking a pawn.

Realities had taken on a dim, unearthly quality. Occasionally a sound from the kitchen would strike him like an unexpected note in a harmony; the whiteness of the bed would flash out like a piece of colour in a subdued painting.

There was a shuffling in the kitchen and the sound of feet going towards the door. The latch lifted with a rasp. He could hear the hoarse, deep tones of a few boys, and the high-pitched, singsong intonations of girls. He knew they were going for a few miles' walk along the roads. He went over and raised the blind on the window. Overhead the moon showed like a spot of bright saffron. A sort of misty haze seemed to cling around the bushes and trees. The outhouses stood out white, like buildings in a mysterious city. Somewhere there was the metallic whirr of a grasshopper, and in the distance a loon boomed again and again.

The little company passed down the yard. There was the sound of a smothered titter, then a playful, resounding slap, and a gurgling laugh from one of the boys.

As he stood by the window he heard someone open the door and stand on the threshold.

'Are you coming, Alice?' someone asked.

Michael James listened for the answer. He was taking in eagerly all outside things. He wanted something to pass the time of waiting, as a traveller in a railway station reads trivial notices carefully while waiting for a train that may take him to the ends of the earth.

'Alice, are you coming?' was asked again.

There was no answer.

'Well, you needn't if you don't want to,' he heard in an irritated tone, and the speaker tramped down towards the road in a dudgeon. He recognised the figure of Flanagan, the football player, who was always having little spats with the girl he was going to marry. He discovered with a sort of shock that he was slightly amused at this incident.

From the road there came the shrill scream of one of the girls who had gone out, and then a chorus of laughter. And against the background of the figure behind him and of young Kennedy he began wondering at the relationship of man and woman. He had no word for it, for 'love' was a term he thought should be confined to story-books, a word to be suspicious of as sounding affected; a word to be scoffed at. But of this relationship he had a vague understanding. He thought of it as a criss-cross of threads, binding one person to the other, or as a web which might be light and easily broken, or which might have the strength of steel cables, and which might work into knots here and there, and become a tangle that could crush those caught in it.

It puzzled him how a thing of indefinable grace, of soft words on June nights, of vague stirrings under moonlight, of embarrassing hand-clasps and fearful glances, might become, as it had become in the case of himself, Kennedy and what was behind him – a thing of blind, malevolent force, a thing of sinister silence, a shadow that crushed.

And then it struck him with a sense of guilt that his mind was wandering from her, and he turned away from the window. He thought how much more peaceful it would be for a body to lie out in the moonlight than in a shadowy room with yellow, guttering candlelight, with a sombre oak bedstead, and five solemn-looking chairs. And he thought again how strange it was that on a night like this Kennedy should come as an avenger seeking to kill rather than as a lover with high hope in his breast.

Murray slipped into the room again. There was a frown on his face and his tone was aggressive.

'I tell you, Michael James, we'll have to do something about it.' There was a truculent note in his whisper.

The farmer did not answer.

'Will you let me go down for the police? A few words to the sergeant will keep him quiet.'

Michael James felt a pity for Murray. The idea of pitting a sergeant of police against the tragedy that was coming seemed ludicrous to him. It was like pitting a schoolboy against a hurricane.

'Listen to me, Dan,' he replied. 'How do you know Kennedy is coming up at all?'

'Flanagan, the football player, met him and talked to him. He said that Kennedy was clean mad.'

'Do they know about it in the kitchen?'

'Not a word.' There was a pause.

'Well, listen here, now. Go right back there and don't say a word about it. Wouldn't it be foolish if you went down to the police and he didn't come at all? And if he does come I can manage him. And if I can't I'll call you. Does that satisfy you?' And he sent Murray out, grumbling.

As the door closed he felt that the last refuge had been abandoned. He was to wrestle with destiny alone. He had no doubt that Kennedy would make good his vow, and he felt a sort of curiosity as to how it would be done. Would it be with hands, or with a gun, or some other weapon? He hoped it would be the gun. The idea of coming to handigrips with the boy filled him with a strange terror.

The thought that within ten minutes or a half-hour or an hour he would be dead did not come home to him. It was the physical act that frightened him. He felt as if he were terribly alone, and a cold wind were blowing about him and penetrating every pore of his body. There was a contraction around his breast bone and a shiver in his shoulders.

His idea of death was that he would pitch headlong, as from a high tower, into a bottomless dark space.

He went over to the window again and looked out towards the barn. From a chink in one of the shutters there was a thread of yellow candlelight. He knew there were men there playing cards to pass the time.

Then the terror came on him. The noise in the kitchen was

subdued. Most of the mourners had gone home, and those who were staying the night were drowsy and were dozing over the fire. He felt he wanted to rush among them and to cry to them to protect him, and to cower behind them and to close them around him in a solid circle. He felt that eyes were upon him, looking at his back from the bed, and he was afraid to turn around because he might look into the eyes.

She had always respected him, he remembered, and he did not want to lose her respect now; and the fear that he would lose it set his shoulders back and steadied the grip of his feet on the floor.

He could not remember what Kennedy looked like. His fancy distorted his enemy's countenance into a thin, grim-lipped face. There was a horrible unreality about him, as about a djinn in the *Thousand and One Nights*.

And then there flashed before him the thought of people who kill, of lines of soldiery rushing on trenches, of a stealthy, cowering man who slips through a jail door at dawn, and of a figure he had read of in books – a sinister figure with an axe and a red cloak.

The moon was well to the westward now. There was still the white, blinding look about the outhouses. They threw heavy, angular shadows. Trees appeared as if etched in black on the ground. There was a chill in the air.

As he looked down the yard he saw a figure turn in at the gate and come towards the house. It seemed to walk slowly and heavily, as if tired. He knew it was Kennedy.

He turned and walked to the door. As he walked he felt he was being watched from behind. In the kitchen someone was speaking slowly and emphatically, as if driving home a point. He opened the kitchen door and slipped outside.

The figure coming up the pathway seemed to swim towards him. Then it would blur and disappear, and then appear again vaguely. The beating of his heart was like the regular sound of a ticking clock. Space narrowed until he felt he could not breathe. He went forward a few paces. The light from the bedroom window streamed forward in a broad, yellow beam. He stepped into it as into a river.

'She's dead,' he heard himself saying. 'She's dead.' And then he knew that Kennedy was standing in front of him.

The flap of the boy's hat threw a heavy shadow over his face, his shoulders were braced, and his right hand, the farmer could see, was thrust deeply into his coat pocket.

'Ay, she's dead,' Michael James repeated. 'You knew that, didn't you?' It was all he could think of saying. 'You'll come in and see her, won't you?' He had forgotten what Kennedy had come for. He was dazed. He didn't know what to say.

Kennedy moved a little. The light from the window struck him full in the face, and Michael James realised with a shock that it was as grim and thin-lipped as he had pictured it. A prayer rose in his throat, and then fear seemed to leave him all at once. He raised his head. The right hand had left the pocket now. And then suddenly he saw that Kennedy was looking into the room, and he knew he could see, through the little panes of glass, the huge bedstead and the body on it. And he felt a desire to throw himself between Kennedy and it, as he might jump between a child and something that would hurt it.

He turned away his head, instinctively – why, he could not understand, but he felt that he should not look at Kennedy's face.

Over in the barn voices rose suddenly. They were disputing over the cards. There was someone complaining feverishly and someone arguing truculently, and another voice striving to make peace. They died away in a dull hum, and Michael James heard the boy sobbing.

'You mustn't do that,' he said. 'You mustn't do that.' And he patted him on the shoulders. He felt as if something unspeakably tense had relaxed, and as if life were swinging back into balance. His voice shook and he continued patting. 'You'll come in now, and I'll leave you alone there.' He took him under the arm.

He felt the pity he had for the body on the bed envelop Kennedy, too, and a sense of peace come over him. It was as though a son of his had been hurt and had come to him for comfort, and that he was going to comfort him. In some vague way he thought of Easter-time.

He stopped at the door for a moment.

'It's all right, laddie,' he said. 'It's all right,' and he lifted the latch.

As they went in he felt somehow as if high walls had crumbled and the three of them had stepped into the light of day.

THE SPANCELED

DANIEL CORKERY

DANIEL CORKERY

Daniel Corkery was born in Cork in 1878. An artist, playwright and a passionate advocate of nationalism and the Irish language, he was an early influence on Sean O'Faolain and Frank O'Connor. His *Synge and Anglo-Irish Literature* and other studies of Gaelic Ireland continue to provoke controversy, but his four collections of short stories, though now largely neglected, established him as one of the leading short story writers of the early twentieth century. He was Professor of English in University College, Cork, from 1931 to 1947 and also a member of the Irish Senate. He died in 1964.

THE PAIR OF them, spanceled in two such different ways, met, or rather slipped into acquaintanceship in the most haphazard way in Mike Larrymore's meadowland. As to her: if you saw only her brow and eyes – so shapely, so guileless, open, clear – your heart would pity her because of her burden; but when you marked the shapeless jaw and mouth – the upper lip, long, full, protruding, the lower dragged a little to one side, as by some influence of the retreating chin – you could not but reflect that, after all, the man, her husband, who on his deathbed spanceled her so effectually with a few lines in his will, might have had his own thought in doing so. Upper and lower face so different, the general effect was strange and uncertain – shyness, wildness, passion seemed to be continually deepening or softening, one into another.

The day her husband, Pat Lenihan, was laid in Kilvurrish, they say she smiled. Her six long years of drudgery were over. Henceforth if she stayed up all night to see that the sow didn't smother her young, or if her day's work happened to be in a dripping mountainy field, clearing it of stones, her wages when the task was done would not be the bitter word of a consumptive who, finding life slipping from him, spent his days in gazing with his hopeless eyes on the three children that played about the earthen floor – in gazing on them, thinking what would happen when he was gone. Quiet enough he died, singing old tunes in a sort of stupor that at the end came to comfort him. Then the biteen of land on the steep-down, rock-strewn hillside was hers; and she was still strong, young, and not uncomely. But if she smiled on that wild wintry day while he was being laid in Kilvurrish, the grave-diggers looking quite black and huge in the sombre sunset, she had not then learnt the terms of the will. That same night when she came to know them she flung his relations from the door, bolted it, and standing in the middle of the turf-lit room, looked wildly from one child to another, as if they were the offspring of some other woman; for the will had made it clear that the land would pass to them on her marrying again.

The shock wore off; indeed the time was not long coming when the few neighbours she knew – the Larrymores, for instance, would make many a half-hidden joke about how she was spanceled. Freely, they laid snares for her: 'Come in here, Maggie,' Mrs Larrymore would say, 'I have as fine a bit of homespun as ever ye seen,' and instead of the bit of woollen would be a young and unsuspecting labouring-boy, who would blush and cover half his face with his hand. 'Isn't he grand,' they'd say, 'and nothing to hinder him – or you.' Simple traps, yet again and again she fell into them. What did it matter when she knew that the young man would learn the story of her life as soon as her back was turned? Thus her very safeguard became in a manner her temptation.

Now, as to the spanceled man who was to meet this spanceled woman: John Keegan his name was. In a far-off parish he was known far and wide as the grabber's nephew. If he were a grabber's son persecution would have been so hard and constant against him that he might have grown up a man of will, a powerful man; the tree, they say, is strengthened by the storm. As it was, he grew up in an atmosphere of distrust rather than enmity. Of course this distrust did often pass into enmity, often became total boycott; but on the falling of the political weather-glass he would quickly slip back again into acquaintanceship with such of the young men as were of a character to feel warm elation in forgiving their country's enemies over a few drinks. Thus he became sly, crafty in his knowledge of human nature: he got into the habit of examining every new face he had to speak with; finally he came to know his own power. He discovered distant public houses, where he found himself mistaken for relatives of the same name – men of spotless character. And soon, of course, he knew how exactly to set gossip on false scents; and found a certain pleasure in watching the faces of his pot-house companions as they traced curious relationships between himself and his own father, between himself and himself! Lower and lower he sank; yet from all this a good girl would have, at least might have, rescued him if the bit of grabbed land had not stood in the way. From bad to worse it went; derelict, it came at last to hang like a millstone around the grabber's neck; it drove him to drink. Then the nephew became a spalpeen, a roving labourer; but in all his wanderings he kept as a light in his heart the thought that he would yet be master of Gurteenruadh, would yet be in a position to ask in marriage someone who would not look at a spalpeen. But that day might yet be far off; meantime he was but a spalpeen, an unsettled man. Thus he, too, was in the way of temptation; he was spanceled to a bit of grabbed land in a boggy valley, as the woman to a bit of rocky soil on a steep-down hillside.

All in two days their intimacy came about. Mike Larrymore had his grass in the inches by the river: his fear was that the water would rise and sweep away his cocks: in years that did not seem any wetter than this it had happened. At last came a day of sunshiny wind and, Sunday though it was, men and horses were sent into the fields to get in the grass. Carts of people returning from Mass upon the road that dipped in festoons midway along the hillside, would pull up, and a man or two would scramble down through the furze, take off their coats, and ask for a fork. The stranger, John Keegan, slid down through the furze-brake in the same uninvited manner and began to work. That night he slept with the other labouring-boys in the barn. Next day he was at work again, the widow by his side, both of them gleaning with long rakes in a far part of the field, and that night he sat in the farmer's kitchen and took a hand at the cards. Whatever else he could do, he was confident of his skill at cards. His merry, never-resting tongue showed as much. It rattled on and on, and whether he won or lost he had his joke. There was scarcely a card in the pack for which he had not some pet name: 'my little do-een' – that is 'my little two', 'my little ace-een' were expressions they all began

presently to use, as also his use of 'old lady' for the queen of
hearts. The widow was playing too, in her silent way, uninter-
ested, slow; she lost game after game. They had often to call
out to her to play, or to hand her the pack with the one word,
'Deal'. She was watching the stranger. Other eyes were watching him also, but with far different thoughts. It is a great card-
playing district, and they began to resent the stranger's winning
of almost every trick. His high spirits vexed them too. He
would need to be reminded of his position. Not by the women,
however; they took his side in the battle that had not yet
declared itself. They saw no reason why a game of cards should
be so solemn and quiet: wasn't it for fun they were at them at
all? Playing silently, the widow did not seem to care whether
or not her brooding on the thought of the stranger's presence
was noticed. She had much to think about. That day in the field
he had poured all the sorrows of his life into her ear, apparently
for no purpose than to relieve his mind. And only the bare
truths of his life he told her; in a vibrant voice however, tender
and rich. And she was on the point of doing as much herself;
but her mouth dried up and she could not speak. Now she
was sorry. Never before had she had any thought that such a
confession could bring her comfort. Maybe tomorrow she
would do what she had failed to do today. And as she watched
him she was experiencing the solace of self-accusation; so that
the sallies of his wit, which made the others laugh out, some
of the men against their will it seemed, were powerless over
her; she scarce gathered their meaning. Presently she caught
Jack Constantine looking at her, making signs to her, nodding
and winking, pointing to her cards. Her face was a blank. All
she could gather from his signs was that he was suspicious of
something in the play. His eyes were hard and fiery, and whenever the stranger played, Jack stretched out his arm and felt
the card with his fingers, as if the sense of sight of itself was
not sufficient to make out its value. Suddenly he jumped up and
leaned right across the table, looking down at the stranger.
'Stand up,' he yelled – the voice of one who has been a long
time smothering his rage.

'What – what?'

'Stand up, will 'oo?'

'Why? For what? – what are you saying?'

'Stand up when you're tolt.'

Others began to rise up also. 'Sit down, Jack. Sit down.'

'Take it aisy.' 'Don't spoil sport.' 'What's up with ye at all?'
– the voices broke in from right and left, some of them however
not over-earnest in the peacemaking.

'He's sitting on a card. I'm after seeing it. 'Tisn't fair; we're
not fools,' Jack Constantine spluttered out to them, though his
eyes seemed incapable of swerving for a moment from the man
he was watching.

The stranger shuffled and stood up. As he did so, all the
cards in his hand fell to the ground. There was no card on his
chair.

'That's it,' Jack cried, lying right across the table and pointing
to a card on the floor.

''Twas in me hand.'

''Twas not in your hand.'

''Twas.'

''Twasn't.'

'Maybe 'tis cheating I am?'

''Tis.'

'I'm not.'

'You are.'

'You needn't believe me.'

'Who'd believe you – a grabber.' The stranger collapsed.

'All right,' he said, and rose and made for the door.

'You're not going?' said Mike Larrymore, rising also; he was
afraid a mistake had been made: Jack Constantine was always
a hot-headed man.

'I'm after being insulted.'

''Tis only a bit of temper.'

'I'm no grabber, nor the son of wan.'

'No, only the nephew,' Jack's voice yelled out; he was in the
midst of a whirl of inquiries.

They saw how the light of the kitchen lamp caught the
stranger's back for a step or two; then he was gone. Mike
Larrymore made for the door.

'You should be more careful, Jack,' he said, following the stranger, 'the man has given his labour.'

Then Constantine gave in detail how he had come at the man's history. The widow listened. How strange it was that she should have heard it all before! No circumstance was different. Again there came over her a wave of warm sorrow that she had not told the man her whole history: somehow it would have comforted her to know that he in his homeless wanderings could sometimes think of her. Around her she heard them talking of his story and his relations; and it seemed to her that they had no right to do so, that they did not know him at all.

Mike Larrymore returned. He told them he couldn't get the stranger to stay: 'He's gone wesht,' he said. 'Wan like him,' a woman said, ''tis in his nature to be wandering about.'

'Something like that he's after saying himself; though 'twas hard put I was to make out what he was saying, down in his throat the talking was.'

They made an effort to renew the game; but the women had gathered about the fire; and every now and then one of them would turn to the players with an inquiry: 'Bill, didn't you know Mike Pat Casey, who was an uncle to Dr Casey of Lisheenaglass?' or something like that. All the time the widow's thought was full of a lonely man going west into the heart of the hills.

'Willy, is the moon up?' she asked at last out of her stupor. Willy laughed.

'What ails you, Maggie?' he said, ''tis after coming round by this time.'

'I'll be going,' she said. The moon would take her safely across the stepping-stones.

When she reached the other side of the river, had entered, as it were, her own lonely land, she stood still for a moment in utter confusion, the very landscape seemed unfamiliar. 'Oh! Oh! Oh!' she moaned, and drew her black shawl close about her and swayed to and fro. Then a sort of calmness suddenly fell on her, and almost without a thought in her head she went up the zig-zag path. Presently she came on her little patch of oats, and then above her she could see her little house: in the moonlight the long, low, white-washed wall, seen through the slender birch and rowan trunks, might have been a line of clothes. Suddenly she noticed that the lamp was not in its usual place; she knew as much by the dullness of the window. In these houses the lamps always shine out exactly at the same angle. She hastened, vague thoughts of her children having risen from their beds chilling her. But the silence reassured her. Before entering she paused, and her eyes were towards the west.

Opening the door she saw the stranger, Keegan, half-rising from a stool to meet her. 'Sh!' he said, noting her astonishment, and pointed to the settle. There lay her youngest child, wrapped in a heap of bedclothes. "Twas crying,' he whispered. She gave no heed to his words. She stared at him with frightened eyes: in her brain a lonely figure was still trudging along the roads. To her surprise this man before her had again seated himself, and with no confusion, by the settle, and was now arranging the disordered mass of clothes. She withdrew quickly through the open door. One glance he shot after her; then with a slow smile he bent again upon the infant. A rustle made him look about. She had returned, was crouching as far from him as possible, in her hand a crazy-looking gun held awkwardly.

'Go on out,' she murmured, with no strength in her voice. In a leap his arms were about her, the gun falling with a rattle on the earthen floor. He heard it, half-stooped to seize it; then something made him glance at the woman's face. Her eyes were shut, the mouth wide open and panting; he felt her whole body trembling from head to foot. As if in very pity he kissed her, babbling old-fashioned love-words at her ear.

And so they leaped from their pit of sorrow, as the spanceled will until time be over; in no other way is it possible for them – this is their sorry philosophy – to revenge themselves on fortune, to give scorn for scorn.

THE DROPPER

PATRICK DOYLE

PATRICK DOYLE

Patrick Doyle was born in Dublin in 1938 and taught for many years in a Dublin secondary school. In 1978 his first short story, published in 'New Irish Writing', won a Hennessy Literary Award. He published four further stories and is now concentrating on writing a novel.

TO BE TREATED like a nothing, treated like dirt! The worm got into Steve as he was starting up the van. He was driving down from the sales yard to the town in response to a message from Quinty Ruane. Heat and itch and the smell of beasts came with him. He hated that damned salesroom; hated the routine of herding cattle in a ring. But most of all he hated the dealers on the rails for chucking spits like bait into the peat around his feet.

Neither could he take to 'The Railway Hotel' which was built in the days when the railway served the town and retained that name although the line was now defunct. Bigshots from the parish sometimes patronised the place. Run by the widow of a national politician, it contended with the new hotel outside the town for wedding receptions and other sundry functions. The lounge was fusty, dim and tight. Well-worn carpets sodded the floor and dusty pewter mugs were displayed on high shelves. Steve pushed his way through a mass of pressing bodies, many of them dealers in from the mart.

Quinty's black head topped the crush. He was standing down at the open end between Hopper Glynn and Callaghan, the entrepreneur.

'Well the dead arose,' Hopper intercepted Steve. 'And where in hell do you hide yourself at all. Here, my call's coming up. Have something special for the day that's in it.'

The Hopper's eyes were glazed, his cheeks aflame with alcohol. Quinty stuck his thumb up and winked at Steve. 'No specials,' Steve declined. 'But I won't say neither to a bottle of stout.'

He could tolerate the Hopper any weather of the week. In

the old days they had played on the parish hurling team. In fact
Hopper had retired after Steve's misfortune, swearing he would
never swing a hurley again. Hopper never changed however
seldom they met up and that was always something worth recit-
ing of a man. Tom Callaghan was another kettle of fish, owning
half the town and so hungry for more that some people swore he
was a front for foreign interests. Quinty was the ticket though, a
big strapping fellow with a head of tight black curls and a style
about him, a class of arrogance, that only a diehard could
take exception to. Except that even Quinty was getting on in
years.

The barman came down the counter to them, his shirtsleeves
rolled back tight into the armpits.

'Very humid weather,' he addressed the company.

'And it's catching me in there, Bill,' Quinty gripped his throat.
'We'll all be supping sorrow unless somebody speaks up.'

'I know my round,' the Hopper was aggrieved. 'One large
stout and three large Jamesons.'

Bill put up the drinks and returned with Hopper's change.

'Busy at the sales?' he looked sideways at Steve.

'Damn the bit I noticed,' muttered Steve.

'That's an odd thing to say and you the middle of the trade.'

'Sure the spits were comin' in at me like sleet,' said Steve.
'Them dealers do it deliberate.'

'Ah you take offence too easily,' Quinty observed. 'As the
fella said – forebearance made a bishop of his reverence. That
so, Tom?'

'Think positive and progress,' murmured Callaghan, his
elbows on the counter to support his big-boned frame. The
heavy bunch of keys on a clip from his waistband seemed posi-
tively diagnostic of the man.

'There,' said Quinty lighting up a cigarette. 'The voice of an
authority.'

'Dunno,' mused Bill with a shake of his head. 'The hardened
twig is difficult to twist. Considering his age I would reckon on
burn-out. They might have the right idea in America. Come
middle-age they just start again; new life, new wife, new husband – the works.'

'Now you have it,' Quinty enthused. 'There's your problem, Stevie – no woman in your life. Get a bucket in your hand before the well runs dry.'

Then Hopper intervened between the low and lazy chuckles. 'Will yiz leave this man alone, boys.'

'All the same,' Bill persisted, 'women are the ballast of the most contrary men.'

Quinty grinned. 'As the mermaid told the sailor and he waddling on deck.'

'G'long to hell,' said Steve.

'Madame around, Bill?' Quinty disengaged.

'She's out the back somewhere, want me to slip out and let her know you're here?'

'No, time enough, Bill,' Quinty declined. 'There's more on your plate with the crowd that's in it.'

Steve settled down to a confab with the Hopper whose modest holding and healthy kids played him out short rope for indulging in the drink. They talked about the changing times, the passing of old ways.

'So no wife yet. Any chance you'll take the plunge?'

'Don't you start,' muttered Steve.

'I'm serious,' said Hopper. 'I mind you and Romy not so many years. You'd a right to strike that ball when you had it on the hop. A nice young gentle woman was Romy then. I think you missed the bus.'

'No,' said Steve. 'By the time they released me from the hospital she'd upped and left for God-knows-where.'

'Well, only you can judge your own luck.'

'Yeah,' Steve admitted. 'Then I even lost the herding beyond in Ruanes. Such is life,' he sighed and, taking his third bottle by the neck, drank it straight to beyond halfway.

'A shame,' agreed the Hopper. 'It paid so well and you got your meals free. Mind me asking how you lost that spot?'

'The old man rubbed me wrong. Got up me back for drinkin' bottles on the job.'

'Still, old Ruane is a most honest man,' said Hopper. 'He could drag his coat through any town in Ireland.'

'Give Quinty his due he tried his best for me,' said Steve.

'But to tell the truth I let me tongue cut me throat. I never funked an argument, you know me form by now.'

Steve drew his hand back over his mouth. He knew the Hopper's mind, the unspoken observation that the world was full of down-and-outs who suffered for their pride.

'Still getting them? Those turns I mean,' and like reflex Hopper stole a glance at Steve's white hair which was swept straight back to cover the old wound. 'That gobshite had you marked. He was looking for you.'

'Yeah,' muttered Steve.

They gave some moments' silence to the fateful incident – a ball dropping into Steve's reaching hand, the goalmouth mêlée, a hurley chopping down like an axe and Steve collapsing.

'A dirty stroke,' said Hopper. 'It's the likes of him has them wearing helmets now. He never had a bit of luck after it, I hear.'

'Look, it takes me all my time to forget the bugger's name. Tell me, how are things with you?' Steve changed the subject.

'Oh I'm into sheep entirely now. That sheephouse I had built was quick to pay its way. I've the ewes in off the grass for a couple of bad months and then, after lambing, they're back out on it again. Mortality is next to nothing now.'

'You feed them silage when they're shacked-up in the house?'

'Indeed,' the Hopper nodded, 'and meal the few weeks before they lamb.'

'That's the way to play the game. No fancy stuff.'

'I'm making ends meet, just about,' the Hopper said. 'There's food on the table and clothes on their backs though I never have a minute to scratch myself.'

'Nor another one to feel the itch,' said Steve.

If he could choose a life he would favour the Hopper's. A parcel of land and a gerry-built house. A good wife and growing kids to slow the passing years. Eating the fruits of your own performance.

'Quinty wants a word with me. You'd hardly reckon why?'

'I don't,' the Hopper shook his head. 'Himself and Callaghan are cooking something up. I was with them but offside them, if you get my drift. That Quinty is a headcase; you should watch your step.'

'Ah, his heart is in the right place,' Steve disagreed. 'He's a great man for the crack.'

'He'd better shape up soon then. The word is out his father's near the pearly gates.' Hopper closed his eyes, dropped his voice and tapped his chest. 'The old pump, you know.'

'Yeah, I heard he got a touch.'

'More bang than touch. Sure he's on his last legs. Quinty stands to get the farm – succession, transference and inheritance. Then his father's old seat on the district council; I reckon some day he'll land that too. You can bet your trousers that's the state of affairs.'

'Quinty a councillor!' Steve guffawed. 'You've a great imagination.'

'Oh Quinty's star is on the up and up,' said Hopper, flushed as a punter on a winning streak. 'He could make it all the way into parliament too. He's young yet and hasn't he the family name. Just the one thing against him.' Suddenly the Hopper reined himself in.

'What's that?' Steve waited.

'Nothing. Only hearsay,' the Hopper evaded.

'A woman?'

'A woman, what else.'

'Well?'

'I'll say no more,' said Hopper.

'Ah g'long to hell. If he beats her with a hammer he's sure to get gold. Is she married?'

'No more,' the Hopper was adamant. 'But tell me I'm wrong and there's no politics at work. Callaghan's not here for the taste of drink. Himself and Quinty's father were just like that,' and Hopper crossed two fingers by way of illustration, nodding to where Quinty and Callaghan were now in conclave with Mrs Carr about halfway up the counter. 'Politics or finance,' he mused.

Mrs Carr, proprietress of the establishment, had bright blue eyes and silver-blond hair. When she smiled her teeth showed white and even, a host of tiny wrinkles coming off the brilliant eyes. The smile always vanished like quicksilver though, marking her gracious but expeditious style.

'Now there's a lady,' the Hopper observed.

'Same again?' asked Steve.

'No, I'm off,' the Hopper hastened and knocked back his drink, the cut of a man who'd just remembered his commitments.

'One for the road then.'

'No way, Steve. I'll catch you again.'

'Not here you won't. Catch me down in Nolans any night of the week. Bet you're off to count the sheep again.'

'Well, the way it is,' the Hopper paused, 'I wouldn't feel easy barrin' I saw them twice a day.'

The lounge was humming. Steve called out for one large bottle. Orders were going over thick and fast.

'Make it two while you're about it,' he told Bill.

'And they say,' Bill muttered, 'there's no money in the country.'

'Aren't they owned by the banks the half of them,' said Steve.

He was seeing himself in the glass behind the counter, the white shock of hair and the pale thin face. I should slop on down to Nolans now, he thought. All that talk and resurrections of the past. We're all dying on our feet and all we can do is pour out history from a bottle. Should've told you, Hopper. How a year ago I drove out to that one-horse town she came from. Quiet as the stars of that frosty night, bejasus. How I drove up the one street and back down again. You'd want to see the changes. New factory and bungalows with lawns in front; but the same old church and same grey houses, me wondering if she lived there now or if she lived at all. Had the divil of a problem to remember what she looked like; not her shape and make but her living image. Didn't spot her of course. Life goes on in its own mortal way and it's no use talking or putting back the clock.

He had just about decided to slip out and down to Nolans when Quinty emerged from the crowd and collared him.

'Pow-wow, Stevie. Let's you and me put our spades together.'

Quinty lit a king-sized cigarette. He was tanked. You could tell by the way he supported himself – steady as a boulder on the lips of a pit.

'That old wooden chalet you've been living in,' said Quinty. 'It's on a grand little site. Build solid walls around the frame, then roof with slates and what have you got? A bungalow. I've seen it done and very cheaply too.' Quinty's throat was as rough as a shagged engine.

'You don't say,' muttered Steve.

'A man in your position need not be out of pocket. Council grants would nearly see you right.'

'Council grants?' Steve remained sceptical.

'No problem,' said Quinty. 'You can do well out of this. Your disability benefit – how much does that pay?'

'Why?' Steve asked him warily.

'I'm considering your welfare.'

'Thirty-nine fifty,' Steve told him.

'With a wife and child you would get a bit more. Or maybe you could have your old job back again.'

'After your father?'

'Sure,' said Quinty. 'You know, he rues the day he ever let you go.'

'Fired me you mean.'

Quinty shrugged. 'We all lose the head one time or another.'

'Why the sudden interest in my welfare?' asked Steve.

'Because I'm looking for a favour. There's a dropper bitch that's giving no end of trouble. Drags home lumps of putrid meat, wherever the hell she digs them up. Running livestock too, or so I'm told. You know how some of them turn queer and scavenge like mad once they've had their first litter.'

'You want me to take her off your hands?' asked Steve.

'No, she'll have to be put down. She's owned by a woman out beyond the Craigstown ridge. About seven miles from here, near the Mullingar road. Do you know that country, Stevie?'

'No, it's back of the beyonds.'

Quinty took a beer-mat and produced a silver biro. 'Here, I'll draw a map. There's a vet in that locality will do the job for you.'

The biro was lost in Quinty's big brown fingers.

'And what's this lady's name?' asked Stevie.

'Now don't pass a brick, my right honourable friend. She's an old flame of yours. Romy Peregrino is the lady's name.'

His shirtsleeved mates on the bookie's corner nodded to Steve as he drove out. They stared with idle curiosity, working up a thirst in the sultry heat before heading down to Nolans for the evening session.

Summer had come late. The verges were in flourish and pale young whitethorns had just begun to blossom. Steve was only coming back to earth. He pushed back his hair, watching himself in the rear-view mirror. The past was catching up on him and drawing him together again. But he could not think straight.

It was hot as a glasshouse inside the van by the time he was climbing up the narrow ridge road. Gorse bloomed brilliantly off the margins. To either side the landscape, low and flat, was smothered by a purple brooding sky. He wondered what her reaction would be. Then, deep down and distant, he could see a housetop nestled among screens of thick green yew. His heart was pumping.

The house was small with green pebble-dashed walls. He drove through a gateway to the side and round into a bit of yard at the back. Anxious and irresolute, he stayed in the van. It was deathly still and quiet outside.

He did not recognise her right away as she emerged from an extension at the rear of the house. She was dressed in red – bright red costume and bright red shoes. Her blouse was low cut, white and frilly. She recognised him slowly, greeting him in her cool phlegmatic way.

'Hello, Stevie,' was all she said as if she'd only seen him yesterday.

'You look well,' he told her, standing like a fool beside the van.

She looked fabulous, her jet-black hair clasped to one side

by a comb, the bright red lipstick setting off her dark complexion. Old emotions choked up behind his tongue.

He said, 'Quinty sent me out to collect the dog.'

'Oh yes, the dog,' she lingered.

He sensed he had never made a difference to her – not now, not ever.

'He's not coming so.'

Steve said, 'No, he's tied up beyond.'

He noticed she was wearing lace gloves. For the withered fingers of her left hand, he supposed.

'Tied up,' she repeated tonelessly. 'Hold on a minute, Stevie.'

He appraised her as she walked back to the house. She was out of place in a mean backyard, her figure unaffectedly sensual, her thighs and shoulders more plump than he remembered.

He cursed himself for the cut of his old clothes and the smell of closely herded beasts that came from them. There was a pair of small outhouses, one of them a toilet, dry and derelict. The second one was bolted and he heard the moans and whinings of a dog inside. He strolled into a wild patch beyond the yard, waist-deep in seed heads and lanky buttercups. It had seen a plough in the distant past for the furrows were deep and regular. She might have had a notion to enhance the place and then for some reason let it go again. A hole had been dug near the boundary fence and a spade left standing in the mound of fresh clay. The heat oppressed him. He was stupid from lethargy, unable to take stock.

Then, hearing voices, he saw her on the path and a young girl wheeling a bicycle beside her. He watched them pause in conversation at the gate, the girl spin the pedals in reverse with her foot, then mount the saddle laughing at some words that passed between them. She waved the girl goodbye and started back up the path.

Steve was in no hurry. He contemplated the sleek black bitch.

'A fine looking animal,' he observed. 'There's the labrador in her.'

She was holding the leash out vertically to keep the dog from her tightly packed skirt.

'Labrador and pointer,' she confirmed.

'A dropper. Is she quarrelsome?'

'Not a bit,' she said.

He smelt rich perfume as she passed him the leash.

'You're in fine shape,' he said, remembering how she used to crave for compliments. 'A real picture,' he added.

'Am I?' she replied stepping back again. A smile was on her lips but nowhere near her dark eyes. He stroked the dog now sitting by his side. The ears were soft as velvet. Her whole body rippled with nervous energy.

'What happened to the pups?' he asked, trying to meet her lovely eyes. She was looking into space.

'Oh, Quinty took them away somewhere.'

'Drowned them I suppose. A mongrel litter, it's the only way,' he said, caressing the dog but watching her. He was tender beyond caution but she was maintaining a cool reserve.

'He likely told you the way to the vet.'

'Oh, sure,' he said and knew she wished him to go. The rebuff turned him hard, made him want to hurt.

'And the hole where I can bury her is up there by the fence.'

'That's right,' she said shortly.

She stood off and watched as Steve was driving out the gate, the dog sitting meekly behind him in the van.

The bungalow was three miles up the road on an elevated site with a southern view. The vet was a fair-haired slim young man and a double garage served as his surgery.

'You're sure about this?' he asked doubtfully.

'She can't control her. Has to keep her locked up.'

They watched her sitting meekly on the dusty concrete floor. The vet was reluctant but finally he said, 'Let's get her up on the table then.'

Steve kept fondling her velvet ears as the vet scraped a patch of her foreleg bare, then tied a piece of bandage high up on the leg. Her soft brown eyes were looking trustingly at Steve. The vet located the vein with his fingers but soon as the needle touched she turned and twisted till finally he had to withdraw.

'No use,' he said. 'She has to be still.'

Now Steve was using both his arms to hold her fast in the sitting position. The plastic cylinder was flecked with blood.

'I'll try the other leg,' the vet decided with obvious distaste for the task in hand. He set to work on the second leg but the same thing happened all over again. 'Only one thing for it,' he capitulated.

So then they had her lying sideways on the table, her head unsupported out over the edge. She kept on looking back at Steve for reassurance and Steve was feeling all tied-up inside. Now the vet was trying for her heart between the forelegs and Steve had a struggle just to keep her down. Feeling the needle, she frisked and jerked but some of the shot had already got home.

Soon her legs were splayed on the concrete floor, her blood set like garnets in the dust about her. She went down as they talked.

'Peregrino,' smiled the vet, 'is not exactly an Irish name.'

'No, it's said she was an infant when her mother brought her over.'

Steve did not disclose his deeper knowledge of the subject – that the mother and her infant, having suffered cruel abuse, had fled from southern Europe to a town near Mullingar where the mother had expired and left her orphaned child in care.

'And now she's renting Tom Callaghan's old house.'

'Callaghan's?' said Steve.

'Oh yes, that humble dwelling is the great man's birthplace. Suppose he keeps possession to remind him where he's come from. Gives him an incentive to stay at the top of the wheel.'

'Throws nothing away,' said Steve. 'Maybe that's why he's a millionaire now.'

'You're joking,' laughed the vet. 'He was worth a million years ago.'

She lay whining and wheezing, her tongue hanging slack from the side of her mouth.

'Though I've never seen Tom next to near the place. Another party visits regularly. I often see his car there.'

'A red Mercedes?' Steve suggested. It was more than just a hunch.

'So you know about herself and Quinty.'

'Who doesn't,' said Steve.

'I gather he takes her off on trips with him. All very discreet of course. Dublin, London, even the States. But then you don't need me to tell you.'

'No,' lied Steve. 'It's been going on for some time now.'

'Oh years,' said the vet. 'Maybe five or six. If they're happy that way then good luck to them. It wouldn't be my cup of tea – all that cloak and dagger stuff.'

'If she's happy,' said Steve.

'True, very true,' agreed the vet. 'But it must be horrid lonely below in that old house.'

There was something else the vet was itching to say but he turned his attention to the dog instead.

He sighed and said, 'This won't be very delicate.'

Then he stooped and injected her low into the stomach.

'Better get her in the sack before old rigor mortis sets.'

The smell of her alive was in the van as Steve drove back. He felt hollow and world-weary.

The house was in darkness. He buried the heavy sack without delay and, the favour done, he rested on the spade. Gentle clouds pressed down on the west where a great yellow mouth consumed the vestiges of light. It was late, too late for Nolans now. The day was ending without consummation.

The headlights opened up the convoluted track as he sped out over the crest of the ridge and began to recall Quinty's chat in the lounge. On impulse he checked, and swung the bonnet towards the ditch. Why not? he thought. A hook well lost to catch a salmon.

His resolve was strong as he left the van and strode across the yard to the door of the extension. He hammered on the opaque glass. The lights came on and then she was unbolting the door.

'Holy Jesus!' she exclaimed.

The jet-black hair was loose to her shoulders and she wore a white silk dressing-gown.

He said, 'The job is done.'

'I hope it was easy on the poor oul' thing.'

'Yeah,' he said. 'Like a long deep sleep.'

She kept her two hands on the door, the fingers of the left one hidden from his view.

He said, 'I wanted you to know I've been making some plans.' But he had to pause because, disturbed from behind, she turned her head and opened back the door. A little child was clinging to her leg and burying its face in the folds of her gown. Disconcerted, he began again.

'I've got some plans for that wooden house of mine. I'm goin' to claim the grants and make a bungalow of her. Do you follow me?'

Tense about the mouth she nodded warily.

'Now,' he nerved himself. 'I pull a few pounds here and there on the side but the welfare cheque is money in me fist. Are you with me?'

'So far,' she said, the withered left hand plunged deep in a pocket, the good hand moulding the small child's skull.

'Is the little one yours?' He peered at the child.

'She is.'

'About four years old I'd nearly say.'

Her mouth was poised to speak but she said nothing.

'I'd say so anyway,' he continued. 'See, if we were to be married I'd be father to the child and the welfare money would amount to more.'

She considered the doorstep. He grew more confident the longer she reflected.

'Or I could even take up the offer of a job. A full day's work is no great burden on me now.'

But when she looked at him again a bitter sneer had corrupted her face.

'Tell Quinty it's no dice,' she addressed him calmly.

'Quinty bedamned,' he said. 'I'm dancing to my own tune.'

'No, he won't get shut of me so easy. The courts will soon be on the side of the child. I've got him and he knows it.'

Steve looked away and studied the full dark yews on the perimeter. So this was life and this his fate. He was jaded, crushed beyond redemption. Not wanting her to see him, he turned his back and stared beyond the still black outlines of the couch grass. The night was still as the dropper's grave.

Then, hard as stone, he turned and asked, 'Any chance you'd have a bottle of stout?'

'Come on,' she left the door for him. 'You look fit for one.'

He followed her inside.

MICHAEL AND MARY

SEUMAS O'KELLY

SEUMAS O'KELLY

Seumas O'Kelly was born in Loughrea, Co. Galway in either 1875 or 1878. He worked on or contributed to many Irish newspapers while also producing short stories, plays, novels and verse. His novella, *The Weaver's Grave*, is considered by many to be not only his best work, but to bear comparison with the best of the *genre* in the English language. His untimely death in 1918 was caused by the shock suffered when the offices of 'Nationality', the newspaper he was editing, was attacked by an anti-Sinn Fein mob celebrating the ending of the Great War.

MARY HAD SPENT many days gathering wool from the whins on the headland. They were the bits of wool shed by the sheep before the shearing. When she had got a fleece that fitted the basket she took it down to the canal and washed it. When she had done washing it was a soft, white, silky fleece. She put it back in the brown sally basket, pressing it down with her long, delicate fingers. She had risen to go away, holding the basket against her waist, when her eyes followed the narrow neck of water that wound through the bog.

She could not follow the neck of yellow water very far. The light of day was failing. A haze hung over the great Bog of Allen that spread out level on all sides of her. The boat loomed out of the haze on the narrow neck of the canal water. It looked, at first, a long way off, and it seemed to come in a cloud. The soft rose light that mounted the sky caught the boat and burnished it like dull gold. It came leisurely, drawn by the one horse, looking like a Golden Barque in the twilight. Mary put her brown head a little to one side as she watched the easy motion of the boat. The horse drew himself along deliberately, the patient head going up and down with every heavy step. A crane rose from the bog, flapping two lazy wings across the wake of the boat, and, reaching its long neck before it, got lost in the haze.

The figure that swayed by the big arm of the tiller on *The Golden Barque* was vague and shapeless at first, but Mary felt her eyes following the slow movements of the body. Mary thought it was very beautiful to sway every now and then by the arm of the tiller, steering a Golden Barque through the twilight.

Then she realised suddenly that the boat was much nearer
than she had thought. She could see the figures of the men
plainly, especially the slim figure by the tiller. She could trace
the rope that slackened and stretched taut as it reached from
the boat to the horse. Once it splashed the water, and there
was a little sprout of silver. She noted the whip looped under
the arm of the driver. Presently she could count every heavy
step of the horse, and was struck by the great size of the
shaggy fetlocks. But always her eyes went back to the figure
by the tiller.

She moved back a little way to see *The Golden Barque* pass.
It came from a strange, far-off world, and having traversed the
bog went away into another unknown world. A red-faced man
was sitting drowsily on the prow. Mary smiled and nodded to
him, but he made no sign. He did not see her; perhaps he was
asleep. The driver who walked beside the horse had his head
stooped and his eyes on the ground. He did not look up as he
passed. Mary saw his lips moving, and heard him mutter to
himself; perhaps he was praying. He was a shrunken, misshaped
little figure and kept step with the brute in the journey over
the bog. But Mary felt the gaze of the man by the tiller upon
her. She raised her eyes.

The light was uncertain and his peaked cap threw a shadow
over his face. But the figure was lithe and youthful. He smiled
as she looked up, for she caught a gleam of his teeth. Then the
boat had passed. Mary did not smile in return. She had taken
a step back and remained there quietly. Once he looked back
and awkwardly touched his cap, but she made no sign.

When the boat had gone by some way she sat down on the
bank, her basket of wool beside her, looking at *The Golden
Barque* until it went into the gloom. She stayed there for some
time, thinking long in the great silence of the bog. When at last
she rose, the canal was clear and cold beneath her. She looked
into it. A pale new moon was shining down in the water.

Mary often stood at the door of the cabin on the headland
watching the boats that crawled like black snails over the narrow
streak of water through the bog. But they were not all like
black snails now. There was a Golden Barque among them.

Whenever she saw it she smiled, her eyes on the figure that stood by the shaft of the tiller.

One evening she was walking by the canal when *The Golden Barque* passed. The light was very clear and searching. It showed every plank, battered and tar-stained, on the rough hulk, but for all that it lost none of its magic for Mary. The little shrunken driver, head down, the lips moving, walked beside the horse. She heard his low mutters as he passed. The red-faced man was stooping over the side of the boat, swinging out a vessel tied to a rope, to haul up some water. He was singing a ballad in a monotonous voice. A tall, dark, spare man was standing by the funnel, looking vacantly ahead. Then Mary's eyes travelled to the tiller.

Mary stepped back with some embarrassment when she saw the face. She backed into a hawthorn that grew all alone on the canal bank. It was covered with bloom. A shower of the white petals fell about her when she stirred the branches. They clung about her hair like a wreath. He raised his cap and smiled. Mary did not know the face was so eager, so boyish. She smiled a little nervously at last. His face lit up, and he touched his cap again.

The red-faced man stood by the open hatchway going into the hold, the vessel of water in his hand. He looked at Mary and then at the figure beside the tiller.

'Eh, Michael?' the red-faced man said quizzically. The youth turned back to the boat, and Mary felt the blush spreading over her face.

'Michael!'

Mary repeated the name a little softly to herself. The gods had delivered up one of their great secrets.

She watched *The Golden Barque* until the two square slits in the stern that served as port holes looked like two little Japanese eyes. Then she heard a horn blowing. It was the horn they blew to apprise lock-keepers of the approach of a boat. But the nearest lock was a mile off. Besides, it was a long, low sound the horn made, not the short, sharp, commanding blast they blew for lock-keepers. Mary listened to the low sound of the horn, smiling to herself. Afterwards the horn always blew like that whenever *The Golden Barque* was passing the solitary hawthorn.

Mary thought it was very wonderful that *The Golden Barque* should be in the lock one day that she was travelling with her basket to the market in the distant village. She stood a little hesitantly by the lock. Michael looked at her, a welcome in his eyes.

'Going to Bohermeen?' the red-faced man asked.

'Ay, to Bohermeen,' Mary answered.

'We could take you to the next lock,' he said, 'it will shorten the journey. Step in.'

Mary hesitated, as he held out a big hand to help her to the boat. He saw the hesitation and turned to Michael.

'Now, Michael,' he said.

Michael came to the side of the boat, and held out his hand. Mary took it and stepped on board. The red-faced man laughed a little. She noticed that the dark man who stood by the crooked funnel never took his eyes from the stretch of water before him. The driver was already urging the horse to his start on the bank. The brute was gathering his strength for the pull, the muscles standing out on his haunches. They glided out of the lock.

It was half a mile from one lock to another. Michael had bidden her stand beside him at the tiller. Once she looked up at him and she thought the face shy but very eager, the most eager face that ever came across the bog from the great world.

Afterwards, whenever Mary had the time, she would make a cross-cut through the bog to the lock. She would step in and make the mile journey with Michael on *The Golden Barque*. Once, when they were journeying together, Michael slipped something into her hand. It was a quaint trinket, and shone like gold.

'From a strange sailor I got it,' Michael said.

Another day that they were on the barque, the blinding sheets of rain that often swept over the bog came upon them. The red-faced man and the dark man went into the hold. Mary looked about her, laughing. But Michael held out his great waterproof for her. She slipped into it and he folded it about her. The rain pelted them, but they stood together, Michael holding the big coat folded about her. She laughed a little nervously.

'You will be wet,' she said.

Michael did not answer. She saw the eager face coming down close to hers. She leaned against him a little and felt the great strength of his arms about her. They went sailing away together in *The Golden Barque* through all the shining seas of the gods.

'Michael,' Mary said once, 'is it not lovely?'

'The wide ocean is lovely,' Michael said. 'I always think of the wide ocean going over the bog.'

'The wide ocean!' Mary said with awe. She had never seen the wide ocean. Then the rain passed. When the two men came up out of the hold Mary and Michael were standing together by the tiller.

Mary did not go down to the lock after that for some time. She was working in the reclaimed ground on the headland. Once the horn blew late in the night. It blew for a long time, very softly and lowly. Mary sat up in bed listening to it, her lips parted, the memory of Michael on *The Golden Barque* before her. She heard the sound dying away in the distance. Then she lay back on her pillow, saying she would go down to him when *The Golden Barque* was on the return journey.

The figure that stood by the tiller on the return was not Michael's. When Mary came to the lock the red-faced man was telling out the rope, and where Michael always stood by the tiller there was the short strange figure of a man with a pinched, pock-marked face.

When the red-faced man wound the rope round the stump at the lock, bringing the boat to a standstill, he turned to Mary.

'Michael is gone voyaging,' he said.

'Gone voyaging?' Mary repeated.

'Ay,' the man answered. 'He would be always talking to the foreign sailors in the dock where the canal ends. His eyes would be upon the big masts of the ships. I always said he would go.'

Mary stood there while *The Golden Barque* was in the lock. It looked like a toy ship packed in a wooden box.

'A three-master he went in,' the red-faced man said, as they made ready for the start. 'I saw her standing out for the sea last night. Michael is under the spread of big canvas. He had the blood in him for the wide ocean, the wild blood of the rover.' And the red-faced man, who was the Boss of the boat, let his eyes wander up the narrow neck of water before him.

Mary watched *The Golden Barque* moving away, the grotesque figure standing by the tiller. She stayed there until a pale moon was shining below her, turning over a little trinket in her fingers. At last she dropped it into the water.

It made a little splash, and the vision of the crescent was broken.

WHAT'S WRONG WITH AUBRETIA?

MARY LAVIN

MARY LAVIN

Mary Lavin was born in 1912 in the USA. She has lived in Ireland since she was eleven, mainly in Co. Meath, next to Bective Abbey – from which came the title of her first collection of short stories, *Tales From Bective Bridge* – and in Dublin. Her two novels, a novelette and numerous short story collections have won her many prestigious awards and a reputation as one of the great short story writers of this century.

THEY WERE STANDING inside the big gates at the entrance to the avenue: the gates that were one more anomaly now as the villas invaded the small fields to either side of the drive.

'Is there to be no end to them?' she cried, as if, because he lived down in one of them, Alan should know.

'I'm not the contractor. I've told you that before,' he said shortly.

'Yours was one of the first to be built though,' she said accusingly, as if this made him a party to the whole scheme. 'They levelled the little upland pasture last week, did you know that? And they're laying down a new road. Villas, villas, villas! They stick up like tombstones all around us. We might as well be living in a cemetery.'

'It can't be worse than when you first had to sell the land. I could understand your being pretty fed-up then.'

'Oh, it wasn't so bad then. We saw it coming, I suppose. And we really didn't realise there would be all this appalling vulgarity.'

'It was really the villas themselves you hated, wasn't it?' he said thoughtfully.

She pulled him up short, though.

'Why the past tense?'

He was a bit startled by the sharpness in her voice, but he answered off-handedly all the same.

'Well, you must be getting used to them by now, no matter what you say.'

'As if I ever could,' she said passionately.

Still, they did not quarrel then. He looked up at the big granite pillars to either side of the gates, wound round with ivy, that

having no more foothold on the stone, flowered and fruited
wildly about the heads of the plaster figures (no noses) that
held aloft the empty iron brackets of long-ago carriage lamps.

'The funny thing is, you know,' he said ruefully, and he
nodded backwards in the direction of the new villas, 'to them
it's this that is the eyesore!' He laid his hand on the granite
pier, and nodded again, this time back at the dark old house in
the trees.

'Is it an eyesore to you then?'

He paused for a minute before he answered her.

'Look here, Vera,' he said then sternly, 'I feel we are on to
something more complicated than aesthetics. Are we?'

'Oh, not necessarily,' she said, but she also had begun to be
uneasy as to where their words were leading them.

'I've felt it before now!' he said quietly. 'I felt it the day you
were sneering at those people in the villa opposite us when
they were planting the aubretia, do you remember?'

'Not sneering! I only asked why it always had to be aubretia!'

'You knew why! Because they didn't have generations behind
them with experience of making terraces and shrubberies – like
you!'

She agreed. 'Maybe so, but I don't see what it has to do with
us now!'

'It has everything to do with us. I felt that day that it might
easily have been *my* family that offended you with their horticul-
tural ignorance – it could easily have been *me*. As a matter of
fact I like aubretia. I don't see what's wrong with it.'

'Oh, for goodness sake,' she cried. She wished passionately
that she could have retracted her own words at the start, but
he went on doggedly.

'It's a question of class, I suppose?' he said.

'Oh, don't be silly,' she cried quickly, too quickly; the words
were barely out of his mouth, and she had anticipated them too
accurately. 'Don't be silly! Not class: taste if you like!'

But he wasn't convinced.

'Taste is the new euphemism for class.'

'Nonsense. There's no such thing as class nowadays; not in
places like this anyway, not in any form.'

'You're right there,' he said. 'It hasn't any form any more. It's formless and vague, like a fog. You get lost in it. At least that's how I'd feel, I'm sure, if I was talking to your father. What does he think of me, by the way?' he asked suddenly. 'He must have noticed my calling for you so often.'

It was so sudden a twist to the conversation that her heart missed a beat. With the simple question, they had soared suddenly above the reach of the small vexations that troubled them.

'I'll have to get to know him, sooner or later,' he said.

'Would you like to come to tea some afternoon', she asked cautiously, 'what about some Sunday afternoon – next Sunday?'

Oh that afternoon! How awful it was. Her father was at his worst.

To begin with, because Alan lived in one of the villas, her father acted as if they were in the relation of tenant and landlord. She was mortified, though she ought to have foreseen it. It was the way he went on all the time since the villas started. He acted as if, erected on his land, he had an interest in them. The way he walked around studying the layout of the foundations, criticising the workmen, questioning the mix of the cement. Of course, he had gone on much the same way years before they ever sold the land, when they first had to let it for grazing. That ought to have been his first come-down, but he never gave in to it. He walked around the pastures as usual, with his stick that had a small hoe at the end, scotching thistles, and prodding the dealer's cattle.

'It's time those pollies went to the sales yard,' he'd say. 'They'll only lose weight in this weather.'

Ah well! it had done no harm to anyone then. But now before Alan she could hardly bear it.

She could see, the minute he came into the room that Alan was thunderstruck at the discrepancy between the old man's squirish notions, and his most unsquirish manners. His manners were at their worst that day. When tea came in, he was the limit. He pounced on the food, re-buttering the buttered bread, clapping two or three slices together and stuffing them into his mouth like a sword swallower. As for his cup, he took it straightaway out of the saucer and set it on the floor between his legs. The only use he made of the saucer was to slop the tea back and forth from it to his cup to cool it. And once, having made it too cold, he reached out and snatched the lid of the silver kettle that swung on its silver tripod over the lighted spirit lamp, and slopped back his whole cupful of tea, regardless of having already drunk some of it, regardless of its being poisoned with too much sugar and cream.

Yet the really awful thing was that it was Alan, and not he, who appeared in a bad light! It was Alan who looked at a disadvantage. Take the way they each acted if she had to stand up for anything, or even half-stand, for any reason. Father, as usual, sat tight. But poor Alan sprang to his feet tirelessly every time, even if she only as much as stirred in her chair to reach for another cup. He must have jumped up a dozen times in this way, till at last it seemed to her that the gesture was drained of courtesy, and had become like an uncontrollable disability – a tic!

'Oh, do sit down; you're like a jack-in-the-box!' she said at last, and she knew she had hurt and perplexed him.

All the same, later that same day, when she was walking part of the way down the driveway with him, on his way home to the villas, she was not prepared for the effect the visit had had upon him. Their relationship seemed unaccountably to have deepened. At the gate he put up his hand to his forehead.

'What are we going to do?' he asked morosely.

'You're not proposing to me, by any chance, are you?' she said caustically, because she, too, was upset, and it was a joyless moment, anyway. It called for bitterness.

'No, I'm not,' he said quietly. But he smiled. 'I'm afraid I took it for granted, right at the start, that you'd have me, if circumstances were otherwise.'

At first his words filled her with such joy that she missed the ominous note at the end.

'– What I mean is this, Vera – we'd have to go away. We couldn't stay here! You can see that!'

'But why on earth . . . why can't . . . ?'

At thirty-four, she had for a long time become unconsciously reconciled to the thought that she would not marry, and in the unexpected, tumultuous happiness of being in love with Alan she hadn't given any thought to the practicalities.

Once or twice it had crossed her mind to wonder where they would live, but it had never seemed urgent. She had even looked around the old house sometimes, and thought how easy it would be to make separate quarters for Father if –

'But why?' she said again.

'Why what?' he said roughly.

'Why would we have to go away? What about your work? And there's father –'

'Oh, there's father all right!' he said sarcastically.

'What do you mean?' she asked, but her next words showed her uneasiness. 'I think lately he looks very –' she hesitated to say he looked old, however, although Alan knew she was the child of a late marriage, – 'very shaken,' she said. 'He needs me.'

'He needs someone. He couldn't stay alone in that great barracks. But it doesn't have to be you. I want you, Vera, but I'm not fool enough to think our marriage would survive long if we stayed around here.' He waved his hand to take in not only the old house and the masses of oppressive ivy, but the entire building estate.

'Tell me one thing,' she said suddenly. 'What are we running away from? This – or that?' and she nodded first at the old house, and then at the villas and the white cement roads that had been laid down, like the runways of an aerodrome, and lit up in all their bareness by bright arc lamps.

'Oh, don't try to be funny,' he said. 'It's the constant comparison I can't stand. You think I hate the old house – that I haven't the taste to appreciate it: it's not that though.' He stared back at it. 'I feel it's brow-beating me all the time: I feel I'm always being measured up against it, and being found short!'

'Oh, for goodness' sake,' she said lamely. 'You told me once that I had a bee in my bonnet about the new villas: it's you that has one I think.'

'Perhaps it's the same bee,' he said drily. 'I didn't honestly notice much difference between one house and another until I met you. I used to hear my mother, and the people next door to us talking about this old house, and saying it ought to have been pulled down – that it spoiled the whole estate.' He laughed suddenly. 'They used to wonder if they could take an action against the builders for leaving it standing to disfigure the land-scape!' She smiled wanly to please him, ' – but outside of casual conversations like that, as I say I was indifferent to all houses; a place to sleep and eat: that's all any house was to me. I dare say I was lacking in perception of some sort, but there you are!'

'Oh no, I wouldn't say that,' she cried. 'That *is* all a house ought to be, I suppose, if –'

'Oh no,' he said then, grimly. 'You can't retract like that, Vera. It was you who opened my eyes. Left to myself, I would probably have thought the villas were the last word. I'd have thought I was doing well by any girl if I provided her with a nice new bungalow. After all, it takes about twenty years of a man's life to pay for one of them.' He was watching her face. 'You never thought of it like that, I suppose? And I'm sure your father never did! It must be a great thing to get to his time of life without ever facing reality. No wonder he's so fit!'

'Oh, do you think he's looking fit?' she cried, not exactly irrelevantly, but with a relevance too deep for him to see. 'I think sometimes lately –'

'Nonsense. I never saw a man of his years look as active and strong. He could see us all down, that man. I shouldn't be surprised if he outlasted the old house too, in the end.'

They had turned at the gate and walked back, so that now they were close to the house, and it loomed over them, darken-ing the starry sky.

'I wonder what will become of it in the end,' he said, almost casually, and she was suddenly chilled to the heart's core by the impersonal note in his voice.

'Do you?' she said coldly. 'It will fall down, in the long run, I dare say.' Then she felt a return of the unaccountable venom the villas roused in her. 'Lovers will make use of it, I suppose! They may complain about us, but I often wonder what they'd do without our avenue – and our shrubs!'

For there was always a couple, or more than one, among

the shrubs in the evenings. She and Alan could sometimes hear muffled voices, or the creak of a twig to one or other side of them. They could even see, indistinctly, some of the less discreet pairs just inside the gate, pressed against each other in the darkness.

'Those are not girls from the new houses!' Alan protested sharply. 'They're servant girls.'

'I thought there were no servant girls needed in the new labour-saving houses?'

'Maybe not,' he said slowly. 'I don't know where they come from, but I resent your inferences.'

'You resent everything I say lately.'

But he didn't take it up. He was still thinking about the lovers.

'I suppose there were always lovers hanging about here, anyway,' he said. 'Someone was telling me that the road behind our house was once a lane, and it was known as Lovers' Lane. That's the way it's marked on an old ordnance map.'

'They had the ditches then, at least,' she said coldly. 'They didn't obtrude themselves on us. They didn't make use of our driveway.'

'You seem to think that a good thing,' he said drily. 'I'm sure they went a lot further with their love-making in the ditches.'

'Well!' she said defiantly. 'I'm sure it was more natural than this – this pushing against each other! And not so revolting!'

'Hhmmm!' said Alan. 'It seems morality also is synonymous with aesthetics!'

But he was less tense. And he even laughed. He probably knew as well as she did that obscurely she resented their own fastidiousness. Only for not wanting to put themselves in the same category as the unseen lovers in the darkness around them, there might have been more body in their own affair. But as it was, they always walked scrupulously apart when they reached the avenue, and at the top of the steps they kissed, by leaning forward towards each other, not moving closer. She, for her part, felt that he was holding back from her, and she felt, too, that it was for reasons other than a respect for her person. Obscurely she felt this too had something to do with the old house. If they had met in some other situation, in another city perhaps, would things have been quite the same?

'Well, Vera, what are we going to do?' he said again.

'We don't have to decide tonight, do we?' she said. 'I must go in. After all, there's no great hurry, is there?'

But he put out his hand.

'Vera, wait! I must tell you something else. I was all right until I met you. I mean I was satisfied with myself, more or less. But you've unsettled me. And whether you come with me or not, I'm going to make a change; to get away from here. As a matter of fact I didn't tell you, but the other day I saw an advertisement for a job abroad. I answered it. And I got a reply. I can take it if I want. What do you think?'

'It might be a solution,' she said cautiously, but even then she was sure he meant that he would go first and, afterwards perhaps, if she could arrange something for her father, or if perhaps – well, in the natural order of events poor father mightn't be so long in it – she'd be following him. She didn't dream for a moment that he intended to make a clean cut.

'But why?' she cried out, when she suddenly realised that he wanted things settled for once and for all. 'Why has everything come to a head so quickly? Why cannot we wait?'

'Wait for what? Till the old man dies? Till –?'

He stopped. But she knew, for all that, exactly what he had been going to say. He wanted her; she didn't doubt it, but he didn't blink the fact that she was four years older than him, and that each year they waited would be a loss, not a gain, to her. He was so terribly practical.

'I see,' she said.

She did see.

When they first met, he was always telling her how he spotted her the first day she was out for a walk on one of the new concrete roads. 'That's the kind of girl for me,' he had said. It made her so happy to hear him say so, but even at the time she noticed that he had not said she was 'the' girl for him, but only 'the kind of girl' for him. He had no time for what she called love, and absolutely none for love at first sight. Doggedly he claimed that men and women selected each other consciously, that it was a reasoned choice. The most he would concede to fate or fortuity was a slight biological attraction between two people that they would have to examine later.

With her it had been entirely different. It was his unlikeness to her friends that she noticed first, but she soon saw that they were only external disparities. And when their eyes met even on that first occasion, she felt that deep inside them was some affinity that when it was brought to light ought to make him hers for ever. In short, she believed in love. But apparently she was wrong. It has been her undoing, that reliance upon a fated bondage. He would not be hampered by any such romantic notions. Indeed, he would not keep up a vague association that could come between him and a new attachment if he met another girl who was also his kind.

'Very well, Alan,' she said. 'If that's the way you want it. But I'll see you again, I suppose – tomorrow?'

Did he hesitate? She couldn't really tell, but he was emphatic enough in his reply.

'Good lord – yes! What do you take me for?'

But what did she take him for? And what was he – to her, now?

A feeling of separateness, and aloneness that she had never known, even before she met him, a feeling of being sundered, came over her as she stood listening to his footsteps going down the drive. She had a sudden desperate longing to run after him, but it seemed that the shrubs were all eyes, hidden eyes, watching her. She felt sick too, and dizzy. She turned and went up the steps. On the top step she had to stand and draw a long breath, holding on to the big brass knob in the middle of the door, the big knob shaped like the head of a lion, and bright from handling except in the tangles of his mane where verdigris had lodged.

While she stood there the whistle of a train shrilled out and she started. Alan could not have got as far as the end of the avenue, and yet that whistle seemed to menace her; to sound his farewell. But he was not going away for several – weeks? Days? She hadn't asked him when he was going! The whistle shrilled again in the sharp night air. He might have been going

tonight for all she knew. But no – he had agreed they would
see each other again. She was nervy and upset, that was all.
She'd see him again, and it wouldn't be a final meeting either.
He wouldn't really go, or if he went he would write, and they
would keep in touch. Yet in spite of all her efforts to reassure
herself, her eyes filled with tears, and when at that moment
the train whistle went for the third time, she steadied herself
against the door. She really was dizzy: and in the darkness she
saw the train rocketing through the night, all lit up like an
excursion train, its golden lights strung loosely together and
swaying gently with the sway of the carriages.

'I must be ill,' she thought in panic, because normally no train
could be seen from the house. There was an old disused railway
line somwhere near, on which a freight car was sometimes
shunted to and fro. But no train. No brightly lighted train.

'I'm sick, or I'm going balmy,' she thought, and she dried her
eyes and turned to stumble into the house.

As she turned, she saw the lights again, clearly this time,
through the few remaining trees that stirred in a light wind,
and made it seem that it was the lights that swayed. But the
lights were not moving at all, for they were in fact the lights of
the new villas, twinkling severally through the branches. Seeing
what they were, her heart was assailed, for they struck an
unexpected note, a sweet elegiac note that ought properly only
to have come from beauty.

COUNTY FOLK

MICHAEL CAMPBELL

MICHAEL CAMPBELL

Michael Campbell was born in Dublin in 1924 and educated at St Columba's and Trinity College, Dublin. He studied law, was called to the Irish Bar, but shortly afterwards turned to writing and journalism as a member of the London staff of *The Irish Times*. All his early stories were published in 'Irish Writing' and in 1956 the first of his six novels appeared. He succeeded to the title of Baron Glenavy on the death of his older brother – the celebrated humorous writer, Patrick Campbell – but the title lapsed on his own death in 1984.

THE STEWARTS ARRIVED at ten thirty; late considering that they had now to drive thirty-five miles. Patricia had been sitting in her evening-frock in the drawing-room for hours, watching mother playing Patience and father smoking his pipe over some book about horses. She had been thinking about Bruce. She could not *see* him. Although her one wish was to see him she could see nothing but a reddish face and a moustache; and Bruce had been much more. She and her mother conversed nervously about nothings, as if they were expecting terrible news, or someone upstairs was dying, or Patricia was leaving home to seek her fortune in the World, or leaving to meet her lover back from the Wars. This last, she kept on realising with a shock, *was* what she was doing.

At nine o'clock Mrs Fitzgerald turned on the News, softly so that it would not infuriate father. To those who listened without prejudice it was the year 1948 and the world was near to a war to end all wars, but it was hard not to be prejudiced in a house in the midst of County Kildare. Conferences were being held, and Notes exchanged; but in Kildare the rain falls softly upon the green fields and upon the cows that stand with their backs to the wind, and the sky is streaked with flying blue-back clouds, and the streams are so full that they provide a perpetual accompaniment to an unchanging world. Only in some of the houses, as in the Fitzgeralds', there are photographs of men in the uniforms of two wars, often three, as a reminder that the news means something even here. There was a photograph of Patricia's brother, Bob, who was killed in the RAF in the Second World War and of her uncle, Fred, who was killed in the First. But mother still listened to the news to read peace into every conference and note.

The Stewarts arrived at ten-thirty, and Patricia, sitting in a red dress in an armchair had for some time been longing to go upstairs, take off the red dress and slip into bed; yes, in spite of Bruce, for after all she could not see him. The Stewarts, he in tails and she in a black satin gown and silver-fox fur, were at the top of their form. They had a drink. Father had risen from his chair in his ragged tweed coat, put down his pipe, and poured it out for them. Father was being almost obsequious. So even he expected this to be *her* night, and blessed the Stewarts for having a Bentley!

Like Bruce, Colonel 'Reggie' Stewart had been in the Guards. He was over six feet tall and very broad, and his voice was always raised. His wife was tall, thin and beautiful, and her voice made a grating sound. They both had much to say. At first it was about the Smith O'Gradys and the home-coming of Bruce. Then it expanded. Reggie had bought a hell of a fine bay gelding of whom he had great hopes, and Charlie was making plans for London as soon as the season recommenced. Their conversation, therefore, almost clashed, but only in a humorous way. At home it had been different.

It was beginning to appear as if they would never leave when Reggie finally downed his glass of nearly neat Irish whiskey and said that they had better be getting along. Mother and Father came to the door and said good-night. Mother made it sound like Good Luck, but father wore a mask of indifference. Unreasonably she liked him for it, while mother's participation was irritating.

The Bentley lay like a slug shining with dew at the bottom of the steps. The three of them sat comfortably in front on the shining brown-leather seat, Charlie on the outside, Patricia captured by two Stewarts. Then, with mother standing under the light and waving, smoothly and silently they were off.

The car travelled at fifty on the narrow road. Its headlights turned it into daylight from hedge to hedge, from wall to wall. Now and then the dark-green trees that stood at either side stretched across to embrace in an arch above them. Reggie seldom troubled to dim the lights. The natives of this green and desert land, old farmers holding bicycles, young farmers holding girls, stood dazzled, unable to see and appreciate the Bentley or the evening-dress of the passengers.

To Patricia the night was peculiarly made of foxes. Her left cheek was constantly brushed by the long silver-black hairs of the fox that hung about Charlie's shoulders, and at the end of the bonnet of the car a silver-model of a fox stood and guided them along the winding road. The model held Patricia's eyes hypnotically as it bobbed from side to side, and almost in a trance all the time she tried to determine her attitude to what was to come. But the more she essayed to direct her thoughts ahead the more they retreated.

Patricia and Bruce became engaged on his last leave. They had grown up together; for although the Smith O'Gradys lived thirty-five miles away, this, in the country, is a neighbourly distance. Countless times they had hunted together, been to the races together, been seen together. She had been to school in England with his two sisters. The attachment had many links, and not the least of these was a physical attraction, for it was not merely a neighbourly engagement. Yet now she could only properly recall the neighbourliness; the other she remembered but could not feel. Profoundly-moving experiences were erased as if they had been superficial. It was inexplicable, and frightening.

She had never looked at anyone else; Bruce was so obviously the best of the 'set'. Bruce, while knowing the importance of hunt balls, county weddings, knew how to take an interest in other things. He bought pictures. When last home he had bought two paintings, originals, by Paul Henry of scenes in the West of Ireland; most people, if they had them at all, only had copies. He read books. Last Christmas he had sent her *None but the Rose*, and *April Lover* by Lucilla Drake. Yes, he was a wonderful person. To regard him as an ordinary, desiring man had always seemed a cheapness.

'What does Pat think?' said Reggie loudly.

'I'm so sorry – what were you saying?' she asked.

'We think we're lost,' replied Charlie, loud and grating.

'Oh dear!' she said. 'Oh, dear, how wonderful – let's get lost, lost, lost; yes, even with Charlie and Reggie, let's get lost!'

'It's all right ladies. Don't worry your fair heads,' said Reggie, 'I'll ask this fellow.'

A man wheeling a bicycle was caught by the headlights and pinned to the side of the road. Nervously peering into the radiance from under his cap he saw that he was required.

'I say,' said Reggie, 'have you any notion where we can find Ballydermot House. It's the Smith O'Gradys' place. It should be somewhere on this road.'

'Yis,' said the man, 'now wait till I tell yeh . . .' He pushed the cap up on his forehead. 'Yeh take the first turn to the lift at the nixt crossroads, and thin yeh keep sthraight on till yeh see the church on the lift and thin it's the first house with the big white geeates on the right.'

'Good man,' said Reggie, 'that's fine. Good-night.'

'Good-night,' said the man. The Bentley pulled away. Patricia reflected that a few years ago the man would have said 'Good-night sorr.' She was glad. She tried to see them as the man had seen them. She could not find an answer; they were either disgusting or impressive. She wondered if Charlie or Reggie ever asked themselves this question, ever, ever; she could not answer this either. She was a little proud of being sensitive, self-critical. Then she was ashamed, because having chosen a part one must play it with heart; the Stewarts at least knew this.

It would have been truer to have said that such complications did not exist for Charlie and Reggie. Reggie, driving much too fast now to see any church on the left, said, 'Of course these fellows will tell you anything . . . The first thing that comes into their heads!'

'Yes, darling,' agreed Charlie, 'but it's rather charming.'

White cottages with thatch, grey cottages with slates, mossy banks, bramble hedges, stone walls, decayed signposts, vast chestnut trees, men, dogs and bicycles, and, yes, a church, a ruin covered with ivy, but definitely a church, sped by. 'Slow darling, for God's sake,' said Charlie. But too late; big white gates on the right appeared and were gone, and Reggie with one hand on the wheel brought the Bentley to a screaming halt one hundred yards beyond. 'Bloody hell!' he said. He backed the car with amazing skill, and they were in through the gates and on to the drive in an instant and the hope that had been aroused in Patricia was gone and her heart was sinking fast.

The drive – she knew it well – seemed endless. In wide bends it passed between the great and ancient trees, and round every bend Patricia expected without reason to see the house. Similes rushed through her mind: going back to school, going into hospital with appendicitis, hunting for the first time. They were inappropriate to a lovers' reunion. The Stewarts – it was their most usual condition, she decided – were unaware. They hoped that the party would be up to scratch. They hoped that they were neither too early nor too late. If they were aware they disguised it well. Mercilessly they swept into the semi-circle of drive in front of the hall-door, among all the shining slugs that were there assembled.

The porch was in darkness and the curtains of the house were drawn. From behind these came an uproar of voices. On the strip of grass in front of the drawing-room windows stood a group of young men and girls, with several children and old men. They stood motionless and silent, watching. Patricia hated them and hated herself. She hurried inside with the Stewarts. She hated them too.

Mr and Mrs Smith O'Grady stood inside the hall-door, unaware of hate, and shook hands with their guests. They were kindly people, and Mrs Smith O'Grady gave Patricia a special look and a special squeeze of the hand to say that *they* knew what the party was really about. Then she turned and looked across the hall which was full of people who stood about with champagne and soup and sandwiches in their hands, and to the broad back of a tall and handsome man she said, 'Bruce. Patricia's here.'

He turned and came quickly. He was excited and happy. 'Hello Pat,' he said, his eyes twinkling, 'it's been a long time.'

'Yes,' she said, looking deeply at him, at his reddish face and moustache, through him, through his pseudo-arrogance, 'much too long.' She was astonished by her self-composure. It made no sense after the agony.

They said no more. She and Charlie went upstairs, leaving Reggie to tell Bruce about the new bay gelding. Pretty young girls and handsome young men were sitting fashionably upon the stairs and they had to apologise for walking there. Then as they reached the landing Patricia looked down across the hall, across the kaleidoscope of many-coloured dresses, white ties and tails, across to where Bruce stood and listened to Reggie. He was decidedly attractive. Did she still love him? She could not say.

The ladies-room was a bedroom that none of the family occupied, and which Patricia had never seen. A four-poster stood at the far end of the room from the door, an anachronism used only by the mice that scampered around the top. The walls were a dark blue that must have been very gloomy in the day-time but now formed a dramatic background, because the room was illuminated by large candles that stood upon tables and upon the dressing-table where four mirrors reflected them in a golden light. Charlie sat at the dressing-table and prepared her face while Patricia wandered about the room. She was aware that it had a distinctive smell; so had the house; she had noticed it when they came in. It was a good smell, a country smell, a smell of turf, of mildew, of candle-grease, of crude tobacco, of polished leather and brass, a smell that dealt roughly with the fake smells that lay shining in little pots and bottles upon the dressing-table or secreted about the bodies of the handsome men and women downstairs. The pictures upon the walls were good pictures too, in the same sense; old prints of hunting scenes, old caricatures of hunting folk, and above the mantel-piece a gentleman in a pink coat and velvet cap. Every picture directly or indirectly was a tribute to the Horse, who was ruler here, and to the nobility and healthiness of his rule. They made Patricia look noble and healthy too, but that would never do, so as soon as Charlie had finished she sat down at the mirror and put on some make-up.

Charlie left the room, saying that they would meet down in the hall. She sat at the mirror, gazing in astonishment. She had put on powder but that did not explain why her face was suddenly deathly white. Then she realised that she was gazing not at herself but at the image of the darkness behind her head. Why she felt like this she would never understand. She was not a sensitive person; and it was merely darkness and flickering candlelight. She sat transfixed, watching it, watching it. She wanted Bruce and almost called out for him. There was silence; not a sound of music or conversation. She was alone, apart. She was not merely out of hearing of the party. She knew that she and the room were away in space and time and yet, curiously, that the music and conversation were near. It was terrifying. Then suddenly a face appeared behind hers in the mirror, so suddenly that she tried to scream but could only gasp. But it was not a ghost; it was Bruce.

He put his arms around her and kissed her on the nape of the neck. Overcome with relief she did not realise what he was doing. He gently raised her up and they stood face to face.

'Why so frightened?' he asked.

'Nothing . . .'

'You thought it was a ghost I suppose?'

'Yes.'

He laughed.

'Perhaps I am,' he said. 'A ghost come back to haunt you. Am I?'

'No.'

'You don't sound very sure.'

'Kiss me,' she said.

As they were leaving the room, moved by a whim she pulled his arm and made him face the painting of the gentleman in the pink coat.

'Who was he?' she asked.

'He was my great-uncle,' he said, 'Matthew Bruce Smith O'Grady. You may notice that he has the family colouring.'

'And the moustache,' she added.

'Exactly. And very handsome too.'

They laughed.

They came out on to the landing. Having already looked across the people below in the hall to discover who they were, she could look at them now with disinterest. She came out on Bruce's arm full of whims, full of fantasy; she loved him. The people were heads of corn, identical, a field of them, as decorative, as irrevocable. It was not a fancy as much as a trick of the memory, for she had spent the afternoon lying in a cornfield watching the heads moving in the breeze. They were a pretty sight, and so were the guests of the Smith O'Gradys. The women wore strapless evening gowns and some of them tiaras, and all had put on self-possession, whilst their men were sleek and proudly attentive; the night was young. Bruce guided her, smiling, privately enjoying her fancy, through the cornfield to the side of the wide, white tablecloth behind which stood four men in white aprons who were doing their best for the harvest.

They drank champagne, excellent champagne, and they clinked glasses and whispered 'To us.'

People gathered round to talk to them, some to give congratulations again. Patricia inwardly gave thanks that she could accept them. But she and Bruce gave nothing to the conversation, because neither had been to the Day's Races. (This was the opening gambit of the night). But they enjoyed their shared ignorance. Bruce had arrived from England that evening; Patricia had spent the afternoon in a cornfield, trying to prepare herself for the agony that had not been an agony.

'I was told to back that damn Ballybrophy Thing,' someone was saying to Bruce, 'and like a fool I let Fitz put me off it.' But Bruce had left to dance with Patricia.

A band of three in white coats gone grey beat out old waltzes. They were *the* Band of the nearest town. Patricia knew two of them by name, and Johnny Reddin who dominated with the accordion she knew in person because he came to help when they were short of men at home on the farm. He smiled at her and tried to squeeze new life from the accordion, but his colleagues were not co-operating. Yet it was wonderful; Patricia thought it wonderful. Bruce was a magnificent dancer and they waltzed and waltzed under the chandelier – there was only one, but it was a good one – and about the long, old room in which there was the same good smell and the same 'good' pictures. There were also large mirrors upon the walls, taste-

less and full of character, so that the dancers saw themselves
and found the sight admirable.

There were others to see them. The room was at a corner
of the house and so there were windows in two walls, and at
each window spectators had gathered. Their faces were
pressed tight to the glass, faces full of most varying emotions.
Patricia was aware of them. In Bruce's arms she liked to be
watched. Oh blessed continuity; nothing in a hundred years was
different, nothing except – she noticed as they swung by – the
radio that stood in the corner.

But the night had to pass. The Band became sleepier and
their white coats more and more grey. The soup and sandwiches were almost consumed, and the champagne was consumed to the last bottle and people began to look less
decorative. Mr and Mrs Smith O'Grady, most tired of all and
not sure whether it had been worthwhile, came back to take
up their places at the hall-door, to receive the thanks that their
guests moulded and brought forth from minds that even when
fresh were not creative. Those of them who had conquered
sleep and champagne wondered at the absence of the son of
the house for whom the party had been given, but most of them
understood. The rooms emptied. The portraits took over. The
Band replaced the instruments in their worn black cases. The
watchers at the windows went home arm in arm, the old men
and small children having departed long ago. The four men who
had replenished the cornfield untied their white aprons, folded
them and put them into cardboard attaché-cases, while the
sleepy servant-girls, whom they ignored as lower-ranking
menials, hunted for cups and plates and glasses. In the largest
drawing-room there had been a turf fire; it was a heap of ashes.
The night was over; but not for Patricia and Bruce. They were
upstairs in Bruce's dressing-room.

Charlie had found Reggie in tête-a-tête with his fifth charming
young girl and persuaded him to leave. She would permit no
more promises to be 'ready in a minute' or – 'I'm just coming
darling'. She had had the hell of an evening on a sofa with a
very fat man called Toby Young who had insisted that she stay
with him and, being very strong and intoxicated, had been

irresistible. Moreover, he had been her first husband – Reggie
was her third – and she feared a scene. God it was tedious!
He talked for hour after hour about his present wife, who was
at the party but kept to another room; she had been married
to a viscount and had decided finally that the change was for
the worse. It was not surprising. It was not interesting. It was
just damn boring. And now of course Patricia was not to be
found; away with that ass of a man, positive pain-in-the-neck
Bruce. God help the poor girl! But she was really just as stupid
so it was probably a sensible match. 'Let them just break it up
for tonight,' thought Charlie. 'Let us all get home to our warm
and comfortable beds.'

'For God's sake go and find Patricia or we'll be here till
doomsday,' she said to Reggie.

'Right,' he said, rubbing his hands; he had spent a wonderful
evening. 'Where is she?'

'Upstairs I suppose, with him,' replied Charlie.

'With who?'

'With Bruce, you idiot.'

'Oh . . . Right.'

He turned and went to the stairs, took them three at a time
and upon reaching the landing roared.

'Pa-tric-ia! Bruce! Patricia?'

He passed out of sight.

There were a number of guests still about the hall, making
a certain amount of noise, but the Smith O'Gradys as they shook
hands heard these cries and shuddered, and many of the guests
as they prepared to shake hands heard them too and thought
that Reggie was overdoing it rather. Charlie stood with them
and reflected that Reggie in a good mood was a bloody awful
nuisance.

After some minutes Reggie, Patricia and Bruce came down
together, Reggie between the others with an arm about each.
All three were exceedingly pleased with themselves, thought
Charlie, and Patricia was unabashed and had of course no understanding that people had been hanging about for hours waiting
for Her Ladyship.

'Found the lost sheep,' bellowed Reggie to the company.

Charlie said nothing. Bruce joined his parents at the door and everyone said good-night, Bruce and Patricia in a lingering way, and Mrs Smith O'Grady gave Patricia a special squeeze of the hand to say that *they* knew what the party had really been about.

'See you tomorrow, Pat,' said Bruce as the three guests stepped out into a cold, windy morning. It was almost light, the most bitter and unfriendly time. They got quickly into the Bentley, and Charlie, shivering inside her silver-fox, put up her window and told Reggie to do the same.

As they moved away down the sweep of the drive Reggie, steering with his left hand, said,'Great party . . . Eh, darling?'

'Rotten, I thought,' said Charlie, her voice more grating than ever.

Patricia was shocked. She could not bear to hear *her* party, her wonderful party, so described. She stayed quiet.

'Oh come off it,' replied Reggie, unmoved, 'you were doing fine. Couldn't separate the old Toby-jug tonight. What do you two talk about anyway?'

'None of your business,' said Charlie.

'The party was all right for Pat, eh?'

'Oh fine,' answered Patricia.

'Our little friend is getting married pretty soon.'

'Really,' said Charlie.

'Yes. We hope so,' said Patricia. They had no doubt of it.

The three were silent, watching the road in the headlights, watching the silver-model of the fox. White cottages, grey cottages, mossy banks, bramble hedges, stone walls, decayed signposts, vast chestnut trees sped by, but men, dogs and bicycles were all in bed. The three were sleepy. They were content not to speak. Reggie was thinking about a blonde in a green dress. Charlie was trying to find a reason, one reason, for preferring Toby Young to Reggie, and was angry with herself and both of them that she could not find one. Patricia closed her eyes and thought about Bruce; about his superiority to other men, about the way he kissed her, about his dancing, his love of books and pictures, his strong arms. Above all she tried to *see* him; and the curious fact was that although she concentrated with all her strength, and although she had only just left him, she could see nothing but a reddish face and a moustache.

ANGLO-IRISH RELATIONS

MAEVE KELLY

MAEVE KELLY

Maeve Kelly was born in 1930 in Co. Clare, and grew up and was educated in Dundalk, Co. Louth. She has lived near Limerick for many years where she has been prominent in the women's rights movement. She won a Hennessy Literary Award in 1972 and has published a collection of poetry, two novels, and two volumes of short stories, *A Life Of Her Own* and *Orange Horses*.

PERHAPS IT IS envy, perhaps it is genuine sadness that makes me think of the days of my youth with a pang. Salad days is how I remember them. That was the time of the musical by Julian Slade. Somewhere among my old records the bright voices are still captured – 'The Things that were Done by a Don' and 'We Said We Wouldn't Look Back'. And in the background the piano tinkling with all the fresh, green enthusiasm of youth.

All summer we played it, until it was ousted by the Goons and 'I'm Walking Backwards to Christmas clonk, clonk'. There were parties and outings and picnics. There were occasional gala events where we dressed up and thought we were beautiful and perhaps we were. One of my friends borrowed my only evening dress to go boating on the Isis with some tipsy, newly fledged graduate from Magdalen College. She was reputed to be the daughter of a Polish count – there were hundreds of them in England after the war – but since I had actually known a genuine Polish countess whose frozen gentility was a far cry from Marietta's gay insouciance, her disguise wore thin very quickly. Not that I minded. But I did mind the loss of the only evening dress which never recovered from its adventures in the muddy depths of Oxford's most famous tributary.

There were other evenings which required no fancy dress, merely an acceptance of the enchantments of Oxford: *Twelfth Night* performed in New College Cloisters, a trip to the Bodleian with an aged uncle who had translated Pliny's letters fifty years before and always checked that his copy was catalogued, a visit to Christ Church where the same aged uncle scowled and complained if a chair had been moved or a pew damaged. He

was then almost eighty years old and he endeared himself to
all of us, who were only his nieces by marriage, because he
was the most blatant lover of Ireland we had ever met. He
used to declare that had he been an Irishman he would have
been a Fenian, and he loved my grandmother when he went to
visit her in Connemara because she confessed that she had
been of that very persuasion in her youth. He knew G. K.
Chesterton, who was at the time a passion of mine (and for
that matter still is), and said he was the sloppiest eater he had
ever known. Since he himself was a fastidious old man, elegantly
handsome, his curl of contempt at the memory of food-slopped
waistcoats was without equal. He had been at college with F. E.
Smith, later Lord Birkenhead, and told me that he was the
wickedest man he had ever met. He himself was a socialist,
the first socialist mayor in the Borough of Willesden, and perhaps that had something to do with it. He was Mayor at the
time of the Coronation of George VI, and his account of the
paper bags with sandwiches tucked under the regal robes of
titular bishops and lords of the realm was hilarious. Pomp and
circumstance were treated with mockery, and the lack of toilet
facilities for all those aged bladders made him by turns angry
and amused when he recounted the other splendours of that
day. Every now and again, when I met up with prejudice
because I was Irish, I was consoled to think that the most
English of Englishmen loved his wife because she was Irish and
shared that affection with me. If all this seems irrelevant I can
shortly make clear that it is not.

And before I go further I must also make clear that I was not
one of Oxford's embryo scholars. One of my great weaknesses
throughout my training as a student nurse was that the smell
of the theatre made me ill and when I qualified after four years,
my knowledge of surgical techniques was so poor I could not
assist at a simple appendectomy. The hospital in Oxford offered
a year's training for nurses who wanted to specialise in surgery. I didn't want to specialise. I didn't want to spend the rest
of my life behind hospital walls. But I had utopian visions of
changing the whole system and to do that I had to learn as
much as I could. The academic and cultural delights of Oxford

were fringe benefits, about the only fringe benefits available. But they were enough for me. I was lucky, I suppose, because a young man with a motor-bike who had got a second in history (considered barely acceptable by the aged uncle who had a formidable intelligence) happened to fall in love with me, or so he said. Although I treated such declarations with a healthy scepticism, I enjoyed his company and we soared across the Cotswolds on his machine, investigating Laurie Lee country and Roman remains and Norman arched churches with equal enthusiasm.

Those excursions were magnificent relief from a life which I began to think was hardly worth living. I still felt ill in the theatre, sometimes hardly able to breathe, and the instruments which everyone else took for granted had for me the appearance of medieval tools of torture. Part of my training involved learning their names and their uses so that I could reel them off with the speed, accuracy and soullessness of an abacus. Then each surgeon had his own particular likes and dislikes. The instrument had to be slapped into his hand with just the right degree of pressure so that no irritation could interfere with the great man's concentration. The fact that I was constantly irritated by the piques and foibles of great men was of no account to anyone, and after a while I began to see myself as a kind of robot, computerised to give satisfaction at all times. But my programming was faulty. The body on the table remained a real live human being, and not, as I tried to convince myself, an anonymous mound of green cloth with an aperture of flesh in the centre. And the deified person beside me was a kind of glorified plumber, a graduate of barber-school days. He could be admired for the risks he took with other people's lives, and therefore for the responsibility he had thrust upon him, but had to be judged as well by the consideration, or lack of it, which he showed to his menials, among them – and way down at the bottom of the list – myself. Once I forgot a particular Allis forceps when I was setting the trolleys for major surgery and the fuss created was almost as bad as when I dropped the radio-active gold on the floor and the theatre had to be vacated for two days. For weeks afterwards the Geiger counters were croaking in odd corners. I was quite sure I would die of leukaemia at an early age since I had got the full blast of the thing.

I certainly felt tired. The boyfriend began to complain.

'I thought you Irish girls were full of the joys of spring.'

'What do you mean, "you Irish girls"? I thought you English boys had impeccable manners,' I countered.

He laughed. 'I told you I was only a scholarship boy.'

That was the first time he had brought up the racial difference. It was almost as if he had said 'you peculiar aliens'. When I mocked him with, 'Take me to your leader,' he didn't think it funny.

'I don't think of you as foreign,' he said. 'But you are different. You don't giggle like the girls I know. And you look at me when I talk to you.'

'I think you are well worth looking at,' I teased and he actually blushed.

'Now look what you've done,' he said. 'Nobody makes me blush but you.' Our little darts of racialist repartee stayed at that level.

But then the letter bombs started, or took up where they had left off. Now and again and without warning, people's hands were blown off because they opened a package. Sometimes they were British hands, sometimes West Indian hands, sometimes even Irish hands, but they were always Irish bombs.

'Your lot are at it again,' he said once, angrily. The aged uncle never said things like that. He merely sighed and looked grim.

'I am not up for bid at auction, lot twenty-two, one average-sized Irish colleen full of queer tricks and trades with thirty bombs up her knickers,' I jeered.

'How crude,' he said reproachfully in his flattened Reading accent.

'That's the kind of response prejudice brings. One can only be crude,' I answered.

'I don't blame you,' he cried. 'You know how I feel about you. You are the first girl I ever loved.'

'What a pity I happened to be an Irish bog-trotter,' I sneered.

'What does that mean? Your background is probably much better than mine,' he said magnanimously. 'I don't feel any social difference.'

'*Oh.*' I seized on the slip. 'Being Irish pulls me down sufficiently to reach your scholarship boy level.'

'Did anyone ever tell you what a damned pompous racist you are?'

Talk about the kettle calling the pot black. I fumed for days. When the chef in the hospital pretended not to understand what he chose to call my brogue I bit his nose off.

'Brogue?' I said. 'What do you mean? Brogue means shoe. Every ignoramus, even those unversed in the subtleties of the Irish language, which is the oldest of the Indo-Europeans, knows a brogue is a shoe.'

'Oi. You speak Erse then?'

Erse my arse I said under my breath. I didn't want to go too far.

'Want some more booter then love, yerrah begorrah,' he called out.

'Not booter. Butter. B-U-T-T-E-R.'

'Oi. She means botter.'

'I don't want botter. I want butter. The stuff they make out of milk.'

'That's cream, you know, love. Don't your Irish cows make cream, then?'

How could one compete against such ignorance?

Then there was the boyfriend's special subject: history. The aged uncle asked him had he got a first and the boyfriend looked suitably scathing at so outmoded a value. When pressed he admitted he hadn't.

'I suppose a second for history is acceptable,' the aged uncle said with a pointed charity.

'From what dusty archives did you drag him?' the boyfriend asked me later. 'Methusaleh in person.'

'He is very fit. And intelligent,' I said loyally.

'When was he at Oxford?'

'In the 1890s I think. He was the same year as F. E. Smith.' The boyfriend looked stunned.

'You look as if you didn't know whether you were shot or poisoned,' I said. 'You could learn a lot from him.'

'I learn more from you,' he said, winking lasciviously.

The aged uncle referred to him as a blurb. 'The fellow's a blurb,' he said confidentially. 'Don't know what you see in him.'

His knowledge of Irish history was certainly limited. When I sneered at the gaps, he explained that he had specialised in European history. That was before the EEC and we were a mini-continent all on our owney-oh out in the Atlantic. And of course our greatest mistake in Ireland was to have left the Empire. He waxed lyrical on the topic.

'What resources do you have? No coal, no minerals to speak of. Thousands of acres of bog. You're mad.'

'Any minerals we had you stole. You ruined our trade to protect your own. Destroyed our forests to save your own. Savaged our religious beliefs to entrench your own. Rapacious plunderers. And left a bastard culture behind you.'

'Some convent you went to. Always wondered what those nuns got up to.'

He enjoyed himself hugely during these encounters. The angrier and more vicious I got, the more he loved it and the more he swore he loved me. He had the intellectual arrogance of the newly conferred with just enough confidence to water it down to acceptable limits. Even so, he had to admit that we came out about even, mainly – though he would never admit it – because his ignorance of Irish affairs was truly abysmal. My own knowledge of European and British history was diffuse, scattered through the centuries in dilettante fashion, but I had enough ingenuity and common sense to keep myself afloat when he tried to drown me in a deluge of facts and dates. Since my education had a much broader base than his, he might confound me with detail but I confused him with generalisations thrown in with abandon. However, on my own ground of things Irish or even medical, I won hands down. He tried to isolate and condemn. I related everything to everything else.

'Facts are facts,' he would say.

'Truth is relative,' I would respond to his despair.

'You are a mere empiricist,' he would yell.

'What's a historian for God's sake? I suppose you call yourself a scientist.'

'It is a science. A most exact and precise science.'

'Secondhand news and biased reporting. That's all history can ever be.'

'What do you know about it? What have you read?'

That's when the going got tough. But I was not to be done down by lists of reading and I capped his personal bibliography with fictitious titles and authors and magnificently imaginative quotations. I quite impressed myself. I began to plan a career as a popular historian. At times I went too far. He collapsed into laughter when I used the lost vernacular.

'Say that again,' he said in mock wonder one pleasant sunny evening in the park. 'It sounds as if you're trying to spit and can't quite manage it.'

'You English are so prejudiced, so how could you possibly escape?'

'I'm British,' he corrected me. 'My mother was Welsh.'

'Being born in a stable doesn't make you a horse,' I threw back.

'Oho. Fee fie fo fum. An expert on Wellington.'

'It's useless talking to you. *Briseann an nadúr tré suile an chait.*'

He fell on the hallowed grass in the hallowed Oxford park and had hysterics. There were some sheep droppings near by and I picked up a small handful and dropped them into his wide open mouth. People have been hanged for less. It took him two weeks to forgive me and he came ostentatiously to one of our awful hospital hops with Marietta.

'Dahling,' she said, 'he's a perfect poppet. How can you throw him over! I love him. I could eat him for dinner. He's simply adorable. And so bwilliant.'

'Does he call you Your Countessness?' I said cattily.

'Weally dahling. There's no need for that. I gave up all claims to title. You know what I suffered. Those dweadful Germans drove all that nonsense out of my head. And you know how poor I am.'

Of course I was filled with remorse and said she could have him for breakfast as well as dinner, if she liked.

'Gluttony, my dear, is a cardinal sin. We Catholics know that.'

She went to the Black Friars for Mass because it was the snob thing to do. I went blatantly to Cowley where they had bingo. If I must play the part, I should play it to the death. I repaid him by going to the Spider's Web, a dreadful dank dungeon where everyone leaped around doing Bill Haley's rock, with a classical scholar who was as bored by me as I was by him. The boyfriend glared from a corner. Marietta had found a Polish count and they were exchanging reminiscences. I smiled radiantly at the classical horror before me as we bounded past the corner, just to prove what a marvellous time I was having. Marietta whizzed off with the definitely suspect count and the body in the corner wilted. My partner thought I was ready for higher things and made noisy advances. I kneed him where it hurt and ran for the bus stop, clutching my handbag and my virtue with equal determination. It began to rain. Miraculously the boyfriend appeared, complete with umbrella which he silently raised over the two of us.

'When all fruit fails, welcome haw,' I said, and he smiled gratefully. Marietta passed with the classical scholar, both of them beaming. I said, 'Let them off, fine weather after them and snow to their heels.'

He collapsed, leaning on the bus stop and laughing so much that the tears trickled out of the corners of his eyes. 'I've missed you.'

Actually I had missed him too, and I felt it only fair to tell him.

'Perhaps we should get married,' he said, but I knew he was only joking and ignored it.

Our reconciliation made life bearable again. I was having a rough time. Our theatre sister had been in the army and brought army discipline to our overloaded routine. She even examined our nails at morning parade. One of her boasts, and also ours, was that there was never a case of cross-infection in our theatre. No porter was allowed inside the swing doors, which meant we had to do the heavy lifting as well as the skilled work. Every eight days one of us was on call for emergencies. There was no such thing as an eight-hour shift. On a busy day you just stayed on. It was bad luck if you got a call at midnight after being on duty until 10 p.m., and I was as susceptible to bad luck as anyone else.

I found the theatre stuffy and blamed the lack of air for my shortness of breath. One night I had a call as I was climbing into bed. The French girl whose turn it was gave some garbled explanation about an abortion and her conscience. 'You should refuse too,' she said, 'but there's no one else around, and I always get the feeling that your religion doesn't mean as much to you as it does to me.'

'You've a bloody cheek,' I said. 'What the hell do you know about it?'

'See what I mean,' she said. 'The language you use,' and she stalked off.

There were new degrees of exhaustion, I decided, never before experienced by man. The boyfriend was off in Norway. He sent a card or letter every day with declarations of love on each one. The next time he made a proposal of marriage I would take him seriously and further the cause of Anglo-Irish relations. I'd even become a British citizen and abandon faith and motherland if I could escape from this dedicated drudgery. Fair exchange was no robbery. Not even for Kathleen Movourneen and all that would I swop life and good health. I was not the stuff of which martyrs were made. Even at twelve years old I had discovered as much about myself. Having seen a gory religious film called *The Twenty-Seven Martyrs of Japan*, amongst other equally gory films which were regularly shown to convent schoolgirls to improve our moral fibre, I decided I would be a permanent coward. If I am ever tied to a stake, I said, or thrown to the lions, I'll have to turn Protestant or Buddhist or heathen or whatever is required at the time. It was a decision I stuck to firmly, and having made up my mind to be a coward, my nighmares of being buried alive in a coffin or being kicked out of heaven because I got there too late, wearing only my vest and bedroom slippers, miraculously ceased. Cowardice has its advantages. My mother almost ruined it by saying she was sure I would get whatever strength was needed in my moment of trial. I didn't want to be strong. I wanted to be a weak, snivelling renegade living a life of ease and comfort. I assured her earnestly there was no hope for me and she gave one of her wondering sighs and said, 'The things you think of.' How could one *not* think of them with the twenty-seven martyrs of Japan groaning behind every bush. And here I was lurching into dedicated uniform after a mere two hours' rest. The time for cowardice and high treason was nigh.

The poor young woman on the trolley in the anaesthetic room was not there for an abortion but because she had had a back-street job done. The smell of infection and her cries of pain were suffocating. She was a beautiful, olive-skinned Italian girl with no English and she cried constantly *O mama mia, O mama mia, O mama mia*, before the anaesthetic delivered her. If I needed any convincing of my cowardice and gutlessness I was confirmed in it when I bawled after it was all over while I scrubbed out the theatre for two hours until even our martinet would have been satisfied. I had four hours' restless sleep before facing the day. Before breakfast I went to see how our patient was faring. She had died just half an hour earlier. I couldn't eat and went straight to theatre. It was my turn in the sterilising room and I carried the first tray of boiled instruments to the surgeon who had already started. Again there was that feeling of suffocation and I had a terrible need to cough. Out on to the newly sterilised instruments came half a pint of my own frothy bright red blood.

Even in my last extremity, as I believed it to be, the look on the surgeon's face gave me enormous satisfaction. As I fell clattering to the floor, still holding on to the tray of instruments, I prayed that some magician with a camera would appear, capture his expression for posterity and have it pasted on the theatre wall to remind him and his successors that nurses bleed too and when they do it's the same colour as anyone else's. I think I must have been hung up on prejudices – class, social, race and all the others. I retired in ignominy having messed up the antiseptic conditions for another while. It had to be someone

Irish – I could imagine everyone saying – who would infect the place with the tubercle bacillus.

I prepared to meet my Maker, reminding her/him that all my intentions had been honourable and imploring him/her to make due and merciful allowances. I was put into a glass-walled room with a spyhole into the office from which I could be observed, while I cried with apparently suicidal intent for three days. They thought I was wallowing in self-pity and that it might be good therapy, but I cried for *Mama mia* and another foreigner who had died in a strange and hostile world, and who had to have a room scrubbed out after her visitation. In the end I was told I would have another haemorrhage if I didn't stop and what a lot of nonsense it was and Streptomycin, Para amino salicylic acid and I.n.a.h. would soon see me as bright as a new penny. As it turned out it wasn't quite as simple as that.

Meanwhile, back at the ranch, the boyfriend's letters and cards piled up. What with bouncing around on his motor-bike through the hills and dales of merry old England I hadn't much time to get very friendly with the other nurses, though there were a few, apart from Marietta, with whom I exchanged groans over conditions of work and the sexual frustrations of nursing sisters. Eventually, after some weeks, Marietta arrived with a new young worshipper in tow, shielded her nostrils against my contamination, and deposited the parcel of mail before fleeing as if from the plague. I shouted after her, 'I'll need my evening dress any day now,' and heard her wistful 'O dahling, don't, you'll make me cwy. It's all so sad. And you're so bwave,' from the safety of the hallway. 'Your lisp is slipping,' I said bitterly. I never saw her again, or only faintly in the distance. And I'm sorry about that too. She was quite a character.

I went through the mail. There were six communications from the boyfriend in Norway and I read them in chronological order as I made out the dates on the postmarks.

The first was full of the usual chirpy nonsense about the scenery and the weather and the people. The second was more interesting. He certainly missed me. I had dug deep into him and he couldn't get me out. He would be at the enclosed address and would I please write and tell him that yes, he and I should be wed forthwith and spend our lives in bliss for evermore together. And just to prove how much he loved me he enclosed a rude doggerel of Ogden Nash's about hips being fleeting or something. The next one was slightly reproachful. He was a master of the reproachful reminder. Perhaps my reply was on the way. Had I not noticed his telephone number? Was I so impoverished I could not spend a few quid on a call about such a momentous matter? But he was certain my letter would arrive, or better still, a telegram, or better still, the phone would ring any moment now.

The fourth had a dash of malice to it. Apparently the Irish government was making perfidious statements which would encourage terrorism in England. He must have had the *Daily Telegraph* posted to him. The fifth was an angry and bitter series of accusations about treachery and disloyalty and betrayal and countries who weren't grateful when other more enlightened countries tried to do them favours, about political traditions, and historical firsts, and Magna Cartas. The aged uncle was right. The fellow was a blurb.

The last letter was a sad acceptance of the inevitable without any reference to history or national pride. He had been a fool. He had been conned. He would know better the next time. He thanked me for giving him such a hard lesson because he was sure it would be of great benefit to him in the difficult years ahead as he made his millions because after all what was there left but money and he was ambitious and he didn't need to be saddled with encumbrances however sexy and attractive and foreign.

He little knew what an encumbrance he had just missed, I thought. Bad enough to be female, but Irish, a nurse, wowee-wowee, and now tubercular. All that was left was to be black. I peered hopefully into the mirror but the pink and white gleamed back at me. If I had even turned pale and interesting it would have been something. The classic tubercular complexion, one of the medics said, after tapping me all over. The haemorrhage had given me a rather neat shade of green, I thought, but it had soon passed.

I turned my face to the wall and contemplated its blankness.

Every now and again a cheerful nurse would dash in, puncture my tail-end with a needleful of raw acid, ram dozens of tablets the size of half crowns down my throat plus hundreds of mini varieties and make me drink another bucketful of milk. The glass doors were left wide open to freeze out the b-b-bacillus since that was the fashion in those days. My pink and white turned to deep violet which was very apt. One of the medics remarked on my name outside my closed door in one of those clear penetrating English voices which can laser beam their way through ten-inch steel. Is it Mauve? What an odd name. Is it Oirish har har? Oh victimised nation! The butt of every joker through the uncountable class structures of English society. Some weeks later when I realised death was not as imminent as I had first imagined and I would therefore not be depending on aliens to get my foreign corpse back to the green isle of my birth, I told him, 'Maeve was a famous queen, a fact which is no mere legend, but is well authenticated historically. I am not deaf. I am not retarded. All that is wrong with me is that the muggy mists of this damp town and the insanitary conditions of your hospitals have aggravated an infection which was at one time so common in this country you managed to spread it all over the world, both to Ireland and the plains Indians and the Eskimos.' I was breathless for two days after that speech but it was worth it.

He said, 'Dear me. She not only bleeds. She talks too.'

I resigned myself to a slow and patient recovery. After the initial shock it was quite pleasant. At least one could look on the bright side of it. Perhaps it is an exaggeration to say it was pleasant, but the days of servitude were temporarily over. Perhaps permanently over. Someone else would have to take up the torch for Florrie and put up with insults and abuse in order to be of service to the sick. History offered possibilities. All one needed was nerve, imagination and plenty of bias. I didn't think about the boyfriend. My lungs felt as if they were filled with lead and when I thought of him the lead shifted over to my heart. I put him out of my mind.

The aged uncle occasionally visited me but his attitude had changed. He seemed to be saying, without putting it into words,

that anyone who could allow themselves to be in such a pre-
dicament was guilty of gross negligence, not to say Catholic
fecklessness. At eighty his pink and white complexion was
unscarred and his round of golf every morning with occasional
triumphant birdies added zest to his disturbingly springing step.
Born more than half a century after him I ebbed and waned and
wilted while he waxed and flowed and thrived disgustingly. Look
at me, his lustrous white hair declaimed. Behold the wholesome, hard-working English gentleman, behind him centuries
of order and good clean living, and fine traditions and noble,
victorious wars and independent thinking and sharp, decisive
intellect and glorious monarchy and the British Way of Life.
Wake up and get on with it. None of this nonsense about being
ill. I was never a day ill in my life. My mother was never a day
ill in her life and she lived to be ninety-nine and three hundred
and sixty days. His father died at thirty but that never merited
a mention. The child has no *joie de vivre*, he said to the aunt
standing bewilderedly beside him. Thank you for coming, I said.
But I'm sure it's too tiring for you. Please don't bother any
more. Tut tut. You're not taking offence at anything I say. You
know I'm just a silly old man. Take no notice, take no notice.
It was good advice to someone with two lungs full of lead. I
took him at his word and he went off in a huff. The British, I
decided, with pleasant prejudice, are a very huffy nation. Shortly
after that visit I opened the door to totter down to the bathroom
and bumped into the boyfriend who was standing outside, a look
of stark terror on his face and a potted plant of freesia in his
hand.

'What,' I asked furiously and rhetorically, 'are you doing here?
And who told you where I was?'

'Marietta.'

'Marietta,' I mimicked. 'La contessa blabbermouth. Trust
her. I'm not allowed visitors. Go away immediately. I'm highly
contagious. You should be wearing a mask even now.'

'The nurse said it was all right.'

'The nurse! The nurse! You know what nurses are. Would
you take the word of a nurse? Menials. Peasants. Is she English
or Irish?'

'Spanish, I think. Knows very little English.'

'Another of the underprivileged.' I coughed deliberately into my handkerchief and he didn't even flinch.

'I was only joking,' I said, when safely back in bed. 'I'm not infectious at all. They've tested my sputum, and I don't even have a cough.'

'I don't care if you are infectious,' he lied nobly. 'And you are more beautiful than ever. And I have been a perfect beast to you. Those terrible letters I wrote and the terrible things I said. And here you were being ill and I didn't know. Why didn't you tell me?'

'It all happened so quickly. And it's not the sort of thing one likes to boast about,' I said. 'And I feel such a failure.'

'You can't help being ill. It's nobody's fault.'

Some kind soul had given me Thomas Mann's *Magic Mountain* to read so I had other ideas.

'I think it is a wilful act of self-destruction.'

'What rubbish,' he said. 'It's just like getting a cold.'

'It's all in the mind,' I said. 'But what's the use of talking? Here I am. I'm stuck with it. I'll just have to get on with it.'

To be fair to the boyfriend, he tried. Anyone less noble would have fled. Marietta, for instance. I could see he was a little anxious and I didn't blame him. I was a little anxious myself. Was I contaminating the air every time I exhaled? I wouldn't borrow books in case I infected the paper. I carried out as many of the aseptic practices I had learned as was humanly possible. If I had known about Howard Hughes I would have had sympathy for his fetishes. Only in this case I myself was the malignant source. Another Typhoid Mary. Thank God no one gave me Kafka's *Metamorphosis* or I would have been properly depressed. It was a new experience in alienation.

The boyfriend tried to resume where he had left off, but it was useless. I had been all alone in the bottom of a sewer and nothing could change that. Besides, he had gone a bit far in his letters. Words like 'perfidy' could not be bandied around so casually. I forgave him, of course. There was no question of holding it against him, but I began to see him in twenty years' time re-enacting British victories on the dining-room table, with war maps instead of Van Gogh prints, Union Jack table mats and dinner service, and myself desperately and secretly wearing the crude tricolour knickers. I began to dream of the green fields of home.

We both knew it was all over when one day I said nostalgically, '*Nil aon tinteán mar do thinteán féin,*' and he didn't laugh. He asked me to translate it. How could you turn firesides and storytelling and warmth and acceptance and common origins and shared disasters into that transfer embroidered 'There's no place like home'? I swore I would join the Gaelic League the minute I got back and I would never utter a word of English again, since it was so ineffectual an instrument for expressing the finer subtleties of the Gael. And I thought of G. K. C. and his sloppy waistcoat with even greater affection. 'The great Gaels of Ireland whom all the gods made mad, for all their wars are merry and all their songs are sad.' I wallowed in euphoric fantasies. One evening on one of the permitted trips out of the san, I called at the Irish Catholic Gaelic League Bingo Hall to watch the merrymaking. I sagged in a corner and a gay, red-haired, blue-eyed Irishman asked me would I bate the floor with him. When I apologised because I just wasn't able he said, 'Well, you poor creature you,' with the proper mixture of sympathy and unconcern. It put everything in perspective. I knew I was lost to the Empire and the boyfriend for ever. It had to be back to the bogs.

We parted good friends. I kept his letters with others in a trunk in an outhouse, always meaning to burn them. When I finally got round to it I discovered generations of mice had used them as nesting material. It seemed a very inappropriate end to Anglo-Irish relations, or Hiberno-English relations – depending on your point of view.

A SORT-OF LOVE STORY

TOM MacDONAGH

TOM MacDONAGH

Tom MacDonagh was born in New York in 1934, of Irish parents who returned to Dublin when he was four. Educated in Synge Street C.B.S., he is now an Executive Officer in the Government's Department of Enterprise and Employment. A prolific short story writer, he has also published a memoir of his youth, *My Green Age*.

CLAIR WAS THIN, that was the first thing I noticed about her the night I met her at the Metropole. She was sitting alone behind a phalanx of men who faced outwards towards the ballroom floor. They admired the girls dancing, and like true heroes they never looked behind. In her black dress and dark hair combed across her forehead she was a picture of composure. She was waiting, waiting for someone to come along. Her whole bearing spoke of resignation and humility, spiced with a little pride. I asked her up and we began a quickstep that took us around the hall under the rotating ball and the flashing lights.

She lived with her mother in a house in Dartry. She played golf at Milltown and worked as a departmental manageress in a fashion store in Grafton Street. A hint of expensive perfume insinuated itself into my mind, and holding her in my arms I was aware both of her age and a quality I can only describe as felicitousness. She whispered the right word at the correct time and she agreed with things. I felt powerful with her, master of a domain and voyeur of all the earthly delights on show that night. She was in her mid-thirties, given to occasional silences, her warm brown eyes resting on me or on some other target behind me. When she spoke I felt she had considered what she was about to say, and I availed of her utterances to admire her all the more.

She drove me home in her car, puffing away on her cigarettes. I apologised for my poverty. She agreed to come out with me, but I musn't get the wrong idea, she was not interested in a relationship. She travelled quite a lot, and was tired most evenings. She looks very frail to be driving a car, I thought, as she sped away.

When we met the following Tuesday she had the film she wanted to see picked out. *The Black Widow*, with Anthony Quinn and Sophia Loren. She didn't go to the pictures often. I'd say it was a rather lowbrow thing for her. For me the cinema was a palace of dreams, a place where I restored myself after being bruised by reality. She got more from the film than myself. I was averse to sentiment. She revelled in the human complications of it all.

We drove up the quays to the Four Courts hotel for a drink. The old city lay dreaming under the weight of its years, and the shadows of ancient tenements peering over the quay walls were like the spectres of the past closing in on whatever little bit of light remained on the river. I was aware of a certain faded grandeur. Railings built to last forever, and domes that reflected the moonlight. Clair drank vodka and white. I stuck to the pint. She showed off her knees. I found myself addressing them. She ran her hands along them. She had been to Canada, working hard and learning the hard way about men and life. She seemed bitter when she spoke of Canada, it was snow all over. I conjured up visions of arctic wastes, emptiness, and despair. She laughed when she told me about the ladies with their tiny shovels lifting their dogs' dirt into plastic bags when they soiled the street.

After that night I took her out to Howth, walked her under the rhododendron shrubs at the Castle, kissed her in a lifeboat shelter at the end of the pier, and brought her home safely in a bus. There was something magical about Howth that night, the houses on the hill hinted at happiness, and at something more, the rare elixir of life itself. The boats in the harbour, the curve of the jetty, the lighthouse exploding every few moments into splashes of light, all were perfect beneath the stars. I looked out to sea, half expecting to see the benign hand of God rising above the waves. Maybe it was all due to the million flowering rhododendrons, our hands meeting as we helped each other up the narrow inclines and over soggy ground, the view of Ireland's Eye from the high ground, the ever-present sea – whatever it was, it was not to be repeated. Every other time in Howth I try for the same feeling and it's not there. Neither, of course, is Clair. It was as if she was afraid of happiness, and all my cajoling could never really budge her from her fixed point, her belief in the essential frailty of human relationships. Embedded in her was a hopelessness I found hard to understand. I was touched by it, but I was alien to it. It grew out of a milieu I couldn't fathom. Something foreign that scared me, that I couldn't probe too deeply. Men were a species she didn't trust. She was making something of her life and wasn't going to imperil it by allowing any emotional attachments to take root. Whatever her needs were she kept them well under wraps. She was dubious of love's pretensions. I liked that about her. Most women have that soft core that melts easily at the sight of a bride, but not her. 'How long will it last?' would be her snide remark.

Her father was a horsey man who left home to fight for Britain in the Second World War and never returned. The war was his excuse for doing a bunk. For Clair, an only child, it was a dark wound. She could convey the loneliness of childhood. No one to play with. Naming her dolls and making them act out her fantasies.

'Sure we all done that,' I said, although I only had a burnt teddy bear to take to bed.

'But we lived in a biggish house. I remember acres of faded carpet, dark furniture that frightened me, and closets I was afraid to open. Everything was so cold ... .' Her voice tailed off at the recollection, her lips pursed together. Her recollections led to silence.

Her mother was a quiet retiring type of person. At least that is how she appeared to me. In her early sixties, she said hello to me once and after that I kept in touch with her only through hearing her footsteps pattering about in her bedroom as I waited for Clair to make a cup of tea. Those footfalls unnerved me. I found myself looking up at the ceiling. What manner of woman was this? In a subtle way she was a damper on romance. There was always a chance she might pop in, intruding into our tea-drinking ceremony.

'Is your mother all right?' I would ask.

'She has a bit of a headache. Nothing serious.' Clair was quiet and abstracted in her own house. The silences between us grew longer. She put on an electric fire and toasted her lovely knees. I eavesdropped on her every syllable. There was no way into her heart. Even the room we sat in was null, empty of personality. There was nothing in this sitting-room that I could relate to her. It all belonged to a bygone era. She examined the tea leaves.

'Anything good in it?'

'Only a camel,' she said.

'One or two humps?'

'Just one.' Her delicate fingers ringed the cup, a slight stain of tea freshened her lips.

'A one-humped camel, I don't know what to make of that.' I was trying to make her smile.

'Probably something to do with a journey,' she said. I didn't tell her what was in mine. The remains stretched out like an archipelago of islands. I suggested she change the brand of her tea. That mouth I sought was refused me, and I shrugged my shoulders at her suggestion that we should not meet again. Walking home from Dartry I got the message about the camel. I was the one to make the journey through the desert of middle-class suburbia. I had been seeing her for two months when she dropped her little bombshell.

But she liked to dance and I met her some months later at a tennis hop. She always dressed well and she stood out in her disdain amongst the paralytic swains. She smiled at me. She took it for granted I would ask her up. She was right. I had to rescue her from this drunken mêlée. Even though I'd had a few myself. She introduced me to a friend. A broad-limbed horsey type with faded blonde hair and rather large front teeth. It was the Night of the Smile. Grins all round. The alternative for me that night was too appalling to contemplate. She exercised a proprietary hold on me. She thought our previous friendship gave her that right. And then again, the conventions of the ballroom worked in her favour. One holds on to what one has. A process of pairing off. The ambience of the floor is such that most accept the myth of finding a mate even though they have reservations which they sublimate in the common hysteria. The band, the music, the dissatisfied faces peering at you, lead you on and lull you into accepting that romance is sacred, that all is for the best in the best of all possible worlds.

I swept her away for a mineral. The wooden palisade around the tennis club gave a view of the courts. Dark lonely trees lived out their lives unaware of our human passions. Girls sat on the fencing, their arms about their boyfriends. We drank the sweet concoction through straws. There was nothing like a woman to make one thirsty. She looked at me once more. Those brown eyes. The slow coming of words. A pale lipstick delineated her lips.

'Why do you come to a dump like this?' I asked. The instant barrage of her eyes.

'For the same reason that you come.'

'Sex and companionship, that's nice to know,' I replied.

'Actually Beryl rang and asked me and I agreed out of the goodness of my heart. Men wouldn't understand a thing like that.'

'You're looking great anyhow, how is your mother?'

'Fine, thanks.'

Only when I had her in my arms did I feel tenderness for her. Her intense fragility, her softness as she leaned ever so slightly into me awoke a fluttering of doves in my head. My eyes jumped the length of the hall. Did she think I was made of stone? God knows what she thought, but she seemed to have relented somewhat in her attitude to me. She was not showing the hard face tonight anyway.

'I'm flying out to Milan on Tuesday. A week at a trade fair,' she informed me.

'Can I come?'

'I'm going with one of our managers,' she said. We sat down. I fought an impulse to tidy her hair. She lit a cigarette. It was nearly 2 a.m. The Sabbath had begun. The lights from the club cut swathes of green across the grounds. The nets faltered under the weight of gravity. The shouts of dancers got lost in the darkness. The National Anthem was an aberration of extremists. Badly played, its military bravura fudged by a tired saxophonist, the beat wilting under the stares of the remaining

dancers, it sank down to an inglorious end. I went with Clair
and Beryl to her car parked in a laneway. Someone was trying
and obviously succeeding in having a pee in the dark. The
women refused to notice anything. She drove down under the
great sprawls of trees, lit up by the street lamps, to Rathmines.
I got out.

'Ring me,' she ordered from the driver's seat.

'Will do.'

I walked down Rathmines aware of couples coming hoofing
it from town, wondering if the melody of her that insinuated its
way into my heart was anything more substantial than the
memory of half-forgotten tunes of adolescence, the reprise of
earlier failures turning up to mock me in the early morning
hours when a man is weakest.

I hesitated to ring her. A twinge of pain, of frustration, had
me galloping in different directions. To greyhound racing, to
cabarets, to other centre-city halls where the girls came from
Finglas and Inchicore, had no cars, and who danced with me
unaware that my mind was on another. The music, the chat, was
enough for them. After each dance they lit up their cigarettes as
if they had been through some terrible ordeal.

'Are you married?' was the only question that interested
them. They had this thing about married men. Being married
gave men potency. I began going on long walks, my veins full
of the allure, the mystery, of this cold girl called Clair. By
ignoring her she had become more real than if I had picked up
the phone and spoken to her. She was everywhere. When my
heart leaped it was for her. When I tried to forget her, something in my blood rebelled and called me back to that cool presence that resided at the centre of my dreams like some inviolate
image of feminine goodness. One evening, by the banks of that
brown, trout-stocked stream called the Dodder, with the birds
darting homewards and a lone water-hen struggling, pulling, it
seemed, its body along by its neck, I ran into Beryl. She had
this massive Afghan hound alongside her, with a mouth like a
shark, and when I foolishly went to pat him he bit me on the
arm. She took me to her home and bathed the tooth marks in
a solution of water and disinfectant. It was soothing to have

this large blonde girl patting my arm. Even the hound looked contrite, wanting to get into the act. I asked her out for a drink and she stopped in her tracks for a moment, looking intently at me. She looked vaguely ill-at-ease and during the few weeks we went out together she always retained that quality. It was rather endearing in a tiresome sort of way. Beryl was as blind as a bat. She had these horrendous spectacles that did nothing for her, in fact she only wore them when driving, and she was in the process of getting contact lenses. She lived her life in the shadows of other people, her parents, her friend, Clair. Nothing I could do could budge her. She was one of nature's second fiddlers. Yet she was kind and her awkward clumsiness evoked a tenderness in me that had me procuring petrol for her and trying to get her to wise up in general. Her parents had a fine house at the back of the Dodder, everything betokened an ease of living that left me smiling and speechless. Her hound was a bitch, Michaela. In a way it was her only friend. Beryl expected nothing and seemed to be surprised at my interest in her. She had little confidence, lived her life in a sort of wasteful humility that made her unhappy.

'How is Clair?' I inevitably asked. She was without guile or tension. She spoke as if she had been waiting for me to mention her. I hated her squalid feminine unawareness. She was myopic in more ways than one. Kissing her was like refuelling in space. She really was awkward.

'Clair is fine, seeing someone else, I believe, of course she's a very attractive girl, why don't you ring her, she seemed a trifle taken aback when I told her you were taking me out.' She apologised for living. She bowed before the altar of Clair. She was a simple girl, didn't want any trouble.

'Did you tell her about bumping into you and being savaged by your brute?'

'I am afraid she found it all rather hilarious.'

And so as I wandered innocently into Beryl I wandered out of her company. I'd say she was glad I didn't force any issues. When I met her later she appeared happier, was a new girl in her contact lenses, full of caressing words and get-up-and-go. She was settling into her Irish spinsterhood, no bother. In some way she had abdicated her rights, had opted for the quiet lonely road of non-involvement. It suited her. One of nature's innocents. She didn't mind that I was seeing Clair again – after all, Clair had seen me first. Her fading maidenhood hung about her like some autumnal rose, blooming in vain as far as this world goes, but she breathed a quality of spirituality, a hint of something far more precious than the obvious delights of the flesh or the successes of this life. A composure. That's what it was. She was the nun in civilian clothing.

I had never seen Clair looking so well. Her eyes sparkled with wickedness. She chided me for not ringing, for taking out Beryl. She knew she was the adored one. It made her cocky.

'Have you ever been bitten by an Afghan hound?' I said by way of self-defence.

Her car seemed made for canoodling, for confidences, for kisses that made my lips ache. On Howth Summit we watched other couples embrace, saw the lights of Dun Laoghaire and Dalkey twinkle like tiny torches held up for the God of Love. What was becoming apparent to her was my infatuation. When I was near her the pain ceased, I revelled in her softness, her laugh, her lips that fed my desire. She had become the loved one. And to give her credit, she responded. She gave her kisses with the unwritten yet obvious qualification that she wasn't in love, but she gave them. She enjoyed a little tenderness, but as long as I understood she had entered a caveat against my submission, everything was hunky-dory.

There were nights when she withdrew into an introspective chill. When she wouldn't let me put my arm around her. When her coldness wounded me to the quick. But I soldiered on, made allowances for her, tried to understand the vagaries of the female system. I remembered the good times then, bringing her back to the real world, bringing her back to my words of reassurance and hope. She could see I loved her. My steadfastness, however, upset her. She couldn't cope, couldn't understand it. She was a daughter of Eve, fickle, unsure, at the mercy of her hormones. My strength undermined her, left her grasping at the moon, the ebb and flow of her blood. Locked in our separate sexuality we gazed across the chasm at each other. It was those times when I should have held her but didn't that rankle even now. Instead, it was a relief to be on my own again, away from love and caring and the whole damn thing.

There were weeks when she would not see me. When only her mother's voice on the phone sympathised with my plight. On walks I saw her standing in every fresh-ploughed field, an immaterial scarecrow that scattered peace of mind, a crucifying figure of elemental pain. Even a dead crow on the road reminded me of her. There was no escape. Madness assailed me. The whole race of women came under attack. I turned my lancet on myself. I saw myself through her eyes. A nobody. As immature as ever. The stuttering lover, never quite ordinary enough to be accepted. Taking me to bed would be like taking a rattlesnake between the covers. When sanity returned I prayed that walking would burn the passion out of me.

This poor Clair persisted in her delicate thumbs-down operation – the neurotic surgeon wielding the scalpel on the drugged victim, inflicting wounds that time only would heal. She would see me on the occasional Thursday evening. In the lounge of the Dartry Inn she would withdraw into herself, smoking and sipping her lager as if it was poisoned. The view outside was of a car park and a small park where children played on swings. The river careered over rusty remains of appliances and vehicles. A bridge tried to put a stop to it all but the water circled its pinioned ramparts, forcing its way through. On the far bank the green chlorophyll of Ireland raised its ragged head. I thought treacherous thoughts. Something was coming to an end. Maybe the guys in the Metropole knew what they were doing in turning their collective backs on her. There was an element of the petulant autocrat about her. Surely she didn't expect a knight in shining armour to arrive? You never knew with women. The older they got, the worse they got. She resented my vast unspoken claim on her. She would never admit she might need me. On such nights I wondered what had happened to her felicity of thought and expression. Our relationship had become an elaborate artificial game. Who was kidding who? Walking her home on the last of these dates to the airless splendour of her semi-detached, aware of our footfalls on the echoing flags of the paths, the quiet domesticity of the middle-class Irish night, the loneliness of my soul, shriven to the size of a pea, aware of her otherness beside me, a body and mind and heart no longer tuned to my liking, aware of rejection, pain and loss, I accepted quite lucidly that she would have to be expelled from my mind by whatever means came to hand. Decision came before insincerity could take root, before the foul rag-and-bone-shop of the heart closed shop altogether.

Years later I saw her in Rathmines. She wore a delicious astrakhan coat to ward off the winter cold. She looked like a sophisticated Russian spy. Alien, almost, amongst the anonymous shoppers. Our eyes met for a moment but her aloof will never yielded. Only a flicker of recognition. She walked on imperiously. My fluttering curiosity died almost as soon as it rose. The past had brushed up against me and passed on. She who had filled my every waking moment had receded into a carefully tended memory. Part of a dream, she found her niche in my panoramic tapestry of remembered dancing partners and failed loves.

SEASCAPE

ANNE ENRIGHT

ANNE ENRIGHT

Anne Enright was born in Dublin in 1962. She studied at Trinity College, Dublin and the University of East Anglia, and made her writing debut with her short story collection, *The Portable Virgin*, which won the 1991 Rooney Award for Irish Literature. She is a Producer/Director in RTE.

HE STOOD LIKE a young seminarian at the water's edge, refusing to see the bodies that were strewn all around him. His eyes rested on the cool line of the horizon, and sweat gathered in the white creases of his face. His only concessions to the sun were the jumper he had removed, which never left his hand, and the thick boots that stood waiting in the sand behind him. He seemed to be standing quite still, but in fact was edging his feet forward, inch by inch. After a while, a thin film of water pulled at his bare toes, and he leapt back. The jump was awkward, and when he turned to walk back up the beach, he had the loping, twisted stride of an old tramp. He belonged to the street, and not to the sea, because his eyes had that puzzled, childish look, and his mouth was hard.

A woman rose from the sea behind him, the water spilling from her shoulders and hair.

'Daniel!' He stooped to pick up his boots, without turning around, so she ran up the slope after him, her body scattering a wet trail on the sand. The swimsuit she wore was azure blue, with a triangle of viridian at the neck, and her wet blonde hair had a greenish sheen in the strong light.

'Daniel,' she said again, catching up with him, 'are you coming in?'

'Nope.' He still didn't turn around.

'You grunter! You pig!' She shook herself at him like a wet dog and he pulled away from the drops. When she was done, he caught her by the arms and pushed her into the sand, then laughed and walked on. There was a moment's shock before she screamed and scrabbled up again, then charged after him up the beach. The old boots banged together in his hand as he evaded her, but when he reached the towels he turned around and let himself be caught. She pushed him down and sat on his chest.

'You need the wash, you old pig. I should throw you in like a drowned cat.'

'I can't swim.'

'You can't swim? Sure everyone can swim. I'll teach you.'

'Of course I can swim.'

'Liar.' She swung off him.

'You are a liar,' she said, picking up the towel, which was yellow like her hair. 'You're always lying to me.'

He lay on his back, his eyes slits in the glare of the sun. He seemed to be watching the sky. She flicked her body with the towel to get rid of the grit that had lodged in the creases, but he still didn't turn around. The laces of the boots were tangled in his hand and there were sweat marks and the marks of her wet body on his thick, old shirt.

'You like it,' he said and rolled on his belly to watch her. She covered herself with the towel to block his gaze.

'And anyway . . . I don't,' and he rolled back again with a small grunt.

He pursed his mouth. 'Pour us a cup of tea, will you?' It was an old joke.

'Pour it yourself, you bad bastard. You're not in your mother's house now.'

She sat there, for what seemed like a long time, and watched him sprawled damply on the sand. She did not stretch out, ignoring the freak weather with the confidence of one who already had the perfect tan. The colours of her swimsuit brightened in the sun.

After a while, she became aware of someone staring. It was a small child, naked as a cherub. He turned away from her when she looked up, and put his hands up to his face, but continued to watch her through his fingers.

'Hello.' She smiled at him and he ducked away at the sound of her voice.

'Look,' he said, suddenly bold, and with one hand still to his face, he pissed delicately on to the sand.

'Lovely,' she said, at a loss – trying not to give the child a complex.

'No, it's not,' he said, 'it's very bold,' and he ran off as his mother lumbered up after him; 'Come back here and I'll give you a belt!'

'That's the woman for you,' she told Daniel, as she caught the struggling child and trapped his legs in a pair of pants.

'A good, pink-skinned Irish ma with strap marks.'

Daniel lay still.

'Strap marks and stretch marks and Dunne's nighties. A fine hoult for you in the bed at night.' Daniel grunted assent.

'Well, take the old shirt off at least. You look like a maggot under a rock.'

'I look,' he said carefully, 'like something the tide washed up.'

Affairs, she thought, should stay in the place where they were conceived, they do not transplant well. He lay on the sand as though it were the gutter, while she turned her patch of towel into a little piece of the Riviera. Her face was drawn with effort.

'All I want,' she finally said, with deliberation and a fake smoothness, 'is an intelligent life. You *know* what I mean.' He turned to face her and his eyes were both puzzled and wary.

'No, I don't,' he said, and then as a small concession, 'it was far from intelligence that I was reared.'

'Well, start now,' she said, 'do my back.' He lifted his head and looked along the beach.

'I will not.'

'Pig.'

She flicked out the towel then lay down on it, with her back to him. After a moment's pause he made his way across to her on his belly.

'Here,' he said, taking the plastic bottle of sun oil from its dug-out in the sand. 'What do I do with this?' He spilt some on his fingertips and slapped it on her back, then moved over the skin like a farmer with a new lamb.

'You're done,' and quietly he lifted the hair from the nape of her neck. He stroked the side of her face, until her breathing eased, his eyes still out to sea.

'Did you see the body in the water?'

'Which one?' Her voice was muffled by her arms.

'With the clothes on.'

'No.'

'Floating on its face.'

'No.' Her voice had an edge to it.

'It was badly swelled. The gas brings them up, you know, after nine days.'

'No, I did not see it.'

'Pity.' His hand left her face, and he lay down the length of her. After a while, he seemed to sleep.

The afternoon wore on, and still neither of them moved. There was something obscene about the two forms lying so close together, one fully dressed and curved around the naked limbs of the other. She looked like a tropical fish in a dirty pond, with a bad old pike to protect her. Everyone around them was busy being amazed by the good weather, playing and shouting and soaking up the sun, but these two were not sunbathing or flirting. They were probably not even asleep.

The heat grew less intense, and as a slight breeze pulled at her hair, she stirred and slipped away from the curve of his body. She sat up and stared around her, as though surprised by what she saw, and then she reached for her bag and started to search around in it. She produced a bundle of postcards and a pen, and shuffled through them to find the right one. It was a picture of a cat in a window, reaching for the blind above her, with the sign 'Guinness is good for you' posted on the wall outside.

> Dear Fiona, (she wrote) the weather is glorious. The lump is being lumpish, haven't seduced him into the sea as yet. Will you check the cat for me? Should never have trusted her with that couple downstairs. We miss ickle pussums, we does, and you too.

She tore it up and took out a fresh one; this had a picture of a donkey and a red-headed girl with a turf creel in her arms.

Dear Fiona, is he psychotic or what? The nights are, as always, amazing, but the weather doesn't seem to suit his sensitive skin. Besides, he keeps on sneaking downstairs to make dubious phone calls. I don't care about An Other Woman . . . maybe, but I keep fantasizing that he's got a kid salted away somewhere. If you see Timmy, say I'm fine, i.e. give him a crack in the gob and tell him I'm sorry. All is . . .

She had run out of space and was writing where the address should go. The breeze had brought up the hairs on her arms, and she paused for a moment to examine them. Then she started to write on the front of the card, over the donkey's face:

I have lovely arms. Not that it makes any difference.

and she abandoned everything where it was and ran off down the strand, into the sea.

She could swim for hours. The water was beautiful, despite the cold, and she aimed straight for the horizon. She felt like diving down, wriggling out of the swimsuit and swimming on and on. The foolish picture of its limp blue and green washed up on the beach drifted into her mind. They might even accuse Daniel of the crime.

She took a breath, grabbed her knees to her chest and bobbed face down on the surface of the water. Slowly, as she ran out of breath, her muscles eased. She blew what was left in her lungs out in an explosion of bubbles, then shot up into the air and took breath. No. She would not be angry. Anger did not suit her. She would carry around instead the chic pain of an independent woman – the woman who did not whinge or demand, or get fat on children.

'I like independent women,' he had said once.

'Bloody sure you do,' she answered. 'They're not allowed to complain.'

The shadows had grown harsher and longer by the time she got out of the water, her hands numb and her legs stiff with the cold. She made her way up the slope heavily, shaking her fingers in front of her. Long before she reached their place, she saw that Daniel had gone. The postcard she had written and left was torn up like the first, the pieces scattered and half-buried in the sand. Among them was his discarded shirt, and a pair of trousers lay broken-limbed and empty on her yellow towel. She yanked at the towel to clear it of debris and the bundle of postcards flew up into the air. Moving slowly, and shivering with the cold she went to each one in turn and picked it up. Daniel had written on the face of them all.

The first was a picture of a Charollais cow on the cliffs of Moher. The sky was a hazy mauve, and the cow, which was right on the edge of the cliff, stared seductively at the viewer. Across the line of the sky he had written, 'A Rathmines Madonna Dreams of The Intelligent Life.' The next was a glossy reproduction of the beach in front of her, the colours artificially bright. Along the curve of the strand were the words, 'Yes, the nights are amazing, but as yet, I have no child.' She stared at it for a long time, and looked around to see where Daniel could be, before picking up the next one. It had an oul fella sitting in a pub, the light bouncing off the polished surface of the bar counter and a fresh, new pint in the shaft of the sun. There was a crudely drawn balloon coming out of the old man's mouth with the words: 'What *is* the difference between a pair of arms?' Finally, there was the beach again, though this time there were footprints drawn along the strand, enormously out of proportion, and a figure in the sea with HELP! coming from it. The caption read, 'O Mary mo chree, I am afraid that the water will claim me back again.'

'All washed up.' The voice came from directly above her, and she gave a start. When she looked up he was there, perfectly dry. He was wearing a pair of navy high-waisted swimming trunks. His body was white as wax and his front was sticky with hair. She was ashamed to look at this body and so looked at his face.

'Oh all right,' she said, and wanted to turn off the sun like a lamp, so they could make love on the beach.

PURE NATURAL HONEY

DERMOT SOMERS

DERMOT SOMERS

Dermot Somers was born in 1947 in Co. Roscommon. His first short stories appeared in 'New Irish Writing' and his first collection, *Mountains And Other Ghosts*, was published in 1990. At the age of twenty-seven he took up climbing and mountaineering, and in the 80s he climbed the classic Alpine series known as the Six Great North Faces, culminating in ascents of the Matterhorn and the Eiger. In 1993 he was a member of the first Irish team to succeed in reaching the top of Everest.

HE FELL OFF her old bike near Legale. No damage done, it was at a standstill anyway. A lady's model – a rusty, black, high-Nelly without gears. Mike was trying to cycle it up the ferociously steep road above the Guinness Estate.

Síle stood leaning on slightly more modern handlebars and watched him with delight. She mopped perspiration and drowning midges from her face, shook back a sunlit mass of curly, brown hair. She looked like an ad for simple, healthy living. Mike was much too vivid to be quite wholesome as he wrestled with the hill, so black-haired, blue-eyed, young and alive that there had to be badness in him somewhere.

His old Volvo had taken these Wicklow hills without strain the day he picked her up hitching to Dublin a month ago. He wore a neat, grey business suit then, white shirt and tie and serious leather shoes. At first glance he so resembled a solicitor that Síle felt like a throwback to the hippies. There were sinister objects – vague plastic torsos – on the back seat. He produced a smile so unexpectedly bright that she tingled with shock. The farmers and businessmen who gave lifts to Síle – she was tall, tangle-headed with clear skin, full lips and a striking wide-eyed face – were always predictable in their manner. Never objectionable, just shades of ordinary. But this one radiated a magnetic sense of energy and humour, barely suppressed – a lively actor playing an accountant.

Síle had her stylised country clothes on against the weather as she hitched; black broad-brimmed hat, brown handknit scarf, tweed waistcoat, lumberjack shirt, jeans and boots, and a good deal of her own handmade jewellery too. She knew she'd overdone it a bit but she felt pleasantly exotic in an old-fashioned way as his neatly cuffed wrist with a severely digital watch changed gears beside her knee.

He looked fit and slim to her appraising eye, no rugby or gaelic brawn; if he played football he'd score quick, clean soccer-goals. For the first time in months Síle was sharply aware of her own singleness. She searched for space to stretch long legs. He glanced in approval, 'Pull back the seat.' She saw plenty of strong, white teeth, an intelligent mouth – and he hadn't dived across her to find her seat-belt.

'Scenery or speed?' The car hesitated slightly at the junction before choosing the mountain road to Dublin.

'Do you live around here?' He began to be predictable, 'You don't sound local.'

'Quite close . . .' Careful, against her instinct, not to give too much information. 'You don't sound local either.'

'Just moved down! I love it even though it's a long drive to Dublin, but I don't go every day . . .'

'Neither do I – I work at home mostly . . .'

'Me too! I've a terrific house. I'm modernising it . . .' Their eager information overlapped, broke off in laughter.

'What do you do? No let me guess. You're . . .' he studied her quizzically and the car wandered, '. . . you're a potter!' He slapped the steering-wheel straight and laughed, not at all unkindly, amused, as if he knew her well already. 'Or a poet! You could easily be a poet, all that hair – and dressed for the imagination, as well as the road.'

'If that's how it works, you must be a computer programmer,' she put him briskly in his place. 'No, I'm not a poet – though I wouldn't mind. I'm not a weaver either, by the way. It's my turn to guess. You're some kind of engineer . . . or is it pharmaceuticals?'

'Pretty good, you must be a gypsy! I design special projects for the countryside,' he ad-libbed gleefully. 'Jails, abattoirs, schools, morgues . . .'

'Oh God, I'll walk, so –' The car breasted the ugly tree line and she stared entranced as the mountains flooded the morning with banked-up waves of colour. 'This is why I live in Wicklow . . .'

'Me too!' he agreed brightly. 'I love all that space. The imagination can breathe . . . And I'm not an engineer. I'm a kind of –' He pretended to wince, ' – Well, a sculptor actually. You'd hate my work though; it's all plastic and steel, and viciously modern.'

He was full of self-mocking relish, 'Anyone who weaves or knits or hurls pots *hates* me!'

'Sculpture? Is that it in the back?'

'God no! Display models for fashion shops! That's just business. They're always looking for something different, so I sell them squares and cubes and it seems to suit them. Clothes aren't made for human beings anymore.'

'Neither is your sculpture by the sound of it. I work in fashion design by the way. For people, not robots. No, don't apologise, I know the sector you mean – though I don't think I'd care to cater for something I didn't approve of!' She looked at him sternly, amazed to be so intimate, and then smiled at the consternation on his face. 'All my work is traditional,' she explained. 'At least, the materials are. Though I try to do something original with them – if I think it's an improvement that is. I'm still a student, so I'm working at various things – fabric, fashion, jewellery – at the moment I'm designing furniture for a diploma project; I'm bringing the chair designs up to town today, and I'll be finished then, free . . .'

'Furniture?! I'm doing my house and studio. Can I see?' He brought the car to an impulsive halt on the verge and turned towards her.

Funny, she didn't feel a bit nervous in a lonely layby with him, just defensive about her work. 'I told you it's very traditional,' she warned. 'Nothing sophisticated, but they're solid and they work, and anyone could have them in a house beside the TV or the dishwasher. That was my brief, and I believe in it too. OK?' she challenged.

'OK,' he agreed absently. 'Let's see. Mm, nice drawing for a start anyway – I could never draw.' He studied her artist's impressions with lively appreciation, and then turned busily to detail.

Síle turned away, suddenly embarrassed that he had her so

easily in the palm of his hand. Was he laughing at her? Unsettling
too to see her work appraised with such detachment as if it
were a business proposition. Until now she had traded among
friends and fellow students. This guy was intriguingly different,
but she was annoyed that she had delivered herself to him for
judgement. He was definitely younger than her, probably no
experience of design at all.

She peered at her drawing again; not much at first to distinguish it from a traditional wooden chair of the more elaborate
kind with a round, inlaid seat and a semi-circular back-support
projecting forward in two sturdy arm-rests. She'd emphasised
all those characteristics, and then altered the proportions for a
more – well, rakish appearance. These chairs looked as if they
were ready to dance and only waiting to be asked.

The motifs to be carved on the wood were semi-original
ideas; they were meant to imply motion, a difficult thing with
something as stable as a chair. Síle felt confused. He was still
studying them, as if memorising the design – or was he
composing something plausible to say?

She turned to look up at Tonelagee, the sun now kindling
the heather to golden warmth, and she seized on the memory
of the heart-shaped lake up there, hidden except to those who
made the effort to walk up the mountain.

'Ever been up to Lough Ouler?' He interrupted her solitude.

'Yes, often, I was just thinking of it – Well, do you like the
chairs?'

'Definitely! Respectable without being genteel. I hate smug-
ness, don't you? I can imagine elderly aunts being tempted to
too much sherry in those. There's a sense of discreet sin about
the shape.'

'Is there?' Síle was amused. 'That doesn't sound like me.
When I sin I'm not a bit discreet – I get carried away . . .'

She stopped, embarrassed again; she didn't usually get
carried away quite so soon. 'Sounds interesting!' he encouraged
innocently with wide-open eyes. She noticed again their compul-
sive colour.

Probably no bluer than ordinary eyes really – it must be the
vivid way they caught the mountain light that brightened them.

She found herself laughing with him, as if they knew something between them that no one else knew.

The other thing about his eyes was the way they distracted attention from the rest of his face, as if they were compensating for a plainness which of course he didn't suffer from at all. He was too dangerous to be left driving around picking up romantic young women and setting them down again as if they were shapes in clear plastic for displaying garments. Síle was veering towards indiscretion and steadied herself for whatever he might do next.

What he actually did was fold the drawings carefully, hand them to her, gaze up Tonelagee with narrowed eyes and murmur, 'Terrific site for a hotel up there!' Then he started the car and drove away. She was relieved, not only that he hadn't made a pass at her and put her in the difficult position of refusing the desirable – but also because she'd have been bitterly disappointed by such predictability. Particularly after he'd liked her chairs.

She was used to being pursued, but how to pursue? Did he live on his own, that was crucial.

'Do you live on –' lost her nerve ' – on the main road?'

'No, up the back behind Annamoe. I can be on the hills in minutes from my door!'

'Lovely! Do you get out much?'

'Not until the studio is finished. I know the hills pretty well though – I used to belong to a mountaineering club in college.

'Hey! . . .' an idea struck him. 'Maybe we could do some walking together!' He turned towards her, beaming with pleasure, and the car almost left the road. 'Look out!' she cried, and threw her hands up in fright.

He fell off the bike again trying to force it straight uphill. Then he got smart and began to zig-zag, a wobble at each verge and a horizontal lurch across the road and back. He might make it that way, but it would take at least a week. A sheep popped its head over the wall agog with critical alarm. He wobbled the wrong way in response and plunged back towards her.

'Let's leave the bikes here at Pier Gates,' Síle pleaded, 'you'll never get to the Sally Gap. We can walk down by the lakes here and up Knocknacloghoge instead – save Lough Ouler for another day.'

'OK, you'd need the muscles of a postman to pedal this.'

'It belonged to a district nurse,' Síle scoffed. 'She used to overtake motor cars! You haven't got the legs for it.'

He stretched long, fine limbs for her inspection, 'Are they up to walking do you think?'

Plunging downhill at the half-walk, half-trot the slope requires he caught her swinging hand and closed his own around it.

'In case I get lost,' he confided.

'Get lost!' she parodied, but she held on tight and gazed with absurd contentment at the quiet lake below, a fringe of forest along the near shore, then a sandy beach and the big house behind it guarded by steep slopes, a boulder field along the far side, and above it a huge, hanging mass of rock. Out of all that tranquil enclosure the lake drained south along a green valley floor between tawny slopes of heather and fern. A second lake, Lough Dan, was partly visible a mile away surrounded by low hills that rolled lazily away on every side without any of the crowding steepness of a mountain range.

'Isn't it beautiful?' she sighed, feeling sentimental and apt. 'It's got everything – trees, water, rock, heather, sand . . .'

'Midges,' he slapped busily at himself. Síle was above minor irritations, only something volcanic or nuclear would disturb her now. She pointed across the valley with her free hand. A small area of hillside lay softly lined with ridges and furrows, blurred by heather, almost re-absorbed into the earth.

'Lazy-beds, the remains of old potato drills. Look at the colour and texture! If you could knit it or weave it just as it is!' she teased longingly. 'Plastic will never mean anything rich like that.'

'Of course it will, when we've lived in a plastic world long enough – then it'll be quite normal . . .

'Look,' he continued briskly, getting it straight, 'you see things in a different way to me, Síle –' And for a terrible moment she thought he meant something more important than the view, '– I mean, we both love the oaks and all that, and we hate the creepy dullness of the conifers, but in a way I walk to get *above* the – claustrophobia of the earth and the bog. Sorry if it sounds pretentious, it's not meant to. I don't look at my feet. Sometimes the ground hems me in with its gravity, it's full of memories and promises of – of decay . . .'

She was staring with profound anxiety and interest, and he laughed nervously at himself. 'Don't get me wrong! I agree the mountains are lovely, that's why I'm out – well, part of the reason –.' He grinned and blushed but didn't stop. 'You like the density and the texture of the mountains Síle, you'd like to wrap them around you like tweed or a plaid rug, but when I look at the hills I like to see space, not substance. I don't think it's the way most people look. To me the landscape sort of gets in its own way sometimes. You know those photographs with huge hunks of geology and vegetation stuffing the frame? – I find that boring, even if the colours and textures are . . . interesting. D'you think I'm a philistine . . . ?'

He watched her worriedly and at the vigorous shaking of her head he plunged on: 'What I like is lots of shifting sky shaped by the profile of the landscape. Wicklow is very friendly that way; it's so rounded and open it lets the sky through in great curves and arcs. A tent of light. And I love the way the lakes reflect it, and make a full circle –'

He seized another strand, '– I'm the same with houses and buildings, I sort of look past them and in between. There's plenty of people concerned with the density of things. I think it's really important to appreciate the spaces – the way light is allowed to make its own designs . . . It doesn't happen at all in Dublin because it's flat and sort of *tight*; if I had to live in a city I'd definitely go for New York . . .'

'I see . . .' Síle broke the flow. 'Town-planning as sculpture –'

'Well, that *is* what I try to do in my work. I know you haven't seen it yet, but that's *it*! It's always groups of objects arranged so that I can emphasise the spaces between them. The trouble is, it results in draining the objects of any meaning in themselves, otherwise they'd take over; you know, as if letters and numbers were just the limits to the space between the ink and meant nothing more than that. See what I mean? –' and he bounded in front of her waving his arms vigorously, '– think of a number, take your own age, twenty-three; I bet you've never examined the shape of that space between the two figures before! Or your name; you make extraordinary patterns between the letters every time you write it. Why shouldn't that be important? I'm trying to liberate that space.'

Síle's hand had cooled by now, and her heart was steady with caution. Was he garrulous – or actually inspired in some hectic way? It was very important that he should not be a sham! She still hadn't seen any of his real work. His house was empty while he rebuilt the big attic as a working space. She was impressed by the enthusiasm of the project, but she needed hard evidence as to what he was. She needed to see his work.

'Maybe you can see my problem now, with the sculpture I mean? People say it's all very well, but they want to buy Objects – they don't want to spend money on Space which they feel they own already! Now if I could make objects that were both valid in themselves *and* definitions of space I'd be on a winner . . .'

'Make a chair!'

'A chair? A Chair! Why a *chair*?'

'It'll give you discipline in structure.' Síle was very firm.

'Good furniture is unobtrusive – it's sort of invisible in a way, and yet it defines a room. You can concentrate all you want on the spaces and shapes within a chair – but if it doesn't work as a seat then it's worse than useless. Burn it! There's nothing worse than a chair that doesn't work . . . except maybe a jug that dribbles. Oh, and that's another idea; I don't want to set you up as a craft centre, but you could design all sorts of pots and jugs that make fantastic statements with the space between them – everybody knows the urn/faces trick – but if they don't pour properly, I'll take a hammer to them . . .'

'A chair!' He sneezed it quietly again, 'Could I make yours, Sile?'

'Mine? Of course! I'd love to see it made. Can you do all that stuff, wood-turning, carpentry . . . ? That's real craftsmanship. Much harder than sculpture.' She grinned.

'Just leave it to me!' He grabbed her hand again, his bright face full of restored confidence.

Mike threw the door open and she walked into his studio screwing up her eyes. She was ambushed again by the vigorous light inside the attic. There was no sign of rafters, roofing felt, or the underside of slate. The white room was full of long windows angled across the hilltops at the sky. Bright surfaces and mirrors intensified the daylight; like passing through a door into foreign weather.

The room was empty still, he'd been working on her chairs. She looked around for the dark, rich wood. Mike was silent for once, and then she realised – they were there . . . She was looking right through them.

A gasp of disbelief and she turned a withering glare on him. He quailed but managed a weak grin. She strode across the room, heels hammering the bare floor. Her chairs all right – but pale, transparent ghosts of her intention, not timber at all, but a thick see-through substance moulded smoothly on to a thin steel frame; a parody of texture – what had he done there? For she saw that the chairs were indeed the colour of some strange kind of wood; a subtle stain had been added to the plastic, and there were traces of texture too, at random; one seat had the undeniably natural grain of wood – though when she felt the surface there was nothing there. Then she saw the mandala from a child's marble embedded within the ghost of a knothole, and she understood the trick – the textures and the marble were all inside, pressed on to internal layers . . .

The seat of the second chair had hints of fine, old lace in it, and a blurred corduroy imprint too as if someone had thought of sitting in it while it was still soft. She ran a fingernail across the furrows and ridges – 'Lazy-beds,' he reminded nervously – but there was nothing there on the surface except that infuriatingly funny blandness. And there was a sense of – well, of Exposure about the glassy chair. She had a disconcerting flash of someone – herself? – sitting naked except for a see-through plastic mac, seen from behind drinking gin?

Mike was still grinning at her – his eyes held the only deep colour in the room – his expression a blend of enquiry, apology, affection and sheer cheek. She knew she was being – not ridiculed or parodied, but . . . laughed at? No, it wasn't that either, and whatever it was she was beginning to mind less as he smiled at her. He simply couldn't resist statement – like the day at Luggala. There it was, embedded in the thick arm-rests of the chairs, that day again – strands of moss, heather, blades of grass, leaf imprints, and somehow as well a stitch motif from the Aran jumpers he detested . . .

. . . But the joke was on him – for the whole thing was beginning to work, in detail if not quite in total. It gave character to the vacant plastic. She followed the exquisite footprints of a bird small as a wren around the rim of a seat until it took flight. It was so meticulously done that it revealed his respect for the materials he satirised as clearly as if she had found a scrapbook of pressed flowers under his bed.

And the colour too, a kind of tawny, golden transparence owed more than a nod of submission to wood. She returned again to a tiny tuft of moss, a few blades of grass, a quartz pebble and a twig or two, arranged so that between them they conjured up a whole landscape; and something warm and permanent – the rhapsody of the scene – settled into her heart.

Mike nudged her attention impatiently downwards. He tilted the chair to show how the legs had been moulded to her design – but as she bent closer she saw that he had infiltrated a joke in the form of tiny labels into the mixture, so that the carved sections of the legs now resembled slender bottles and jars stacked on top of each other. The labels were transparent of course – strings of old-fashioned print just beneath the surface.

A plumply tubular section near the seat read Pure Natural Honey, and she giggled helplessly because the smooth plastic with its delicate, mellow stain did indeed look fit to spread on bread – home-made brown of course. There was even an uncanny trace of something like honeycomb stirred in. Just below it, the next section was labelled Vintage Cider Vinegar, the same colour was equally apt and the taste of honey turned apple-sharp and sour in her mouth. He'd caught her lifestyle exactly, for another label announced Twelve Year Old Whiskey and without effort the rich substance glowed amber.

There was Lemon Tea as well, complete with rind, and a plain section of leg at the floor that contained either wine or urine – but the two words, and samples, were so remarkably similar that she didn't dwell on that, in case he was taking the p . . .

'OK,' she surrendered, stifling laughter. 'OK, you win; though I wouldn't sit in one! I don't see why you changed the shape –' She pointed at the D-shaped seat and a missing arm, '– was the symmetry too much for you?'

He danced in front of her, beaming with relief and pride, grabbed a chair and swung it between them. He sat down solidly, braced his left arm on the single arm-rest, grabbed a sketch-pad to his knee, and with elaborate motions showed how he could sketch freely without any obstruction to his right elbow. It made devastating sense.

'That's all very well for you!' Síle fought to the end, 'but it's selective design. One-offmanship! What about me – I'm left-handed?'

'I know! And this is the Ciotog-model; this is *your* chair!' He pressed her into the other one, taking a delicate liberty while he did so, and she found her left arm unrestricted while her right was supported. The opposite to his.

He thrust the sketch-pad at her, drew his chair across and placed it down beside her. The cutaway sides of the seats butted perfectly together, while the two interrupted back-rests now made a continuous arc. It was an intimate double-seat. Síle slapped her forehead; she had just spotted the purpose and the punch line. As they sat pressed warmly together, he slid his arm along the joint back-rest and tightened it round her shoulders, 'We're armchair mountaineers!'

'Wait a second, hold on –' she was still a designer, 'what about a normal couple, right-handers, how will they get on . . . ?'

'Who cares?' He shrugged her firmly against him. 'Let them make their own chairs.'

THE WHITE HOUSE

MICHAEL CURTIN

MICHAEL CURTIN

Michael Curtin was born in Limerick in 1942. All his early stories appeared in *The Irish Press* 'New Irish Writing' page and he was joint winner of the Writers' Week Short Story Award in 1972. In recent years he has published four novels which received wide praise.

AROUND THE TIME de Valera gave Churchill his answer George Ellis bought the White House. George worked in the Customs and when he inherited a couple of thousand pounds he thought it would be a good idea to buy a small pub. His wife, the former Madge Brilly, was thrilled. They had been married only a few months and the kitchen sink had no attraction whatsoever for her. She was a gay, charming, liberated woman devoted to the Arts, and stolid George was a refreshing contrast to the wild young men who adored her. Now that she was married, running a pub would give her something to do. Characteristically, George continued in the Customs until he was sure the pub could yield a comfortable living. By that time he had discovered he loathed serving in the bar. Particularly with the clientele Madge had amassed. All the customers were either writers, actors or painters or thought they were writers, actors or painters. He decided to hold on to his job and left the pub in Madge's capable hands. He had to help out occasionally at night but his heart was never in it. Still, the extra income was comforting.

Madge Brilly's bridesmaid and fellow flapper of the time was Nan Daly. She was among Madge's first customers. Nan, at nineteen, was regarded as an outstanding local actress. She was constantly exhorted by all who knew her to seek fame and fortune further afield. She wore trousers, smoked an odd cheroot and drank a pint as good as a man. Yet there was nothing masculine about her. She was in fact so beautiful that the few men around who might have been worthy of her were so conscious of their deficiencies in her presence that they immediately smothered their desires. Those who made no secret of their admiration were such rubbernecks that there

was no danger of their feelings being hurt by a rebuff. Madge
was to spend years promoting the cause of every extrovert and
deep poet who lent a tone to the bar, but Nan would only
laugh and point out that she was waiting for someone more on
George's line. When George would be in the bar they would
have a great joke about it. Madge would say that Nan could
have him – that he had no interest in the theatre, that he was
only interested in his golf and rugby – she didn't know how she
married such a Philistine.

It never occured to Nan to try and conquer the world. She
enjoyed acting – just as she enjoyed singing or listening to one
of the pub poets. She had no desire to emigrate or live on beans
or be had by an impresario, as she fondly imagined was the
statutory apprenticeship of the stars. She was quite happy to
put in her day at the office and rehearse at night, or drop in to
the White House for an evening with the literati. Now and
again she went out with one of Madge's recommendations and
sometimes she was kissed. She never went further than that
– no one did at the time, at least no one with any sense. These
little affairs scarcely ever lasted more than three dates.

Doggie Doyle clarified her emotions. He wore a cravat and
was known to be a lady-killer. He was a sporty type but his
heart was in the right place and he was drawn to the White
House. Madge looked upon his gall as charm and raved about
him. He walked Nan home from the pub one night and before
she knew where she was he was courting her deftly against
the door. He was neither clumsy nor eager and knew when and
where and how subtly to massage. Nan went to bed out of
breath. She relived her contact with Doggie and found to her
amazement she was thinking of George. It was weeks before
she could accept it. She was in love with George. She remained
in love with him for thirty years.

On the odd night that George did potter about behind the
counter Nan's heart did not beat any faster. This was what she
loved about him, she decided. She could be relaxed and natural
in his presence. George was unaware of her existence other
than that she was a friend of Madge's and he tolerated her as
amiably as he did the other odd bods who laid bare their souls

in front of the fire. Nan accepted the cruel twist of fate that
attracted her to the unattainable. She threw herself into the
theatre. When she was not acting she was producing. She had
affairs and inevitably, as time passed, she sometimes allowed
a relationship to reach its natural climax. She enjoyed herself
but always surrendered to the thought that if such pleasure
could be had from a liaison with a vacuous artist, what paradise
the droll George would surely provide. She did not feel envious
of Madge. On the contrary, she was drawn closer to her. Madge
had such good taste. Oh George, George!

The golden age of the White House was in the early fifties.
Still without bingo and television and sensing the approach of
the technological age and its inevitable concomitant of slipping
standards, the people flocked to the bedside of the dying relative
– the theatre. When she was not rehearsing or acting Nan Daly
held court around the fire. The passage of years had eroded
her armour and now in her full maturity she drank like a fish
and, her beauty mellowing, was more available. But her dream
of romance died hard and whenever she did succumb, George
still hovered in her imagination in the platonic background.
Doggie Doyle had become a bit of an arty buff and brought his
sporty friends in with him. They were reasonably well behaved
and Madge, in her moments of weakness, welcomed their presence because they drank a lot and, unlike the pure artist, they
had the money to pay for it. The White House was now well
known as the sanctuary of every bastard descendant of the
Muse incestuously listening to one another's recitations of
poetry or snippets from books of the mind.

The gradual decay of progress became apparent in the early
sixties and culminated with the invasion of the post-Beatle,
battle-dressed, proxy orphans of the Vietnam war. Conversation was replaced with the strident strumming of people over-
coming. Sloppy, anaemic, tubercular, draped on high stools,
they wailed: 'We shall overcu-uh-um, we shall overcu-uh-um.'
The drama group creaked at the seams. The gradual influx of
younger members on to the committee was reflected in the
choice of productions. Nan Daly, who had wallowed between
Coward and O'Casey for almost a quarter of a century, was

expected to mother angry young heroes with the vocabularies of sailors. She declined. However much she now indulged herself in private life she would not take down her spiritual pants on the stage. So Nan, Doggie Doyle and the rest of the fading old guard were pushed into the background of the White House, their gentility insignificant amidst the vocal rabble of the media age. But as with all rabble of any age their roots were shiftless and the early seventies revealed the White House camp, jaded and devoid of 'go'. The old guard came back to power, joined this time by a new devotee, Billy Whelan.

Billy Whelan's discovery of the White House had been inevitable. His family owned the local newspaper and a talent for composition at school seemed to pre-destine his career. The paper's narrow spectrum gave rise to the jack of all trades and Billy became a gifted obituarist, critic and sporting correspondent who, with facility, wrote ill of nobody – and despised himself for it. He was clean-shaven, good looking, well dressed and polite – a refreshing change to the White House from the recent trash. Madge was mad about him. Doggie Doyle was thrilled to have him as a source of inside information on the sporting world. He even got on well with George. Nan Daly liked him instinctively but then she was a very easy person to get along with. Billy thought they were a quaint lot and he secretly prided himself on his friendship with them. Not for Billy the world of the discothèque, the speculation about drugs, the naked indulgence in unabashed sex. Only with this vanishing breed could he be distracted from the sense of his own uselessness. He did not know what he wanted, only that he wanted to do better. He acted with the drama group and with little effort he was commendable. Maybe he would become an actor. There was little enough to it, he imagined, except hard work and a bit of luck. Or a writer. More hard work and luck.

Billy did not have a girlfriend. He was shy with girls. At least with the girls with whom he came in contact. They were not shy. They could curse and swear with an insouciance they never learned at their mothers' knee. He felt fragile in such company. He dreamed of a maiden whose hand he could hold and at whom he could smile coyly with excitement. He dreamed in vain. The shy maidens were dead and gone, hounded out of existence by the unquiet revolution of bad taste. He noticed old men and women standing on crowded buses; football fanatics chanting obscenities; women polluting conversation by their tolerance of its vulgarity and frequently by their very entrance into it. He smiled sadly at the introduction of plastic milk bottles; they would reduce breakages. Even at his tender age he could recollect when a clip on the ear reduced breakages. It distressed him that people for whom the American Dream had come true and who had houses with seven bedrooms preferred margarine to butter. Every evidence of change for the worse he noted and found himself looking down his nose at the world.

Nan and Doggie and a few other cronies often took drink back to Nan's flat when the pub closed. It was a gathering of the lonely and displaced and although Billy was always invited and sometimes went, they were amazed that he did not seem to have something better to do. Nan felt particularly inhibited by Billy's presence at these late night sessions. It wasn't that in his absence hair was let down or anything of that nature but she felt her fading stature should not be exposed to the young. In the pub, where the talk was general, she lost no caste, but the intimate nature of the late-night gatherings highlighted her frailty and sadness. Billy was witty in a cynical way in the pub but his droll observations of the present day merely reminded Nan and the others of their own actual suffering of what he joked about.

There were a few bottles still standing one night when Doggie and everyone except Nan and Billy had passed their quota. When they had all staggered home poetically and Billy and Nan were alone the drink made her bold enough to quiz him. What was he going to do with himself? Was he going to continue with his obituaries and court cases until he inherited the paper? Had he no desire to go out and conquer the world and all the rest of it? Why hadn't a fine young man like himself not got a fine young girl to look after? Billy told her. He destroyed the local customs and neighbourliness and stultification. He lamented the dearth of women of character. He admitted his burning desire to change the world. Why hadn't Nan – a fine woman, he gallantly conceded – why hadn't she married? Why was there nothing now in her life except tippling in the White House? Was everyone blind that no one appreciated her? Nan laughed. He was a terrible flatterer. No, he meant it, he assured her. The conversation died for a while as they gulped the remaining bottles. Nan found herself talking about George. How she had always persuaded herself that she loved him. Billy only half heard her. He gathered she had never come across the magic person he himself was sure he sought.

Billy blurted out secrets he would never confide in a contemporary. With so much insurance Nan trotted out some of her own peccadilloes. Like youngsters surreptitiously flicking through the pages of a dirty book they charged the atmosphere with their exchange of confidences. Nan was sprawled on an armchair while Billy sat erect and excited on the sofa. He was staring at her and she acknowledged it. She beckoned him but he wasn't sure. She motioned her head again and this time though still unsure he rose and stumbled over to her. She drew him to her and they slipped slowly down the armchair on to the floor.

Billy was still asleep on the floor when Nan went out to work. He woke with dry lips and a cigarette cough. He remembered everything and blushed with the recollection. He threw water on his face and tidied himself as best he could but he was a nervous wreck at work that day and the usual platitudinous speculations flew anything but freely from his typewriter. When he finished late that night he knew he needed a drink badly but was afraid to go into the White House. Yet he knew a drink anyplace else would make him worse. The usual crowd, including Nan, were there before him. Nan was as relaxed as ever and greeted him as though nothing had happened but he wasn't his usual witty self. Nervously he spoke when he was spoken to and when he tried to engage Nan's eyes she avoided him. Apparently it had been a drunken bout and no more. He had better forget about it like a true sophisticate. But he couldn't forget about it. For days he relived it and after a week, fortified once more by drink, he followed Nan home from the pub. She stopped when he caught up with her.

'Can I come up with you?' he blurted out. She nodded.

They vowed that every night would be the last night. They felt as remorseful as two teenagers tempting fate. But something grew between them gradually that was more than the sum of what they had mutually to offer. Finally, through tears, Nan said one night: 'I love you Billy Whelan. Oh God, I love you.' There were no more maidens for Billy to hold hands with and smile coyly at with excitement and for Nan there was no George in the platonic background.

And then Madge died.

She died with little originality, suffering an early morning stroke while stacking up the shelves in the pub. A pensioner in for his constitutional malt found her. The newspaper office was just around the corner and Billy heard the news within the hour. He rang Nan but she had already known and had gone to the pub to see what she could do. Billy made a few more phone calls and a large gathering were soon on the scene protesting to one another that Madge had seemed in great form the last time they saw her. The efficient undertaker set plans in motion to have her boxed by the night, and the death notice, together with a hasty appreciation from Billy, appeared in the evening paper. He would do her justice in the weekend edition. Nan looked after the bar during the day and when they took Madge to the church that night Doggie Doyle went behind the counter. There seemed to be a tacit understanding that the White House should not close on such an occasion. Billy, Nan and Doggie served the bar after the funeral. The place was crowded. George was there. He felt he had to be there with these people keeping the pub open for him. Although he couldn't understand why the pub shouldn't be closed. Maybe Madge would have wished it open, as they said, but he didn't know. It was most peculiar. People he had never met came up to him and shook his hand and told him they knew her well. Acquaintances Nan hadn't seen for years turned up. It was more than Madge's wake – it was the wake of a way of life long since dead but only now interred.

She had a huge funeral the following day but what with pressure of business and various other excuses only a hard core went back to the pub. They had no pressure of business or if they had they said to hell with it. Madge Brilly was dead. Or Madge Ellis as she is now. Or was. George faced up to his responsibilities. If the pub didn't close yesterday there seemed little point in closing it today. Although he would have to hire someone to tend it. He couldn't have that bunch turning it into a poets' co-op. Nan took the death very badly. She got so drunk Billy had to carry her home. He did it without the subterfuge they normally resorted to as though he was performing a corporal work of mercy and had nothing to hide. He had to put her to bed and felt the increased intimacy that such a personal deed effects.

Pathetically George installed a farmer's daughter as barmaid. She was coarse and insensitive and was constantly rebuked by Nan for spilling drink or forgetting to put briquettes on the fire or humouring the knobs of the old wireless to a pop music station. They grew testier every day at the sight of her and when George dropped his bombshell it was a welcome relief. He was selling the pub. An auctioneer pal of his had a client. A returned exile who had spent ten years in the States as a contractor. He felt he could 'make a go' of the place. On the last night they presented George with a hastily commissioned drawing of the pub, gratefully executed by one of the younger artists who appreciated the opportunity to make some recompense for the slate that had died with Madge. George thought it was a nice gesture. Obviously it was the thought rather than the unintelligible impressionism of the sketch that counted. He stood to the house and there was much drunken speech-making.

The new owner was friendly in the uninhibited American way. He had a distressing habit of constantly cleaning the counter. Little by little he effected small improvements. He blocked up the fireplace and put in a gas fire. He tantalised them with his contemplation of which corner would be most suitable for a colour television. He had a lovely transistor that had access to BBC One, Two, Three and Four. The old wireless with the face like a chapel door, from which Dev's voice once rallied the nation, stood silent in the background. Finally he closed the pub for renovation.

The White House was closed for a month and Nan and Billy

and Doggie no matter where they went could not feel at home. When it reopened the exterior was scarcely affected. A coat of fresh paint brightened the Tudor façade. Nan opened the door with a sense of anticipation. The high stools were gone. Every place she looked she saw covered leather seats with little tables in front of them. She blinked at the gaudy colours of the television. Billy was standing at the bar watching her stocktaking. She walked towards him and noticed, over his shoulder on the wall where the old posters advertising the drama group used to hang, a splendid dart board. Her face coloured and her lips trembled. 'Good Christ,' she said.

There was a complete reversal in their relationship. Up to now Billy had been ever eager and impatient for the rendezvous in her flat but with the death of the White House Nan began to need him more. She consumed him. She rang him during the day, something she had never done before. She brought him into the flat earlier and made him stay later. The natural outcome was that Billy's enthusiasm began to wane. It was grand to drop into the White House and pick her up when he felt like it but meeting her in other pubs where their relationship was obvious and the atmosphere less liberal was another matter. Luckily Nan sensed what was happening and she had the maturity to know what to do. On a night when he was in a particularly hot mood from drink she refused him.

'What's the matter, Nan?

'I want you to do something for me, Billy.'

'I'd kill a dragon for you, Nan.'

'I want you to go away.'

'Go away? Now?'

'Yes. This very minute. Tilt your hat at a rakish angle on your head and hop on a boat. Go away and become a dishwasher or an elevator operator or sleep in a telephone box or whatever is the thing to do. Go away before I drag you down with me. Do you understand?'

'You're tired of me. You want to cast me aside and take up with someone else.'

'Billy, I'm serious. Give up that crummy job and go away and become something.'

When he realised she was in earnest the words began to go to his head. She flattered him outrageously about the talent he had. He could become a great writer if he broadened his horizon and gave himself a chance to develop instead of contracting in the arms of an old hag. Billy was glad she had the character to bring it out in the open. He knew he would have to leave sometime – leave Nan at any rate; they were being whispered about in pubs. They talked till four in the morning. Nan assured him she would manage quite well without him. Billy did not know whether he should make a final overture.

'Do you want me to stay?' he asked. Nan shook her head.

He paused at the door for a minute and said: 'Thanks for everything.'

Nan forced a smile. 'If I was only your age what a great time we'd have.' She said it airily. He could not think of a suitable reply. She motioned her head for him to go and, relieved, he blew her a kiss.

After he left she sat folded in the armchair, chain-smoking, and letting the ash fall carelessly on her breast.

WATCH OUT FOR
PARADISE LOST

MICHAEL COADY

MICHAEL COADY

Michael Coady was born in Carrick-on-Suir, Co. Tipperary in 1939. *The Irish Press*' 'New Irish Writing' published his first poems in 1970 and his first story in 1973. He won a number of awards, including the Writers' Week Short Story Award and the Patrick Kavanagh Poetry Award. He is currently engaged in exploring areas of creative connection between poetry and prose, memory and time, people and place.

NO MAN CAN taste the whole wine? By God, old Donne went for it anyway. Sermons and seduction. Body and soul. God in woman. Up and at it with a metaphysical will.

> *Full nakedness! All joyes are due to thee*
> *As souls unbodied, bodies uncloth'd must be*
> *To taste whole joyes . . .*

He stretched his legs down in the bed and adjusted the book on his chest.

'John.'

'Hmm?'

'John!'

He turned his head and looked across the room. She was sitting in her slip at the dressing-table, smearing something around her eyes.

'What is it?'

She unscrewed the lid from another jar.

'Talk to me.'

'Just hold on a minute. I'm in the middle of something. The Dean of St Paul's trying to get his mistress into bed.'

> *To teach thee, I am naked first; why then*
> *What needst thou have more covering than a man?*

Some boyo.

'John, will you put away the book and listen to me?'

'Hmm?'

'You never listen.'

He put the book down and blinked across at her. 'Alice, are you going to spend the night out there? Come to bed and stop fussing.' He moved over and turned the clothes back at her side. Page lost again.

She opened a drawer. 'I looked into Patrick's room. His mouth was open and he had half the bedclothes out on the floor.'

He searched for the page. 'He's all right. I put him to bed at eight o'clock and he was asleep halfway through the King's New Clothes. What would you do if you had a houseful, instead of one and a bit?'

The page. Love's War.

Here let me war; in these arms let me lie
Here let me parlie, batter, bleed and die.

A cold draught of air sneaked under the bedclothes. What the hell was she doing? 'Alice! Are you going to stay out there all night?' He sat up and faced towards her. 'What's the matter with you?'

Twitch of the shoulders. After eight years you knew the signs. Trough of low pressure approaching. Sometimes he came in to find her crying her eyes out over some old film full of rose-covered studio cottages, idyllic weekends, sobbing violas and Ronald Colman saying goodbye in foggy railway stations. And, oh my God, the night he brought her to Jane Eyre. Half the cinema turning around in their seats to look at her in the floods. As delicately tuned as a bloody fiddle.

'John!' Tears ran down her cheeks and plopped on to a framed photograph which she held in her hands. His mouth opened in astonishment. She made a sudden dive for the bed and buried herself against him, heaving with great sobs and covering his chest hair in a mixture of tears and skin conditioner. Oh God, oh John Donne.

'Alice, will you for goodness sake tell me what's the matter?' Something was digging painfully into his gut. The photograph. He patted her on the back and drew the clothes around her. 'Come on. Talk to me about it. And take that picture away before you do me an injury.'

She relaxed a little. He felt a tear run down all the way to his navel. After a while the talk would come. And probably go on for hours. What would Donne have done?

'Aw now Alice . . . Did I say something? Did I do something?'

Under his neck she shook her head, disentangled an arm and held out the photograph, then turned on her back, her eyes half closed, their lids awash.

It was a picture of herself. He remembered taking it one day in the woods, before they were married. Her face framed in fresh-green branches. Whitethorn blossom he had confettied in her hair. Smiling; a girl. Sweet lovers at their play.

He studied it for a while, remembering, then leaned over and stroked her wet cheek. 'Alice . . . There's no doubt about it. You were the Queen of the May.'

She sobbed.

'And listen to me – you're the same girl now as you were that day.' Dammit, it was true. Put her in a gymslip and she was seventeen again.

'You're,' she swallowed, looking up at him in bitterness, 'you're only trying to pacify me. I was a girl then. I'm a woman now. Twenty-nine. With stretch marks. And little wrinkles coming around my eyes.'

'Stretch marks? What in God's name are you talking about? You were always a woman. And you'll always be a girl. Nothing to do with stretch marks. Or wrinkles. You could still be seventeen.'

'Don't. I'm not a child.'

Irishwomen never believe compliments. He twisted towards her and John Donne fell out on the floor. 'Listen to me, Alice. I mean it. You haven't changed a bit and you'll still be beautiful when I'm pushing up nettles. You'll live forever. Look at your grandmother – eighty-three and still getting her hair done to go to bingo every week. Now come on and don't be acting like a' – it came out before he could stop himself – 'like a child.'

She opened her swollen eyes and looked up at him in utter hatred. 'You and your bloody poetry.'

'What!'

'It's only all talk with you. You don't live any of it. You're in a rut and you don't even know it.'

'For God's sake what has poetry got to do with it? What are you talking about?'

'All the romance is gone out of you, that's what. If I'm not changed, then you must be. Something is missing anyway.'

'Romance!'

'Call it what you like. You think you have everything worked out, everything finished and in its place. No more adventure or taking a chance or doing something unusual. And then when you're drunk enough you go on about poetry and stuff . . .' She glared. 'You're only a big fake.'

'Alice, listen. You're upset. Can't you try to relax and go to sleep? In the morning things always look different. You can't expect life to be like a fairytale.'

'What do you know about it? You think it's all fixed and done now. The only place you want to live is between the covers of a bloody book. Because it's nice and safe.'

'What the hell am I supposed to do – ride up on a white horse and serenade under your window? A semi-detached knight in shining armour? You were always the same. Life must be magic all the time. Rabbits out of hats and leaps through flaming hoops. You notice, ladies and gentlemen, that while I perform this trick the fingers never leave the hand. Watch carefully while I turn the mortgage and the nappies into a magical –'

She reached over suddenly and gave him a vicious pinch in his unprotected paunch. He gasped. She was always a girl who could pinch. With the nails, and leave a mark.

'Holy God!' He jumped out on to the floor. 'You little bitch!' He dragged the coverlet from the bed and draped it around himself. He was angry, but he felt a mad urge to laugh, which made him angrier still. 'Assaulted in my own bloody bed, after I spend the night at home to leave you out with your women friends. I'm going downstairs. For a drink.' He stumbled over the book on the floor, reached down and tossed it at her from the doorway. 'Romance! Try the Dean. Still standing up and saluting after four hundred years.'

Passing the mirror in the hallway he saw himself, flushed in his toga, questing wine, making a wild face at his own reflection. Mr John O'Brien M. A., H. Dip. Ed., looking like a goat dragged through a bush. The unsuspected dramas that go on inside the mortgaged privacies. As sure as God the cupboard would be bare. Give them romance and they want security. Give them security and they want romance. Search. Empty whiskey bottle and one stale beer since Christmas. Drawer of cabinet. Insurance policies; bulwarks against adventure. Life insurance, fire insurance, car insurance, mortgage insurance. Insurance insurance? All risks and personal liability. Keep at bay the lizard in the grass, arm against the tiger in the dark. The unexpected foreseen, forestalled.

Take life and multiply by age, profession, number of dependents, congenital defects, original sin. Express in terms of possibility divided by probability, allow for earthquakes, floods, wars, racial characteristics, climatic variation, longitude and latitude. Relate to profit-curve of company. Press button. Say sixty pounds a week. Sleep safe. With benefits. Family provided for in the event of. Go gentle and dead safe into that good night, easy in your mind. Large and representative attendance present at the final obsequies. Quiet and unassuming disposition. Exemplary family man and dedicated in his profession. Generations of past pupils attest. Love of books and cultivation of the highest ideals as embodied in the enduring outpourings of the great poets.

No drop to be had but this flat beer. Wait a minute. Yesterday in the garage. Beside the driftwood and the back numbers of *The Times Lit. Supp.* A gallon of the stuff. Dark red in a big dusty jar. Elderberry? From the château of Brother O'Rourke, science master. Swinging chalk-stained soutane and bare ankles. 'Socks, Mr O'Brien. Unhealthy. The enemy of clear thinking. The unimpeded circulation of the blood from the brain to the extremities. *Mens sana* yes? Essential. A few moments of your time in the science room after school. I'd like you to taste some dandelion for acidity.' Two dozen bottles exploding in his room one night. Community sleep disturbed. Wine flowing out under the door and down the monastic stairs. Resignation of housekeeper.

Kitchen door to garage locked. Security. Key God knows where. Lateral thinking into play. Slip out front door and across patch of grass, toga flapping over his night-nakedness. Old Vermin's light still on next door. Worrying about his repayments. Up-and-over lock broken. Thank God for small mercies. Grope in the dark. There it is. Lug out, pull down door behind. Twitch of Vermin's curtain above. Vocal member of Laurel Grove Residents' Association. 'Through the chair, Mr Chairman. Tree-planting would be a visual amenity but there's the problem of leaves in the autumn, and the danger of encouraging vermin in the estate.' Poor bastard. Nightmaring about birds, snails, caterpillars and primeval forest advancing on his tenth of a territorial acre while he sleeps.

Prise bung out with screwdriver and pour gurgling dark-red glass. O'Rourke, eccentric celibate, from your grave you come to my aid. Temperature, acidity, fermentation. 'Any port in a storm of course, but a good body, Mr O'Brien, is everything, while I prefer my bouquet to be modest and unobtrusive.' Dark juice of the elderberry, work of monkish hands, bring me the true, the blushful visions. The king sits in Dunfermline town, drinking the blude-red wine. Fill again and bedamned.

Safe between the covers of a book she said. Do something unusual. Warm glow kindling in the innards. Romance and adventure. First they fix the balls and chains and then they wait for you to perform triple somersaults and other astounding tricks. Woo them constantly with wonders, keep the canker from the rose. See how the fermentings of yesteryear release in the fullness of time and chance their glow, their sun and solace. O'Rourke, mad cleric, you weren't the worst of them. 'The Tuatha de Danaan type, Mr O'Brien. Easily distinguishable in the physiognomy of the midlander. Don't you think? Try another drop, though it won't be at its best for another couple of months. A second opinion is always interesting and the community are all abstainers. Except Sullivan who has no time for anything except big black bottles of stout. A Kerryman of course.'

O'Rourke, sad celibate, I drink to your memory. Rotting now in the clay while I taste the water you reddened. 'Married life must have its consolations, Mr O'Brien, though we choose otherwise. Who can know the greater wisdom? *The tragedy of sexual intercourse is the perpetual virginity of the soul.* Mr Yeats was it? I am unlettered in these matters; a celibate scientist standing aside from the hurly-burly of human relations.'

And she above now, mourning the loss of wonder, of magic and surprise. Crying for golden lads and lasses, still sad music. Link by cosy link the chains are forged; the horizons narrow down to a small town with a hill over it, a river, a bridge, tight streets. Thirty pairs of young eyes in a classroom. What is the poet trying to say in these lines? Can you find a parallel in your own experience? Revise Wordsworth, look up 'Lycidas', brush up on the sonnets and watch out for *Paradise Lost.* Sir, what use is poetry? Chalk, duster, syllabus; another thirty pairs of eyes next September. Brilliant lad; choice of Electricity Supply Board, civil service, teaching profession. Grateful past pupils owe their success. Weep no more ye shepherds.

Toes and knees turning chilly. Go up to her. Bring jug of wine and extra glass. Capitulate. Human comfort. No man is an. Paddy Cleary in the pub. Folk wisdom. 'Listen, you're an educated man and tell me if I'm wrong. In the long run what have we in this life only the few bottles every night and the wife's arse warm beside us in the bed? Listen, there's a lot of people over in the cemetery would like to be like us. Am I right or am I wrong?'

Gather thy shroud about thee, bear gifts to the nuptial chamber. I come with wine for wooing, unsteady but ardent; fain would I gather rosebuds.

Her forehead frowning over John Donne.

'Alice, I'm cold.'

She closed the book and looked. 'Mother of God, would you look at the cut of him! Where did you get that stuff?'

He put down the two glasses on the bedside table and poured. 'O'Rourke, the late brother. Master of science, maker of wine; the cracked cleric who refused to wear socks. Elderberry and two years old. I found it in the garage.'

'I heard the front door. It's a pity I didn't think of locking it after you and leave you out there in your shift.'

He sat down on the bed and drank. 'It's not bad stuff at all. When you get used to it. Try some.'

'Wouldn't it be great! Locked out on the road and nothing on him but a bed spread. I'd wet myself laughing. Imagine the boys in school hearing about it, not to mention Vermin.'

He handed her a glass and she gulped it back, making a face.

'The trouble with old Vermin is he has no sense of irresponsibility. You wouldn't do that to me anyway. Leave me naked and alone, at the mercy of middle-class outrage?'

'That's what amuses me about you. That really kills me. Which class do you think *you* are?'

'I don't dream about double-glazing and holidays in Tenerife anyway. Or worry about the golf handicap or whether to order red or white. Let us be thinking about life and love and death, not about mowing lawns and washing cars. I have immortal longings in me.'

'That's only your excuse to get out of doing things. You're no different from any of the rest of them. Except that you can't hammer a nail or paint a door.'

'Alice, I'm famished with the cold. Would you think of shoving over in the bed before I get my death? When I have thoughts that I might cease to –'

'Give me some more of that stuff. I might as well be drinking, seeing as you are.'

He topped up two glasses. She moved to make room for him as he turned the clothes back. Flash of white thighs by God. Home is where the heat is. The dead O'Rourke's elderberry setteth us on. He was wont to lace, to fortify. 'Rather potent, Mr O'Brien. Needs more time to mellow. The Roman civilisation. A pity we missed it. You remember Horace? The cask of Falernian. Loved his wine. *Falernum*, neuter noun. Ah yes, the Mediterranean, a pity. The white light, the terraced vine; *O fons Bandusiae.* Our own ancestral experience distilled a dark fatalism Mr O'Brien. Caught in a pincer movement between endless troughs of low pressure from the west and Anglo-Saxon injections of puritanism from the east. A people shaped by constant rain and colonial humiliations. We have something of the Mediterranean instinct but without the climate to match. So we drink whiskey for oblivion rather than joy. Are we a lost tribe in the wrong place? Try the dandelion. A little dry? Sullivan refuses to taste, even on feast-days. A Kerryman. Black porter. Extraordinary.'

Love and wine. Illusions to distract us from the dark? Still, the best illusions we've got. Leaning on elbows, the warmth of her soft beside him. And dead O'Rourke – my God, yes – O'Rourke is here, a part of this communion. He reached and put a hand on her stomach. 'Alice, you're lovely.' Yeast of life, his, hers, swelling within.

She jumped at his cold touch and the elderberry splashed over her neck, trickled down towards her breasts.

'You chancer. An hour ago you wouldn't look at me. Stuck in your bloody book. Now you're three sheets in the wind and getting worked up. The eyes are dancing in your head you eejit.'

'Alice, I meant it, honest to God.' He stroked the soft, blue-veined skin of her shoulder, sitting upright and speaking with a sudden passionate clarity. 'This is the terrible, Godawful truth, Alice. We lie all these average nights together, never knowing how many nights there will be for us, except that in the end, in the final wind-up the two of us will be stretched together in a bloody grave. A hole in the ground for Christsake. A black hole in the bloody ground. Jesus think of it. Just think of it!'

'Thinking is poisonous. You're giving me the creeps. We won't know anything anyway. It's while we're here that matters. And you ignore me half the time.'

'Sometimes I'm blind. It's hard to see the important things clearly all the time. Alice –' he reached '– give us a feel . . .'

Her face turned scarlet. She could still blush, after eight years. Blushed, but did not draw away.

'Oh God John it's not fair. You take me for granted. You expect me to be there waiting for you when you want me. It wasn't always like this. You used to give time to me. You used even sing to me. It's a long time since that happened.'

First on the roadside outside a country pub one night in

summer. Still half strangers to each other, but something was
sealed in the singing of that song of Burns which came unbidden
into his head on a summer night. Unspoken then but sealed. In
a song by the roadside.

'I remember, Alice. I remember. Bobby Burns had a hand
in it.' And knew all about it. The silver tassie and the pint of
wine, ploughland and red lips and candlelight, winds and tides
of meetings and partings, the boat rocking at the pier of Leith,
the need to sing.

'Drink, Alice. The last of O'Rourke's wine. I'll sing for you
now.'

'You'll wake the child. And the neighbours. It's all hours.'
But smiling.

'To hell with all the neighbours. I'll sing for you now and let
the dead rise if they're able.' Clearing his throat to let out the
song, he leaned warm and tipsy over her, singing as he did first
in a moment of recognition shared on a country road one summer night.

> O my love is like a red, red rose
> That's newly sprung in June;
> O my love is like a melody
> That's sweetly played in tune.

His voice lifted, affirming love till all the seas gang dry and
rocks melt with the sun. Suddenly her hand reached up to stop
his mouth.

'Whisht! Listen!'

Whimper. Next room. My child, my son.

'Mammy! Mammy!'

She stiffened, alert on an elbow. Girl. Mother.

'Easy, Alice. He'll go to sleep again; he's only dreaming.'

'Mammy! Mammy!'

'All right love. I'm coming.'

Gone to comfort him. Fare thee well my bonnie lass. Head
throbbing. Grey light creeping cold under curtains. Thirty pairs
of eyes. Sir, what use is poetry?

AIMEZ-VOUS COLETTE?

ITA DALY

ITA DALY

Ita Daly was born in Drumshanbo, Co. Leitrim in 1944 and lives in Dublin. She taught English and Spanish in St Louis Convent, where she had received her secondary education. She has written four novels, two children's books, and a collection of short stories, *The Lady With The Red Shoes*.

AS I WALK to school in the morning, or go for my groceries at the weekend, or perhaps pay a visit to the local public library, I often wonder – do I present a figure of fun? I should I suppose: provincial schoolmistress; spinster; wrong side of forty. Certainly I must seem odd to those pathetic rustic minds to whom any woman of my age should be safely wed, or in a nunnery, or decently subdued by her continuing celibacy. I teach in a convent. No ordinary convent, mind you, for the nuns are French, and as you might expect this gives the school a certain cachet among our local bourgeoisie. Most of the girls are boarders – day girls are tolerated with an ill grace – and many of them spring from quite illustrious lines. The leading merchant has two daughters here; the doctor and the dentist three apiece. Even the surgeon in the county hospital has sent his Melissa to us.

The town in which I work and live is one of those awful provincial Irish towns which destroys without exception anyone of any sensitivity who must live there. It is every bit as narrow, snobbish and anti-thought today as it was twenty years ago. It is the sort of town which depraved Northerners – Swedes, Dutch and the like – are captivated by. They always assure us, on departing, that our unique attitude towards life and our marvellous traditions must be preserved, at all costs, against encroaching materialism.

As you may have guessed, I do not like this town: neither, however, does it make me unhappy. Unhappiness, I am beginning to realise, is a condition of the young. I realise it more as I spend a whole day – sometimes as much as a week – without being actively unhappy myself. Even those mediocrities who surround me do not upset me excessively any more. At most I occasionally feel something a little sharper than irritation at their absurd attempts at liberalism. Such as collections and fasts outside church doors for the Biafrans, when every mother within twenty miles would lock up her daughter if a black man came to town. And would be encouraged by their priests to do so.

But on the whole, as I said, I live life with a modicum of enjoyment. I have a small house, and a cat. I grow vegetables and flowers and I buy beautiful and expensive clothes in Dublin and London. I cook well, and I enjoy a glass of wine with my meals. I have no friends, but I do not feel the need of them. When I leave the victim daughters of the bourgeoisie behind, having duly carried out my daily efforts at subversion with the help of Keats and Thomas, I return to my little house and close my door on the outside world. Then I read. As Miss Slattery in the public library says, I am a terrible reader. I prefer the French to the English novel, and with the best, the most sophisticated and subtle minds for company, why should I care about an Ireland that continues to rot in obscurantism and neurosis?

I particularly like the novels of Colette. I have always been drawn to her work. She creates an ambience which I have never found elsewhere, except in poetry. Indeed I often think that if it were not for Colette, I should have left this wretched place years ago. But her books are so peopled with village school-mistresses, leading romantic and smouldering lives in some distant town, I may foolishly have thought that something similar might happen to me, here in *my* distant Irish town. But Irish towns are not French towns. Or perhaps the whole point is that they are: if I were living deep in the Midi, teaching the daughters of the local bourgeoisie at the local Lycée, I would perhaps find myself surrounded by just such nonsense and stupidity as I do here. It is, after all, the romantic vision of Madame Colette which transforms and enhances.

I have often thought of writing myself. I am sure I could, for I consider myself to be intelligent and perceptive enough and my retired life is ideally suited to such an occupation. I have hours of undisturbed solitude, all the bodily comforts that I need, and a job which if dull is not overtaxing – and yet I have never written. Not a line, not even an elegy for Sitwell, my dear cat, when he died last spring aged twelve years.

Of course, really, I know perfectly well why I do not write; why I will never write. I have nothing to write about. Now I appreciate that this may seem a lame excuse to many; a writer, they will say, a real writer, can write about anything. Look at Jane Austen. Jane Austen, I notice, is always cited in this context, why I don't know, as she has always seemed to me an excessively sociable person with a myriad human relationships. While, by comparison, I am a hermit. It is true that I work and live among people but my relationships with them are invariably tangential. I never exchange a word with my headmistress, my girls, my butcher, except in the course of business. And I have lived like this for twenty years. Before that, it is true, there was the odd relationship which may appear to have had slightly more substance: a shadowy involvement with my parents, the occasional girlish exchange during my years at a gloomy and indifferent boarding school. On the whole, however, my life could be said to be arid. But, be assured, I do not use the word pejoratively. I am pleased with this aridity. Just as I like the dryness of my skin. I cannot abide clammy skin – it makes me quite ill to come into contact with. But when my hand brushes my cheek and I feel and hear the dry rasp, I experience something akin to pleasure.

In my entire life there is only one incident about which I could write. No, it was not an incident, it was an interlude – a period of joy. I could write about it with ease, for I recall it often and I remember it still with clarity though its pain is no longer as sharp.

Can you imagine me at twenty? I have always been a plain woman, but whereas nowadays I seldom think of this, even when I look in my mirror, at twenty it was the overriding factor in my life. At school I had never thought about my looks – I don't think any of us did. Cleverness was what counted, and anyway, nobody who spent nine months of the year in the same greasy gymfrock and washed her hair every two months could

have any pretensions to prettiness. And when I left my boarding
school and went, clutching my county council scholarship, to
pursue my studies at university in Dublin, my terror was so
overwhelming that it blotted out every other sensation from
my consciousness. As I stood for the first time in the Great
Hall of the college, I literally trembled from head to foot.

Today my most outstanding character trait is probably my
independence, but in those days I was like a puppy. I became
a slave to anybody who threw me a kind word. Perhaps this is
why I dislike dogs so much. I prefer my cats – elegant independent beasts, who stalk off, indifferent to all shows of affection.
Every time I see a silly pup, wagging his tail furiously, even
when he is being kicked out of the way, I am reminded of myself
at twenty.

I was staying at Dominican Hall, where I lived for my four
years at university. Initially I was even too shy to have tea
with the others in the dining-room and I would buy a bun and
an apple and eat them by myself in my bedroom. Then, after
about a month, I began to venture downstairs and eventually I
became accepted. People came to know my name and they'd
nod to me as I crossed the green. I was even included in the
tea-time conversations. I was a good listener, and quite a subtle
flatterer (though to be fair to myself, I think it was often genuine
admiration on my part). I did not make a close friend, but this
new-found camaraderie was quite enough. Then, as I gained
confidence, and was known even to timidly initiate a conversation myself, I began to realise that I was finding much of my
companions' conversation unintelligible. It was all about boys,
love affairs and dating; unknown territory to me. Just as I had
never thought about my looks, so I had never thought about
boys. But now I did. I even began to notice them as I sat in
the lecture halls, and it was easy to see what interested the
other girls so greatly. Suddenly I was caught up in the excitement of potential romance, just like all the rest. I stopped thinking of myself as an outsider. I felt I was becoming normal.

I began to pay visits to Woolworths, to buy lipsticks and
powder and even a home permanent. I could discuss such pur-
chases with the other girls, even sometimes offer them advice

on bargain hunting. I woke up every morning with a feeling of anticipation, and instead of going straight to the library, increasingly I found myself going for coffee and a gossip.

At this stage, the question of boyfriends was largely academic as few of the girls actually had one, but we all talked about them constantly. I believed I was attractive to boys. I think I trusted in the magic properties of the make-up I used and I felt that each time I clumsily applied my morning mask I was being liberated from myself and my inadequacies. Of course I was still too shy to actually look directly at boys, but whenever I had to pass a group of them I felt sure that they were all looking at me.

Eventually it was decided (by whom I cannot now recall) that I should join some of the other girls at the Friday evening student dance. I was overwhelmed. I felt far more nervous than I had ever felt sitting for an examination. But I was determined to go, so I took myself in hand and was ready, painted and coiffured, at the appointed time on the Friday.

I went to three dances before I would allow myself to admit that something was wrong. The first night, I was genuinely puzzled. As the evening wore on I couldn't understand why nobody was asking me to dance. Maybe because I didn't know the place and looked awkward as I blundered around searching for the Ladies. Maybe because these boys only danced with the regulars, the girls who came here every week, and they would have to get used to my face before they asked me. At the end of the night I had convinced myself that there was no need to worry and indeed I was looking forward to the next Friday when I would avoid so many mistakes and would surely emanate a new confidence.

But the following week it was the same story, and the week afterwards. That night when I came home I locked myself in the bathroom and stood in front of the mirror. A heavy, rather stupid-looking face stared back at me. The skin was muddy, the hair dull and limp. Even to my novice eyes the inexpertly applied make-up appeared garish and pathetic. The dress which I had chosen with such care hung in sad folds over my flat bosom. I felt myself blush – a deep blush of shame. What a spectacle I must have made of myself. What a fool I must have looked, standing there with a hopeful, grateful expression on my lumpy face, waiting to be asked to dance.

I think most people, when they look back on their youth, find, or pretend to find, these intense emotions rather amusing. It seems to me that this is just another aspect of the sentimentalisation of youth which is so commonly indulged in in middle age. I know that the misery I experienced that night was far greater than anything I have experienced, or could experience, since.

I left the bathroom and I took my lipstick, my powder and my cheap perfume, made a bundle of them, and threw them over the railings into the bushes in Stephen's Green. I resumed my earlier habits, and returned to my reading in the library, where I kept my eyes firmly downcast in case by chance I should meet the pitying gaze of some of those boys whom I had so beseeched at those dances. I took my tea earlier to make sure of avoiding contact with my friends. They never appeared to miss me, and I suppose they were relieved to be rid of someone whom they had tolerated only out of kindness. How had I ever imagined that I could fit in amidst their gay and careless chatter – I, who carried around with me a smell of deprivation and humility which singled me out from these confident grocers' daughters?

I became a most serious student, and it was in this period of my life that I developed my taste for vicarious living. I did not have to totally relinquish my world of romance, for now I found it in the pages of Flaubert, and Hardy and Stendhal.

After a time I became less actively unhappy, and once I could close my door on the world at night I knew peace. I was no longer tormented by my ugliness and ineptitude – there was nobody there to sneer at my clumsy attempts at man-catching – and my antidote against loneliness continued to give me solace as I read late into the night. But with the coming of spring and the longer evenings, I began to feel restless. An animal stirring perhaps? I found myself gazing around the library, daydreaming, instead of reading the books lying in front of me. It was in this manner, one day, that I first noticed Humphrey. I was toying with a pencil, idly thinking of nothing, when it rolled away from me across the table. As I retrieved it, again idly, I happened to glance at the man sitting opposite. He had been staring at me, but quickly looked away. It must have been the embarrassment with which he looked away that first aroused my interest, for after that I noticed him practically every day, and he always seemed to find a seat near mine. Sometimes I would catch him gazing at me; at other times he would be totally involved in his work.

At this period there were quite a number of African students at the university, but I think Humphrey was the blackest man I had ever seen. He was quite small, with a rather large head covered in fuzzy down, and long, curiously flat arms. He seemed very ugly to me, but I was flattered by his obvious interest in me and I had all sorts of fiercely-held liberal attitudes which must have affected my reaction towards him. I pitied him too, for I thought that anyone who could find me an object of interest must be desperate indeed.

Soon, when I found him looking at me I would look back, not quite smiling, but in a reasonably friendly manner. I took to saying, 'Excuse me,' vaguely in his direction when I left the table. Then one day we literally bumped into each other outside the library door and both of us involuntarily said hello. After this we always exchanged greetings and then about a month later as we sat working I found a note pushed across the table towards me. It read (and I still remember the wording clearly): 'Dear Miss, would you care to break into your morning studies and refresh yourself with a cup of coffee?'

We were soon meeting regularly. As if by agreement, though neither of us ever mentioned it, we never met outside, and we never went anywhere. But every Saturday afternoon at about four o'clock, I would catch the bus to Rathmines, to Humphrey's bed-sitting-room. He lived in a large run-down house, at the top of a hill, just off the Rathmines Road. The house seemed to be let out entirely to African and Indian students, and I can still recall vividly the strong, individual aroma that filled it. It was made up of exotic cooking smells and perspiration and stale perfume. All the other students seemed to entertain their girlfriends on Saturday afternoons too, and I got to know some of them (though we never spoke) as we travelled on the bus or stood on the doorstep together. Their approach was either furtive or brazen and I was sure that I was the only undergraduate among them. It made me very angry that these girls should feel that they had to act like this, and also, that these boys should have to have such girlfriends; but when I thought of myself and remembered my own ugliness I was often reminded of a favourite saying of one of the students in Dominican Hall as she prepared for the Friday night dance – 'Any port in a storm.'

Perhaps this was true for me initially, but as I got to know Humphrey I began to realise that he was a person of unusual qualities. He was very gentle – he didn't seem to have any aggression in his make-up at all. He laughed often and easily. He was a cultivated person, and whereas I was a crammer – with my peasant equation: learning equals getting on – he was a scholar.

Each Saturday when I arrived he would very formally shake hands and take my coat and make me comfortable. Then we would sit and talk, I with ease for the first time in my life, discovering too that I could be witty and interesting and that Humphrey obviously thought so. We always listened to music, and I was taught to understand something of its magic. We would sit for hours, listening to string quartets and looking out over the darkening roof-tops. During these periods I grew genuinely to like Humphrey. He seemed so lonely and yet so calm sitting there in the shadowy room. I admired his calm, and my natural kindness and crude radicalism made me suffer what I imagined he was suffering.

Later, when it was quite dark and the light was put on and the spell broken, he would make me a chicken stew. It was of a most spicy, succulent oiliness which I have never tasted since and have never been able to capture in my own cooking. Afterwards he would kiss me and fondle me for half an hour, maybe an hour, and then I'd get up, put on my coat and catch my bus home.

Oh, they were marvellous evenings – oases of brightness in

my grey, dull weeks. His kisses healed me, and if they excited him, I never knew. I was too young, too unconscious, for the relationship to have been a sexual one, even in texture. And I am so glad now that I was unschooled in the sex manuals with their crude theories of the potency of the black man. Our relationship was a relationship of love.

I had never in my life been given a present, not even by my parents who were too busy struggling to keep me at school to have been able to pay for presents. Now Humphrey gave them to me. He would suddenly present me with a flower, or a hairband, or a book. He taught me to open myself, he told me I was pretty, and while I was with him I believed it, for I knew by the way he looked at me that *he* believed it. Most of the time in that bed-sitting-room, I was happy. I learned to forget myself and my tortured inadequacies.

I don't know how I thought it would end. I knew at the back of my mind that I would not marry Humphrey, but I never really admitted it to myself – I kept it well out of sight and continued to enjoy the present.

Then one Saturday, about three weeks after he had duly carried off a double first in History and Politics, Humphrey handed me a large white envelope as I came in the door. It was an invitation to any of Mr Ozookwe's friends to the forthcoming conferring ceremonies, and afterwards, to a cup of tea with the President of the College.

'Well,' said Humphrey, 'we'll buy you a new hat. I know exactly the kind you should wear . . .'

This was a shock – I had never thought of it. Not once. I began to feel sick. I thought of all those girls in Dominican Hall, and all the boys who had ignored me at those Friday night dances. I thought of me in my finery, and their comments and their sneers. So this was all I could produce. This was where I ended up. Humphrey was no longer my kind, gentle friend – he was a black man.

'Humphrey, no,' I said, 'you know how I hate social occasions. I won't even go to my own conferring – if I ever get that far.' The little joke could not disguise the panic in my voice. 'I'll tell you what – afterwards, we could . . .' but the expression on his face stopped me. He looked as if he was in physical pain. But his voice was gentle when he spoke.

'Yes, I see,' he said. 'I should have seen all along – it was stupid of me. I am sorry for embarrassing you. I think you'd better go now, please.'

Well, of course, I changed my mind the next day. Humphrey would be going away, it was the least I could do for him, give him this. I would miss him. I would sorrow after him.

I wrote to him but he did not reply. I called at his house, and the second time an Indian answered the door and told me that he had moved, left no address. I never saw him again. He may have been killed in the Biafran War (he was an Ibo), or he may be rich and prosperous, living somewhere in Nigeria, with several wives perhaps. I hope, do you think, that he has forgotten me?

THE WREATH

FRANK O'CONNOR

FRANK O'CONNOR

Frank O'Connor was born in Cork in 1903. He had no great formal schooling and was largely self-taught. He took part in the Irish Civil War on the Republican side and his experiences provided the material for his celebrated first collection of short stories, *Guests Of The Nation*. He wrote four more collections as well as novels, biographies, criticism, autobiography, a book on Shakespeare and translations of Irish poetry. He died in 1966.

WHEN FATHER FOGARTY read of the death of his friend, Father Devine, in a Dublin nursing home, he was stunned. He was a man who did not understand the irremediable. He took out an old seminary group, put it on the mantelpiece and spent the evening looking at it. Devine's clever, pale, shrunken face stood out from the rest, not very different from what it had been in his later years except for the absence of pince-nez. He and Fogarty had been boys together in a provincial town where Devine's father had been a schoolmaster and Fogarty's mother had kept a shop. Even then, everybody had known that Devine was marked out by nature for the priesthood. He was clever, docile and beautifully mannered. Fogarty's vocation had come later and proved a surprise, to himself as well as to others.

They had been friends over the years, affectionate when together, critical and sarcastic when apart. They had not seen one another for close on a year. Devine had been unlucky. As long as the old Bishop, Gallogly, lived, he had been fairly well sheltered, but Lanigan, the new one, disliked him. It was partly Devine's own fault. He could not keep his mouth shut. He was witty and waspish and said whatever came into his head about colleagues who had nothing like his gifts. Fogarty remembered the things Devine had said about himself. Devine had affected to believe that Fogarty was a man of many personalities, and asked with mock humility which he was now dealing with – Nero, Napoleon, or St Francis of Assisi.

It all came back: the occasional jaunts together, the plans for holidays abroad that never took place, and now the warm and genuine love for Devine which was so natural to Fogarty welled up in him, and, realising that never again in this world would he be able to express it, he began to weep. He was as simple as a child in his emotions. When he was in high spirits he devised practical jokes of the utmost crudity; when he was depressed he brooded for days on imaginary injuries: he forgot lightly, remembered suddenly and with exaggerated intensity, and blamed himself cruelly and unjustly for his own shortcomings. He would have been astonished to learn that, for all the intrusions of Nero and Napoleon, his understanding had continued to develop when that of cleverer men had dried up, and that he was a better and wiser man at forty than he had been twenty years before.

But he did not understand the irremediable. He had to have someone to talk to, and for want of a better, rang up Jackson, a curate who had been Devine's other friend. He did not really like Jackson, who was worldly, cynical, and something of a careerist, and he usually called him by the worst name in his vocabulary – a Jesuit. Several times he had asked Devine what he saw in Jackson but Devine's replies had not enlightened him much. 'I wouldn't trust myself too far with the young Loyola if I were you,' Fogarty had told Devine with his worldly swagger. Now, he had no swagger left.

'That's terrible news about Devine, Jim, isn't it?' he said.

'Yes,' Jackson drawled in his usual cautious, cagey way, as though he were afraid to commit himself even about that. 'I suppose it's a happy release for the poor devil.'

That was the sort of tone that maddened Fogarty. It sounded as though Jackson were talking of an old family pet who had been sent to the vet's.

'I hope he appreciates it,' he said gruffly. 'I was thinking of going to town and coming back with the funeral. You wouldn't come, I suppose?'

'I don't very well see how I could, Jerry,' Jackson replied in a tone of mild alarm. 'It's only a week since I was up last.'

'Ah, well, I'll go myself,' said Fogarty. 'You don't know what happened him, do you?'

'Ah, well, he was always anaemic,' Jackson said lightly. 'He should have looked after himself, but he didn't get much chance with old O'Leary.'

'He wasn't intended to,' Fogarty said darkly, indiscreet as usual.

'What?' Jackson asked in surprise. 'Oh no,' he added, resuming his worldly tone. 'It wasn't a sinecure, of course. He was fainting all over the shop. Last time was in the middle of Mass. By then, of course, it was too late. When I saw him last week I knew he was dying.'

'You saw him last week?' Fogarty repeated.

'Oh, just for a few minutes. He couldn't talk much.'

And again, the feeling of his own inadequacy descended on Fogarty. He realised that Jackson, who seemed to have as much feeling as a mowing machine, had kept in touch with Devine, and gone out of his way to see him at the end, while he, the devoted, warm-hearted friend, had let him slip from sight into eternity and was now wallowing in the sense of his own loss.

'I'll never forgive myself, Jim,' he said humbly. 'I never even knew he was sick.'

'I'd like to go to the funeral myself if I could,' said Jackson. 'I'll ring you up later if I can manage it.'

He did manage it, and that evening they set off in Fogarty's car for the city. They stayed in an old hotel in a side-street where porters and waiters all knew them. Jackson brought Fogarty to a very pleasant restaurant for dinner. The very sight of Jackson had been enough to renew Fogarty's doubts. He was a tall, thin man with a prim, watchful, clerical air, and he knew his way around. He spent at least ten minutes over the menu and the wine list, and the head waiter danced attendance on him as head waiters do only when they are either hopeful or intimidated.

'You needn't bother about me,' Fogarty said to cut short the rigmarole. 'I'm having steak.'

'Father Fogarty is having steak, Paddy,' Jackson said suavely, looking at the head waiter over his spectacles with what Fogarty called his 'Jesuit' air. 'Make it rare. And stout, I fancy. It's a favourite beverage of the natives.'

'I'll spare you the stout,' Fogarty said, enjoying the banter. 'Red wine will do me fine.'

'Mind, Paddy,' Jackson said in the same tone, 'Father Fogarty said *red* wine. You're in Ireland now, remember.'

Next morning they went to the parish church where the coffin was resting on trestles before the altar. Beside it, to Fogarty's surprise, was a large wreath of roses. When they got up from their knees, Devine's uncle, Ned, had arrived with his son. Ned was a broad-faced, dark-haired, nervous man, with the anaemic complexion of the family.

'I'm sorry for your trouble, Ned,' said Fogarty.

'I know that, Father,' said Ned.

'I don't know if you know Father Jackson. He was a great friend of Father Willie's.'

'I heard him speak of him,' said Ned. 'He talked a lot about the pair of ye. Ye were his great friends. Poor Father Willie!' he added with a sigh. 'He had few enough.'

Just then the parish priest came in and spoke to Ned Devine. His name was Martin. He was a tall man with a stern, unlined, wooden face and candid blue eyes like a baby's. He stood for a few minutes by the coffin, then studied the breastplate and wreath, looking closely at the tag. It was only then that he beckoned the two younger priests towards the door.

'Tell me, what are we going to do about that thing?' he asked with a professional air.

'What thing?' Fogarty asked in surprise.

'That wreath,' Martin replied with a nod over his shoulder.

'What's wrong with it?'

''Tis against the rubrics,' replied the parish priest in the complacent tone of a policeman who has looked up the law on the subject.

'For heaven's sake, what have the rubrics to do with it?' Fogarty asked impatiently.

'The rubrics have a whole lot to do with it,' Martin replied with a stern glance. 'And, apart from that, 'tis a bad custom.'

'You mean Masses bring in more money?' Fogarty asked with amused insolence.

'I do not mean Masses bring in more money,' replied Martin who tended to answer every remark verbatim, like a solicitor's letter. It added to the impression of woodenness he gave. 'I mean that flowers are a pagan survival.' He looked at the two young priests with the same anxious, innocent, wooden air. 'And here am I, week in, week out, preaching against flowers, and a blooming big wreath of them in my own church. And on a priest's coffin, what's more! What am I to say about that?'

'Who asked you to say anything?' Fogarty asked angrily. 'The man wasn't from your diocese.'

'Now, that's all very well,' said Martin. 'That's bad enough by itself, but it isn't the whole story.'

'You mean because it's from a woman?' Jackson broke in lightly in a tone that would have punctured any pose less substantial than Martin's.

'I mean, because it's from a woman, exactly.'

'A woman!' said Fogarty in astonishment. 'Does it say so?'

'It does not say so.'

'Then how do you know?'

'Because it's red roses.'

'And does that mean it's from a woman?'

'What else could it mean?'

'I suppose it could mean it's from somebody who didn't study the language of flowers the way you seem to have done,' Fogarty snapped.

He could feel Jackson's disapproval of him weighing on the air, but when Jackson spoke it was at the parish priest that his coldness and nonchalance were directed.

'Oh, well,' he said with a shrug. 'I'm afraid we know nothing about it, Father. You'll have to make up your own mind.'

'I don't like doing anything when I wasn't acquainted with the man,' Martin grumbled, but he made no further attempt to interfere, and one of the undertaker's men took the wreath and put it on the hearse. Fogarty controlled himself with difficulty. As he banged open the door of his car and started the engine his face was flushed. He drove with his head bowed and his brows jutting down like rocks over his eyes. It was what Devine had called his Nero look. As they cleared the main streets he burst out.

'That's the sort of thing that makes me ashamed of myself, Jim. Flowers are a pagan survival! And they take it from him, what's worse. They take it from him. They listen to that sort of stuff instead of telling him to shut his big ignorant gob.'

'Oh, well,' Jackson said tolerantly, taking out his pipe, 'we're hardly being fair to him. After all, he didn't know Devine.'

'But that only makes it worse,' Fogarty said hotly. 'Only for our being there he'd have thrown out that wreath. And for what? His own dirty, mean, suspicious mind!'

'Ah, I wouldn't go as far as that,' Jackson said, frowning. 'I think in his position I'd have asked somebody to take it away.'

'You would?'

'Wouldn't you?'

'But why, in God's name?'

'Oh, I suppose I'd be afraid of the scandal – I'm not a very courageous type.'

'Scandal?'

'Whatever you like to call it. After all, some woman sent it.'

'Yes. One of Devine's old maids.'

'Have you ever heard of an old maid sending a wreath of red roses to a funeral?' Jackson asked, raising his brows, his head cocked.

'To tell you the God's truth, I might have done it myself,' Fogarty confessed with boyish candour. 'It would never have struck me that there was anything wrong with it.'

'It would have struck the old maid all right, though.'

Fogarty turned his eyes for a moment to stare at Jackson. Jackson was staring back. Then he missed a turning and reversed with a muttered curse. To the left of them the Wicklow mountains stretched away southwards, and between the grey walls the fields were a ragged brilliant green under the tattered sky.

'You're not serious, Jim?' he said after a few minutes.

'Oh, I'm not suggesting that there was anything wrong,' Jackson said, gesturing widely with his pipe. 'Women get ideas. We all know that.'

'These things can happen in very innocent ways,' Fogarty said with ingenuous solemnity. Then he scowled again and a blush spread over his handsome craggy face. Like all those who live mainly in their imaginations, he was always astonished and shocked at the suggestions that reached him from the outside world: he could live with his fantasies only by assuming that they were nothing more. Jackson, whose own imagination was curbed and even timid, who never went at things like a thoroughbred at a gate, watched him with amusement and a certain envy. Just occasionally he felt that he himself would have liked to welcome a new idea with that boyish wonder and panic.

'I can't believe it,' Fogarty said angrily, tossing his head.

'You don't have to,' Jackson replied, nursing his pipe and swinging round in the seat with his arm close to Fogarty's shoulder. 'As I say, women get these queer ideas. There's usually nothing in them. At the same time, I must say *I* wouldn't be very scandalised if I found out that there was something in it. If ever a man needed someone to care for him, Devine did in the last year or two.'

'But not Devine, Jim,' Fogarty said, raising his voice. 'Not Devine! You could believe a thing like that about me. I suppose I could believe it about you. But I knew Devine since we were kids, and he wouldn't be capable of it.'

'I never knew him in that way,' Jackson admitted. 'In fact, I scarcely knew him at all, really. But I'd have said he was as capable of it as the rest of us. He was lonelier than the rest of us.'

'God, don't I know it?' Fogarty said in sudden self-reproach. 'I could understand if it was drink.'

'Oh, not drink!' Jackson said with distaste. 'He was too fastidious. Can you imagine him in the d.t.'s like some old parish priest, trying to strangle the nurses?'

'But that's what I say, Jim. He wasn't the type.'

'Oh, you must make distinctions,' said Jackson. 'I could imagine him attracted by some intelligent woman. You know yourself how he'd appeal to her, the same way he appealed to us, a cultured man in a country town. I don't have to tell you the sort of life an intelligent woman leads, married to some lout of a shopkeeper or a gentleman farmer. Poor devils, it's a mercy that most of them aren't educated.'

'He didn't give you any hint who she was?' Fogarty asked

incredulously. Jackson had spoken with such conviction that it impressed him as true.

'Oh, I don't even know if there was such a woman,' Jackson said hastily, and then he blushed too. Fogarty remained silent. He knew now that Jackson had been talking about himself, not Devine.

As the country grew wilder and furze bushes and ruined keeps took the place of pastures and old abbeys, Fogarty found his eyes attracted more and more to the wreath that swayed lightly with the hearse, the only spot of pure colour in the whole landscape with its watery greens and blues and greys. It seemed an image of the essential mystery of a priest's life. What, after all, did he really know of Devine? Only what his own temperament suggested, and mostly – when he wasn't being St Francis of Assisi – he had seen himself as the worldly one of the pair, the practical, coarse-grained man who cut corners, and Devine as the saint, racked by the fastidiousness and asceticism that exploded in his bitter little jests. Now his mind boggled at the idea of the agony that alone could have driven Devine into an entanglement with a woman; yet the measure of his incredulity was that of the conviction he would presently begin to feel. When once an unusual idea broke through his imagination, he hugged it, brooded on it, promoted it to the dignity of a revelation.

'God, don't we lead terrible lives?' he burst out at last. 'Here we are, probably the two people in the world who knew Devine best, and even we have no notion what that thing in front of us means.'

'Which might be as well for our peace of mind,' said Jackson.

'I'll engage it did damn little for Devine's,' Fogarty said grimly. It was peculiar; he did not believe yet in the reality of the woman behind the wreath, but already he hated her.

'Oh, I don't know,' Jackson said in some surprise. 'Isn't that what we all really want from life?'

'Is it?' Fogarty asked in wonder. He had always thought of Jackson as a cold fish, and suddenly found himself wondering about that as well. After all, there must have been something in him that attracted Devine. He had the feeling that Jackson, who was, as he recognised, by far the subtler man, was probing him, and for the same reason. Each was looking in the other for the quality that had attracted Devine, and which, having made him their friend might make them friends also. Each was trying to see how far he could go with the other. Fogarty, as usual, was the first with a confession.

'I couldn't do it, Jim,' he said earnestly. 'I was never even tempted, except once, and then it was the wife of one of the men who was in the seminary with me. I was crazy about her. But when I saw what her marriage to the other fellow was like, I changed my mind. She hated him like poison, Jim. I soon saw she might have hated me in the same way. It's only when you see what marriage is really like, as we do, that you realise how lucky we are.'

'Lucky?' Jackson repeated mockingly.

'Aren't we?'

'Did you ever know a seminary that wasn't full of men who thought they were lucky? They might be drinking themselves to death, but they never doubted their luck? Nonsense, man! Anyway, why do you think she'd have hated you?'

'I don't,' Fogarty replied with a boyish laugh. 'Naturally, I think I'd have been the perfect husband for her. That's the way Nature kids you.'

'Well, why shouldn't you have made her a perfect husband?' Jackson asked quizzically. 'There's nothing much wrong with you that I can see. Though I admit I can see you better as a devoted father.'

'God knows you might be right,' Fogarty said, his face clouding again. It was as changeable as an Irish sky, Jackson thought with amusement. 'You could get on well enough without the woman, but the kids are hell. She had two. "Father Fogey" they used to call me. And my mother was as bad,' he burst out. 'She was wrapped up in the pair of us. She always wanted us to be better than everybody else, and when we weren't she used to cry. She said it was the Fogarty blood breaking out in us – the Fogartys were all horse dealers.' His handsome, happy face was black with all the remorse and guilt. 'I'm afraid she died under the impression that I was a Fogarty after all.'

'If the Fogartys are any relation to the Martins, I'd say it was most unlikely,' Jackson said, half amused, half touched.

'I never knew till she was dead how much she meant to me,' Fogarty said broodingly. 'Hennessey warned me not to take the Burial Service myself, but I thought it was the last thing I could do for her. He knew what he was talking about of course. I disgraced myself, bawling like a blooming kid, and he pushed me aside and finished it for me. My God, the way we gallop through that till it comes to our own turn! Every time I've read it since, I've read it as if it were for my mother.'

Jackson shook his head uncomprehendingly.

'You feel these things more than I do,' he said. 'I'm a cold fish.'

It struck Fogarty with some force that this was precisely what he had always believed himself and that now he could believe it no longer.

'Until then, I used to be a bit flighty,' he confessed. 'After that I knew it wasn't in me to care for another woman.'

'That's only more of your nonsense,' said Jackson impatiently. 'Love is just one thing, not half a dozen. If I were a young fellow looking for a wife I'd go after some girl who felt like that about her father. You probably have too much of it. I haven't enough. When I was in Manister there was a shopkeeper's wife I used to see. I talked to her and lent her books. She was half crazy with loneliness. Then one morning I got home and found her standing outside my door in the pouring rain. She'd been there half the night. She wanted me to take her away, to "save" her, as she said. You can imagine what happened to her after.'

'Went off with someone else, I suppose?'

'No such luck. She took to drinking and sleeping with racing men. Sometimes I blame myself for it. I feel I should have kidded her along. But I haven't enough love to go round. You have too much. With your enthusiastic nature you'd probably have run off with her.'

'I often wondered what I would do,' Fogarty said shyly.

He felt very close to tears. It was partly the wreath, brilliant in the sunlight, that had drawn him out of his habitual reserve and make him talk in that way with a man of even greater reserve. Partly it was the emotion of returning to the little town where he had grown up. He hated and avoided it; it seemed to him to represent all the narrowness and meanness that he tried to banish from his thoughts, but at the same time it contained all the nostalgia and violence he had felt there; and when he drew near it again a tumult of emotions rose in him that half-strangled him. He was watching for it already like a lover.

'There it is!' he said triumphantly, pointing to a valley where a tapering Franciscan tower rose on the edge of a clutter of low Georgian houses and thatched cabins. 'They'll be waiting for us at the bridge. That's how they'll be waiting for me when my turn comes, Jim.'

A considerable crowd had gathered at the farther side of the bridge to escort the hearse to the cemetery. Four men shouldered the shiny coffin over the bridge past the ruined castle and up the hilly Main Street. Shutters were up on the shop fronts, blinds were drawn, everything was at a standstill except where a curtain was lifted and an old woman peered out.

'Counting the mourners,' Fogarty said with a bitter laugh. 'They'll say I had nothing like as many as Devine. That place,' he added, lowering his voice, 'the second shop from the corner, that was ours.'

Jackson took it in at a glance. He was puzzled and touched by Fogarty's emotion because there was nothing to distinguish the little market town from a hundred others. A laneway led off the hilly road and they came to the abbey, a ruined tower and a few walls, with tombstones sown thickly in quire and nave. The hearse was already drawn up outside and people had gathered in a semicircle about it. Ned Devine came hastily up to the car where the two priests were donning their vestments. Fogarty knew at once that there was trouble brewing.

'Whisper, Father Jerry,' Ned muttered in a strained excited voice. 'People are talking about that wreath. I wonder would you know who sent it?'

'I don't know the first thing about it, Ned,' Fogarty replied, and suddenly his heart began to beat violently.

'Come here a minute, Sheela,' Ned called, and a tall, pale

girl with the stain of tears on her long bony face left the little
group of mourners and joined them. Fogarty nodded to her.
She was Devine's sister, a schoolteacher who had never married. 'This is Father Jackson, Father Willie's other friend. They
don't know anything about it either.'

'Then I'd let them take it back,' she said doggedly.

'What would you say, Father?' Ned asked, appealing to
Fogarty, and suddenly Fogarty felt his courage desert him. In
disputing with Martin he had felt himself an equal on neutral
ground, but now the passion and prejudice of the little town
seemed to rise up and oppose him, and he felt himself again a
boy, rebellious and terrified. You had to know the place to realise
the hysteria that could be provoked by something like a funeral.

'I can only tell you what I told Father Martin already,' he
said, growing red and angry.

'Did he talk about it too?' Ned asked sharply.

'There!' Sheela said vindictively. 'What did I tell you?'

'Well, the pair of you are cleverer than I am,' Fogarty said.
'I saw nothing wrong with it.'

'It was no proper thing to send to a priest's funeral,' she
hissed with prim fury. 'And whoever sent it was no friend of
my brother.'

'You saw nothing wrong with it, Father?' Ned prompted
appealingly.

'But I tell you, Uncle Ned, if that wreath goes into the graveyard we'll be the laughing stock of the town,' she said in an
old-maidish frenzy. 'I'll throw it out myself if you won't.'

'Whisht, girl, whisht, and let Father Jerry talk!' Ned said
furiously.

'It's entirely a matter for yourselves, Ned,' Fogarty said
excitedly. He was really scared now. He knew he was in danger
of behaving imprudently in public, and sooner or later, the story
would get back to the Bishop, and it would be suggested that
he knew more than he pretended.

'If you'll excuse me interrupting, Father,' Jackson said
suavely, giving Fogarty a warning glance over his spectacles.
'I know this is none of my business.'

'Not at all, Father, not at all,' Ned said passionately. 'You were the boy's friend. All we want is for you to tell us what to do.'

'Oh, well, Mr Devine, that would be too great a responsibility for me to take,' Jackson replied with a cagey smile, though Fogarty saw that his face was very flushed. 'Only someone who really knows the town could advise you about that. I only know what things are like in my own place. Of course, I entirely agree with Miss Devine,' he said, giving her a smile that suggested that this, like crucifixion, was something he preferred to avoid. 'Naturally, Father Fogarty and I have discussed it already. I think personally that it was entirely improper to send a wreath.' Then his mild, clerical voice suddenly grew menacing and he shrugged his shoulders with an air of contempt. 'But, speaking as an outsider, I'd say if you were to send that wreath back from the graveyard, you'd make yourself something far worse than a laughing stock. You'd throw mud on a dead man's name that would never be forgotten for you the longest day you lived . . . Of course, that's only an outsider's opinion,' he added urbanely, drawing in his breath in a positive hiss.

'Of course, of course, of course,' Ned Devine said, clicking his fingers and snapping into action. 'We should have thought of it ourselves, Father. 'Twould be giving tongues to the stones.'

Then he lifted the wreath himself and carried it to the graveside. Several of the men by the gate looked at him with a questioning eye and fell in behind him. Some hysteria had gone out of the air Fogarty gently squeezed Jackson's hand.

'Good man, Jim!' he said in a whisper. 'Good man you are!'

He stood with Jackson at the head of the open grave beside the local priests. As their voices rose in the psalms for the dead and their vestments billowed about them, Fogarty's brooding eyes swept the crowd of faces he had known since his childhood and which were now caricatured by age and pain. Each time they came to rest on the wreath which stood at one side of the open grave. It would lie there now above Devine when all the living had gone, his secret. And each time it came over him in a wave of emotion that what he and Jackson had protected was something more than a sentimental token. It was the thing that had linked them to Devine, and for the future would link them to one another – love. Not half a dozen things, but one thing, between son and mother, man and sweetheart, friend and friend.

BROTHERLY LOVE

GILLMAN NOONAN

GILLMAN NOONAN

Gillman Noonan was born in Kanturk, Co. Cork in 1937. He worked at various jobs in Germany and Switzerland as well as taking part in archaeological digs. All his early stories appeared in 'New Irish Writing' and in 1975 he won the Writers' Week Short Story Award. He has published two collections.

WHEN DAVE PHONED from Clonakilty, where he was travelling for his firm, to say he had met a 'marvellous girl' and was contemplating marriage, I was sceptical, to say the least. In my experience of the brother's courtships there had been so many marvellous girls who for various reasons had turned out to be disappointments. *Two* had even decided to become nuns after walking out with him for a while. That had been a particularly trying time – though a practising Catholic himself, Dave had become neurotically convinced he was the kind of man who drove women to vows of chastity. One man reassuring another of his virility without recourse to practical demonstration proved a formidable task, so this time I was reluctant to become involved – particularly in the kind of brotherly 'vetting' he had inveigled me into on previous occasions. He seemed to think that I – a widower of fifty and fifteen years his senior – was an all-time sage in the matter of assessing the wifely qualities of young women. It was above all, I think, the happiness of my marriage that had impressed him. Having selected the best of all women for myself, there was no reason why I shouldn't help him do the same. It was useless my arguing that 'vetting' did not help much, that happiness with a woman in this life is usually in the fall of the dice.

'You must come down and meet her,' he pleaded on the phone.

'I'm working,' I said.

'You can work down here. I'll get you a nice quiet room where you can write all day if you wish. I just want you to have a look at her.'

The crudity of the expression made me shudder. Did he think

I was something of a male chauvinist jobber who in the best
tradition of the Irish street fair could cast an eye on a woman's
haunch and say: 'There's breeding in that one all right, brother,
take her'?

'Please,' he went on, 'just this last time.'

I relented. Having completed the first draft of some children's
stories, I felt in need of a break. The clean surf of Inchadonny
strand beckoned – but it would be the last time, I resolved.
The next morning I locked my cottage, drove into Dublin to
visit my son and daughter who are both married with young
children, and then headed south . . . The weather brightened
on the way, and when I stopped in front of the hotel in Clonakilty
the late afternoon sun had a steady continental heat that augured
well. The brother must have been on the look-out in the bar
for he appeared at once.

'Hi, Tom,' he called in a very American kind of way. 'Have
a nice trip?'

He looked fatter and balder than when I had last seen him,
perhaps because he had shaved off his moustache. His rather
big lips seemed to portrude farther than ever, giving him the
expression of an eager duck.

'What's all this about marriage?' I said, leaning against the
car and going straight into battle.

'No lark,' he said seriously. 'This is for real. You'll like her.
Come on, she's in the lounge, her name is Twinkle.'

Twinkle turned out to be diminutive and young – scarcely
out of her teens, I imagined – with long blonde hair and large
eyes, one of which was slightly out of focus giving her a con-
cussed look as if she had just fallen off a horse. I liked the look
of her.

'Hi,' she smiled, thus explaining all the hi-ing.

'Twinkle's mother was Irish, a Slattery from near Clon.' The
fool was warming to her pedigree even before I was seated.

'A drink,' I ordered. 'A large Irish with a drop of water.'

Dave went up to the bar and I could see him watching us in
the mirror. It was a familiar situation and I swore I was not
going to make any hasty pronouncements. Even if I grew to
dislike the girl, I was going to be guarded in my comments. I

was not, after all, his marriage broker. Like or dislike hardly entered my head as I listened to Twinkle recount details of her travels from Idaho where she had lived with an uncle until he died. She seemed no different from any of the young Americans I had met who, while in Ireland, wanted to trace some Irish forebear, fitting together the jigsaw of identity that in conversation seemed of such casual interest to them but was always, one sensed, much more than that.

'How long have you known each other?' I asked her.

'About three weeks,' she said. 'I was in difficulties.'

'Oh?'

'In the sea. Dave saved my life.'

'Heavens.'

She expelled smoke. 'Yes, crazy, isn't it?'

Here we had all the ingredients of a romance à la Dave. 'There must be a happening of some kind in love, don't you agree?' he had once remarked to me. How could I tell him that in marriage the happenings were usually of a different kind? In an old-boyish way he was still madly in love with love. The older he got and the closer he seemed to epitomise the cliché figure of the sales rep, the more obsessed he became with the idea of a lasting and truly romantic relationship. It was a need with which I truly sympathised. The four years I had been a widower had weighed on me. I knew loneliness and loss, but from the brother's point of view I had at least found happiness before losing it again. To his mind it was infinitely worse never to have found it. I, moreover, would be taken seriously by a woman if I asked her to marry me. *He* had to get around the 'randy rep' image first, and even then the girl often refused to believe he didn't have a wife tucked away somewhere and was only chatting her up. Dave, I realised now listening to him paint the future, had sold Twinkle a fairy tale and she was believing it.

'I've had my eye on a little cottage near the strand for a long time,' he said. 'It will be ideal for us. I'll get McGregor to base me here permanently so I'll never be far afield and Twinkle won't become a grass widow like the wives of most travellers.' He squeezed her hand reassuringly and she smiled at him.

'Won't you be lonely down there?' I ventured to her. 'It's miles from the town.'

'Oh, no,' she smiled. 'I love isolation.'

'Twinkle paints,' the brother interjected with a gleam in his eye as if to say: That's a quare one for you, Mr Writer. Dave knew as much about painting as I knew about Idaho.

'Only water-colours,' said Twinkle.

'You must show me some of your work,' I smiled lamely.

'Oh, she will, she will,' said Dave. 'I'll be away for most of the day so you'll have plenty of time to get to know each other.'

We did have a lot of time together in the days to follow. After breakfast Dave went off on his rounds and Twinkle and I drove down to the beach in my battered old VW. In the evenings we had dinner together, after which we either all went for a walk or to the pictures, rounding off the day with a few drinks. At first Twinkle and I were very formal with each other. I set up my small folding table in a quiet spot and concentrated on polishing my stories, she went off with her books and brushes to her own favourite nook. We had a hamper lunch and she prepared it, making very straight comments on the kind of things she liked and asking me about my preferences.

'Do you like pizza?' she would ask.

'I love pizza.'

'A pity you can't get it here, isn't it?'

'It sure is.'

Lapsing so easily into her style of conversation, I was tempted to follow up with paternal riders to the effect that as the years went by she would find there was so much else it was a pity she could not get in this lonely corner of the south, but I checked myself. Why shouldn't they have their idyll for as long as it lasted? To waggle the didactic finger at other people's happiness was anyway the height of casuistic arrogance.

Later, Twinkle showed me her paintings – animal-like abstractions of the landscape that to my untutored eye were not at all bad – and from then on conversation became more natural between us. In a halting, preoccupied way she spoke of her family and I pieced together a childhood that must have been very unhappy, with a father in and out of a mental home and a mother who carried on with men in his absence. Eventually the mother took to drink and died of it while Twinkle was still in her mid-teens. The father being then permanently detained in the home, she was packed off to a bachelor uncle who didn't seem to care what she did once she kept out of his way.

It was a sad but typical enough story that, for me, was all the more unreal since I had no true conception of the place out of which it had been so carelessly etched. But whatever tangle of love and inherited guilt had sent her across the Atlantic, it was clear that Twinkle was now a girl with a mission, and this was the dimension that concerned me most – alarmed me indeed when in a wedding photo of her parents I noticed a marked resemblance between her father and Dave. God above! Did she really believe that Fate was offering her a rose-rimmed canvas on which all the smears of the past could be transformed, expiated even? I found this hard to believe considering her extremely dry and cryptic remarks on many things. Yet each evening when Dave sketched in a little more of the pretty scene she seemed to accept it as if he was merely corroborating what she already knew.

She was a marvellous audience for Dave's long monologues on politics and religion sublimated in his mystique of love. She hadn't a clue, of course, at least not within the heady Irish context of this brew. Once she interrupted to ask him who de Valera was. He nearly quacked into his beer. It couldn't have been worse if she had asked him who was Jesus Christ. There followed a long lecture on Dev from which I politely withdrew. When I joined them a little later he was still pouring it out and she was still lapping it up, under no apparent strain. She seemed to think that all Irishmen were thus passionately committed to the history of their country and that the sooner she started generating the same fervour the better.

She found the formula of Irish religion as embodied by Dave more puzzling since it impinged on sex and romance, two concepts the brother held strictly at arm's length when he was confident that a future bride was at the receiving end of his attentions. I was sure Dave entertained hopes of converting her but I didn't intend to be around when that campaign was launched. Indeed the situation was sufficiently trying: the nice quiet room Dave got me was separated from his own by what must have been a paper-thin wall because I went through agonies trying to drown the noises he felt obliged to make in the name of high passion suspended under the Almighty's watchful eye. The very thought of his old-young duck face necking like a sixteen-year-old in the next room was driving me batty.

Part of the trouble was that they waited for *me* to go to bed before slipping into the room – why they couldn't have done their courting in her room I failed to understand. It was really just smooching but Dave worked up enough steam to put any rutting buffalo in the shade. I could hear him heightening the tension with an ooh and a mmmmm and an umpf only to cease at some theologically crucial point with a 'No, no . . .' or a 'We mustn't . . .' gasp '. . . not yet.' Grace must flow with courtship of a bride-to-be, and for Dave marrying in the blessed state of grace and romance was paramount to the restoration of the Irish language and the re-unification of the country under a government of true Republicans of his choice.

I suppose, depending on one's view of divine surveillance, this is quite in order, but to a girl of Twinkle's background it was bound to be puzzling. She was seeking terms of reference and approached the problem over lunch on the beach in a less than subtle way.

'Did you sleep with your wife before you married?' she asked between mouthfuls of lettuce-and-egg sandwich.

'No. I'd say few people had sex before marriage at that time.'

'Would you now?'

'Perhaps . . . perhaps not.'

The pickings were meagre there. Sucking her teeth, she probed more boldly. 'What do you do for sex?'

'Do I look as if I have to go to extraordinary lengths to get it?'

'Don't you worry about religion?' she persisted. 'It's very important in Ireland, isn't it?'

I almost laughed at the understatement. 'For some people rather too important.'

'But you do have religious . . . compunctions about sex?'

'I think at my time of life I have less a sense of sin than a sense of ugliness. That's a moral feeling too, I suppose.' I could have gone on like this for hours feeling very urbane and superior. She fell silent so I prodded a little. 'It's a question of degree. Dave, I know, is more concerned with principle than I.'

'Is there anything wrong with that?' she flew at me. 'Dave is good.'

'Unlike me?'

She pouted, plucking at the sand. My tone had already put a slight crack in the idyll. 'Dave,' she said aggressively, 'is the first man that ever took me at face value.' (He was probably afraid to ask, I thought unkindly). 'The first man to offer me something . . . beautiful.'

'Indeed.' I felt she was acting now and disliked her for it.

'Yes, he has principles, not like most men. I respect that.' She looked up at me defiantly. 'Other men I felt I had to tell them everything about me, not Dave. It's what I am now that matters to him. He's *genuinely* good.'

What she felt she had to tell 'other men', to whose number I now apparently belonged, came out a little later in a faintly accusing tone, as if I were partly to blame. She had been raped when she was sixteen and had had two abortions, one the following year and one when she was nineteen. I let it all come without saying a word. What was there to say? If such things were happening every day to girls from 'good' homes, why should they arouse surprise in Twinkle's unhappy, perhaps tragic, past life? She could have told Dave and it would only have sharpened the edge of his zeal to save a lost soul. Indeed, *I* also firmly believed that Dave was a good man. I felt sure he would do all in his power to realise the dream. What worried me was what would happen to Twinkle when the romance of the cottage and the isolation wore off. It was probably all selfishness on my part – I didn't want an unhappy brother on my hands.

Twinkle's 'other men' view of me expressed itself that evening in an even more ardent attention to Dave's philosophising. Eyeing me with occasional malice, she exclaimed and enthused with him, altogether creating a bizarre, upended picture of courtship: he the balding adolescent full of schmaltz and wet kisses, she the actress, the creature of experience and detachment turning over the passion offered her like a toy she had once played with for real. But I saw she was on edge, and that night and later her tension expressed itself in a growing reluctance for Dave's particular brand of non-sex. I was able to read undisturbed by the sighs of battle between the spirit and the flesh.

As the hours passed on the beach, however, Twinkle's hostility showed all the signs of a counter-flirtation, and I began to feel guilty at the thought that this might be what I had wanted to happen all along. From my role as clearing house for her unromantic, 'normal' self – the self she would probably have shown Dave had they met in a crowded Dublin pub surrounded by her youthful friends – I found myself being provocatively lured as a potential lover. In some gutsy physical way I felt she wanted to humiliate me for being so aloof, perhaps debasing herself as well for playing at Romance she would have spurned in other circumstances. The complications entailed in stealing the brother's girl, however unintentionally, were simply too appalling to be considered. I decided to leave, having accomplished (or almost) what I had probably intended from the start: to break the sugary holiday-affair spell and introduce them to each other as real people. They could take it from there.

Like all weak people I wavered. Alarm at a woman's approaches is all confused with vanity to which men, I'm convinced, are even more prone than women. If the brother was balding and looked like a duck, I still had at least a fine thatch of steel-grey hair and looked no worse than a scholarly owl. Moreover, my mild flirtations since my wife's death had given me the confidence of the clinical lover – a new thing for me even at fifty. I felt I could pluck the bud and discard it with ill-effects no worse than the nostalgia of the middle-aged savant

for a brighter passion. I fear I was beginning to delude myself
as a kind of sophisticated degenerate.

Still, all flirtation remains safe and indulgent theory until a
young girl with long blonde hair – and looking like the girls in
the advertisements – runs up to you in your warm hollow in the
dunes, stretches out beside you panting, squirms and mutters
something about the constriction of clothes and that even on
barges on the Seine now sunbathing *au naturelle* was the thing
– and there and then whips off the monstrously confining chain
of her tiny bra. Whatever reaction she expected of me – repri-
mand at which she would have scoffed or attraction which she
would have rebuffed – at the time I merely remarked on the
Irish weather being a fairly reliable deterrent to such exposure.
But I was genuinely disturbed. Nudity is not taken to kindly in
Ireland. On the beach people were passing by – sometimes
appearing out of nowhere and climbing over us – and I was
afraid that at any moment the local vice squad in the person of a
blushing young Garda would appear and cover Twinkle's minute
breasts and startlingly large nipples with his blue tunic.

Still, for all the baiting it was also a peculiarly childish act. A
little later she was up and off again into the sea, complete with
bra. She would have laughed at the idea, but I suspected I had
become – at least for now – to some extent a father figure who
would see to it that she did the right thing. What bothered me
was the extent to which the father figure would do the right
thing himself.

Several times I renewed my resolve to leave that evening
but Twinkle – then and on the days to follow – made it increasingly difficult. She still acted as though the cottage by the sea
and all that went with it were still within her grasp, but I sensed
her unrest as each afternoon progressed and the hour came for
her to return to the hotel and talk about it. On the point of
departure she would want another dip, and then of course to
dry out we would walk miles along the beach. Often she made
me detour to a lovely old thatched pub at a crossroads where
we drank pints of stout. She teased me, calling me her sugar
daddy. Once with the locals looking sombrely at us from under
their peaked caps she kissed me full on the mouth and made

an erotic thing of wiping the line of froth from my upper lip with her little finger which she then licked teasingly with the tip of her tongue. She was having a great time dangling me on a string, and although I resented it I kept coming back for more.

Dave naturally noticed the change and worried, becoming more and more silent with her. When Twinkle was in the loo one evening about ten days after my arrival, I suggested that perhaps I was a gooseberry and should leave.

'No, no!' he exclaimed. 'She likes you. She told me so. It's something else.'

'Ah, dammit, maybe she wants to be alone with you again.' My sense of guilt was really working.

'No, it's something else.'

He looked up and saw Twinkle talking to a group of men at the bar, one hand resting casually on the arm of a well-dressed young man with thick black curls.

'I've seen her talking to that fellow several times,' Dave said ominously.

'Yes, he seems quite a nice bloke.'

'I know what's nice about him.' His eyes never left them. 'He's a commercial gentleman too, one of these sharp dandified blades from Dublin.'

'I think he's moving on tomorrow.'

I felt it was the last conversational lifeline I could throw before something happened, and I was right. Dave heaved himself to his feet and crossed over to the group. I rose unsteadily behind him – we had both been drinking more than was good for us. Dave quietly moved Twinkle to one side and gave the young man's patterned shirt front a gentle shove. I knew his style. He was one of those patriotic Irishmen who would knock the bloody Brits into the sea with one clout if he got the chance, but when it came to real action he was good at shoving.

'Stay away from my girl,' he demanded.

I had the sensation that we were all going to go for our guns. The young man looked at him calmly and said: 'Who're you and who's your girl?'

'You know damn well who I am' (shove) 'and who she is' (shove).

The trouble with shoving, of course, is that it is insulting to a man's dignity, like a slap on the face. This the young man seemed to think too because his first return shove was accompanied by his fist to the region of Dave's left eye. Dave stumbled back against me and then against a barman who was passing with a bowl of soup. The two collapsed backwards in a desperate hug.

I had begun to feel sorry for my sins. A real Irish set-to was brewing, and it would surely have boiled over only that at some crucial moment in Dave's recovery Twinkle laughed. It was a nervous laugh, immediately smothered, but since she was standing with her back to the young man it was obviously directed at the brother. Dave stopped in his tracks, looked at her with profound sadness (relief too, I suspected: it would have been an unfair fight) and strode from the room, a sorry sight with his big behind spattered with vegetable soup. The young man turned to Twinkle and shrugged in apology. With a little cry she hurried out after Dave.

I went for a long walk feeling like the original Judas. By the time I returned I was fully determined to confess everything to Dave (though what I had to confess was still very vague, nothing really had happened). It was better to lose Dave's friendship than his trust. But he had locked himself into his room with a bottle of whiskey and a piece of raw beef he had sent down for and was seeing no one, not even Twinkle.

I had a large nightcap that nearly stood me on my head and climbed under the covers, but I couldn't sleep. At about three in the morning I was still trying to read when Twinkle appeared in a blue nightdress and crept in beside me. She was inclined to tremble and I put my arm around her, comforting her as best I could but saying nothing. I think we were both beginning to realise the dangers of tampering with rose-covered cottages.

We must have nodded off because the next thing I recall is the door opening and Dave in his striped pyjamas, looking woebegone and haggard, approaching the bed as if there was a time bomb in it. My involuntary start at seeing him woke Twinkle and she raised herself on one elbow, with her other arm and tangled strands of her hair thrown across my chest.

We all went into a kind of freeze that could have lasted any length of time at that unreal hour, while the comedy of it flickered darkly in my mind with silly opening lines such as 'Now, Dave, it's not what you think . . .' But before I had a chance to utter any of them he retreated as spectrally as he had appeared. If he had passed out through the wall I wouldn't have been surprised.

After some more uneventful sleep I felt Twinkle leaving the bed, and I awoke fully shortly afterwards to find the sun quite warm in the room and the hands of my little clock at ten. I shaved and packed with unusual abandon, after which I called on Dave and found him making coffee with his tiny immersion heater. He was still in his pyjamas and looked like a man who was well and truly on the batter.

'Look,' I began, 'I'm leaving. About last night . . .'

'Forget it,' he said. 'It was all my fault.'

'Indeed it was,' I rounded on him. 'You've been messing about with that girl like a pious fifteen-year-old. Last night you locked your door to her, sulking. She only wanted to comfort you. Any real man would have taken her in and made love to her.'

'With this eye?' he cried.

The eye was indeed scarcely visible in its pouch of puffed and multi-hued flesh, but I still failed to make the connection with the successful performance of the love act.

'What do you think a healthy intelligent girl like Twinkle is to make of your carry-on?' I felt real anger rise in me. 'You have the typical Irish hole-and-corner approach to love. You can't even touch the body of the girl you want to marry without feeling sinful about it. A beautiful act, a beautiful creature, and you behave like a mean little fat spider weaving webs of sin around everything, debasing love to some kind of horrible exercise in degrees of passion to be discussed in whispers in the stale air of the confessional! Maybe this is how you can court an Irish girl who has been reared in the belief that her body is something dirty and evil, but for all she has gone through Twinkle certainly doesn't think that about her body – and she probably *knows* more about the wicked world at first hand than the two of us together. Do you think girls of her generation want to be treated like dolls? Oh, yes, she admired your great show of restraint but by God I think there's a limit, and when that limit has been reached a woman wants proof that she is loved as a woman and an individual and not as a soul in transit that must be kept on ice until it can start producing babies. Twinkle isn't *real* for you, she's a myth you take to adorn your own self-exalting male spiritual temple. I think you must be in love with virginity, a soft-boiled saint all runny with your own soulful importance.'

It was a great speech, the best I had ever made. I heard the universal applause of enlightened women. Dave hung his head and said nothing. His condition had probably nothing to do with priests or religion. In him had crystallised the reflexes of generations of rural Irish courtships in dark doorways and fragrant hedges where caresses had been honed by a morally brainwashed society to a fine ethic of tolerance, with ultimate union suspended like a chalice from the stars.

I was pole-axed therefore, when he looked up at me with his one good eye and said in a voice of doom: 'All right so, we'll do it tonight.' It was his tone that made me feel I had just brutally destroyed something, an iconoclast who had shattered an altar of conceit and pomp only to realise that for some it may have had a deep and pure significance. At the back of it all, though, I suspect I was feeling a tinge of jealousy. Twinkle had been almost mine too.

'You can't,' I said tersely.

'Why not?'

'She won't let you.'

'Why won't she let me? Sure I had to hold her back.'

'She will hate you for ever for relinquishing your principles.'

'I'll let her seduce me.'

'I bet you haven't a chance.'

'Who says?' And this time he looked at me with cyclopean suspicion.

But Twinkle was nowhere to be found. Her bulky knapsack was gone, she had left without even leaving a note. At the reception desk we were told she had paid her bill in full. The main street was astir with forenoon shoppers. We stood at the door feeling like people waiting for a funeral.

'Maybe it's serious,' Dave said suddenly.

'What?'

'Maybe she'll do something foolish. I was just thinking of when I plucked her out of the sea.'

'You mean she was trying to drown herself?

'It's possible, and now in her great loss she'll try it again.'

'What loss?' I laughed and he looked at me, hurt. In the eleventh hour we had become rivals after all.

We drove down to the beach but except for a few families it was deserted. Up and down the coast with us, but there was no sign of Twinkle. That night on our way back to Clon we pulled up at a point overlooking a small cove. In the light of the full moon we saw a couple moving along the silvered apron of the tide. For both of us Twinkle was rapidly fading into just such a romantic setting. Recalling her naked body beside me on the warm sand, I realised that Dave and I were really two of a kind in our inability ever to drink of pleasure without diluting it. I would have said so too to him and it might have made things better between us, but I sensed he was still dreaming; and anyway, I doubt if he would have understood.

BANK HOLIDAY

JOHN McGAHERN

JOHN McGAHERN

John McGahern was born in Dublin in 1934 and raised in Co. Roscommon. He has written five novels and three short story collections and is acknowledged throughout the literary world as one of Ireland's leading writers.

IT HAD BEEN unusual weather, hot for weeks, and the white morning mist above the river, making ghostly the figures crossing the metal bridge, seemed a certain promise that the good weather was going to last beyond the holiday. All week in the Department he had heard the girls talking of going down the country, of the ocean, and the dances in the carnival marquees. Already, across the river, queues were forming for the buses that went to the sea – Howth, Dollymount, Malahide. He, Patrick McDonough, had no plans for the holiday, other than to walk about the city, or maybe to go out into the mountains later. He felt a certain elation of being loose in the morning, as if in space. The solid sound of his walking shoes on the pavement seemed to belong to someone else, to be going elsewhere.

A year ago he had spent this holiday in the country, among the rooms and fields and stone walls he had grown up with, as he had spent it every year going back many years. His mother was still living, his father had died the previous February. The cruellest thing about that last holiday was to watch her come into the house speaking to his father of something she had noticed in the yard – a big bullfinch feeding on the wild strawberries of the bank, rust spreading in the iron of one of the sheds – and then to see her realise in the midst of speech that her old partner of the guaranteed responses was no longer there. They had been close. His father had continued to indulge her once great good looks long after they had disappeared.

That last holiday he had asked his mother to come and live with him in the city, but she had refused without giving it serious thought. 'I'd be only in the way up there. I could never fit in with their ways now.' He had gone down to see her as often as he was able to after that, which was most weekends, and had paid a local woman to look in on her every day. Soon he saw that his visits no longer excited her. She had even lost interest in most of the things around her, and whenever that interest briefly gleamed she turned not to him but to his dead father. When pneumonia took her in a couple of days just before Christmas, and her body was put down beside her husband's in Aughawillian churchyard, he was almost glad. The natural wind now blew directly on him.

He sold the house and lands. The land had been rich enough to send him away to college, not rich enough to bring him back other than on holiday, and now this holiday was the first such in years that he had nowhere in particular to go, no one special to see, nothing much to do. As well as the dangerous elation this sense of freedom gave, he looked on it with some of the cold apprehension of an experiment.

Instead of continuing on down the quays, he crossed to the low granite wall above the river, and stayed a long time staring down through the vaporous mist at the frenzy and filth of the low tide. He could have stood mindlessly there for most of the morning but he pulled himself away and continued on down the quays until he turned into Webb's Bookshop.

The floor in Webb's had been freshly sprinkled and swept, but it was dark within after the river light. He went from stack to stack among the second-hands until he came on a book that caught his interest, and he began to read. He stood there a long time until he was disturbed by the brown-overalled manager speaking by his side.

'Would you be interested in buying the book, sir? We could do something perhaps about the price. The books in this stack have been here a long time.' He held a duster in his hand, some feathers tied round the tip of a cane.

'I was just looking.'

The manager moved away, flicking the feathers along a row of spines in a gesture of annoyance. The spell was ended, but it was fair enough: the shop had to sell books, and he knew that if he bought the book it was unlikely that he would ever give it the same attention again. He moved to the next stack, not wanting to appear driven from the shop. He pretended to inspect other volumes. He lifted and put down *The Wooing of Elisabeth McCrum*, examining other books cursorily, all the time moving towards the door. It was no longer pleasant to remain. He tried to ignore the manager's stare as he went out, to find himself in blinding sunshine on the pavement. The mist had completely lifted. The day was uncomfortably hot. His early excitement and sense of freedom had disappeared.

Afterwards he was to go over the little incident in the bookshop. If it had not happened would he have just ventured again out into the day, found the city too hot for walking, taken a train to Bray as he thought he might and walked all day in the mountains until he was dog-tired and hungry? Or was this sort of let-down the inescapable end of the kind of elation he had felt walking to the river in the early morning? He would never know. What he did know was that once outside the bookshop he no longer felt like going anywhere and he started to retrace his steps back to where he lived, buying a newspaper on the way. When he opened the door a telegram was lying on the floor of the hallway.

It was signed 'Mary Kelleher', a name he didn't know. It seemed that a very old friend, James White, who worked for the Tourist Board in New York, had given her his name. There was a number to call.

He put it aside to sit and read through the newspaper, but he knew by the continuing awareness of the telegram on the table that he would call. He was now too restless to want to remain alone.

James White and he had met when they were both young civil servants, White slightly the older – though they both seemed the same age now – the better read, the more forthright, the more sociable. They met at eight-thirty on the Friday night of every week for several years, the evening interrupted only by holidays and illnesses, proof against girlfriends, and later wives, ended only by White's transfer abroad. They met in bars, changing only when they became known to the barmen or regulars, and in danger of losing their anonymity. They talked about ideas, books, 'the human situation', and 'reality and con-

sciousness' often surfaced with the second or third pint. Now
he could hardly remember a sentence from those hundreds of
evenings. What he did remember was a barman's face, white
hair drawn over baldness, an avid follower of Christy Ring; a
clock, a spiral iron staircase to the Gents, the cold of marble
on the wristbone, footsteps passing outside in summer, the
sound of heavy rain falling before closing time. The few times
they had met in recent years they had both spoken of nothing
but people and happenings, as if those early meetings were
some deep embarrassment: that they had leaned on them too
heavily once and were now like lost strength.

He rang. The number was that of a small hotel on the quays.
Mary Kelleher answered. He invited her to lunch and they
arranged to meet in the hotel foyer. He walked to the hotel,
and as he walked he felt again the heady, unreal feeling of
moving in an unblemished morning, though it was now past
midday.

When she rose to meet him in the foyer, he saw that she
was as tall as he. A red kerchief with polka dots bound her
blonde hair. She was too strong boned to be beautiful but her
face and skin glowed. They talked about James White. She had
met him at a party in New York. 'He said that I must meet you
if I was going to Dublin. I was about to check out of the hotel
when you rang.' She had relations in Dundalk that she intended
to look up and Trinity College had manuscripts she wanted to
see. They walked up Dame Street and round by the Trinity
Railings to the restaurant he had picked in Lincoln Place. She
was from Mount Vernon, New York, but had been living in
Chicago, finishing her doctorate in medieval poetry at the University of Chicago. There were very pale hairs on the brown
skin of her legs and her leather sandals slapped as she walked.
When she turned her face to his, he could see a silver locket
below the line of the cotton dress.

Bernardo's door was open on to the street, and all but two
of the tables were empty.

'Everybody's out of town for the holiday. We have the place
to ourselves.' They were given a table for four just inside the
door. They ordered the same things, melon with Parma ham,

veal Milanese, a carafe of chilled white wine. He urged her to have more, to try the raspberries in season, the cream cake, but she ate carefully and would not be persuaded.

'Do you come here often?' she asked.

'Often enough. I work near here, round the corner, in Kildare Street. An old civil servant.'

'You don't look the part at all, but James White did say you worked in the civil service. He said you were quite high up,' she smiled teasingly. 'What do you do?'

'Nothing as exciting as medieval poetry. I deal in law, industrial law in particular.'

'I could imagine that to be quite exciting.'

'Interesting maybe, but mostly it's a job – like any other.'

'Do you live in the city, or outside?'

'Very near here. I can walk most places, even walk to work.' And when he saw her hesitate, as if she wanted to ask something and did not think it right, he added, 'I have a flat. I live by myself there, though I was married once.'

'Are you divorced? Or am I allowed to ask that?'

'Of course you are. Divorce isn't allowed in this country. We are separated. For something like twenty years now we haven't laid eyes on one another. And you? Do you have a husband or friend?' he changed the subject.

'Yes. Someone I met at college, but we have agreed to separate for a time.'

There was no silence or unease. Their interest in one another already far outran their knowledge. She offered to split the bill but he refused.

'Thanks for the lunch, the company,' she said as they faced one another outside the restaurant.

'It was a pleasure,' and then he hesitated and asked, 'What are you doing for the afternoon?' not wanting to see this flow that was between them checked, though he knew to follow it was hardly wise.

'I was going to check tomorrow's trains to Dundalk.'

'We could do that at Westland Row around the corner. I was wondering if you'd be interested in going out to the sea where the world and its mother is in this weather?'

'I'd love to,' she said simply.

It was with a certain relief that he paid the taxi at the Bull Wall. Lately the luxury and convenience of a taxi had become for him the privilege of being no longer young, of being cut off from the people he had come from, and this was exasperated by the glowing young woman by his side, her eager responses to each view he pointed out, including the wired-down palms along the front.

'They look so funny. Why is it done?'

'It's simple. So that they will not be blown away in storms. They are not natural to this climate.'

He took off his tie and jacket as they crossed the planks of the wooden bridge, its legs long and stork-like in the retreated tide. The rocks that sloped down to the sea from the Wall were crowded with people, most of them in bathing costumes, reading, listening to transistors, playing cards, staring out to sea, where three tankers appeared to be nailed down in the milky distance. The caps of the stronger swimmers bobbed far out. Others floated on their backs close to the rocks, crawled in sharp bursts, breast-stroked heavily up and down a parallel line, blowing like walruses as they trod water.

'I used to swim off these rocks once. I liked going in off the rocks because I've always hated getting sand between my toes. Those lower rocks get covered at full tide. You can see the tidal line by the colour.'

'Don't you swim anymore?'

'I haven't in years.'

'If I had a costume I wouldn't mind going in.'

'I think you'd find it cold.'

She told him of how she used to go out to the ocean at the Hamptons with her father, her four brothers, their black sheep Uncle John who had made a fortune in scrap metal and was extremely lecherous. She laughed as she recounted one of Uncle John's adventures with an English lady.

When they reached the end of the Wall, they went down to the Strand, but it was so crowded that they had to pick their way through. They moved out to where there were fewer people along the tide's edge. It was there that she decided to wade in the water, and he offered to hold her sandals. As he walked with her sandals, a phrase came without warning from the book he had been reading in Webb's: 'What is he doing with his life, we say: and our judgement makes up for the failure to realise sympathetically the natural process of living.' He must indeed be atrophied if a casual phrase could have more presence for him than this beautiful young woman, and the sea, and the day. The dark blue mass of Howth faced the motionless ships on the horizon, seemed to be even pushing them back.

'Oh, it's cold,' she shivered as she came out of the water, and reached for her sandals.

'Even in heatwaves the sea is cold in Ireland. That's Howth ahead – where Maud Gonne waited at the station as Pallas Athena.' He reached for his role as tourist guide.

'I know that line,' she said and quoted the verse. 'Has all that gone from Dublin?'

'In what way?'

'Are there . . . poets . . . still?'

'Are there poets?' he laughed out loud. 'They say the standing army of poets never falls below ten thousand in this unfortunate country.'

'Why unfortunate?' she said quickly.

'They create no wealth. They are greedy and demanding. They hold themselves in very high opinion. Ten centuries ago there was a national convocation, an attempt to limit their powers and numbers.'

'Wasn't it called *Drum* something?'

'*Drum Ceat*,' he added, made uneasy by his own attack.

'But don't you feel that they have a function – beyond wealth?' she pursued.

'What function?'

'That they sing the tired rowers to the hidden shore?'

'Not in the numbers we possess here, one singing down the other. But maybe I'm unkind. There are a few.'

'Are these poets to be seen?'

'They can't even be hidden. Tomorrow evening I could show you some of the pubs they frequent. Would you like that?'

'I'd like that very much,' she said, and took his hand. A whole day was secured. The crowds hadn't started to head home yet, and they travelled back to the city on a nearly empty bus.

'What will you do for the rest of the evening?'

'There's some work I may look at. And you? What will you do?'

'I think I'll rest. Unpack, read a bit,' she smiled as she raised her hand.

He walked slowly back, everything changed by the petty confrontation in Webb's, the return to the flat, the telegram in the hallway. If he had not come back, she would be in Dundalk by now, and he would be thinking about finding a hotel for the night somewhere round Rathdrum. In the flat, he went through notes that he had made in preparation for a meeting he had with the Minister the coming week. They concerned an obscure section of the Industries Act. Though they were notes he had made himself he found them extremely tedious, and there came on him a restlessness like that which sometimes heralds illness. He felt like going out to a cinema or bar, but knew that what he really wanted to do was to ring Mary Kelleher. If he had learned anything over the years it was the habit of discipline. Tomorrow would bring itself. He would wait for it if necessary with his mind resolutely fixed on its own blankness, as a person prays after fervour has died.

'Section 13, paragraph 4, states clearly that in the event of confrontation or disagreement . . .' he began to write.

The dress of forest green she was wearing when she came down to the lobby the next evening caught his breath; it was shirtwaisted, belling out. A blue ribbon hung casually from her fair hair behind.

'You look marvellous.'

The Sunday streets were empty, and the stones gave out a dull heat. They walked slowly, loitering at some shop windows. The doors of all the bars were open, O'Neills and the International and the Olde Stand, but they were mostly empty within. There was a sense of a cool dark waiting in Mooney's, a barman arranging ashtrays on the marble. They ordered an assortment of sandwiches. It was pleasant to sit in the comparative darkness, and eat and sip and watch the street, and to hear in the silence footsteps going up and down Grafton Street.

It was into this quiet flow of the evening that the poet came, a large man, agitated, without jacket, the shirt open, his thumbs hooked in braces that held up a pair of sagging trousers, a brown hat pushed far back on his head. Coughing harshly and pushing the chair around, he sat at the next table.

'Don't look around,' McDonough leaned forward to say.

'Why?'

'He'll join us if we catch his eye.'

'Who is he?'

'A poet.'

'He doesn't look like one.'

'That should be in his favour. All the younger clerks that work in my place nowadays look like poets. He is the best we have. He's the star of the place across the road. He's practically resident there. He must have been thrown out.'

The potboy in his short white coat came over to the poet's table and waited impassively for the order.

'A Powers,' the order came in a hoarse, rhythmical voice. 'A large Powers and a pint of Bass.'

There was more sharp coughing, a scraping of feet, a sigh, muttering, a word that could have been a prayer or a curse. His agitated presence had more the sound of a crowd than the single person sitting in a chair. After the potboy brought the drinks and was paid, the poet swung one leg vigorously over the other, and with folded arms faced away towards the empty doorway. Then, as suddenly, he was standing in front of them. He had his hand out. There were coins in the hand.

'McDonough,' he called hoarsely, thrusting his palm forward. 'Will you get me a packet of Ci-tanes from across the road?' he mispronounced the brand of French cigarettes so violently that his meaning was far from clear.

'You mean the cigarettes?'

'*Ci*-tanes,' he called hoarsely again. 'French fags. Twenty. I'm giving you the money.'

'Why don't you get them here?'

'They don't have them here.'

'Why don't you hop across yourself?'

'I'm barred,' he said dramatically. 'They're a crowd of ignorant, bloody apes over there.'

'All right. I'll get them for you.' He took the coins but instead of rising and crossing the road he called the potboy.

'Would you cross the road for twenty Gitanes for me, Jimmy? I'd cross myself but I'm with company,' and he added a large tip of his own to the coins the poet had handed over.

'It's against the rules, sir.'

'I know, but I'd consider it a favour,' and they both looked towards the barman behind the counter, who had been following every word and move of the confrontation. The barman nodded that it was all right, and immediately bent his head down to whatever he was doing beneath the level of the counter, as if to disown his acquiescence.

Jimmy crossed, was back in a moment with the blue packet.

'You're a cute hoar, McDonough. You're a mediocrity. It's no wonder you get on so well in the world,' the poet burst out in a wild fury as he was handed the packet, and he finished his drinks in a few violent gulps, and stalked out, muttering and coughing.

'That's just incredible,' she said.

'Why?'

'You buy the man his cigarettes, and then get blown out of it. I don't understand it.'

'It wasn't the cigarettes he wanted.'

'Well, what did he want?'

'Reassurance, maybe, that he still had power, was loved and wanted after having been turfed out across the way. I slithered round it by getting Jimmy here to go over. That's why I was lambasted. He must have done something outrageous to have been barred. He's a tin god there. Maybe I should have gone over after all.'

'Why didn't you?'

'Vanity. I didn't want to be his messenger boy. He could go and inflate his great mouse of an ego somewhere else. To hell with him. He's always trouble.' She listened in silence as he ended. 'Wouldn't it be pleasant to be able to throw people their bones and forget it?'

'You might have to spend an awful lot of time throwing bones if the word got around,' she smiled as she sipped her glass of cider.

'Now that you've seen the star, do you still wish to cross the road and look in on the other pub?'

'I'm not sure. What else could we do?'

'We could go back to my place.'

'I'd like that. I'd much prefer to see how you live.'

'Why don't we look in across the road, have one drink if it's not too crowded,' and he added some coins to the change still on the table. 'It was very nice of them to cross for the Gitanes. They're not supposed to leave their own premises.'

The door of the bar across the way was not open, and when he pushed it a roar met them like heat. The bar was small and jammed. A red-and-blue tint from a stained glass window at the back mixed weirdly with the white lights of the bar, the light of evening from the high windows. A small fan circled helplessly overhead, its original white or yellow long turned to ochre by cigarette smoke. Hands proffered coins and notes across shoulders to the barmen behind the horseshoe counter. Pints and spirit glasses were somehow eased from hand to hand across the three-deep line of shoulders at the counter the way children that get weak are taken out of a crowd. The three barmen were so busy that they seemed to dance.

'What do you think?' he asked.

'I think we'll forget it.'

'I always feel a bit apprehensive going in there,' he admitted once they were out on the street again.

'I know. Those places are the same everywhere. For a moment I thought I was in New York at the Cedar Bar.'

'What makes them the same?'

'I don't know. Mania, egotism, vanity, aggression . . . people searching madly in a crowd for something that's never to be found in crowds.'

She was so lovely in the evening that he felt himself leaning towards her. He did not like the weakness. 'I find myself falling increasingly into an unattractive puzzlement,' he said, 'mulling over the old, useless chestnut, What *is* life?'

'It's the fact of being alive, I suppose, a duration of time, as the scholars would say,' and she smiled teasingly. 'Puzzling out what it is must be part of it as well.'

'You're too young and beautiful to be so wise.'

'That sounds a bit patronizing.'

'That's the last thing I meant it to be.'

He showed her the rooms, the large living-room with the oak table and worn red carpet, the brass fender, the white marble of the fireplace, the kitchen, the two bedrooms. He watched her go over the place, lift the sea shell off the mantel-piece, replace it differently.

'It's a lovely flat,' she said, 'though Spartan to my taste.'

'I bought the place three years ago. I disliked the idea of owning anything at first, but now I'm glad to have it. Now, would you like a drink, or perhaps some tea?'

'I'd love some tea.'

When he returned he found her thumbing through books in the weakening light.

'Do you have any of the poet's work?'

'You can have a present of this, if you like.' He reached and took a brown volume from the shelf.

'I see it's even signed,' she said as she leafed through the volume. 'For Patrick McDonough, With love', and she began to laugh.

'I helped him with something once. I doubt if he'd sign it with much love this evening.'

'Thanks,' she said as she closed the volume and placed it in her handbag. 'I'll return it. It wouldn't be right to keep it.' After several minutes of silence, she asked, 'When do you have to go back to your office?'

'Not till Tuesday. Tomorrow is a Bank Holiday.'

'And on Tuesday what do you do?'

'Routine. The Department really runs itself, though many of us think of ourselves as indispensable. In the afternoon I have to brief the Minister.'

'On what, may I ask?'

'A section of the Industries Act.'

'What is the Minister like?'

'He's all right. An opportunist, I suppose. He has energy, certainly, and the terrible Irish gift of familiarity. He first came to the fore by putting parallel bars on the back of a lorry. He did handstands and somersaults before and after speeches, to the delight of the small towns and villages. Miss Democracy thought he was wonderful and voted him in top of the poll. He's more statesmanlike now of course.'

'You don't sound as if you like him very much.'

'We're stuck with one another.'

'Were you upset when your marriage failed?' she changed.

'Naturally. In the end, there was no choice. We couldn't be in the same room together for more than a couple of minutes without fighting. I could never figure out how the fights started, but they always did.'

'Did you meet anyone else?'

'Nothing that lasted. I worked. I visited my parents until they died. Those sort of pieties are sometimes substitutes for life in this country – or life itself. We're back to the old subject and I'm talking too much.'

'No. I'm asking too many questions.'

'What'll you do now that you have your doctorate?'

'Teach. Write. Wait on tables. I don't know.'

'And your husband or friend?'

'Husband,' she said. 'We were married but it's finished. We were too young.'

'Would you like more tea, or for me to walk you back to the Clarence? . . . Or would you like to spend the night here?'

She paused for what seemed an age, and yet it could not have been more than a couple of moments.

'I'd like to spend the night here.'

He did not know how tense his waiting had been until he felt the release her words gave. It was as if blank doors had slid back and he was being allowed again into the mystery of a perpetual morning, a morning without blemish. He knew it by now to be an old con trick of nature, and that it never failed, only deepened the irony and the mystery. 'I'll be able to show you the city tomorrow. You can check out of your hotel then if you wish. And there are the two rooms . . .' he was beginning to say when she came into his arms and sealed his lips.

As he waited for her, the poet's sudden angry accusation came back. Such accusations usually came to rankle and remain long after praise had failed, but not this evening. He turned it over as he might a problem that there seemed no way round, and let it drop. If it was true, there was very little that could be done about it now. It was in turn replaced by the phrase that had come to him earlier by the sea's edge; and had he not seen love in the person of his old mother reduced to noticing things about a farmyard?

'I hope you're not puzzling over something like "life" again,' a teasing call came from the bedroom.

'No. Not this time.' He rose to join her.

In the morning they had coffee and toast in the sunlit kitchen with the expectation of the whole day waiting on them. Then they walked in the empty streets of the city, looked through the Green before going to the hotel to bring her things back to the flat.

The following days were so easy that the only anxiety could be its total absence. The days were heightened by the luxury and pleasure of private evenings, the meals she cooked that were perfection, the good wine he bought, the flowers; desire that was never turned aside or exasperated by difficulty.

At the end of the holiday, he had to go back to the office, and she put off the Dundalk visit and began to go to the Trinity Library. Many people were not back in the office, and he was able to work without interruption for the whole of the first morning. What he had to do was to isolate the relevant parts of the section and reduce them to a few simple sentences.

At the afternoon meeting the Minister was the more nervous. He was tall and muscular, small blue eyes and thick red hair, fifteen years the younger man, with a habit of continually touching anybody close to him that told of the large family he grew up in. They went over and over the few sentences he had prepared until the Minister had them by rote. He was appearing on television that night and was extremely apprehensive.

'Good man,' he grasped McDonough's shoulder with relief when they finished. 'One of these evenings before long you must come out and have a bite with us and meet the hen and chickens.'

'I'll be glad to. And good luck on the TV. I'll be watching.'

'I'll need all the luck I can get. That bitch of an interviewer hates my guts.'

They watched the television debate together in the flat that evening. The Minister had reason to be apprehensive. He was under attack from the beginning but bludgeoning his way. As he watched, McDonough wondered if his work had been necessary at all. He could hardly discern his few sentences beneath the weight of the Minister's phrases. 'I emphatically state . . . I categorically deny . . . I say without any equivocation whatsoever . . . Having consulted the best available opinions in the matter,' (which were presumably McDonough's own).

'What did you think?' he asked when he switched off the set.

'He was almost touching,' she said carefully. 'Amateurish maybe. His counterpart in the States might be no better, but he certainly would have to be more polished.'

'He was good at handstands and somersaults once,' he said, surprised at his own sense of disappointment. 'I've become almost fond of him. Sometimes I wish we had better people. They'll all tell him he did powerfully. What'll we do? Would you like to go for a quick walk?'

'Why don't we,' she reached for her cardigan.

Two days later she went to Dundalk, and it wasn't certain how long she intended to remain there. 'I guess I've come so far that they'll expect me to stay over the weekend.'

'You must please yourself. You have a key. I'll not be going anywhere.'

They had come together so easily that the days together seemed like a marriage without any of the apprehension or drama of a ceremony.

When he was young he had desired too much, wanted too much, dreaded and feared too much, and so spread his own fear. Now that he was close to losing everything – was in the direct path of the wind – it was little short of amazing that he should come on this extraordinary breathing space.

Almost in disbelief he went back in reflection to the one love of his life, a love that was pure suffering. In a hotel bedroom in another city, unable to sleep by her side, he had risen and dressed. He had paused before leaving the room to gaze on the even breathing of her sleep. All that breath had to do was frame one word, and a whole world of happiness would be given, but it was forever withheld. He had walked the morning streets until circling back to the hotel he came on a market that was just opening and bought a large bunch of grapes. The grapes were very small and turning yellow and still damp, and were of incredible sweetness. She was just waking when he came back into the room and had not missed him. They ate the grapes on the coverlid and each time she lifted the small bunches to her mouth he remembered the dark of her armpits. He ached to touch her but everything seemed to be so fragile between them that he was afraid to even stir. It seemed that any small movement now could bring calamity. Then, laughing, she blew grape seeds in his face and, reaching out her arms, drew him down. She had wanted their last day together to be pleasant. She was marrying another man. Later he remembered running between airport gates looking for flights that had all departed.

It was eerie to set down those days beside the days that had just gone by, call them by the same name. How slowly those days had moved, as if waiting for something to begin: now all the days were speeding, slipping silently by like air.

Two evenings later, when he let himself into the flat and found Mary Kelleher there, it was as if she had never been away.

'You didn't expect me back so soon?'

'I thought you'd still be in Dundalk, but I'm glad, I'm delighted.' He took her in his arms.

'I had as much of Dundalk as I wanted, and I missed you.'

'How did it go?'

'It was all right. The cousins were nice. They had a small house, crammed with things – religious pictures, furniture, photos. There was hardly place to move. Everything they did was so careful, so measured out. After a while I felt I could hardly breathe. They did everything they possibly could to make me welcome. I read the poems at last,' she put the book with the brown cover on the table. 'I read them again on the train coming back. I loved them.'

'I've long suspected that those very pure love sonnets are all addressed to himself,' McDonough said. 'That was how the "ignorant bloody apes and mediocrities" could be all short-circuited.'

'Some are very funny.'

'I'm so glad you liked them. I've lived with some of them for years. Would you like to go out to eat? Say, to Bernardo's?' he asked.

'I'd much prefer to stay home. I've already looked in the fridge. We can rustle something up.'

That weekend they went together for the long walk in the mountains that he had intended to take the day they met. They stopped for a drink and sandwiches in a pub near Blessington just before two o'clock, and there they decided to press on to Rathdrum and stay the night in the hotel rather than turn back into the city.

It was over dinner in the near empty hotel dining-room that he asked if she would consider marrying him. 'There's much against it. I am fifty. You would have to try to settle here, where you'll be a stranger,' and he went on to say that what he had already was more than he ever expected, that he was content to let it be, but if she wanted more then it was there.

'I thought that you couldn't be married here,' her tone was affectionate.

'I meant it in everything but name, and even that can be arranged if you want it enough.'

'How?'

'With money. An outside divorce. The marriage in some other country. The States, for instance.'

'Can't you see that I already love you? That it doesn't matter? I was half-teasing. You looked so serious.'

'I am serious. I want it to be clear.'

'It is clear and I am glad – and very grateful.'

They agreed that she would spend one week longer here in Dublin than she had planned. At Christmas he would go to New York for a week. She would have obtained her doctorate by then. James White would be surprised. There were no serious complications in sight. They were so tired and happy that it was as if they were already in possession of endless quantities of time and money.

SAM

ANNE DEVLIN

ANNE DEVLIN

Anne Devlin was born in Belfast in 1951 and lives in England. She won the 1984 Samuel Beckett Award for TV Drama and in 1986 the George Devine Drama Award, and has published a collection of short stories, *The Way-Paver*.

WHAT BOTHERED ME most about Sam, in those last few days before I left him, was his total exposure. All his emotions seemed to be on the surface. He would suddenly stop in the middle of the street, pull me towards him and put his hands up my skirt. Or he would lean across the table in the restaurant at lunch time, grab me by the collar and plunge his tongue down my throat. I got most of his lunch that way as well.

'Do you want the rest of this cherry?' I asked, extracting the stone from my mouth.

'Tinker, tailor, soldier, sailor, rich man,' he said, counting five stones on his pudding plate. 'No, you keep it. I don't fancy being poor.'

I found this behaviour faintly baffling; I had been used to more reserve from my lovers in public places. (I said public.)

The following day he came to meet me in the street outside the china shop opposite the City Hall.

'Sam, you're out of control.'

'What?' he said, beaming innocently.

'Your fly is undone.'

'So it is,' he said, hitching himself up. His hands went immediately to my bum. He pulled me towards him and groaned: 'Oh, you feel so good.' I wriggled free, as the soldiers at a nearby checkpoint looked on.

I had come back to Belfast to kill myself, failing that I decided the next best thing was to love Sam. I told Sam I loved him. I told myself that I loved Sam; the problem was I didn't. Like most adolescents of twenty-seven and a half, I thought if you insisted something was true often enough it would begin to happen. I was indulging in childish beliefs again. I was also very bored. Nothing had ever lived up to the promise of my university days. I married another student who also read English. He turned himself into a successful journalist. We moved from Scotland, where we'd both been to university, to London, where he took a job with one of the better Sunday papers and that's when our troubles began. I had loved Scotland and hated England. I was terribly lonely and he soon got bored with me. Or was it the other way round: I was terribly lonely and I soon got bored with him?

We didn't have any children because he said he wanted to establish his career first. I should have taken the hint then. But I have always been a bit slow to see how I irritated people. A whole whispering campaign could be going on around my head and I would not notice. It took the girl from the next-floor apartment, a feminist who ran a battered-wives hostel in Islington, to say: 'He's left you, hasn't he?' I looked aghast and said: 'Don't be ridiculous, he's only gone to work.' 'No. I mean he's lost interest.'

His first complaint was that I was too withdrawn; no one ever came to visit us. So I changed. Immediately I launched a series of parties; filled the flat with weekend guests; organised theatre tickets; joined a women's consciousness-raising group and took up yoga. Then he said I was too demanding and he wanted a quiet life. I began to feel confused. I went to see an analyst. A year later I left a note on the kitchen table, it read: 'I hope you find what you are looking for. I wish you all the best for the future.' Actually I think it was my lack of ambition which bothered him. All I ever wanted to do was read, bring up children and make jam. I should have written that note to myself.

When I returned to Belfast after eight years away, five of them married, I had no career and no job, however menial, to go to. I thought I might go back to university, because that was the last time I remembered being happy; except I had no idea what

I would do when I got there. The day I got off the boat my father said: 'Well, I'm glad that's over. I never liked him anyway.'

My father was a widower living alone. I suddenly saw my dilemma. My father was arthritic, my mother had worn herself away nursing him. He was glad I was back. But I was determined that two men weren't going to take advantage of my confusion. I told him I was getting a job.

'What do you need a job for? I've got money. You can live here for nothing. Sure I'd only have to pay a home-help.'

Mothering my father didn't appeal to me. In sheer panic at the prospect of what lay before me, I walked into an insurance office that afternoon at the bottom of Castle Street above the fish shop and took a job as a telephonist. I got on very well until the rest of the girls in the office discovered I had a degree – they stopped speaking to me. I was sitting outside the City Hall on a bench one lunch hour crying into my sandwiches when I met Sam.

'Oh dear. I'm sure it can't be as bad as all that,' a voice said. I had given up caring. I didn't even look up: 'It is. I've left my husband. I'm living with my father, and the girls in the office won't speak to me.' I completed this announcement with a great shuddering sob.

'Look, dry your eyes,' he said, taking a large, grubby hanky from his pocket. I accepted the hanky and his offer of a cup of tea just over the road. I discovered that he worked in a library and was writing a novel.

'What's your subject-matter?' I said. 'Or am I not allowed to ask?'

'War,' he said firmly.

I decided to ignore this. I invited him to come on a peace march with me. After the second peace march I decided to seduce him.

'I'll go to bed with you,' I said.

He was panic-stricken. I've never seen a man so frightened. 'Actually,' he said, 'I'm a virgin.'

'At least,' I said, retreating wildly, I wasn't sure if I could

cope with the responsiblilty of it, 'I don't think we should go on
seeing each other if this relationship is to be purely platonic. It
isn't fair on me emotionally.'

He agreed that it wasn't.

My analyst told me – I had an analyst in London after my
marriage broke up – to have as much sex as possible, it would
be good for me. It was with this in mind that I set out to seduce
Sam. What I had not allowed for was the effect of as much sex
as possible on Sam. We used to meet on Friday night after
work and go to his house. We would go to bed immediately,
make love, and then get up and have our evening meal – though
not all of it; then back to bed, make love, get up and have
our pudding; then back to bed again. In the morning, after
love-making, we would cook and eat a hearty breakfast and
then go back to bed before lunch. By teatime on Saturday, the
bedroom had a very high aroma and I would be beginning to
feel bloated.

I can't think why I didn't leave him earlier; I suppose I was
rather fascinated by his gluttony. It was as though for the first
time in his life someone had said to Sam: 'Eat as much as
you like.' And Sam was so overwhelmed by the offer he ate
compulsively and couldn't stop. My husband, the journalist, had
been so terrified of vulgarity he never allowed me to eat apples
or toast in bed. I never realised what a deprivation this was
until I met Sam. We were two of a kind, we ate our heads off.
And he had the most dramatic effect on my personality in other
ways.

I dressed up every time I saw him. On some occasions I pretended I was Mae West and would slink along pouting when I
knew he was looking my way. It was the best game I had played
in years, I had a whole range of outfits that suddenly became
clothes I wore when making love to Sam; a whole range of
colours I could only associate with him. I seem to remember
they were varying shades of fuchsia and lilac. My psychedelic
suits were impressive enough even to win the admiration of
the girls in the office, enough to minimize the handicap of having

a degree. On the day I was to move in with him, I arrived in a shocking pink suit, green suede shoes and boa, reeking of Miss Dior. He opened the door to me, aglow with emotion, bent over to kiss me and banged his head on the lintel. It was classic Sam luck. It was also due to the fact that he was six foot three. Did I mention that before?

He was six foot three and he lived in the smallest house I have ever seen. 'Eh, why did you buy it, Sam?' I asked during my Mae West phase. I had had my hair cut three times in three months. The latest blonde perm had left me uncertain as to whether he would prefer me as Mae West or Marilyn Monroe. I decided on Mae West for myself. She was what you might call a survivor.

'It was different – cottagey, you know.' He kept his head bent while we stood in the kitchen. 'I may have to lower the floor a little,' he said.

'Lower the floor?' I said. 'Why not raise the roof?'

The floor in the kitchen was already a foot below the outside step. The kitchen had one skylight window and gave the impression of being underground. It had been a weaver's cottage, recently modernised; but cheaply done; modernisation did not dispel my feeling of being buried alive once inside it. However, I suppressed my unease about the place: after all, I had wanted to get away from father.

'Raise the roof?' Sam said. 'I hadn't thought of that.'

The next day was Saturday, it rained heavily and the water from the roof poured into the drain outside the front door. The drain overflowed into the hall. I was in the kitchen at the time and heard the water gushing; unfortunately I went to investigate. I had to ring Sam at work.

'Eh, Sam, I hate to worry you but the kitchen's flooded. Could you come home and help bail out the water?'

Two hours later, when I had almost finished bailing water from the kitchen bucket by bucket into the sink, and thinking this is the last straw, two ambulance men appeared with Sam on a stretcher. He had slipped on the steps outside the library in the rain, slipped a disc and broken his ankle. Sam's luck had

struck again. I thought of abandoning him then and going back
to father, but it seemed a bit mean walking out on him when
he was down. I stayed on.

Yet it wasn't so much that Sam was a danger to himself. I could
cope with that, but he could also innocently project a certain
destructiveness like radar on to anyone or anything else within
his range; consequently he was extremely dangerous to be
with. For instance, he was very fond of tomato juice and used
to drink it by the gallon at meal time. One evening while we
were eating he knocked over his glass, the rim cracked as it
hit the table top and tomato juice poured over on to my lap,
leaving an indelible red stain on my blue cotton dress, worn for
the first time that evening. And he was often drawn to the most
fragile object in the room: like the time he attempted to remove
a very small scratch from an old china plate which had belonged
to my mother. The plate was rather beautiful, so I had it
mounted on the wall. Despite protestations from me, Sam took
a piece of steel wool to the scratch and then a knife. The result
was not the removal of the scratch but a gash ten times the
size across the face of the plate. 'My hand slipped,' he said.
    Another day at the open-air fitness centre at the park, I was
moving along some parallel bars, shifting along on the strength
of my arms alone. Sam couldn't wait until I was finished before
it was his turn, he jumped up after me on the bars and began
to move rapidly along the same short space. He knocked me
clean off the bars, a drop of six foot, on to the grass below. I
wasn't expecting the jolt, as he had already declined to get on
them in the first place. I fell awkwardly. I think he said something like: 'Oops, sorry. That was me,' and continued to finish
the length of the bars before he stopped. He got off looking
very pleased with himself, and then said: 'What's wrong with
you?' I was kneeling on the grass nursing a crumpled limb and
said in a voice of subdued rage: 'Sam, I think you've broken
my wrist.' So it should come as no surprise that on the following
Sunday, during a spell of sunny weather when Sam suggested
he might take a look on the roof and try to mend the broken
guttering, I fled out of the house.

'Couldn't you pay someone to do the job properly?' I asked. He accused me of having no confidence in him. I decided if Sam was on the roof I'd prefer to be outside the house rather than in. I put on my bikini, took a rug and lay on the grass at the far end of the garden, well clear of the house. Half an hour later I was sitting in the casualty ward of the Royal Victoria with blood pouring from my head. Sam managed to knock the ladder clean away from the roof – it was a direct hit. I should have left then, but the extraordinary thing was that I was so fascinated by the escalating violence of our relationship that I was spellbound into staying. I had read Freud at university, so I knew there was no such thing as an accident. He was full of remorse this time and brought me roses, said he'd never forgive himself and that he had a problem with objects.

And then it happened. We had very little money, but one day Sam went out and bought himself a very expensive piece of kitchen equipment. I was faintly surprised, we had been living on beans and eggs for months in one form or another and only ate meat occasionally. I looked apprehensively at the heavy, shiny stainless-steel blade and said: 'Eh, Sam, what's the meat cleaver for?'

'Chopping the legs off crabs,' he said. 'There's a recipe in *The Sunday Times* for fish soup.' (I wouldn't let him buy the other paper for personal reasons. I am capable of that.) 'I fancied making it some time. It recommended a cleaver for the crab, so I thought I'd better get one.'

My occult sign was a crab – the spell broke.

I finally resolved to leave.

He was smiling when I said at breakfast several days later: 'Eh, Sam, I don't think we'd better see each other again.'

'All right,' he said pleasantly, and trod on my toe.

He went off to work as usual. There were no scenes, he offered no resistance to my departure. This surprised me. I thought the least he could do was throw himself on the kitchen floor at my feet and plead with me not to leave. As I had no immediate alternative, I went back to father. Sam was still

smiling when he knocked at my door the next day. I was furious.
Not with Sam, but with father. I had only just moved back and
already he was making incredible demands on me.

'Yes?' I roared as I opened the hall door to him.

He was standing there grinning at me. My toe reacted in
apprehension; I felt a slight stabbing in it. Had he brought the
meat cleaver?

'Hello,' he said.

'Sam,' I said, changing into the alluring creature I always was
with him. A few minutes earlier a vision of me in the kitchen
rowing with father would have shattered that image completely.
No, he would have to find someone else to water the cabbages
and take the dog for a walk. Yes, I was only staying until I
found a place of my own. Of course I couldn't commit myself
to my whereabouts the day after tomorrow, I had yelled at my
father. Standing at the door with Sam grinning manically at me,
his hands behind his back, I wasn't sure if I'd be alive the day
after tomorrow.

'I'm in the shit!' Sam said.

I concurred with this.

'I want you back,' he said. 'I'll do anything. I'll even lose
weight.'

'Sam,' I said, trying to interrupt, but he continued.

'I'll be a great writer one day when my novel is published. I
know I'll never do better than you and you'll never do better
than me. We have to make the best of what we've got. Anyway,
I'd like to have a family with you. So what do you say?'

It was father's voice behind me in the hall yelling – 'Who's
that you're keeping standing at the door?' – which drove me
over the threshold.

'Yes. All right, Sam,' I said, playing for time. 'But come back
tomorrow. I'm a bit busy with father.'

He was still smiling when I closed the door. He was still
there in the morning when I went to bring in the milk. And he
came back every night for a week and stood in the street until
the fanlight in the hall went out. And he went away. He went
away.

A PORNOGRAPHER WOOS

BERNARD MacLAVERTY

BERNARD MacLAVERTY

Bernard MacLaverty was born in Belfast in 1945. His first book, *Secrets*, a collection of short stories, won an award from the Scottish Arts Council. Since then he has published two further collections and two novels, one of which, *Lamb*, became a highly acclaimed film.

I AM SITTING on the warm sand with my back to a rock watching you, my love. You have just come from a swim and the water is still in beads all over you, immiscible with the suntan oil. There are specks of sand on the thickening folds of your waist. The fine hairs on your legs below the knee are black and slicked all the one way with the sea. Now your body is open to the sun, willing itself to a deeper brown. You tan well by the sea. Your head is turned away from the sun into the shade of your shoulder and occasionally you open one eye to check on the children. You are wearing a black bikini. Your mother says nothing but it is obvious that she doesn't approve. Stretchmarks, pale lightning flashes, descend into your groin.

Your mother sits rustic between us in a print dress. She wears heavy brogue shoes and those thick lisle stockings. When she crosses her legs I can see she is wearing pink bloomers. She has never had a holiday before and finds it difficult to know how to act. She is trying to read the paper but what little breeze there is keeps blowing and turning the pages. Eventually she folds the paper into a small square and reads it like that. She holds the square with one hand and shades her glasses with the other.

Two of the children come running up the beach with that curious quickness they have when they run barefoot over ribbed sand. They are very brown and stark naked, something we know again is disapproved of, by reading their grandmother's silence. They have come for their bucket and spade because they have found a brown ogee thing and they want to bring it and show it to me. The eldest girl, Maeve, runs away becoming incredibly small until she reaches the water's edge. Anne, a year younger, stands beside me with her Kwashiorkor tummy. She has forgotten the brown ogee and is examining something on the rock behind my head. She says 'bloodsuckers' and I turn round. I see one, then look to the side and see another and another. They are all over the rock, minute, pin-point, scarlet spiders.

Maeve comes back with the brown ogee covered with sea-water in the bucket. It is a sea-mat and I tell her its name. She contorts and says it is horrible. It is about the size of a child's hand, an elliptical mound covered with spiky hairs. I carry it over to you and you open one eye. I say, 'Look.' Your mother becomes curious and says, 'What is it?' I show it to you, winking with the eye farthest from her but you don't get the allusion because you too ask, 'What is it?' I tell you it is a sea-mat. Maeve goes off waving her spade in the air.

I have disturbed you because you sit up on your towel, gathering your knees up to your chest. I catch your eye and it holds for infinitesimally longer than as if you were just looking. You rise and come over to me and stoop to look in the bucket. I see the whiteness deep between your breasts. Leaning over, your hands on your knees, you raise just your eyes and look at me from between the hanging of your hair. I pretend to talk, watching your mother, who turns away. You squat by the bucket opening your thighs towards me and purse your mouth. You say, 'It is hot,' and smile, then go maddeningly back to lie on your towel.

I reach over into your basket. There is an assortment of children's clothes, your underwear bundled secretly, a squash-bottle, sun-tan lotion and at last – my jotter and biro. It is a small jotter, the pages held by a wire spiral across the top. I watch you lying in front of me shining with oil. When you lie your breasts almost disappear. There are some hairs peeping at your crotch. Others, lower, have been coyly shaved. On the inside of your right foot is the dark varicose patch which came up after the third baby.

I begin to write what we should, at that minute, be doing. I have never written pornography before and I feel a conspicuous bump appearing in my bathing trunks. I laugh and cross my legs and continue writing. As I come to the end of the second page I have got the couple (with our own names) as far as the hotel room. They begin to strip and caress. I look up and your mother is looking straight at me. She smiles and I smile back at her.

She knows I write for a living. I am working. I have just peeled your pants beneath your knees. I proceed to make us do the most fantastical things. My mind is pages ahead of my pen. I can hardly write quickly enough.

At five pages the deed is done and I tear the pages off from the spiral and hand them to you. You turn over and begin to read.

This flurry of movement must have stirred your mother because she comes across to the basket and scrabbles at the bottom for a packet of mints. She sits beside me on the rock, offers me one which I refuse, then pops one into her mouth. For the first time on the holiday she has overcome her shyness to talk to me on her own. She talks of how much she is enjoying herself. The holiday, she says, is taking her out of herself. Her hair is steel-grey darkening at the roots. After your father's death left her on her own we knew that she should get away. I have found her a woman who hides her emotion as much she can. The most she would allow herself was to tell us how, several times, when she got up in the morning she had put two eggs in the pot. It's the length of the day, she says, that gets her. I knew she was terrified at first in the dining room but now she is getting used to it and even criticises the slowness of the service. She has struck up an acquaintance with an old priest whom she met in the sitting-room. He walks the beach at low tide, always wearing his hat and carries a rolled pac-a-mac in one hand.

I look at you and you are still reading the pages. You lean on your elbows, your shoulders high and, I see, shaking with laughter. When you are finished you fold the pages smaller and smaller, then turn on your back and close your eyes without so much as a look in our direction.

Your mother decides to go to the water's edge to see the children. She walks with arms folded, unused to having nothing to carry. I go over to you. Without opening your eyes you tell me I am filthy, whispered even though your mother is fifty yards away. You tell me to burn it, tearing it up would not be safe enough. I feel annoyed that you haven't taken it in the spirit in which it was given. I unfold the pages and begin to read it again. The bump reinstates itself. I laugh at some of my artistic attempts – 'the chittering noise of the venetian blinds', 'luminous pulsing tide' – I put the pages in my trousers pocket on the rock.

Suddenly Anne comes running. Her mouth is open and screaming. Someone has thrown sand in her face. You sit upright, your voice incredulous that such a thing should happen to your child. Anne, standing, comes to your shoulder. You wrap your arms round her nakedness and call her 'Lamb' and 'Angel' but the child still cries. You take a tissue from your bag and lick one corner of it and begin to wipe the sticking sand from round her eyes. I watch your face as you do this. Intent, skilful, a beautiful face focused on other-than-me. This, the mother of my children. Your tongue licks out again wetting the tissue. The crying goes on and you begin to scold lightly giving the child enough confidence to stop. 'A big girl like you?' You take the child's cleaned face into the softness of your neck and the tears subside. From the basket miraculously you produce a mint and then you are both away walking, you stooping at the waist to laugh on a level with your child's face.

You stand talking to your mother where the glare of the sand and the sea meet. You are much taller than she. You come back to me covering half the distance in a stiff-legged run. When you reach the rock you point your feet and begin pulling on your jeans. I ask where you are going. You smile at me out of the head hole of your T-shirt, your midriff bare and say that we are going back to the hotel.

'Mummy will be along with the children in an hour or so.'

'What did you tell her?'

'I told her you were dying for a drink before tea.'

We walked quickly back to the hotel. At first we have an arm around each other's waist but it is awkward, like a three-legged race, so we break and just hold hands. In the hotel room there are no venetian blinds but the white net curtains belly and fold in the breeze of the open window. It is hot enough to lie on the coverlet.

It has that special smell by the seaside and afterwards in the bar as we sit, slaked from the waist down, I tell you so. You smile and we await the return of your mother and our children.

FEMALE FORMS

EMMA COOKE

EMMA COOKE

Emma Cooke was born in Portarlington, Co. Laois in 1934. She lived for many years in Limerick City before moving in 1987 to Killaloe, Co. Clare, where she is very involved with local writers, groups. Her short stories have appeared widely, and she has published one collection, *Female Forms*, and three novels.

TALBOT'S GIRL OF the moment was a young woman in her early twenties. A schoolteacher in her first job. She was engaged to another schoolteacher; a boy who lived in a far off part of the country and whom she hoped to marry directly after Christmas. In the meantime she met Talbot.

She was a fat girl with a bottom that seemed ready to burst out of the jeans she wore whenever she was not wearing her school-going skirts. She had sandy hair, a freckled face and gold stars in her ears. The gold stars were the only touch of glamour about her. She was a very ordinary girl with sturdy legs, square hands, and a heart that went thumpie, thumpie, thumpie as regular as clockwork. (She had once been captain of a camogie team.) Even the way she felt about Talbot was run-of-the-mill for a girl who was engaged to a fellow schoolteacher with a fuzzy beard who wore white socks, tweed jackets with elbow patches and corduroy trousers; a fellow who played Gaelic games and always sang 'She Moved Through The Fair' after his fourth pint.

Talbot sang 'I'll Do It My Way' in the best Old Blue-eyes manner and drank either hot whiskeys or wine or Dubonnet with a twist of lemon. He never sang anything in her company but she had heard him and seen him, once, before she knew him personally. She had been out with some female companions celebrating the ending of the school year in a well-known downtown restaurant. Talbot had been across the way with a group of dark-suited men who were all, like himself, middle-aged and mildly drunk. Even that first night in the smoky restaurant she had observed from a distance, but minutely, the black wings of hair that sprang back from his temples and his rather fleshy lips

mouthing the corny words. When he had finished he laughed at
his own absurdity and called the waiter, who hurried to bend
soothingly over his shoulder. She had twisted the ring with its
three diamonds on her engagement finger and felt an aching
need for – she did not know what. Excitement?

Nowadays if she ever tried to think of Talbot and her fiancé
in the same context she experienced a drowning sensation, as
if she was being pushed under by an ice floe. Only one thing
was clear: what was happening between herself and Talbot had
nothing to do with her fiancé. It was outside the bounds of their
relationship. She had slept with her fiancé several times and
knew that he felt sexual intercourse had 'no harm in it', so long
as the couple involved 'knew where they stood'. With Talbot
such points were irrelevant. He wanted her and that was that.

Last thing at night she cold-creamed her face. She did it as
thoroughly as she greased soufflé dishes (she was an enthusiastic cook). She dabbed rosettes of grease here and there over
the planes of her skin and then spread and rubbed the stuff into
the crevices around her eyes and nose. Next she rubbed it all
off again with cotton-wool balls. It took an eternity. Talbot
watched from his side of the bed. He remembered a girl from
a previous relationship who used to massage her scalp for five
minutes every night before she lay down. Each woman had her
own special rituals. He knew that questioning them was useless.
He yawned. His mouth was full of the taste of curry spiked
with cider. The girl's cooking was distressingly way out. At first
he had been charmed. It was such a contrast to her simplicity in
other matters.

'My tongue is burning,' Talbot said plaintively.

'It's that new curry paste,' the girl said. 'If you like I'll go to
the kitchen for ice cubes and you can suck one.'

'No thank you, my pet,' Talbot said. In his imagination the
crystal lump melted on his tongue, cooling it into a rancid jelly.
He shivered at her lack of sensitivity. Desire, which had been
mounting in him with each slap of her palms against her chubby
face, subsided. He rolled on his back, aware of her shallow
breathing but only wanting her now in fits and starts. There
had been enough women over the past few years for him to

recognise immediately the symptoms that heralded the beginning of the end.

He let his mind range over the girl's predecessors. They appeared frame by frame, frozen in attitudes that might have won prizes if photographed and called 'Pictures of dejection'.

As for the girl, she lay there, waiting, confident that at any moment Talbot would turn and tweak one of her curls as a preliminary to taking her on his search for the source of pleasure. She did not know that her time for carrying the torch had run out. Talbot fingered the sleeve of her jacket. She was the first girl he had ever slept with who wore pyjamas. Until tonight they had amused him. Now the brushed nylon felt like a heavy barrier, instead of cosy and inviting to his nervous fingers. The fabric had become as impenetrable as the thicket that once surrounded the Sleeping Beauty – and he was past being a cavalier prince; as dense as the blue silk impregnated with lily-of-the-valley perfume in which someone called Daphne became embalmed last year after she sat on the marble coffee table in his sitting room and buckled one of its brass legs.

It was not just the new hot curry paste. Alison, who, in spite of her name, was dusky, long-haired and wore a jewel in one of her nostrils, had made curries that clove to the roof of the mouth like early morning cinders. She had also burnt incense, which he hated, in the bedroom. She had survived while his mouth singed.

It was not the indigestibility of the cider that the girl had added as an afterthought. Mary, who could cook nothing but Welsh Rarebit, had lasted her time in spite of his allergy to cheese. Nevertheless, they had each subscribed to this sudden antipathy.

The glow from the street light outside his house picked out the glinting star in the girl's earlobe. Alison's bespangled nostril had finally appeared as exactly what it was – a mutilation. Mary, who, in spite of her unbalanced diet, had been disgustingly healthy and athletic (although not a camogie captain) sometimes went out for a jog before bed. Talbot's nose wrinkled as he remembered how it had made her sweat.

Talbot took his hand away from the girl's sleeve. He shifted

apart from her. The girl felt words she wanted to speak con-
gesting in her throat. Silly words. 'Well.' 'Colossal.' 'Like.' 'Not
really.' It would have made no difference. Nothing she could
have said would have made any difference. If he had wanted to
Talbot could have told her so. They lay there and up from the
harbour came the 'whoo-whoo' of foghorns.

'Whoo-whoo' they blew through Talbot's head, in one ear and
out the other. He shivered, feeling a goose step over his grave.
His hand slipped under the girl's pyjama jacket and sought her
left breast. She was a curvy girl, built for comfort, but he felt
as if he was scrabbling at an ant hill.

A pause. Then, 'Don't touch me,' the girl said in a vibrant
voice. Talbot took her at her word and withdrew his hand. The
girl had not meant to speak like that. The words had burst out
against her wishes. Now she found her remonstrance echoing
through the room. 'Don't touch me.' 'Don't touch me.' She
always said the wrong thing. She felt appalled at herself. She
would never make a go of life.

She lay beside Talbot like a dying duck, upsetting him. His
forehead throbbed for want of a lily-white hand, for want of
Nance. He saw Nance's fringe and her pale oval face. 'Go away,
Talbot,' she said. Nance with her silken eyes, her bared breast,
her voice muffled by a closed door.

Drifting, the girl caught a snowflake. 'I must give you back
your umbrella, Talbot,' she said. They had met in a storm.
Then her nose had been tipped with scarlet. He had wanted to
bite it. Now, grains of her talcum powder gritted his nostrils,
suffocating him. She used a bargain-counter brand that conjured
up cauldrons of marmalade. Talbot winced at the orange bubbles
forming in his head. He imagined being stuck in a tent with her,
or a cheap hotel building such as she would spend her honeymoon in on the Costa del Sol. Talbot pictured her there – spiking
her legitimate pleasures by ogling the swarthy waiter who
scooped her evening hamburger on to her plate while her husband bent his sunburnt back over a glass of hooch.

Talbot squinted to see the luminous hands of the alarm clock
pin-pointing the night. As he made out the time a corner of the
blanket poked a finger in his eye. He turned his back on the

girl, who looked at him, humped in the gloom, and snapped, 'It's all right for you.' She had no idea what it was that was all right, or why; but she had needles of steel wool in her fingers from scouring Talbot's saucepans and tomorrow she had to prepare Christmas tests for her pupils.

Talbot and the girl, sheeted in hard lines, their insides flannelled with curry, ruminated on the girl's outcry. Embarrassment quilted the girl with a heavy flush that seared her plumpness and made her want to cry. She cried, rooting for a tissue from the bedside table and sending her jar of cream clattering to the ground. Her awkwardness and her sobs beat against Talbot like thorny twigs. He hated them when they cried. 'What are you crying for?' he asked.

'I can't make head or tail of you,' the girl sobbed.

'Go to sleep,' Talbot said, 'we'll talk about it in the morning.'

The girl remembered her pupils' tests. She wished that she was in her own flat, in her own bed with her fiancé and her bunny nightdress case for company while her jeans dripped on the clothes-horse in the bath.

Talbot wished that he had his bed to himself – even if the shadow spreading on the wall were to crystallise into Nance. Nance shivering against the harshness of his voice, her face filmed from her long trek in the night air, a hank of hair in her hand, her fringe a ludicrous adornment on her shorn head, spite in her eyes. He tried to imagine Nance as she must be now; threading her way through an alien crowd on some strange pavement, her hair cropped but silvered here and there like his own. Or maybe she coloured it. He conjured up a sea-green Nance.

The girl remembered that her heart belonged elsewhere and tumbled into a sort of doze. Nerves twitched in Talbot's arms and legs. He closed his eyes and Nance came churning out of the blackness, spewing hailstones.

It was Nance's fault that he lived like this. It was Nance who had turned him into an ageing cradle-snatcher with eccentric tastes. If she had stayed there would have been no reason for other female companionship. No reason, especially, for this girl who lacked even a modicum of modishness and was likely to turn up anywhere dressed for trench warfare. He wondered what the hell the girl had seen in him. He was far too old and fastidious for her. The first night he met her he had looked no further than her delectable nose that shone with the comfort of a nursery lamp in the rain. Now he could hardly wait to see the end of her freckles and scratchy jumpers. He supposed that Nance would laugh if she knew.

The only part of Talbot that was asleep was a leg. He lay parched with thirst and afraid to fetch a glass of water in case he woke the girl and brought on a wave of tantrums. He was one-legged Ahab chasing Moby Dick. He was Talbot pursuing Nance through the holes in the lace curtain. Strip the wallpaper piece by piece to make sure she had not slipped behind it. Count the Nances one by one jumping off a cliff on their honeymoon on the Atlantic coast while he sat on the sea wall with a poke full of periwinkles and a pin.

Talbot had known the girl for two months. A pocket handkerchief of modern life. In her own way she recognised it for what it was. A disposable tissue.

Things were different from when he and Nance were young. Maybe it was due to the increase of traffic in the streets! The general concourse and dispersion. Talbot had once looked away momentarily from the red light at a traffic stop and seen a girl wave at him from the back seat of a car and dreamt erotically of her for the following three nights in a row. A striped bandana she wore, the gap between her front teeth, a small bruise or shadow on her forehead, her starfish fingers splayed on the glass were as firmly fixed in his mind as the bumps, bulges and locknit underwear of the woman who had taught him in kindergarten. He would recognise her if she knocked on his office door tomorrow. And yet, she didn't matter a damn!

'Nothing matters a damn to you, Talbot. You just don't want to know,' Nance said. News had come that her sister had a tumour. He was so glad that it was not Nance who had been pointed out that he could not even pretend sorrow or hide his nonchalance about the fate of the children.

He was barely awake. He heard her stumbling around the room. He heard the click of a suitcase catch.

'Where are you going?' he asked.

'To the bathroom,' the girl said stiffly. The click was made by her setting the cold-cream jar back in its place. When she lurched against the bedpost he could have strangled her.

The girl was gone for so long that Talbot felt a wind whistle up the gap where she should have been. He heard her moving about and the flush of the cistern. When he was a child he used to be frightened in bed in the dark; afraid to put his hand out in case it touched the inside of a coffin. He remembered the story in the Christmas annual that had given him the idea. Even now, in reasonable middle-age, he could not obliterate completely that boyhood pang of uneasiness. When the girl came back, shuffling like an old crone in an effort at quietness, he had stopped disliking her. The drag on the sheets as she climbed back beside him was like a caress. 'Are you OK?' he asked.

Nance was constantly prowling about at night. Sometimes he used to hear a small cracking noise that turned out to be her biting her nails in the small hours.

'I've got my period,' the girl said. 'I'm sorry.'

'That doesn't matter,' Talbot said, finding it in him to wish her well.

'We *are* friends, aren't we?' the girl said.

'Yes,' he said, 'yes.'

'You hate me for it, don't you?' Nance said. 'You hate me. You hate me. You hate me.' She had a habit of cobbling her conversations with repetition.

'I stole it. I stole it. I stole it.'

'He gave it to me. He gave it to me. He gave it to me.'

Nance laughed like a water-spout. She scurried to her dressing table and rooted through its muddle. She tossed out a letter. 'He loves me. He loves me. He loves me.'

Talbot left the house, the skin of his face pulled tight as a drum. They had been married for eight years. The man in question was a widower who lived nearby. Retired. Ludicrous. Talbot saw him every morning as he left for work, walking to the shop for a newspaper. A clockwork man in a raincoat and a tartan cap carrying a shopping bag.

When Talbot returned that evening Nance met him in the hall. She had cut her hair. She said that she had just stayed long enough to let him see! She pirouetted slowly, giving him the full benefit of the nape of her beautiful neck. Talbot's hands itched for a chopper. He brushed past her, managing to remain silent, managing to climb the stairs. Two days later she had taken her leave. He accosted the widower, catching the man in the act of putting on his galoshes on a wet morning. The man straightened himself. His back hurt sometimes. He was as bewildered as Talbot. He was old enough to be Nance's father. He had never meant it to happen. His breath came in sharp puffs. He had a muffler that matched his cap. He was going into hospital next week for a check-up on doctor's orders. His teeth were too straight for comfort.

'The heat must be gone off,' Talbot said.

'Do you find it cold?' the girl said.

'Frozen.'

'I'm sorry about my period,' the girl said.

She could have saved herself the trouble. She waited. She sent out a feeler. 'Good-night, Talbot!' You so-called heart-throb, she thought when no answer came back. You old clown, she thought. He always wore bright pyjamas, bright enough for a harlequin. A strange contrast after his businesslike waistcoats and impeccable collars. She was glad she was getting married to a man who slept in his pelt.

The creepers gossiped against the walls of the house. Talbot hacked them out by the roots at the weekends. He built bon-fires. The newspaper that carried the widower's death notice faded to yellow on the dining-room window-sill. Talbot did not miss it when the daily woman took it for a kneeler.

The daily woman was a vast creature. She and Talbot only met on Friday evenings when Talbot gave her her money. Apart from what he could see – bandaged legs, skinned knuckles, cross-overall bemedalled with safety pins, steel hairclip, fierce chin, odd sprouts of hair, fur bootees – he knew nothing about her. The whirr of dishwasher, clothes washer, vacuum cleaner restricted their exchanges to nods and shrugs. She kept her slippers under the stairs. The sight of them, quiet as a pair of blue mice, sometimes surprised Talbot in the act of getting a bottle of wine from his modest store. She had been with him for years, almost since Nance walked out. There was a time, now blurred in Talbot's memory, and then the woman on her knees scrubbing the kitchen floor and a new smell, a mixture of mustiness, sweat and Jeyes Fluid around the place. He had no idea that he was going to be lost without her when she left. He thought as little of her as he thought of the girls who accepted a shake-down over the years. He was already washed up – thanks very much!

'I hope you rot, Talbot,' Nance said. She stood with one foot already out of the door. She wore a hooded jacket that they had bought the year before in Tunisia. A crimson thing edged with white whorls of wool. Its hood covered her spiky, messed-up hair. With a tapestry bag rolled up under her arm like a prayer mat she looked as purposeful as a pilgrim.

'Are you going to him?' Talbot asked.

'I might and I mightn't,' Nance said.

'How will you manage for money?' Talbot asked.

Nance sighed. When she bent her head the hood hid her expression. She made a gesture with the tapestry bag. 'There's a stain on the carpet.' She peeped sideways at him. 'But it's not my concern. Sure it's not, Talbot?'

He could think of nothing to say to her.

Nance fumbled in her pocket and took out a latchkey. She dropped it into a green bowl on the hall table. 'You can keep your bloody cocoonery,' she said. When she had gone the house seemed full of the sound of ticking clocks. He was sure she would return before morning.

Slivers of Nance, the cleaning woman, the girl beside him, other girls, danced around Talbot. The mattress creaked. His pillow turned into a concrete breast. Yards of hair plumed the darkness. His skin burst out in hives.

He remembered a girl who called herself Miss Everest and went on display in the Fun Palace. Years ago. Years and years ago – before he ever knew Nance. He visited the exhibition several times and spoke to Miss Everest through a tube as she lay packed in ice cubes in a transparent coffin. He tried to date

her. He breathed on the ice and it misted over. He was still a
virgin. It was a huge joke.

'I am asleep,' he muttered when the girl whispered was he
sick.

He wondered if Miss Everest had many relations. Nance had
dozens. Especially aunts, sisters, girl cousins, grandmothers,
a mother, bridesmaids. They sucked up Nance. He was powerless against their magnetism. He stood outside her family house
while the women sat in conclave, smoke pouring from the parlour
chimney. 'Nothing doing,' said a pony-tailed messenger, slamming the door in his face. He stumbled home, wondering what
other men did in such circumstances. He raked over his acquaintances in search of one he could speak to about love. It was
impossible. He went out and met his first woman since Nance.
A woman with a loud voice. He brought her home. She shouted
down his ticking clocks. She was most unhappy – or so she
said. She had a fur jacket that moulted and she was far from
innocent. Her uncle was a well-known politician – or traditional
musician – Talbot had forgotten which.

The girl was asleep, breathing freely. Talbot cooled his still
burning mouth by licking the ice off Miss Everest. Her de-
frosting body had the dull, uninteresting sheen of plastic and
furred his tongue. The pressure which had been gathering under
Talbot's rib cage and across his brow evaporated. Every bit of
him was as limp as stale lettuce. The scrapings and hammerings,
which could have been Nance trying to get in, did not prevent
him from dropping off. Secret things – now hot, now cold –
wriggled from tunnels and vanished.

The girl skated easily across the surface of the early morning.
She stopped by the bed. 'I might as well be off,' she said. It
was early – only half-past seven. The cup of tea she had brought
tilted in her hand so that it slopped into its saucer. 'Oh God!
I'm sorry,' she said but made no other attempt at amends,
just put it down on Talbot's locker in which he kept his Italian
shoes and clean handkerchiefs. She had to take a bus to
her flat, change her clothes, take out her bike and cycle to
school.

'I suppose . . .' Talbot began. He was barely awake.

'You can let me know,' the girl said, forgetting all the memorable phrases of farewell she had composed over half a grapefruit down in the kitchen. 'I left half a grapefruit for you in the fridge,' she said.

'Don't forget to check the back door,' Talbot said. He had an obsession about the back door and thieves and blackguards. Nance's widower had slipped in and out through the back door. He was sure of that. The cleaning woman was guardian of it now.

In the half-light, with a duffle coat over her jeans and jumper, the girl looked vague and lumpish. Her cute nose, her curvy bottom, her grin, had been blocked out. It was no longer clear to Talbot that she was as cuddlesome as a baby spaniel. 'I'll ring,' he said. The girl pulled her scarf up over her chin and muttered something into it.

'It was an experience,' the girl said to herself later. She was a cheerful girl, not given to jibbing at such hand-outs as came her way. Also, her future was by no means bleak. Her fiancé was anxious to name the day. They had the deposit for a house. She was not likely to bump into Talbot west of the Shannon. He would be a memory, thin as a widower's finger, falling softly across her marriage, blurring its harsher edges and softening its certainties. She would remember him fondly.

Talbot ate his breakfast with only the hum of the refrigerator and scrape of chair leg on tiled floor for company. He went to great lengths over his grapefruit, removing the pith and dicing the segments as neatly as any high-class chef. He threw the cherry the girl had stuck on it into the kitchen bin. This last act put him in good humour. He felt that he had scored a winner. Upstairs, he hummed as he threw yesterday's draggled shirt into the bath with his handerkerchiefs. The bed sheets were probably spotted with the girl's blood. He did not investigate. That was the cleaning woman's job. He had to be about the day's business.

He printed a request for toothpaste on one of his business cards and left it, with a pound note, on his marble table where the woman would be sure to see it. He frowned at the small wedge of cardboard under the buckled leg. Then he left for the city. It was as if he had forgotten Nance completely.

The grapefruit shell lay on the kitchen table all day. The cherry mouldered in the bin. A fly rubbed its hind legs over a scattering of sugar. Talbot's breakfast chair stood askew.

The girl's fiancé phoned her at work, long distance. His voice crackled, rough as his tweedy jackets, over the wire and made her feel warm. 'I miss you too,' she said. She did. Dreadfully.

Talbot's dirty linen lay in the bath, attended only by a black spider that eventually tumbled down the waste pipe. The cleaning woman stood in a queue at the airport with a suitcase in one hand and a slip of paper with her son's London address printed on it tucked in the folder with her one-way ticket. She was wishing she had worn her bootees. Her feet were murdering her. She was wishing she had followed her own good judgement and travelled by boat.

The smell of curry lingered in the stairwell of Talbot's house. The unswept floors waited for a slippered footprint. A paper bag blew against the locked back door. It rustled like a woman's petticoat. A drainpipe creaked like an old man's bones. The brushes and mops stood sentinel in the broom cupboard. And a few rags. Old bits of things that the cleaning woman had found at the back of the hot press. A felted-up jumper. A buttonless blouse. It was the kind of day that would make anyone feel desperate if they had nowhere to go.

THE HUSBAND

MARY DORCEY

MARY DORCEY

Mary Dorcey was born in Dublin in 1950 and is a founder member of Irish Women United and the first Irish Gay Rights group. She has published two collections of poetry and a book of short stories, *A Noise From The Woodshed*, which latter won the 1990 Rooney Award for Irish Literature.

THEY MADE LOVE then once more because she was leaving him. Sunlight came through the tall, Georgian window. It shone on the blue walls, the yellow paintwork, warming her pale, blonde hair, the white curve of her closed eyelids. He gripped her hands, their fingers interlocked, his feet braced against the wooden footboard. He would have liked to break her from the mould of her body; from its set, delicate lines. His mouth at her shoulder, his eyes were hidden, and he was glad to have his back turned on the room; from the bare dressing-table stripped of her belongings, and the suitcase open beside the wardrobe.

Outside other people were going to Mass. He heard a bell toll in the distance. A man's voice drifted up: 'I'll see you at O'Brien's later', then the slam of a car door and the clatter of a woman's spiked heels hurrying on the pavement. All the usual sounds of Sunday morning rising distinct and separate for the first time in the silence between them. She lay beneath him passive, magnanimous, as though she were granting him a favour, out of pity or gratitude because she had seen that he was not, after all, going to make it difficult for her at the end. He moved inside her body, conscious only of the sudden escape of his breath, no longer caring what she felt, what motive possessed her. He was tired of thinking, tired of the labour of anticipating her thoughts and concealing his own.

He knew that she was looking past him, over his shoulder towards the window, to the sunlight and noise of the street. He touched a strand of her hair where it lay along the pillow. She did not turn. A tremor passed through his limbs. He felt the sweat grow cold on his back. He rolled off her and lay still,

staring at the ceiling where small flakes of whitewash peeled
from the moulded corners. The sun had discovered a spider's
web above the door; like a square of grey lace, its diamond
pattern swayed in a draught from the stairs. He wondered how
it had survived the winter and why it was he had not noticed it
before. Exhaustion seeped through his flesh bringing a sensation of calm. Now that it was over at last he was glad, now
that there was nothing more to be done. He had tried everything
and failed. He had lived ten years in the space of one; altered
himself by the hour to suit her and she had told him it made no
difference, that it was useless, whatever he did, because it had
nothing to do with him personally, with individual failing. He
could not accept that, could not resign himself to being a mere
cog in someone else's political theory. He had done all that he
knew to persuade, to understand her. He had been by turns
argumentative, patient, sceptical, conciliatory. The night when,
finally, she had told him it was over he had wept in her arms,
pleaded with her, vulnerable as any woman, and she had
remained indifferent, patronising even, seeing only the male he
could not cease to be. They said they wanted emotion, honesty,
self-exposure but when they got it, they despised you for it.
Once, and once only, he had allowed the rage in him to break
free; let loose the cold fury that had been festering in his gut
since the start of it. She had come home late on Lisa's birthday,
and when she told him where she had been, blatantly, flaunting
it, he had struck her across the face, harder than he had
intended so that a fleck of blood showed on her lip. She had
wiped it off with the back of her hand, staring at him, a look of
shock and covert satisfaction in her eyes. He knew then in his
shame and regret that he had given her the excuse she had
been waiting for.

He looked at her now, at the hard pale arch of her cheekbone.
He waited for her to say something, but she kept silent and he
could not let himself speak the only words that were in his
mind. She would see them as weakness. Instead, he heard
himself say her name, 'Martina,' not wanting to, but finding it
form on his lips from force of habit: a sound – a collection of
syllables that had once held absolute meaning, and now meant

nothing or too much, composed as it was of so many conflicting memories.

She reached a hand past his face to the breakfast cup that stood on the bedside table. A dark, puckered skin had formed on the coffee's surface but she drank it anyway. 'What?' she said without looking at him. He felt that she was preparing her next move, searching for a phrase or gesture that would carry her painlessly out of his bed and from their flat. But when she did speak again there was no attempt at prevarication or tact. 'I need to shower,' she said bluntly, 'can you let me out?' She swung her legs over the side of the bed, pushing back the patterned sheet, and stood up. He watched her walk across the room away from him. A small mark like a circle of chalk dust gleamed on the muscle of her thigh – his seed dried on her skin. The scent and taste of him would be all through her. She would wash meticulously every inch of her body to remove it. He heard her close the bathroom door behind her and, a moment later, the hiss and splatter of water breaking on the shower curtain. Only a few weeks ago she would have run a bath for them both and he would have carried Lisa in to sit between their knees. Yesterday afternoon he had brought Lisa over to her mother's house. Martina had said she thought it was best if Lisa stayed there for a couple of weeks until they could come to some arrangement. Some arrangement! For Lisa! He knew then how crazed she was. Of course, it was an act – a pretence of consideration and fair-mindedness, wanting it to appear that she might even debate the merits of leaving their daughter with him. But he knew what she planned, all too well.

He had a vision of himself calling over to Leinster Road on a Saturday afternoon, standing on the front step ringing the bell. She would come to the door and hold it open, staring at him blankly as if he were a stranger while Lisa ran to greet him. Would Helen be there too with that smug, tight, little smile on her mouth? Would they bring him in to the kitchen and make tea and small talk while Lisa got ready, or would they have found some excuse to have her out for the day? He knew every possible permutation, he had seem them all a dozen times on

television and seventies' movies, but he never thought he might
be expected to live out these banalities himself. His snort of
laughter startled him. He could not remember when he had last
laughed aloud. But who would not at the idea that the mother
of his child could imagine this cosy Hollywood scenario might
become reality? When she had first mentioned it, dropping it
casually as a vague suggestion, he had forced himself to hold
back the derision that rose to his tongue. He would say nothing.
Why should he? Let her learn the hard way. They would all say
it for him soon enough: his parents, her mother. The instant
they discovered the truth, who and what she had left him for,
they would snatch Lisa from her as ruthlessly as they would
from quicksand. They would not be shackled by any qualms of
conscience. They would have none of his need to show fine
feeling. It was extraordinary that she did not seem to realise
this herself; unthinkable that she might, and not allow it to
influence her.

She came back into the room, her legs bare beneath a shaggy
red sweater. The sweater he had bought her for Christmas.
Her nipples protruded like two small stones from under the
loose wool. She opened the wardrobe and took out a pair of
blue jeans and a grey corduroy skirt. He saw that she was on
the point of asking him which he preferred. She stood in the
unconsciously childish pose she assumed whenever she had a
decision to make, however trivial: her feet apart, her head tilted
to one side. He lay on his back watching her, his hands inter-
laced between the pillow and his head. He could feel the blood
pulsing behind his ears but he kept his face impassive. She was
studying her image in the mirror, eyes wide with anxious vanity.
At last she dropped the jeans into the open case and began to
pull on the skirt. Why – was that what Helen would have
chosen? What kind of look did she go for? Elegant, sexy, casual?
But then they were not into looks – oh no, it was all on a higher,
spiritual plane. Or was it? What did she admire in her anyway?
Was it the same qualities as he, or something quite different,
something hidden from him? Was she turned on by some reflection of herself or by some opposite trait, something lacking in
her own character? He could not begin to guess. He knew so

little about this woman Martina was abandoning him for. He had left it too late to pay her any real attention. He had been struck by her the first night, he had to admit, meeting her in O'Brien's after that conference. He liked her body; the long legs and broad shoulders and something attractive in the sultry line of her mouth. A woman he might have wanted himself in other circumstances. If he had not been told immediately that she was a lesbian. Not that he would have guessed it – at least not at first glance. She was too good-looking for that. But it did not take long to see the coldness in her, the chip on the shoulder, the arrogant, belligerent way she stood at the bar and asked him what he wanted to drink. But then she had every reason for disdain, had she not? She must have known already that his wife was in love with her. It had taken him a year to reach the same conclusion.

She sat on the bed to pull on her stockings, one leg crossed over the other. He heard her breathing – quick little breaths through her mouth. She was nervous then. He stared at the round bone of her ankle as she drew the red mesh over it. He followed her hands as they moved up the length of her calf. Her body was so intimately known to him he felt he might have cast the flesh on her bones with his own fingers. He saw the stretch marks above her hip. She had lost weight this winter. She looked well, but he preferred her as she used to be – voluptuous: the plump roundness of her belly and arms. He thought of all the days and nights of pleasure that they had had together. She certainly could not complain that he had not appreciated her. He would always be grateful for what he had discovered with her. He would forget none of it. But would she! Oh no. She pretended to have forgotten already. She talked now as though she had been playing an elaborate game all these years – going through ritual actions to please him. When he refused to let her away with that kind of nonsense, the deliberate erasure of their past, and forced her to acknowledge the depth of passion there had been between them, she said, yes, she did not deny that they had had good times in bed but it had very little to do with him. He had laughed in her face. And who was it to do with then? Who else could take credit for it? She did not dare to answer, but even as he asked the question he knew the sort of thing she would come out with. One of Helen's profundities – that straight women use men as instruments, that they make love to themselves through a man's eyes, stimulate themselves with his desire and flattery, but that it is their own sensuality they get off on. He knew every version of their theories by now.

'Would you like some more coffee?' she asked him when she had finished dressing. She was never so hurried that she could go without coffee. He shook his head and she walked out of the room pulling a leather belt through the loops of her skirt. He listened to her light footsteps on the stairs. After a moment he heard her lift the mugs from their hooks on the wall. He heard her fill the percolator with water, place it on the gas stove and, after a while, its rising heart beat as the coffee bubbled through the metal filter. He hung on to each sound, rooting himself in the routine of it, wanting to hide in the pictures they evoked. So long as he could hear her moving about in the kitchen below him, busy with all her familiar actions, it seemed that nothing much could be wrong.

Not that he believed that she would really go through with it. Not all the way. Once it dawned on her finally that indulging this whim would mean giving up Lisa, she would have to come to her senses. Yes, she would be back soon enough with her tail between her legs. He had only to wait. But he would not let her see that he knew this. It would only put her back up – bring out all her woman's pride and obstinacy. He must tread carefully. Follow silently along this crazy pavement she had laid, step by step, until she reached the precipice. And when she was forced back, he would be there, waiting.

If only he had been more cautious from the beginning. If only he had taken it seriously, recognised the danger in time, it would never have reached this stage. But how could he have? How could any normal man have seen it as any more than a joke? He had felt no jealousy at all at the start. She had known it and been incensed. She had accused him of typical male complacency. She had expected scenes, that was evident, wanted them, had tried to goad him into them. But for weeks he had refused to react with anything more threatening than good-humoured sarcasm. He remembered the night she first confessed that Helen and she had become lovers: the anxious, guilty face, expecting God knows what extremes of wrath, and yet underneath it there had been a look of quiet triumph. He had had to keep himself from laughing. He was taken by surprise, undoubtedly, though he should not have been with the way they had been going on – never out of each other's company, the all-night talks and the heroine worship. But frankly he would not have thought Martina was up to it. Oh, she might flirt with the idea of turning on a woman but to commit herself was another thing. She was too fundamentally healthy, and too fond of the admiration of men. Besides, knowing how passionate she was, he could not believe she would settle for the caresses of a woman.

Gradually his amusement had given way to curiosity, a pleasurable stirring of erotic interest. Two women in bed together after all – there was something undeniably exciting in the idea. He had tried to get her to share it with him, to make it something they could both enjoy but, out of embarrassment, or some misplaced sense of loyalty, she had refused. He said to tease her, to draw her out a little, that he would not have picked Helen for the whip and jackboots type. What did he mean by that, she had demanded menacingly. And when he explained that as, obviously, she herself could not be cast as the butch, Helen was the only remaining candidate, she had flown at him, castigating his prejudice and condescension. Clearly it was not a topic amenable to humour! She told him that all that role playing was a creation of men's fantasies. Dominance and submission were models the women had consigned to the rubbish heap. It was all equality and mutual respect in this brave new world. So where did the excitement, the romance, come in, he wanted to ask. If they had dispensed with all the traditional props what was left? But he knew better than to say anything. They were so stiff with analysis and theory the lot of them it was impossible to get a straightforward answer. Sometimes he had even wondered if they were really lesbians at all. Apart from the fact that they looked perfectly normal, there seemed something overdone about it. It seemed like a public posture, an attitude struck to provoke men – out of spite or envy. Certainly they flaunted the whole business unnecessarily, getting into fights in the street or in pubs because they insisted on their right to self-expression and that the rest of the world should adapt to them. He had even seen one of them at a conference sporting a badge on her lapel that read, 'How dare you presume I'm heterosexual.' Why on earth should anyone presume otherwise unless she was proud of resembling a male impersonator?

And so every time he had attempted to discuss it rationally they had ended by quarrelling. She condemned him of every macho fault in the book and sulked for hours, but afterwards they made it all up in bed. As long as she responded in the old manner, he knew he had not much to worry about. He had even fancied that it might improve their sex life – add a touch of the unknown. He had watched closely to see if any new needs or tastes might creep into her love-making.

It was not until the night she had come home in tears that he was forced to re-think his position.

She had arrived in, half drunk at midnight after one of their interminable meetings, and raced straight up to bed without so much as greeting him or going in to kiss Lisa good-night. He had followed her up, and when he tried to get in beside her to comfort her, she had become hysterical, screamed at him to leave her alone, to keep his hands away from her. It was hours before he managed to calm her down and get the whole story out of her. It seemed that Helen had told her that evening in the pub that she wanted to end the relationship. He was astonished. He had always taken it for granted that Martina would be the first to tire. He was even insulted on her behalf. He soothed and placated her, stroking her hair and murmuring soft words the way he would with Lisa. He told her not to be a fool, that she was far too beautiful to be cast aside by Helen, that she must be the best thing that had ever happened to her. She was sobbing uncontrollably, but she stopped long enough to abuse him when he said that. At last she had fallen asleep in his arms, but for the first time he had stayed awake after her.

He had to admit that her hysteria had got to him. He could see then it had become some kind of obsession. Up to then he had imagined it was basically a schoolgirl crush, the sort of thing most girls worked out in their teens. But women were so sentimental. He remembered a student of his saying years ago that men had friendships, women had affairs. He knew exactly what he meant. You had only to watch them, perfectly average housewives sitting in cafés or restaurants together, gazing into each other's eyes in a way that would have embarrassed the most besotted man, the confiding tones they used, the smiles of flattery and sympathy flitting between them, the intimate gestures, touching each other's hand, the little pats and caresses, exasperating waiters while they fought over the right to treat one another.

He had imagined that lesbian love-making would have some of this piquant quality. He saw it as gently caressive – tender and solicitous. He began to have fantasies about Martina and Helen together. He allowed himself delicious images of their tentative, childish sensuality. When he and Martina were fucking he had often fantasised lately that Helen was there too, both women exciting each other and then turning to him at the ultimate moment, competing for him. He had thought it was just a matter of time before something of the sort came about. It had not once occurred to him in all that while that they would continue to exclude him, to cut him out mentally and physically, to insist on their self-sufficiency and absorption. Not even that night lying sleepless beside her while she snored, as she always did after too many pints. It did not register with him finally until the afternoon he came home unexpectedly from work and heard them together.

There was no illusion after that, no innocence or humour. He knew it for what it was. Weeks passed before he could rid his mind of the horror of it; it haunted his sleep and fuelled his days with a seething, putrid anger. He saw that he had been seduced, mocked, cheated, systematically, cold-bloodedly by assumptions she had worked carefully to foster; defrauded and betrayed. He had stood at the bottom of the stairs – his stairs – in his own house and listened to them. He could hear it from the hall. He listened transfixed, a heaving in his stomach, until the din from the room above rose to a wail. He had covered his ears. Tender and solicitous had he said? More like cats in heat! As he went out of the house, slamming the door after him, he thought he heard them laughing. Bitches – bloody, fucking bitches! He had made it as far as the pub and ordered whiskey. He sat drinking it, glass after glass, grasping the bowl so hard he might have snapped it in two. He was astounded by the force of rage unleashed in him. He would have liked to put his hands around her bare throat and squeeze it until he'd wrung that noise out of it.

Somehow he had managed to get a grip of himself. He had had enough sense to drink himself stupid, too stupid to do anything about it that night. He had slept on the floor in the sitting room and when he woke at noon she had already left for the day. He was glad. He was not going to humiliate himself by fighting for her over a woman. He was still convinced that it was a temporary delirium, an infection that, left to run its course, would sweat itself out. He had only to wait, to play it cool, to think and to watch until the fever broke.

She came back into the room carrying two mugs of coffee. She set one down beside him giving a little nervous smile. She had forgotten he had said he did not want any.

'Are you getting up?' she asked as she took her dressing gown from the back of the door, 'there's some bread in the oven – will you remember to take it out?'

Jesus! How typical of her to bake bread the morning she was leaving. The dough had been left as usual, of course, to rise overnight and she could not bring herself to waste it. Typical of her sublime insensitivity! He had always been baffled by this trait in her, this attention, in no matter what crisis, to the everyday details of life and this compulsion to make little gestures of practical concern. Was it another trick of hers to forestall criticism? Or did she really have some power to rise above her own and other people's emotions? But most likely it was just straightforward, old-fashioned guilt.

'Fuck the bread,' he said and instantly regretted it. She would be in all the more hurry now to leave. She went to the wardrobe and began to lift down her clothes, laying them in the suitcase. He watched her hands as they expertly folded blouses, jerseys, jeans, studying every movement so that he would be able to recapture it precisely when she was gone. It was impossible to believe that he would not be able to watch her like this the next day and the day after. That was what hurt the most. The thought that he would lose the sight of her, just that. That he would no longer look on while she dressed or undressed, prepared a meal, read a book or played with Lisa. Every movement of her body familiar to him, so graceful, so completely feminine. He felt that if he could be allowed to watch her through glass, without speaking, like a child gazing through a shop window, he could have been content. He would not dare express it, needless to say. She would have sneered at him. Objectification she would call it. 'A woman's body is all that ever matters to any one of you, isn't it?' And he would not argue because the thing he really prized would be even less flattering to her – her vulnerability, her need to confide, to ask his advice in every small moment of self-doubt, to share all her secret fears. God how they had talked! Hours of it. At least she could never claim that he had not listened. And in the end he had learned to need it almost as much as she did. To chat in the inconsequential way she had, curled together in bed, sitting over a glass of wine till the small hours, drawing out all the trivia of personal existence: the dark, hidden things that bonded you forever to the one person who would hear them from you. Was that a ploy too? a conscious one? or merely female instinct? to tie him to her by a gradual process of self-exposure so that he could not disentangle himself, even now when he had to, because there was no longer any private place left in him, nowhere to hide from her glance, nowhere that she could not seek out and name the hurt in him. This was what had prompted her, an hour earlier, on waking, to make love with him: this instinct for vulnerability that drew her, like a bee to honey, unerringly to need and pain: this feminine lust to console; so that she had made one last generous offering – handing over her body as she might a towel to someone bleeding. And he had taken it, idiot that he was; accepted gratefully – little fawning lap-dog that she had made of him.

She was sitting at the dressing-table brushing her hair with slow, attentive strokes, drawing the brush each time from the crown of her head to the tips of her hair where it lay along her shoulder. Was she deliberately making no show of haste, pretending to be doing everything as normal? It seemed to him there must be something he could say; something an outsider would think of immediately. He searched his mind, but nothing came to him but the one question that had persisted in him for days: 'Why are you doing this? I don't understand why you're doing this.' She opened a bottle of cologne and dabbed it lightly on her wrist and neck. She always took particular care preparing herself to meet Helen. Helen, who herself wore some heavy French scent that clung to everything she touched, that was carried home in Martina's hair and clothing after every one of their sessions. But that was perfectly acceptable and politically correct. Adorning themselves for each other – make-up, perfume, eyebrow plucking, exchanging clothes – all these feminine tricks took on new meaning because neither of them was a man. Helen did not need to flatter, she did not need to patronize or idolize, she did not need to conquer or submit, and her desire would never be exploitative because she was a woman dealing with a woman! Neither of them had institutionalized power behind them. This was the logic he had been taught all that winter. They told one another these fairy stories sitting round at their meetings. Everything that had ever gone wrong for any one of them, once discussed in their consciousness-raising groups, could be chalked up as a consequence of male domination. And while they sat about indoctrinating each other with this schoolgirl pap, sounding off on radio and television, composing joint letters to the press, he had stayed at home three nights a week to mind Lisa, clean the house, cook meals, and read his way through the bundles of books she brought home: sentimental novels and half-baked political theses that she had insisted he must look as if he was to claim any understanding at all. And at the finish of it, when he had exhausted himself to satisfy her caprices, she said that he had lost his spontaneity, that their relationship had become stilted, sterile and self-conscious. With Helen, needless to say, all was otherwise – effortless and instinctive. God, he could not wait for their little idyll to meet the adult world, the world of electricity bills, dirty dishes and child-minding, and see how far their new roles got them! But he had one pleasure in store before then, a consolation prize he had been saving himself. As soon as she was safely out of the house, he would make a bonfire of them – burn every one – every goddamn book with the word woman on its cover!

She fastened the brown leather suitcase, leaving open the lock on the right hand that had broken the summer two years ago when they had come back from Morocco laden down with blankets and caftans. She carried it across the room, trying to lift it clear of the floor, but it was too heavy for her and dragged along the boards. She went out the door and he heard it knocking on each step as she walked down the stairs. He listened. She was doing something in the kitchen but he could not tell what. There followed a protracted silence. It hit him suddenly that she might try to get out of the flat, leave him and go without saying anything at all. He jumped out of bed, grabbed his trousers from the chair and pulled them on, his fingers so clumsy with haste he caught his hair in the zip. Fuck her! When he rooted under the bed for his shoes, she heard and called up: 'Don't bother getting dressed, I'll take the bus.' She did not think he was going to get the car out and drive her over there surely? He took a shirt from the floor and pulled it on over his head as he took the stairs to the kitchen two at a time. She was standing by the stove holding a cup of coffee. This endless coffee drinking of hers, cups all over the house, little white rings marked on every stick of furniture. At least he would not have that to put up with any longer.

'There's some in the pot if you want it,' she said. He could see the percolator was almost full, the smell of it would be all over the flat now, and the smell of the bloody bread in the oven, for hours after she was gone.

'Didn't you make any tea?'

'No,' she said and gave one of her sidelong, maddening looks of apology as though it was some major oversight, 'but there's water in the kettle.'

'Thanks,' he said, 'I won't bother.'

He was leaning his buttocks against the table, his feet planted wide apart, his hands in his pockets. He looked relaxed and in control at least. He was good at that – years of being on stage before a case of students. He wondered if Helen would come to meet her at the bus stop, or was she going to have to lug the suitcase alone all the way up Leinster Road? He wondered how they would greet each other. With triumph or nervousness? Might there be a sense of anti-climax about it now that she had final committed herself after so much stalling? Would she tell Helen that she had made love with him before leaving? Would she be ashamed of it and say nothing? But probably Helen would take it for granted as an insignificant gesture to male pride, the necessary price of freedom. And suddenly he wished that he had not been so restrained with her, so much the considerate, respectful friend she had trained him to be. He wished that he had taken his last opportunity and used her body as any other man would have – driven the pleasure out of it until she had screamed as he had heard her that day, in his bed, with her woman lover. He should have forced her to remember him as something more than the tiresome child she thought she had to pacify.

She went to the sink and began to rinse the breakfast things under the tap.

'Leave them,' he said, 'I'll do them,' the words coming out of him too quickly. He was losing his cool. She put the cup down and dried her hands on the tea towel. He struggled to think of something to say. He would have to find something. His mind seethed with ridiculous nervous comments. He tried to pick out a phrase that would sound normal and yet succeed in gaining her attention, in arresting this current of meaningless actions that was sweeping between them. And surely there must be something she wanted to say to him? She was not going to walk out and leave him as if she was off to the pictures? She took her raincoat from the banister and put it on, but did not fasten it. The belt trailed on one side. She lifted up the suitcase and carried it into the hallway. He followed her. When she opened the door, he saw that it was raining. A gust of wind caught her hair, blowing it into her eyes. He wanted to say, 'Fasten your coat – you're going to get cold.' But he did not and he heard himself ask instead:

'Where can I ring you?' He had not intended that, he knew the answer. He had the phone number by heart.

She held open the door with one hand and set down the case. She stared down at his shoes and then past him along the length of the hallway. Two days ago he had started to sand and stain the floorboards. She looked as if she was estimating how much work remained to be done.

'Don't ring this weekend. We're going away for a while.'

He felt a flash of white heat pass in front of his brain and a popping sound like a light bulb exploding. He felt dizzy and his eyes for a moment seemed to cloud over. Then he realised what had happened. A flood of blind terror had swept through him, unmanning him, because she had said something totally unexpected – something he had not planned for. He repeated the words carefully, hoping she would deny them, make sense of them.

'You're going away for a while?'

'Yes.'

'Where to for Godsake?' he almost shrieked.

'Down the country for a bit – to friends.'

He stared at her blankly, his lips trembling, and then the words came out that he had been holding back all morning:

'For how long? When will you be back?'

He could have asked it at any time, he had been on the verge of it a dozen times and had managed to repress it because he had to keep to his resolve not to let her see that he knew what all this was about – a drama, a show of defiance and autonomy. He could not let her guess that he knew full well she would be back. Somewhere in her heart she must recognise that no one would ever care for her as much as he did. No one could appreciate her more, or make more allowances for her. She could not throw away ten years of his life for this – to score a political point – for a theory – for a woman! But he had not said it, all morning. It was too ridiculous – it dignified the thing even to mention it. And now she had tricked him into it, cheated him.

'When will you be back?' he had asked.

'I'll be away for a week, I suppose. You can ring the flat on Monday.'

The rain was blowing into her face, her lips were white. She leaned forward. He felt her hand on his sleeve. He felt the pressure of her ring through the cloth of his shirt. She kissed him on the forehead. Her lips were soft, her breath warm on his skin. He hated her then. He hated her body, her woman's flesh that was still caressive and yielding when the heart inside it was shut like a trap against him.

'Goodbye,' she said. She lifted the case and closed the door after her.

He went back into the kitchen. But not to the window. He did not want to see her walking down the road. He did not want to see her legs in their scarlet stockings, and the raincoat blown back from her skirt. He did not want to see her dragging the stupid case, to see it banging against her knees as she carried it along the street. So he stood in the kitchen that smelled of coffee and bread baking. He stood over the warmth of the stove, his head lowered, his hands clenched in his pockets, his eyes shut.

She would be back anyhow – in a week's time. She had admitted that now. 'In a week,' she had said, 'ring me on Monday.' He would not think about it until then. He would not let himself react to any more of these theatrics. It was absurd, the whole business. She had gone to the country, she was visiting friends. He would not worry about her. He would not think about her at all, until she came back.

HOW TO WRITE A
SHORT STORY

SEAN O'FAOLAIN

SEAN O'FAOLAIN

Sean O'Faolain was born in Cork in 1900 and his international reputation rests securely on his mastery of the short story. At home, however, he is also honoured for his untiring work, mainly through his editorship of *The Bell* monthly, to rid Ireland of obscurantism and repression. His writing, apart from stories, included novels, biographies, autobiography, drama, travel and criticism. He died in 1991.

ONE WET JANUARY night, some six months after they had met, young Morgan Myles, our county librarian, was seated in the doctor's pet armchair, on one side of the doctor's fire, digesting the pleasant memory of a lavish dinner, while leafing the pages of a heavy photographic album and savouring a warm brandy. From across the hearth the doctor was looking admiringly at his long, ballooning Gaelic head when, suddenly, Morgan let out a cry of delight.

'Good Lord, Frank! There's a beautiful boy! One of Raphael's little angels.' He held up the open book for Frank to see. 'Who was he?'

The doctor looked across at it and smiled.

'Me. Aged twelve. At school in Mount Saint Bernard.'

'That's in England. I didn't know you went to school in England'.

'Alas!'

Morgan glanced down at twelve, and up at sixty.

'It's not possible, Frank!'

The doctor raised one palm six inches from the arm of his chair and let it fall again.

'It so happened that I was a ridiculously beautiful child.'

'Your mother must have been gone about you. And,' with a smile, 'the girls too.'

'I had no interest in girls. Nor in boys either, though by your smile you seem to say so. But there was one boy who took a considerable interest in me.'

Morgan at once lifted his nose like a pointer. At this period of his life he had rested from writing poetry and was trying to write short stories. For weeks he had read nothing but

Maupassant. He was going to out-Maupassant Maupassant. He was going to write stories that would make poor old Maupassant turn as green as the grass on his grave.

'Tell me about it,' he ordered. 'Tell me every single detail.'

'There is nothing to it. Or at any rate, as I now know, nothing abnormal. But, at that age!' – pointing with his pipe-stem. 'I was as innocent as . . . Well, as innocent as a child of twelve! Funny that you should say that about Raphael's angels. At my preparatory school here – it was a French order – Sister Angélique used to call me her *petit ange*, because, she said, I had "*une tête d'ange et une voix d'ange.*" She used to make me sing solo for them at Benediction, dressed in a red soutane, a white lacy surplice and a purple bow tie.

'After that heavenly place Mount Saint Bernard was ghastly. Mobs of howling boys. Having to play games; rain, hail or snow. I was a funk at games. When I'd see a fellow charging me at rugger I'd at once pass the ball or kick for touch. I remember the coach cursing me. "Breen, you're a bloody little coward, there are boys half your weight on this field who wouldn't do a thing like that." And the constant discipline. The constant priestly distrust. Watching us like jail warders.'

'Can you give me an example of that?' Morgan begged. 'Mind you, you could have had that, too, in Ireland. Think of Clongowes. It turns up in Joyce. And he admired the Jesuits!'

'Yes, I can give you an example. It will show you how innocent I was. A month after I entered Mount Saint Bernard I was so miserable that I decided to write to my mother to take me away. I knew that every letter had to pass under the eyes of the Prefect of Discipline, so I wrote instead to Sister Angélique asking her to pass on the word to my mother. The next day old Father George Lee – he's long since dead – summoned me to his study. "Breen!" he said darkly, holding up my unfortunate letter "you have tried to do a very underhand thing, something for which I could punish you severely. Why did you write this letter *in French*?"' The doctor sighed. 'I was a very truthful little boy. My mother had brought me up to be truthful simply by never punishing me for anything I honestly owned up to. I said "I wrote it in French, sir, because I hoped you wouldn't be able to understand it." He turned his face away from me but I could tell from his shoulders that he was laughing. He did not cane me, he just tore up the letter, told me never to try to deceive him again, and sent me packing with my tail between my legs.'

'The old bastard!' Morgan said sympathetically, thinking of the lonely little boy.

'No, no! He was a nice old man. And a good classical scholar, I later discovered. But that day as I walked down the long corridor, with all its photographs of old boys who had made good, I felt the chill of the prison walls!'

'But this other boy?' Morgan insinuated. 'Didn't his friendship help at all?'

The doctor rose and stood with his back to the fire staring fixedly in front of him.

(He rises, Morgan thought, his noble eyes shadowed. No! God damn it, no! Not noble. Shadowed? Literary word. Pensive? Blast it, that's worse. 'Pensive eve!' Romantic fudge. His eyes are dark as a rabbit's droppings. That's got it! In his soul . . . Oh, Jase!)

'Since I was so lonely I suppose he *must* have helped. But he was away beyond me. Miles above me. He was a senior. He was the captain of the school.'

'His name,' Morgan suggested, 'was, perhaps, Cyril?'

'We called him Bruiser. I would rather not tell you his real name.'

'Because he is still alive,' Morgan explained, 'and remembers you vividly to this day.'

'He was killed at the age of twenty.'

'In the war! In the heat of battle.'

'By a truck in Oxford. Two years after he went up there from Mount Saint Bernard. I wish I knew what happened to him in those two years. I can only hope that before he died he found a girl.'

'A girl? I don't follow. Oh yes! Of course, yes, I take your point.'

(He remembers with tenderness? No. With loving kindness!

No! With benevolence? Dammit, no! With his wonted chivalry
to women? But he remembered irritably that the old man sitting
opposite to him was a bachelor. And a virgin?)

'What happened between the pair of ye? "Brothers and companions in tribulation on the isle that is called Patmos"?'

The doctor snorted.

'Brothers? I have told you I was twelve. Bruiser was eighteen. The captain of the school. Captain of the rugby team.
Captain of the tennis team. First in every exam. Tops. Almost
a man. I looked up to him as a shining hero. I never understood
what he saw in me. I have often thought since that he may
have been amused by my innocence. Like the day he said to
me, "I suppose, Rosy," that was my nickname, I had such rosy
cheeks, "suppose you think you are the best-looking fellow in
the school?" I said, "No, I don't, Bruiser. I think there's one
fellow better looking than me, Jimmy Simcox."'

'Which he, of course, loyally refused to believe!'

The old doctor laughed heartily.

'He laughed heartily.'

'A queer sense of humour!'

'I must confess I did not at the time see the joke. Another
day he said, "Would you like, Rosy, to sleep with me?"'

Morgan's eyes opened wide. Now they were getting down
to it.

'I said, "Oh, Bruiser, I don't think you would like that at all.
I'm an awful chatterbox in bed. Whenever I sleep with my Uncle
Tom he's always saying to me, 'Will you, for God's sake, stop
your bloody gabble and let me sleep.'" He laughed for five
minutes at that.'

'I don't see much to laugh at. He should have sighed. I will
make him sigh. Your way makes him sound a queer hawk. And
nothing else happened between ye but this sort of innocent
gabble? Or are you keeping something back? Hang it, Frank,
there's no story at all in this!'

'Oh, he used sometimes take me on his lap. Stroke my bare
knee. Ruffle my hair. Kiss me.'

'How did you like that?'

'I made nothing of it. I was used to being kissed by my elders

– my mother, my bachelor uncles, Sister Angélique, heaps of people.' The doctor laughed. 'I laugh at it now. But his first kiss! A few days before, a fellow named Calvert said to me, "Hello, pretty boy, would you give me a smuck?" I didn't know what a smuck was. I said, "I'm sorry, Calvert, but I haven't got one." The story must have gone around the whole school. The next time I was alone with Bruiser he taunted me. I can hear his angry, toploftical English voice. "You are an innocent mug, Rosy! A smuck is a kiss. Would you let *me* kiss you?" I said, "Why not?" He put his arm around my neck in a vice and squashed his mouth to my mouth, hard, sticky. I thought I'd choke. "O Lord," I thought, "this is what he gets from playing rugger. This is a rugger kiss." And, I was thinking, "His poor mother! Having to put up with this from him every morning and every night." When he let me go, he said, "Did you like that?" Not wanting to hurt his feelings I said, imitating his English voice, "It was all right, Bruiser! A bit like ruggah, isn't it?" He laughed again and said, "All right? Well, never mind. I shan't rush you."'

Morgan waved impatiently.

'Look here, Frank! I want to get the background to all this. The telling detail, you know. "The little actual facts" as Stendhal called them. You said the priests watched you all like hawks. The constant discipline, you said. The constant priestly distrust. How did ye ever manage to meet alone?'

'It was very simple. He was the captain of the school. The apple of their eye. He could fool them. He knew the ropes. After all, he had been there for five years. I remember old Father Lee saying to me once, "You are a very lucky boy, Breen, it's not every junior that the captain of the school would take an interest in. You ought to feel very proud of his friendship." We used to have a secret sign about our meetings. Every Wednesday morning when he would be walking out of chapel, leading the procession, if that day was all right for us he used to put his right hand in his pocket. If for any reason it was not all right he would put his left hand in his pocket. I was always on the aisle of the very last row. Less than the dust. Watching for the sign like a hawk. We had a double check. I'd then find a note in my overcoat in the cloakroom. All it ever said was, "The same place." He was very careful. He only took calculated risks. If he had lived he would have made a marvellous politician, soldier or diplomat.'

'And where would ye meet? I know! By the river. Or in the woods? "Enter these enchanted woods ye who dare!"'

'No river. No woods. There was a sort of dirty old trunk room upstairs, under the roof, never used. A rather dark place with only one dormer window. It had double doors. He used to lock the outside one. There was a big cupboard there – for cricket bats or something. "If anyone comes," he told me, "you will have time to pop in there." He had it all worked out. Cautious man! I had to be even more cautious, stealing up there alone. One thing that made it easier for us was that I was so much of a junior and he was so very much of a senior, because, you see, those innocent guardians of ours had the idea that the real danger lay between the seniors and the middles, or the middles and the juniors, but never between the seniors and the juniors. They kept the seniors and the middles separated by iron bars and stone walls. Any doctor could have told them that in cold climates like ours the really dangerous years are not from fifteen up but from eighteen to anything, up or down. It simply never occurred to them that any senior could possibly be interested in any way in a junior. I, of course, had no idea of what he was up to. I had not even reached the age of puberty. In fact I honestly don't believe he quite knew himself what he was up to.'

'But, dammit, you must have had some idea! The secrecy, the kissing, alone, up there in that dim, dusty boxroom, not a sound but the wind in the slates.'

'Straight from the nuns? *Un petit ange*? I thought it was all just pally fun.'

Morgan clapped his hands.

'I've got it! An idyll! Looking out dreamily over the fields from that dusty dormer window? That's it, that's the ticket. Did you ever read that wonderful story by Maupassant – it's called *An Idyll* – about two young peasants meeting in a train, a poor, hungry young fellow who has just left home, and a girl with her first baby. He looked so famished that she took pity on him like a mother, opened her blouse and gave him her breast. When he finished he said, "That was my first meal in three days." Frank! You are telling me the most beautiful story I ever heard in my whole life.'

'You think so?' the doctor said morosely. 'I think he was going through hell all that year. At eighteen? On the threshold of manhood? In love with a child of twelve? That is, if you will allow that a youth of eighteen may suffer as much from love as a man twenty years older. To me the astonishing thing is that he did so well all that year at his studies and at sports. Killing the pain of it, I suppose? Or trying to? But the in-between? What went on in the poor devil in-between?'

Morgan sank back dejectedly.

'I'm afraid this view of the course doesn't appeal to me at all. All I can see is the idyll idea. After all, I mean, nothing happened!'

Chafing, he watched his friend return to his armchair, take another pipe from the rack, fill it slowly and ceremoniously from a black tobacco jar and light it with care. Peering through the nascent smoke, Morgan leaned slowly forward.

'Or did something happen?'

'Yes,' the doctor resumed quietly. 'Every year, at the end of the last term, the departing captain was given a farewell dinner. I felt sad that morning because we had not met for a whole week. And now, in a couple of days we would be scattered and I would never see him again.'

'Ha, ha! You see, you too were in love!'

'Of course I was, I was hooked,' the doctor said with more than a flicker of impatience. 'However . . . That Wednesday as he passed me in the chapel aisle he put his right hand in his pocket. I belted off at once to my coat hanging in the cloakroom and found his note. It said, "At five behind the senior tennis court." I used always to chew up his *billet doux* immediately I read it. He had ordered me to. When I read this one my mouth went so dry with fear that I could hardly swallow it. He had put me in an awful fix. To meet alone in the boxroom was risky enough, but for anybody to climb over the wall into the seniors' grounds was unheard of. If I was caught I would certainly be flogged. I might very well be expelled. And what would my mother and father think of me then? On top of all I was in duty bound to be with all the other juniors at prep at five o'clock, and to be absent from studies without permission was another crime of the first order. After lunch I went to the Prefect of Studies and asked him to excuse me from prep because I had an awful headache. He wasn't taken in one bit. He just ordered me to be at my place in prep as usual. The law! Orders! Tyranny! There was only one thing for it, to dodge prep, knowing well that whatever else happened later I would pay dearly for it.'

'And what about him? He knew all this. And he knew that if *he* was caught they couldn't do anything to him. The captain of the school? Leaving in a few days? It was very unmanly of him to put you to such a risk. His character begins to emerge, and not very pleasantly. Go on!'

The doctor did not need the encouragement. He looked like a small boy sucking a man's pipe.

'I waited until the whole school was at study and then I crept out into the empty grounds. At that hour the school, the grounds, everywhere, was as silent as the grave. Games over. The priests at their afternoon tea. Their charges safely under control. I don't know how I managed to get over that high wall, but when I fell scrambling down on the other side, there he was. "You're bloody late," he said crossly. "How did you get out of prep? What excuse did you give?" When I told him he flew into a rage. "You little fool!" he growled. "You've balloxed it all up. They'll know you dodged. They'll give you at least ten on the backside for this." He was carrying a cane. Seniors at Saint Bernard's did carry walking-sticks. I'd risked so much for him, and now he was so angry with me that I burst into tears. He put his arms around me – I thought, to comfort me – but after that all I remember from that side of the wall was him pulling down my short pants, holding me tight, I felt something hard, like his cane, and the next thing I knew I was wet. I thought I was bleeding. I thought he was gone mad. When I smelled whiskey I thought, "He is trying to kill me." "Now run," he ordered me, "and get back to prep as fast as you can."'

Morgan covered his eyes with his hand.

'He shoved me up to the top of the wall. As I peered around I heard his footsteps running away. I fell down into the shrubs on the other side and I immediately began to vomit and vomit. There was a path beside the shrubs. As I lay there puking I saw a black-soutaned priest approaching slowly along the path. He was an old, old priest named Constable. I did not stir. Now, I felt, I'm for it. This is the end. I am certain he saw me but he passed by as if he had not seen me. I got back to the study hall, walked up to the Prefect's desk and told him I was late because I had been sick. I must have looked it because he at once sent me to the matron in the infirmary. She took my temperature and put me to bed. It was summer. I was the only inmate of the ward. One of those evenings of prolonged daylight.'

'You poor little bugger!' Morgan groaned in sympathy.

'A detail comes back to me. It was the privilege of seniors attending the captain's dinner to send down gifts to the juniors' table – sweets, fruit, a cake, for a younger brother or some special protégé. Bruiser ordered a whole white blancmange with a rose cherry on top of it to be sent to me. He did not know I was not in the dining hall so the blancmange was brought up to me in the infirmary. I vomited again when I saw it. The matron, with my more than ready permission, took some of it for herself and sent the rest back to the juniors' table, "with Master Breen's compliments." I am sure it was gobbled greedily. In the morning the doctor saw me and had me sent home to Ireland immediately.'

'Passing the buck,' said Morgan sourly, and they both looked at a coal that tinkled from the fire into the fender.

The doctor peered quizzically at the hissing coal.

'Well?' he slurred around his pipe-stem. 'There is your lovely idyll.'

Morgan did not lift his eyes from the fire. Under a down-draught from the chimney a few specks of grey ashes moved clockwise on the worn hearth. He heard a car hissing past the house on the wet macadam. His eyebrows had gone up over his spectacles in two Gothic arches.

'I'm afraid,' he said at last, 'it is no go. Not even a Maupassant could have made a story out of it. And Chekhov wouldn't have wanted to try. Unless the two boys lived on, and on, and met years afterwards in Moscow or Yalta or somewhere, each with a wife and a squad of kids, and talked of everything except their schooldays. You are sure you never did hear of him, or from him, again?'

'Never! Apart from the letter he sent with the blancmange and the cherry.'

Morgan at once leaped alive.

'A letter? Now we are on to something! What did he say to you in it? Recite every word of it to me! Every syllable. I'm sure you have not forgotten one word of it. No!' he cried excitedly. 'You have kept it. Hidden away somewhere all these years. Friendship surviving everything. Fond memories of . . .'

The doctor sniffed.

'I tore it into bits unread and flushed it down the WC.'

'Oh, God blast you, Frank!' Morgan roared. 'That was the climax of the whole thing. The last testament. The final revelation. The summing up. The *document humain*. And you "just tore it up!" Let's reconstruct it. "Dearest Rosy, As long as I live I will never forget your innocence, your sweetness, your . . ."'

'My dear boy!' the doctor protested mildly. 'I am sure he wrote nothing of the sort. He was much too cautious, and even the captain was not immune from censorship. Besides, sitting in public glory at the head of the table? It was probably a place-card with something on the lines of, "All my sympathy, sorry, better luck next term." A few words, discreet, that I could translate any way I liked.'

Morgan raised two despairing arms.

'If that was all the damned fellow could say to you after that appalling experience, he was a character of no human significance whatever, a shallow creature, a mere agent, a catalyst, a cad. The story becomes your story.'

'I must admit I have always looked on it in that way. After all it did happen to me . . . Especially in view of the sequel.'

'Sequel? What sequel? I can't have sequels. In a story you always have to observe unity of time, place and action. Everything happening at the one time, in the same place, between the same people. *The Necklace. Boule de Suif. The Maison Tellier.* The examples are endless. What was this bloody sequel?'

The doctor puffed thoughtfully.

'In fact there were two sequels. Even three sequels. And all of them equally important.'

'In what way were they important?'

'It was rather important to me that after I was sent home I was in the hospital for four months. I could not sleep. I had constant nightmares, always the same one – me running through a wood and him running after me with his cane. I could not keep down my food. Sweating hot. Shivering cold. The vomiting was recurrent. I lost weight. My mother was beside herself with worry. She brought doctor after doctor to me, and only one of them spotted it, an old, blind man from Dublin named Whiteside. He said, "That boy has had some kind of shock," and in private he asked me if some boy, or man, had interfered with me. Of course, I denied it hotly.'

'I wish I was a doctor,' Morgan grumbled. 'So many writers were doctors. Chekhov. William Carlos Williams. Somerset Maugham. A. J. Cronin.'

The doctor ignored the interruption.

'The second sequel was that when I at last went back to Mount Saint Bernard my whole nature changed. Before that I had been dreamy and idle. During my last four years at school I became their top student. I suppose psychologists would say nowadays that I compensated by becoming extroverted. I became a crack cricket player. In my final year I was the college champion at billiards. I never became much good at rugger but I no longer minded playing it and I wasn't all that bad. If I'd been really tops at it, or at boxing, or swimming, I might very well have ended up as captain of the school. Like him.'

He paused for so long that Morgan became alerted again.

'And the third sequel?' he prompted.

'I really don't know why I am telling you all this. I have never told a soul about it before. Even still I find it embarrassing to think about, let alone to talk about. When I left Mount Saint Bernard and had taken my final at the College of Surgeons I went on to Austria to continue my medical studies. In Vienna I fell in with a young woman. The typical blonde Fräulein, handsome, full of life, outgoing, wonderful physique, what you might call an outdoor girl, free as the wind, frank as the daylight. She taught me skiing. We used to go mountain climbing together. I don't believe she knew the meaning of the word fear. She was great fun and the best of company. Her name was Brigitte. At twenty-six she was already a woman of the world. I was twenty-four, and as innocent of women as . . . as . . . '

To put him at his ease Morgan conceded his own embarrassing confession.

'As I am, at twenty-four.'

'You might think that what I am going to mention could not happen to a doctor, however young but, on our first night in bed, immediately she touched my body I vomited. I pretended to her that I had eaten something that upset me. You can imagine how nervous I felt all through the next day wondering what was going to happen that night. Exactly the same thing happened that night. I was left with no option. I told her the whole miserable story of myself and Bruiser twelve years before. As I started to tell her I had no idea how she was going to take it. Would she leave me in disgust? Be coldly sympathetic? Make a mock of me? Instead, she became wild with what I can only call gleeful curiosity. "Tell me more, *mein Schätzerl*," she begged. "Tell me everything! What exactly did he do to you? I want to know it all. This is *wunderbar*. Tell me! Oh do tell me!" I did tell her, and on the spot everything became perfect between us. We made love like Trojans. That girl saved my sanity.'

In a silence Morgan gazed at him. Then coldly:

'Well, of course, this is another story altogether. I mean I don't see how I can possibly blend these two themes together. I mean no writer worth his salt can say things like, "Twelve long years passed over his head. Now read on." I'd have to leave her out of it. She is obviously irrelevant to the main theme. Whatever the hell the main theme is.' Checked by an ironical glance he poured the balm. 'Poor Frank! I foresee it all. You adored her. You wanted madly to marry her. Her parents objected. You were star-crossed lovers. You had to part.'

'I never thought of marrying the bitch. She had the devil's temper. We had terrible rows. Once we threw plates at one another. We would have parted anyway. She was a lovely girl but quite impossible. Anyway, towards the end of that year my father fell seriously ill. Then my mother fell ill. Chamberlain was in Munich that year. Everybody knew the war was coming. I came back to Ireland that autumn. For keeps.'

'But you tried again and again to find out what happened to her. And failed. She was swallowed up in the fire and smoke of war. I don't care what you say, Frank, you *must* have been heartbroken.'

The doctor lifted a disinterested shoulder.

'A student's love affair? Of thirty and more years ago?'

No! He had never inquired. Anyway if she was alive now what would she be but a fat, blowsy old baggage of sixty-three? Morgan, though shocked, guffawed dutifully. There was the real Maupassant touch. In his next story a touch like that! The clock on the mantelpiece whirred and began to tinkle the hour. Morgan opened the album for a last look at the beautiful child. Dejectedly he slammed it shut, and rose.

'There is too much in it,' he declared. 'Too many strands. Your innocence. His ignorance. Her worldliness. Your forgetting her. Remembering him. Confusion and bewilderment. The ache of loss? Loss? *Lost Innocence*? Would that be a theme? But nothing rounds itself off. You are absolutely certain you never heard of him again after that day behind the tennis courts?'

They were both standing now. The rain brightly spotted the midnight window.

'In my first year in Surgeons, about three years after Bruiser was killed, I lunched one day with his mother and my mother at the Shelbourne Hotel in Dublin. By chance they had been educated at the same convent in England. They talked about him. My mother said, "Frank here knew him in Mount Saint

Bernard." His mother smiled condescendingly at me. "No, Frank. You were too young to have met him." "Well," I said, "I did actually speak to him a couple of times, and he was always very kind to me." She said sadly, "He was kind to everybody. Even to perfect strangers."'

Morgan thrust out an arm and a wildly wagging finger.

'Now, *there* is a possible shape! Strangers to begin. Strangers to end! What a title! *Perfect Strangers.*' He blew out a long, impatient breath and shook his head. 'But that is a fourth sequel! I'll think about it,' as if he were bestowing a great favour. 'But it isn't a story as it stands. I would have to fake it up a lot. Leave out things. Simplify. Mind you, I could still see it as an idyll. Or I could if only you hadn't torn up his last, farewell letter, which I still don't believe at all said what you said it said. If only we had that letter I bet you any money we could haul in the line and land our fish.'

The doctor knocked out the dottle of his pipe against the fireguard, and throating a yawn looked at the fading fire.

'I am afraid I have been boring you with my reminiscences.'

'Not at all, Frank! By no means! I was most interested in your story. And I do honestly mean what I said. I really will think about it. I promise. Who was it,' he asked in the hall as he shuffled into his overcoat and his muffler and moved out to the wet porch, the tail of his raincoat rattling in the wind, 'said that the two barbs of childhood are its innocence and its ignorance?' He failed to remember. He threw up his hand. 'Ach, to hell with it for a story! It's all too bloody convoluted for me. And to hell with Maupassant, too! That vulgarian oversimplified everything. And he's full of melodrama. A besotted Romantic at heart! Like all the bloody French.'

The doctor peeped out at him through three inches of door. Morgan, standing with his back to the arrowy night, suddenly lit up as if a spotlight had shone on his face.

'I know what I'll do with it!' he cried. 'I'll turn it into a poem about a seashell!'

'About a seashell?'

'Don't you remember?' In his splendid voice Morgan chanted above the rain and wind: – '"*A curious child holding to his ear /*

The convolutions of a smoothlipped seashell / To which, in silence hushed . . ." How the hell does it go? ". . . *his very soul listened to the murmurings of his native sea."* It's as clear as daylight, man! You! Me! Everyone! Always wanting to launch a boat in search of some far-off golden sands. And something or somebody always holding us back. "The Curious Child." *There's* a title!'

'Ah, well!' the doctor said, peering at him blankly. 'There it is! As your friend Maupassant might have said, *"C'est la vie!"'*

'La vie!' Morgan roared, now on the gravel beyond the porch, indifferent to the rain pelting on his bare head. 'That trollop? She's the one who always bitches up everything. No, Frank! For me there is only one fountain of truth, one beauty, one perfection. Art, Frank! Art! And bugger *la vie!'*

At the untimely verb the doctor's drooping eyelids shot wide open.

'It is a view,' he said courteously and let his hand be shaken fervently a dozen times.

'I can never repay you, Frank. A splendid dinner. A wonderful story. Marvellous inspiration. I must fly. I'll be writing it all night!' – and vanished head down through the lamplit rain, one arm uplifted triumphantly behind him.

The doctor slowly closed his door, carefully locked it, bolted it, tested it, and prudently put its chain in place. He returned to his sitting-room, picked up the cinder that had fallen into the hearth and tossed it back into the remains of his fire, then stood, hand on mantelpiece, looking down at it. What a marvellous young fellow! He would be tumbling and tossing all night over that story. Then he would be around in the morning apologising, and sympathizing, saying, 'Of course, Frank, I do realise that it was a terribly sad experience for both of you.'

Gazing at the ashes his whole being filled with memory after memory like that empty vase in his garden being slowly filled by drops of rain.

THE RETURN

EDNA O'BRIEN

EDNA O'BRIEN

Edna O'Brien was born in Co. Clare in 1930. Love in all its forms has been the dominant theme of her many novels and short stories since her celebrated first novel, *The Country Girls*, appeared in 1960. Since 1959 she has lived in London, which, with Co. Clare, has been the setting of most of her work.

THE LIGHT IS stunning, being of the palest filtered gold, and the clouds are like vast confections made of spun sugar, ruminative orbs that seem to stand in the air, to dally, as if they were being held and willed by some invisible puppeteer. Streams of sunshine issue over the fields and the earth far below – fields that have been mown, others that have been harvested, and still others exuding a ravishing life-giving ochre colour. Sometimes a range of mountains comes into view and the peaks covered with last year's snow shine with an awesome silverwhite brightness. The little houses, the winding rivers, and the ordered fields seem detached from the currents of everyday life, like objects planted in an unpeopled world. All is suspended, and I think how harmonious a life can be. 'I do not want to land,' I say, and wonder if the force and fierceness of the airliner as it mows through the air has the same impact as the plow piercing the earth and slicing a passage through it. As I wend my way home, all sorts of thoughts come to mind, idle and drifting like thistledown. For no reason I think of a peculiar and timid woman who featured in my childhood and who used to sit at her piano and sing whenever visitors descended on her. Though they complained about her screeching voice, they were glad that she performed for them, that she allowed for no gaps in the conversation, and that she gave them something to mock. One year she acquired a pair of peacocks, of whom she was absurdly proud, even boastful. The female contracted an ailment by which she kept her eggs embedded inside her, and, though wanting to, she could not give lay. The mistress was childless, too, and this caused her to cry when she saw the girls decked out in their gauzy veils and the boys, like little men in new suits, in the chapel at their First Holy Communion. Suddenly I think of a peacock's feather and in its centre an eye so blue, so riveting, that I am reminded of those china eyes that they sold on my holiday island, supposed to keep evil away. This blue is metallic and belongs to a zone in the bowels of the sea, where the spirits of the Nereids are said to dwell. The sea by which I sat and lulled myself on my holiday did not seem at all ominous. It was always inviting, and in the scorching town it was as soothing and beneficial as a baptismal font. Life there would have been intolerable without it. The town itself was seething with heat and the small houses were like white cubes that bristled in the heat. The only haven was inside the Byzantine church, whose dun-gold quiet suggested dusk – as dusk in which moths flew about and the faces of saints carved on burnished wood looked out at visitors with a resigned and temperate beauty.

A gnarled old beggar woman presided at the church door and upon receiving a coin she ranted in ecstasy, delivering a mixture of dirge and song. The narrow cobbled streets were free of automobiles, and in the square thin well-bred donkeys were tethered to the one tree, ready to cart the scalding visitors up the steep hill to the acropolis, and if necessary down again. Once I went there at evening time and it was as if its pillars, its spaces, and its buff stone fragments looking out to sea defied every other standard of beauty and composure. I did not do much sightseeing. It was the harbour to which I veered – the harbour with a life that varied with the hours, so that in the morning breeze its ripples were like minnows on the surface and, later on, its blue was so hard, so glittering, it resembled priceless jewellery. I used to love to watch the liners gliding in, suave and white in comparison with the ferry, which looked clumsy, like a two-decker bus. Then there were the pedal boats with their sedate passengers, and all of a sudden there would be the single sail of a surf boat, like the torn wing of a giant butterfly, dipping down as some embarrassed novice lost his bearings. Two rival groups of children made sand-castles. Walking by them, I would suddenly think of my lover's children and wonder pointlessly what games they were playing on their summer vacation. I was trying to forget him, or at least to suspend the mixed memories of our times together. The two years I had known him had brought such an artful combination of pain and pleasure that I welcomed a rest, and while forbidding myself to think of him I settled for happy ruminations about his children. I imagined how I would woo them with boiled sweets and various small packets containing whistles and water pistols and other distractions. I wondered what they looked like and if they had his eyes – eyes that can be so piercing or so mild, depending on his mood, eyes that almost always contradict the cursoriness of his manner and lead one to believe that things are sweeter than he dares to admit. I shall not meet them. It is true that I have accepted all the rules and all the embargoes. Of course these rules have not been expressly stated, but one knows them, for they are in the air, like motes. It is the same with the future. He and I do not discuss it. It is as if we were prisoners – two cloistered people for whom each meeting is the only one they can count on. Once he raised the question of our past. He said we should have met when we were both younger, both fresher. I do not agree. I believe we should have met when we met, but I did not voice this, because I have acquired the habit of saying little – at least, little of any moment. Perhaps because there is so much to say. Or perhaps we do not venture, lest our frail edifice should topple. I cannot help but think of the sand-castles the children make with such resolve and such pugnaciousness, and yet when they are called in at dusk they know that the sea in all its vehemence will wash their efforts away. And yet the next day they commence again with exactly the same hope and the same gusto.

While I was on the island, I believed that I had become indifferent to him, but now as I head for home I am not nearly so confident. As we fly across Europe, I can feel the chill in the air, and from time to time I put my hand up to lower the draught through the ventilator. I say to myself, 'This is the air of Yugoslavia,' or 'This is the air of Italy,' or 'Soon it will be the air of Belgium,' and I think what a marvel to tread the air of several countries, to have one's body borne forward while one's mind harks back to another place. I did not want to leave my little villa. I felt such a pang, and I thought, Why abandon all this beauty and why jeopardize this hard-won harmony? The villa, though secluded, had a fine view of the bay, a terrace with splashes of bright bougainvillaea in clay urns, and at night the smell of orange blossom was so strong and so heady that it was like another presence, pleasing and drugging the senses. Then, in the morning, the flutes of morning glory, so blue and so ethereal, were like heralding angels. Then, too, life in the harbour recommenced. The visitors would file down the dusty tracks and appoint themselves under the straw umbrellas, and soon there would be bodies, or rather, heads, bobbing in the water alongside the pink buoys, as the sun became hotter and hotter and the sand began to glisten, then sizzle.

Down there, though I was among people, I had a sense of space, of aloofness. The sun shone with such a merciless dedication that even one chink in the straw umbrella could lead to a bad burn. It was a question of lathering oneself with cream, taking a dip, and then hurrying back to the shelter that seemed like a little ark redolent of straw. Across the harbour there were two mountains facing each other, and each in turn had the benefit of the sun. When one was bathed in gold, the other was grey and pitiful, like a widow gathering her weeds about her for the night. This contrast brought to mind his wife's situation and my own: one in a state of happiness at the other's expense, yet the happy one always knowing the precariousness of her situation, just as the mountains had to settle for alternations of light and dark. Still, I was able to banish those thoughts, to rout out those daggers and apply my eyes and thence my mind to nature. In the glaze of sunshine one could wrest one's mind from thought, and it was just like pulling a blind down and shading a room. It was a sparse island, with no crops and with stunted trees that teetered on the barren slopes. There were no dogs, and the cats were thin and ratlike.

When evening came, I would sit on my terrace admiring the stars, so clear and so particular, like flowers on an immense soft navy-blue down. Music from the two rival discothèques and the ceaseless mechanical creak of the cicadas were the only

jarring sounds. The lights from the other houses and the bracelet of lights from the three restaurants reminded me of the life
of the town – a life that I could partake of had I the inclination.
But I did not stir. I used to sit there and think that I was free
of him, and tell myself that I had arrived at that sane and happy
state of detachment. Indeed, had he sent a telegram to say that
he was arriving, I would have sent one back to say that it was
impossible. I did not want him there – not then. But now, as I
near home and I see precisely the soft spill of his brown hair
or one hand in his trousers pocket as he enters my house
abruptly, or a look that for all its prurience is also priestly, I
know that I am being dragged back to a former state, and it is
as if the reins have slipped from my grasp. These forgotten
gestures start up a rush of other moments that I can scarcely
call memories, since they are more palpable and more real than
the passenger next to me. I see the moment when my lover
looked at my new dress on its hanger, looked at it with such
longing, then reached out almost to touch it, as if imagining or
dreading the delight that it would give others to see me in it.
For some reason I am reminded of dull suburban gardens and
how from packets of spring seeds so randomly scattered the
hollyhocks come up tall and defiant, parading their strength and
causing one to think that nature is indeed sovereign. In my
garden last spring it was a tulip, a red tulip with a black centre,
and when the petals opened and I saw its fiendish black face it
was like seeing a caricature of a painted devil. 'Oh, you little
strange devil,' I used to say to it, and wonder how it came to
be there – if the birds had planted it or if its seed was in the bag
belonging to the Breton hawker who sells onions. He knocks on
my door three or four times a year, and, holding the bunches
of onions aloft, he is like a bishop waving a censer. In the
morning light the skins are a beautiful pink, like pearls that have
been lightly tinted, whereas in contrast the garlic he carries is
the colour of raw dough. He always reeks of cognac, and out
of embarrassment or pity I give him another, and then fret over
his progress on his push bicycle. One time he asked me if he
could leave an empty sack in the garden, and it is possible that
as he shook it out the seed of the red tulip lodged there.

Last night I was free. Last night I was certain that I had
conquered rashness, and today I am proven wrong. Last night
something happened to strengthen my conviction, to make me
thankful for my independence. I wanted to buy some figs to
bring home, so I went on an excursion to the town. You can't
imagine how I avoided the town for the whole week. It was
like a furnace down there, with people bumping into each other
and more people spilling from coaches and clamouring for cold
drinks and souvenirs and shade. I found a shop away from the
main square, where there were all kinds of fruit, including the
figs that I had hoped for. There were two kinds of figs, and,
guessing my dilemma, the proprietor, who was pale and
extremely gentle, told me to help myself. He touched my wrist
as he gave me a paper bag, and the touch seemed to say, 'Be
generous. Take both kinds.' After I had paid him, I dallied for
a moment, though I do not know why. Perhaps I was a little
lonely at not having spoken to anyone for a week, or perhaps
I was rehearsing my re-emergence into the world. All of a sudden, he did a charming thing. He took a little liqueur bottle from
a glass case and opened it with one wrench. It was a red liqueur,
like a cordial, and we drank it in turn. As other customers came
in, he weighed tomatoes or peaches or whatever, and spoke
to them in English or German or Italian, then resumed his
conversation with me. He spoke of the contrast between life
on that island in the summer and in the winter. All or nothing,
he said. In the summer he worked eighteen or twenty hours a
day, and in the winter he did indoor tasks, such as painting or
carpentry, and played cards with the men in the café. An old
woman came into the shop, laughing and licking her lips. She
was not the customary old woman in black, with a bony face
and legs like spindles; rather, she was fat and lascivious. She
turned her back to me and pointed to her open zipper, then
gestured to me to do it up. I tried, but it was broken. She kept
gesturing and laughing, and I think in reality she asked so that
he and I could see her flesh. Her flesh was soft and brown, like
a mousse. Some children came in and stepped behind the counter to help themselves to cold drinks from the refrigerator, and
I assumed that they were his children or his nieces and

nephews. He must have always avoided the sun to have a face so pale, and he had very beautiful smooth eyelids, which he kept lowered most of the time. He did not ask me to stay, but I felt that he did not want me to go just yet. I had already told him that I was leaving the following morning and that because of a bungle in my air ticket I had to go to another island, and he had smiled and said that with my colouring I would like the other island, as it was green and leafy. He liked it, he said. It was as if we had a bond, disposed as we were to a bit of shade, to tillage, and to fields. He pulled an airmail envelope from a new packet and started to draw on it in order to show me where the other island was. I had stepped behind the counter and was standing next to him, studying this funny little drawing, when a woman glided in and at once asked me sharply how the owner of my rented villa was. She was a small woman wearing canvas shoes, and everything about her was pinched and castigating.

'Your wife,' I said.

'My wife,' he said.

In an instant I saw their story; it was as if a seer had unfolded a scroll and told me how the man had come from the city, how he had married this thin woman, how the shop was in her name, and how he worked eighteen hours a day, had sired these lovely children, and was always watched. His wife gathered up a sheaf of the brown paper bags that were strewn all over the counter and started to put them in order, and by doing so she told him that he had no right to be slacking, that he had no right to be talking to foreign women. Then she sniffed the empty liqueur bottle and with a grunt tossed it towards the rubbish bin. Thinking that I would probably never see them again, I shook hands with them both and muttered something about the beauty of the island, as if to temper her spleen.

I went alone to the nearest restaurant, ordered a half bottle of white wine, and drank it slowly, and ordered grilled prawns, which I peeled and ate at my leisure, musing about this and that, thinking how lucky I was to be my own mistress, to be saved the terrible inclination of wanting to possess while being possessed, of being separated from myself while being host to another. I so relished my freedom that I even remarked to

myself how nice it was that no other fingers dabbled in the glass
finger bowl. I thought, I have arrived at a new state, a height
which is also a plateau. To drive the matter home, as I walked
up the hill to my secluded house I overheard an English couple
having a ghastly drunken row behind an open door. Four-letter
words were hurled from one to the other with such vehemence
and such virulence that at each utterance the selfsame word
carried different and mounting degrees of hatred; I was afraid
they would come to blows, and perhaps they did. I went and
sat on my terrace, and found to my surprise that a liner had
anchored for the night. Its tiny windows were like strips of
gold, and all of a sudden I was reminded of the interior of the
Byzantine church, and for some reason, alone in the hushed
night, I genuflected and said a prayer. Never had the bay
seemed so beautiful or so safe, with the pair of sable mountains
enfolding it. Now at last they were identical, consumed yet distinctive, in the dark. I delayed going to bed even though I knew
I must be up at five.

When I wakened this morning, the cocks had not yet begun
to crow. The driver came to collect my luggage, and we went
on tiptoe through the town, past all those tiny fortresses, with
owners bound in sleep and countless dreams. Driving along,
we witnessed the dawn, and at first sky and sea were merged,
a pearled vista so pale and so fragile that one knew that it could
– indeed, that it would – be vanquished. Its beauty brought to
mind every intrepid, virginal thing. Even as one looked it was
vanishing, or at least altering, becoming a vision or a passing
dream. The little churches perched on the hilltops were like
tiny beehives, and the earth gave off a breath of moisture and
repose. But it was to the sky one looked, and looking at it the
realization of my love came back to me in one unheralded burst
of sadness. Beauty and sadness must be what love is founded
on, I thought. Then the sky became rosier, the light seeming
to flaunt itself, no longer tentative, as a river of red shot across
the heavens, making a gash. The dawn itself was bleached and
milky, with scarcely any light at all, and the sun rose, shy and
timid, bringing that discharge of emotion inseparable from any
birth. At the airport, the driver and I had coffee, and then he

conveyed me to a small twin-engined airplane whereby I was whisked to that other island, which by comparison was tropical. There were white goats tethered in the fields next to the landing strip, and the sight of these and the little trees and shrubs reminded me of my native land. I had a four-hour wait, and so I sat outside on a step, and presently some young soldiers came to talk to me and tried to inveigle me to dance by putting on their transistor radio and performing some idiotic capers. They plied me with offers of coffee and cigarettes. They were dark, their dark eyes small and busy, and from the sun's constant glare they had wrinkled like raisins. Even then I did not believe that I was going home. I felt I would be detained there, and I did not in the least object.

It is evening when our plane lands. It is not dark, but it seems so in comparison with that far-off scorching island. It is as if all the sun has been snatched from here, and involuntarily I think of autumn and the hexagonal street lights in my square which will go on a fraction earlier each evening. My fellow-passengers and I wait for our luggage, stare at the monitor to see which bay our bags will arrive at, and sometimes looking at each other involuntarily look away, as if we have done wrong. We are slipping back into our old lives. He is not here, nor did I expect him to be, but it has started up, not quite as pain or fret but as a sense of resumption. Already I feel the imminence of his next visit, and I think how it will appear as if he had vacated the place only minutes before. The future looms, mirroring the selfsame patterns of the past – his occasional visits, the painful vigils in-between, the restraints we have imposed upon ourselves – and I wonder how much longer I shall be able to endure it.

THE COMPOUND ASSEMBLY
OF E. RICHTER

HUGO HAMILTON

HUGO HAMILTON

Hugo Hamilton was born in Dublin in 1953. His father was Irish and his mother German. He lived in Germany and Austria during the late 1970s and then returned to Dublin, working in the recording business and publishing. His first short stories appeared in 'New Irish Writing' in 1986 and he has since published two highly praised novels.

FRANK MURRAY WOKE up to the sound of hammering. He half hoped that the noise would abate or that sleep would win back its grip. But the window was open and the noise persisted. It quickly distinguished itself from any other sound as that of scaffolding. The enclosed courtyard amplified it. Even though Frank was on the fourth floor it seemed as if they were erecting scaffolding right outside his window. In Germany, nobody sleeps during the day. Even those who work at night lie in bed at their own peril in the morning.

He tried to shut the window without getting up. From his bed, or his mattress on the floor, he reached up and pushed on the frame with his fingers. He caught sight of the workmen in grey and blue overalls. They were further away than he thought. They were working on the opposite face of the court-yard. It wasn't enough to close out the noise and he had to reach further to lock the handle. In doing this, his body became uncovered. The duvet only covered half his thighs, breaking the nocturnal spell of warmth. His naked body, like sensitive photographic paper, had been exposed to daylight. He locked the window and drew himself back under the duvet. It turned steel into rubber.

He couldn't sleep again. He coiled his knees up and held his shoulders with his hands. The sound still penetrated the window. He stretched his legs and found both the bed and duvet were too short. It was useless. He resolved to get up.

Frank rehearsed the next ten minutes of the day in his mind. Going to the shop next door to buy some rolls and apricot jam. Opening the door of the apartment. Descending the stairs. Seeing the rows of mailboxes which faced him on the way down,

each with its metal door and small glass window through which
he might see a letter from home but which more often turned
out to be circulars and postal advertising which he then regularly
stuck into somebody else's letter box. Seeing that many of the
metal doors had been prised open by owners who'd lost their
keys. Checking with his longest fingers to make sure there
wasn't a letter from home which, whenever one did arrive, he
kept unopened in his pocket for hours, sometimes even till
evening when he would find a secluded pub where he could
read and slowly get drunk with his letter. Cautiously removing
his fingers from under the sharp metal door. Emerging out into
the courtyard where the climate is thick with work, shouts,
commands, hammering and where German workers belittle
each other with diligence. Seeing how far they had got with the
scaffolding. Walking through the outer door into the street.
Lifting one jar of apricot jam but then replacing it again in prefer-
ence for another brand.

On his way back from the shop carrying a white plastic bag,
Frank saw a woman's back beside the mailboxes. She had just
locked her metal door and begun to turn around. He had seen
her before in the same position. She was always locking her
letter box. The stairs were ahead of him. The rise between
the third and fourth step bore a warning. *Vorsicht*! On Tuesdays,
the stairs are freshly polished. On Tuesdays, the climate
indoors is clean but highly slippery.

With one foot already flung into the first part of his ascent,
Frank pronounced the obliged greeting clearly. *Guten Morgen*!
It was addressed at the woman's back and seemed to rebound
off her shoulders. It came back abbreviated. *Morgen*!

His feet had already passed the warning sign, entering the
second phase of ascent, taking steps in doubles. The plastic
bag with apricot jam and rolls swung forward in counterbalance.
His left foot had just pushed off the step when she addressed
him again from below.

'*Sind Sie der Herr der so schön die Flöte spielt?*' He stopped
and his left foot recanted. He turned and made a quick transla-
tion: – Are you the gentleman who so lovely the flute plays?
He brought back the other foot to the step below and fumbled

an answer. *Ja*! It was always a pleasure to hear comments about his music. It was always a compliment to be asked about his nationality. It was good to be Irish in Germany. As long as they didn't want to know about Northern Ireland or the EEh-Er-Ah (IRA). As long as they stuck to music or the cliffs of Moher or smoked salmon or Heinrich Böll or donkeys or red hair and freckles and the agrarian state.

Frank smiled over the banister at her and nodded to secure his answer. He welcomed any compliment. But she didn't smile back at him. She had clutched her keys to her chest and looked straight up at him. He waited for a moment to see if the question of nationality would arise. But there was something wrong with her expression. It held more accusation than admiration.

'Wenn ich diesen Lärm weiter höre, kommt die Polizei.' The last word was enough. If she heard any more of this noise, she would call the police. The sudden conversion of an admirer into an enemy had left him completely stunned and awkwardly poised on the stairs. His feet, drawn by compliment, were still subconsciously coming back down. Frank said nothing.

'Sie wohnen bei Evelyn Richter, nicht wahr?' He wasn't quite sure whether this was meant to confirm that he was living with Evelyn Richter or staying with Evelyn Richter. There was a big difference. Evelyn Richter was the name on his mailbox. That much was right. He was living in her apartment, but in his own separate room. Werner, Evelyn's boyfriend, was living with her.

Frank wasn't about to start explaining anything to the woman with the keys to her chest who had led him into a trap. The glare of her questions over the banisters had registered an insult with him and he turned to continue his climb with redoubled speed.

When Evelyn herself heard about the incident, she created too much of a fuss. At teatime that evening she became very excited.

'Unglaublich! It is unbelievable,' she said. She was laying the table at the time. She used wooden boards instead of plates. Her cutlery matched. She placed another board with an assortment of ham, sausage and cheese on the table. She had also

chopped some radishes which looked like white coins with red rims. Ten pfennig pieces.

'I will go to this woman and tell her she has nothing to say. She has not the right to say this to you. It is unbelievable.'

Evelyn shook her head. She had straight sandy hair which normally hung to one side. Whenever she looked at someone, she had the habit of slanting her head sideways.

'Wait! I will tell this to Werner when he comes. This woman will hear something from us.'

Frank rarely saw Evelyn's eyes because she wore tinted brown glasses. He was leaning against the radiator with his arms folded. She told him to sit down and placed the earthenware teapot on a candle-lit warmer. Frank asked where Werner was and heard he was visiting his mother. There was a small two-pronged fork lying along the board with the ham. It often looked so decorative that Frank didn't think he should disturb it. He lifted the fork and speared a slice of smoked ham, separating it from the next layer. Evelyn asked him to describe the woman.

'Ach, . . . this is Frau Klempner. We know this woman. She is always looking and talking to the *Hausmeister*.' Evelyn made a duck's beak with her hand to describe.

'Do you know this word, "*plappern*"?'

'It sounds very much like the word prattle in English,' Frank explained, thinking of yet another word, 'babble'. Again, there was a white sheen across Evelyn's glasses. Her mime often explained things much better than her words.

Frank would have ignored the incident or passed it off as one more example of German life to be handed on as a gift or a passing joke to some other fellow musician travelling in Germany. His instinct told him to keep playing his pipes and whistles even louder in spite of this Frau Klempner. But Evelyn made more of it. She treated him as a helpless musician affronted by a typically tyrannical German woman. All art and music had been assaulted by this philistine, Frau Klempner. For Frank, even though it was comforting to be defended by a young woman, the incident was amusing. For Evelyn, it was an attack on freedom. It even infringed her own privacy.

'I don't ask her to close her windows when she's cooking and the stink of onions is everywhere in the courtyard.'

Werner was far more rational. He laughed and said Frau Klempner should be ignored. She had no authority. He seemed tired and sat back in the sofa with his beer. He dismissed the whole thing with a wave of his hand which looked as though he was declining the offer of cake.

'This old one. She has nothing to say.'

Evelyn sat down facing Werner with her knees on the sofa. Her shoes had dropped to the floor. Werner had a layer of froth on his moustache. Evelyn reached over and lifted some of the froth clinging to her finger and put it in her own mouth. Werner then placed his own finger across his moustache and caught the remaining froth with his lower lip.

Three sides of the wide courtyard are covered with windows. The other is a wall clung with scaffolding. Some of the walls between the windows are peeling. Some of the windows have a white sheen across them. The workmen have gone home leaving behind an aftersound of planks and shouts.

Frank saw Evelyn coming across the courtyard in a long coat. He was on his way out while she was coming in. She carried a leather bag which was meant more for documents than for personal things. She looked different. It was the first time he had seen her wearing that coat. It was the first time he had seen her at a distance, walking towards him. She seemed smaller. The new perspective of the open courtyard with its windows and scaffolding made her look compact. He saw her as somebody he didn't know.

The furniture in her apartment makes Evelyn Richter stand out. The immured dimensions of her apartment give an illusion of size. Tables, chairs, sofa, the 18-inch television set alter her shape. The height of the pictures hung in her apartment make her seem more friendly. The poster in the kitchen of the Folies Bergère. The shoes beside the sofa make her younger, more like a child. In the courtyard, she looks smaller, fuller, more official and unknown.

She looks like part of the underground throngs. An individual

observed on a crowded train. An unknown person with an imagined unlimited biography. A person in a long beige coat carrying
a leather bag. A rather official-looking bag. A person without
gender on the way home from work. A person who buys a
monthly ticket. A young woman with a public smile for the ticket
vendor.

She looks like a person whose mother might own a dachshund
or a red setter. A person who has just bought some cheese or
unsalted butter at the cheese shop. Who paused briefly before
putting her U-Bahn ticket into her bag. Who thought she was
being stared at by an elderly man on the U-Bahn. Who avoids
making eye contact on the underground trains. Whose view of
two children is blocked by someone standing in front of her on
the U-Bahn. Who glances at the headlines of the evening paper
in someone else's hands and who looks away again because it's
unmannerly and would also form an association with the man
sitting down with his evening paper. Who holds on firmly to the
vertical bar on the U-Bahn whenever she can't get a seat. Who
looks at the familiar, numberless clock on her way out of the
U-Bahn station. Who held her bag against the counter of the
cheese shop with her knee while she took out her purse. Who
heard the combined surge of traffic behind her after she had
crossed the road. Who had hoped that the green man would
stay green a little longer.

A person who has just placed a packet of Danish cheese along
with a packet of unsalted butter into a rather official-looking
bag. Who passes the wine shop without hesitation. Passes the
Eros centre without noticing it. Who has never even been inside
a sex shop. Passes a Turkish woman in the street with her
child and wonders how a Turkish woman can wear so many
layers of clothes, even in spring. Who thinks Turkish children
look pretty. Feels a slight dampness under her arms. Thought
Danish cheese would be nice for tea. Never eats garlic. Who
has never been to South America but would love to go. Who
has never been to Ireland but who knows somebody from Ireland. Who has no wish to go to Turkey ever because there are
so many Turkish people living in Berlin. Never speaks about
school and never associates with any of her old classmates.

Who hates a man called Dieter Opp and who hopes she will never see him again. Who is not too keen on her parents coming to visit her in Berlin.

For whom the conglomerate smell of cheeses at the cheese shop becomes too much after a few minutes. Who emerges from the cheese shop and glances right and left looking for inspiration before continuing her journey home. Who loves Greek food and Greek music. Finds Irish music haunting and medieval. Cannot stand eastern music. Who used to like South American music but who has gone off it somewhat lately. Finds Irish people more European than a lot of Italians. Finds unsalted butter much more pleasant than the salted ones. Finds it incomprehensible that her brother would join the army, particularly after what happened to their father during the war. Whose father refuses to speak about the war. Who writes a letter to her brother asking him not to join the army but receives no answer from him.

Has a general phobia about posting letters which causes a moment of fear and irreversible helplessness once the letter disappears. Once had an older man from Charlottenburg for a boyfriend but put an end to it because he began to remind her too much of her father. Who still tends to compare all boyfriends with her father. Who can't help thinking about her own letter at the bottom of the yellow post-box. Who always insists on discussing all her previous affairs and relationships with any new boyfriend and expects them to do the same. Who tends to bite with abject ferocity at that moment when approaching rapture with her lover. Who was warned many times by one man never again to use her teeth but forgets herself sometimes, causing him once to walk out in the middle of the night saying he would never be back, but did return a week later and was no longer welcome. Though he managed to sleep with her once more, she made sure she didn't bite him on that final turn. Who has a steady relationship which has gone on for the past few years with one man. Who is in no rush to have a baby. Who has orgasms. Who does not bite her current boyfriend.

Is in possession of a sad feature in her eyes which illuminates a paternal longing in all men. Whose strange blend of sadness and comical appearance is noticed on the U-Bahn. Whose skin attracts mosquitoes. Whose eyes are normally hidden by her lightly tinted glasses. Who has a slight tendency to put on weight around the thighs and who suppresses this with regular swimming followed by saunas. Whose hand firmly clutches the bar on the U-Bahn between the grip of an older man and that of a younger man. Who doesn't notice the collection of knuckles along the bar. Who is observed in detail by the younger man looking at her knuckles and following her wrist along the sleeve to trace its owner. Whose head is turned away from the young man on the U-Bahn who has been studying her arm, her hair and her knuckles and contemplated pressing on one of her knuckles to make her turn around so that he could see if the face matched what the hair and knuckles promised. Whose face with its sad look does belong to the knuckles along the vertical bar.

Who received an expensive camera once from her current partner in the early days of their relationship and only shot two rolls of colour film on their first holiday after which she abandoned it. Who would very dearly like to gain possession of a particular photograph which was taken years ago on a time release which shows her smiling and clutching a bottle of champagne while being embraced from behind by Dieter Opp with his hand inside her pink knickers and his chin resting on her left shoulder glancing downwards at her naked breasts. Who is known in the cheese shop. Who carries a bag which does not look like it contains anything such as Danish cheese or unsalted butter. Of whom it is often difficult to tell whether she's looking straight ahead or downwards. Who knows what time it is. Whose hand holds the handle of her bag. Who pushes the heavy front door of the house with her shoulder. Who wears a knee-length coat. Whose arms are inside the coat. Whose hair touches the collar of the coat. Whose chin is round. Whose feet touch the ground. Who has eyes. Who can speak. Breathes, hears, sees in front of her. Is an inhabitant of Berlin.

The windows on all three sides look out on to the courtyard. The tenants can all see out on to their courtyard which has a cluster of olive trees along with some flower boxes as its central feature. It is difficult to tell when people are actually looking out on to their courtyard. Some windows are left open. The tenants are discouraged from hanging out washing through the windows.

Evelyn and Frank meet in the courtyard some ten metres away from the centre. They stop and talk for a moment. The courtyard with all its windows forces them to meet as strangers or people who just know each other vaguely. Frank is in a rush and has a box containing his instruments under his arm. With a clenched fist he tries to indicate running or lateness or hurry. Evelyn has stopped and is holding her bag with both hands. Frank tries to leave on a humorous note.

'What have you done to Frau Klempner? I haven't seen her in weeks. Have you done away with her?'

Evelyn smiles and shakes her head.

'Nothing! I leave her alone.' Evelyn has transferred her bag to the left hand.

The phone rang in the room, suspending his playing in mid-reel. There did follow just two more notes but they had already lost power. The instrument had been winded. The drones lost their momentum and expired. Even the invisible beat was over-powered by the new beat of the phone.

He placed his hand, holding the chanter, under the drones and walked over to the phone in a stoop. Placing one thigh and buttock on the armrest of the sofa, he cradled the pipes in his lap with his arm. The other leg, bound around the thigh with a leather piece like an eye-patch, was poised for balance, knee bent, ready to raise him up again. The green velvet bag with its meretricious tassels, exhaled with a final sigh of unmusical breath. He crouched over the table and picked up the white receiver.

'*Bei Richter,*' he answered. It was Werner. He spoke in a calm, unhurried English. It was unusual to talk to Werner on the phone and Frank had to visualize his moustache before he could speak. He wondered if Werner had left something behind. But Werner was very conversational. Frank explained that he was keeping the evil spirit of Frau Klempner away with the sound of his uillean pipes.

'You have no concert tonight?' Werner asked. It amused Frank that all performances, even though most of his took place in small pubs, were referred to as concerts. He had taught Evelyn to call them 'gigs'.

'No, there's nothing on tonight. No concert.'

'Frank . . . if you have no plans tonight, we could meet us somewhere. I have something to discuss with you. Can we meet us in the restaurant Zum Römer. You know this one?'

Frank agreed and asked what they were going to discuss.

'We will talk about this at dinner, Zum Römer. Can we say eight o'clock?'

Frank closed his eyes and began to play again but he couldn't regain the drive of the music. He couldn't concentrate. It wasn't the first time Werner had formally announced that he was going to discuss something. Usually it was quite straightforward. The first thing was the matter of phone calls. Werner had asked him instead of leaving money beside the phone, to record them all in a booklet beside the phone which they could add up at the end of the month. Then there was the matter of a token rent for the room. Then there was the business of the cheese. This had been split into two issues. The fact that it was unfair to take the last piece of cheese without replacing it with more. Cheese was there to be eaten but only on condition that successors were provided for as well. The other issue concerned the way the cheese was cut, which was also with successors in mind. Cheese should not be approached from all sides at once and should never be cut between knife and thumb. They had many discussions which often spilled over into broader issues, preoccupied mainly with the difference between Germany and Ireland. Only once had the discussion gone too far when Frank had said: 'The only thing wrong with Germany is that it's not surrounded by water.' All other occasions had been more than friendly and disciplined.

When Frank arrived at the restaurant, Werner and Evelyn were already sitting at a table. He was surprised to see Evelyn there. He was also surprised to see that the Römer was otherwise empty. His memory of the Römer was that of a crowded restaurant. It was early. Frank made his way over to them as directly as possible. At one stage, he was forced to walk sideways between two chairs but keeping his destination in sight. He could have carried on along the wall behind Evelyn and Werner which showed the blanched sunlit steps leading down into the warm olive-lined streetscape of southern Italy. Werner shook hands.

'I have ordered a pizza for myself. You should have one too and a nice beer.' The waiter, having stalked Frank's diagonal progress across the restaurant, timed the moment with the sliding menu. At the same time, Evelyn raised her glass of red wine to her lips. Things were unusually formal. A decision was made and the waiter left, coming back moments later with a beer for Frank.

'The pizza here is the best in all Berlin,' Werner said. 'Nearly as good as in Italy.'

'Well, I've never been to Italy so I couldn't comment.'

'Ah, you must go! Evelyn and I, we have been in Italy three times since we met. It is very expensive but we like it very much.' Frank's eyes travelled from Werner to Evelyn and then on to the beer in front of him and in another circle back to Werner and then on to Evelyn again who was nodding in agreement.

'Of course. Italy is the best country for holidays,' she said.

Werner's pizza arrived followed shortly by Frank's pizza. The waiter had brought an extra plate for Evelyn who said she could only manage a small corner. As Werner began to cut a triangular slice, she repeated; not so much, not so much. Frank suggested it might be easier to cut a pizza with a pair of scissors. They laughed. It allowed Frank to slow down the circle which his eyes made around the table from Werner over to Evelyn and down to his own beer and on to Werner's pizza and Werner himself and back to Evelyn who was sitting up with her back straight, looking down at the geometric slice on the plate in front of her. Frank's own pizza gave him something to concentrate on. Werner's moustache appeared to be damp and curled into his mouth at one point. Evelyn cut a small triangle from the big triangle and raised it to her mouth on a fork.

It doesn't take long to eat a pizza. The only things left on Frank's plate are two olive stones. On Werner's, the stems of three chilli peppers. Beyond Evelyn, on the wall, there is a pillar beyond which there is a woman bearing an urn on her way down to a hot plaza. Frank's beer is half full. Werner leans back in his chair and dusts off any possible crumbs from his trousers with his hand.

'Frank, . . . I think you are waiting for me to discuss this with you now. It is something very important to me and to Evelyn also. For two weeks now, I have been thinking. In the beginning I thought it was only in my mind, but now I think I am right. I think Evelyn is falling in love with you.'

With thumb and forefinger, Werner parts his moustache to each side. Frank looks at Evelyn who has her elbows on the table. Her hair has partly fallen over her face. He looks at the ashtray on the table and then back to Werner.

'I have spoken to Evelyn about this. It is true. She has also agreed that something is happening to her. Frank, . . . I don't want to make an accusation against you. I am not angry with you. But I think I must talk to you about this openly.'

Werner continues to explain. It has caught Frank like a compliment which he cannot instinctively deny. He could say nothing.

'I think about this every day now. All the time I think it is going to end with me and Evelyn. I think she will be in love with you very soon. I cannot stop it and I must talk to you before this happens.'

Evelyn has said nothing either. It looks almost as if she is incapable of acting involuntarily. Unharnessed. Why could she not just speak for herself? Frank's first impulse was to turn to Evelyn and ask her directly whether this was true. But her silence had already admitted it. Frank had to say something. At the same time, he didn't want to insult Evelyn by renouncing interest.

'Werner, I must say, this is a total surprise to me. I can tell you honestly, this is the first time anything of the sort entered my head.' It was too much of a defence.

'But I am not accusing you, Frank. I will not make you feel like a criminal that has betrayed me. I like you. I want to be your friend. But I think something is going to happen between Evelyn and you and this would make me very sad.'

Frank tries to assure Werner that there is no intentional threat on his side. He cannot speak for Evelyn. Evelyn is still looking at the table in front of her.

'Don't worry, Werner. I have no intention of causing any trouble like that.' Frank wonders what effect this has on Evelyn. Werner continues.

'You see, Evelyn and I, we love each other very much. We never talk about the future but we are very much in love. If this comes to an end, I cannot stop it . . . All the time, I think this will happen. I think it is going to end with us. Evelyn and I have talked about this. She has said you are very attractive. You are very sympathetic. I think this myself. You are a good friend . . . But for Evelyn, I think you are also attractive in a sexual way. I know this is very natural and I cannot stop it. But this will be a tragedy for me.'

Frank's gaze resumes its lap of the table from Werner around to Evelyn in the hope that she will say something. When she remains silent he brings his eyes down to his glass which is now almost empty. The more she continues to be silent, the more he is compelled to dissociate himself from her. But he doesn't want to dissociate himself.

Evelyn has not looked at Frank. Frank cannot look at Evelyn for too long because it would implicate him. Her silence makes him an accomplice. Frank cannot look at his beer for too long because it would confirm a plot. He cannot speak directly to Evelyn because it might be seen as collusion. Anything, even a sideways glance between them, would confirm an ongoing conversation. Frank cannot look at Werner for too long without saying something to deny it. He cannot deny it because he cannot speak for Evelyn. He cannot speak for Evelyn if she hasn't told him what's on her mind. He cannot look at the woman with the urn for too long because it might signify disinterest.

He cannot speak to Evelyn with Werner at the table. He cannot speak to Werner without talking about Evelyn.

Frank must find a way to talk to Evelyn through Werner. Or to Werner through Evelyn. He could talk to his beer with both of them.

'Look, Werner, I will tell you the truth. Evelyn happens to be one of the most beautiful women that I have ever met. I can say that unreservedly. I think you're very lucky. But Evelyn is also a good friend. And so are you. I like Evelyn very much, but that's where it stays. I couldn't possibly imagine anything further happening between us.'

Frank wonders if he is expected to offer to move out of the apartment. But this would also signify admission. He hasn't said enough. But the more he says the more he will admit duplicity. He will soon touch on the ultimate truth that he can imagine anything. Frank is not bereft of desire. He cannot play the eunuch.

Evelyn is playing with a cardboard match which she has torn from the gratis matches; '*Zum Römer, Italianische gerichte*'. Is she trying to tie a knot with the match? She must know that people can see the shape of her breasts through the jumper. Frank's eyes are trespassing. He is caught red-handed. He can only imagine being caught. Imagine being caught coming out of the Eros shop just at that moment when Evelyn is passing by. Imagine being caught in Werner and Evelyn's bedroom. He remembers being caught in an orchard; while he was hiding behind a hedge, the owner was standing right behind him.

Nothing has changed. Except that the restaurant has become more populated now. The more they sit there, the more the real possibilities become extant in their expressions. The more they discuss it the more it becomes true. Frank must take on Evelyn's silence. He must find out whether she is just enjoying a compliment or whether she really has something for him. Frank must speak to Werner on Evelyn's behalf. Perhaps a double negative somewhere might stir the veracity of her silence.

'Listen, Werner,' Frank knows how to look earnest. 'You have absolutely nothing to worry about. You don't have to worry about me and you certainly don't have to worry about Evelyn either. She may have a passing attraction for me, though I haven't noticed. But she really loves you. Anyone can see that. If she was in any way interested in me, we wouldn't be sitting around the table here. It would have been out in the open long ago. She would have said something. I definitely think it's all your imagination, Werner.'

Frank is talking for Evelyn as if she has no mind. He becomes her mouthpiece. Frank can say what she wants to say. He can make her say what she doesn't want to say. He can make her say what Werner wants to hear. He can make her say what he himself wants to hear. He can say what she never intended to say. He can make her say what she wants Werner to hear. He could make her say what she wants to say but doesn't want Werner to hear. He can say what she wants Frank to hear. He can also make her say what she doesn't want to hear herself say. He can provoke her. As long as she says nothing herself, she assents.

'Total fantasy! Any attraction that Evelyn has for me is entirely her love for Irish music. She also likes to speak English. Like everyone else, Evelyn enjoys the company of a foreigner. She loves the music and is fascinated by the way musicians live. In that way, I represent something new. Something carefree maybe. But Evelyn has much more definite views about men. I don't fit into her scheme and never would either. I'm not even her type of man. Evelyn thinks I'm too skinny. I'm too unhealthy. Evelyn would say I'm too much of a man's man. She thinks I'm too much in love with beer and music and good crack. I wouldn't be her sort in a million years.'

The sight of his empty glass between his hands gives Frank the first chance to move outside the circle. He holds his glass up in the air and looks towards the bar. A fishing net hangs over the bar, floating aloft with bottle-green buoys, illuminated with blue-green nautical lights from the midnight Adriatic.

It was almost noon when Evelyn got up. She opened the window and let in the wet, gritty sounds of cement and plastering. It came in repeated sounds of slapping cement. Shovels turning moist cement piles with a sideways slice. A repeated dash of cement against the wall followed by semicircular or circular sounds of levelling. Trowels scooped matter from mortar boards.

Evelyn's breasts rippled like fine plaster. Her hair fell to one side like sand. She turned away from the window and her thighs and bottom shimmered with movement. With one leg already in her trousers, she had to hop on that foot to get into the other side. The skin beneath her white knickers was somewhere between powder and liquid. Somewhere between solid state and fluid, held together by surface tension. As soon as she pulled her trousers up, it became more solid. Her back bent forward as she stepped into her shoes. It looked matt varnished. A light blue jumper hid the remaining skin from the warm daylight. Evelyn first put on her glasses before she turned to speak in a soft, semi-fluid voice. She left behind a cool metallic taste.

THE PARADISE LOUNGE

WILLIAM TREVOR

WILLIAM TREVOR

William Trevor was born in Mitchelstown, Co. Cork, in 1928. He started out as a sculptor but turned to writing in the 1950s. His second novel, *The Old Boys*, brought him wide recognition and won the Hawthornden Prize, the first of his many awards. He has continued to produce a flow of highly praised novels and short stories, and his own television adaptations of some of the latter have become classics of the small screen.

ON HER HIGH stool by the bar the old woman was as still as a statue. Perhaps her face is expressionless, Beatrice thought, because in repose it does not betray the extent of her years. The face itself was lavishly made up, eyes and mouth, rouge softening the wrinkles, a dusting of perfumed powder. The chin was held more than a little high, at an angle that tightened the loops of flesh beneath it. Grey hair was short beneath a black cloche hat that suggested a fashion of the past, as did the tight black skirt and black velvet coat. Eighty she'd be, Beatrice deduced, or eighty-two or -three.

'We can surely enjoy ourselves,' Beatrice's friend said, interrupting her scrutiny of the old woman. 'Surely we can, Bea?'

She turned her head. The closeness of his brick-coloured flesh and of the smile in his eyes caused her lips to tremble. She appeared to smile also, but what might have been taken for pleasure was a checking of her tears.

'Yes,' she said. 'Of course.'

They were married, though not to one another. Beatrice's friend, casually dressed for a summer weekend, was in early middle age, no longer slim yet far from bulky. Beatrice was thirty-two, petite and black-haired in a blue denim dress. Sunglasses disguised her deep-rust eyes, which was how – a long time ago now – her father had described them. She had wanted to be an actress then.

'It's best,' her friend said, repeating the brief statement for what might have been the hundredth time since they had settled into his car earlier that afternoon. The affair was over, the threat to their families averted. They had come away to say goodbye.

'Yes, I know it's best,' she said, a repetition also.

At the bar the old woman slowly raised a hand to her hat and touched it delicately with her fingers. Slowly the hand descended, and then lifted her cocktail glass. Her scarlet mouth was not quite misshapen, but age had harshly scored what once had been a perfect outline, lips pressed together like a rosebud on its side. Failure, Beatrice thought as casually she observed all this: in the end the affair was a failure. She didn't even love him any more, and long ago he'd ceased to love her. It was euphemism to call it saying goodbye: they were having a dirty weekend, there was nothing left to lift it higher than that.

'I'm sorry we couldn't manage longer,' he said. 'I'm sorry about Glengarriff.'

'It doesn't matter.'

'Even so.'

She ceased to watch the old woman at the bar. She smiled at him, again disguising tears but also wanting him to know that there were no hard feelings, for why on earth should there be?

'After all, we've been to Glengarriff,' she said, a joke because on the one occasion they'd visited the place they had nearly been discovered in their deceptions. She'd used her sister as an excuse for her absences from home: for a long time now her sister had been genuinely unwell in a farmhouse in Co. Meath, a house that fortunately for Beatrice's purpose didn't have a telephone.

'I'll never forget you,' he said, his large tanned hand suddenly on one of hers, the vein throbbing in his forehead. A line of freckles ran down beside the vein, five smudges on the redbrick skin. In winter you hardly noticed them.

'Nor I you.'

'Darling old Bea,' he said, as if they were back at the beginning.

The bar was a dim, square lounge with a scattering of small tables, one of which they occupied. Ashtrays advertised Guinness, beer-mats Heineken. Sunlight touched the darkened glass in one of two windows, drawing from it a glow that was not unlike the amber gleam of whiskey. Behind the bar itself the rows of bottles, spirits upside down above their global measures, glittered pleasantly as a centre-piece, their reflections gaudy in a cluttered mirror. The floor had a patterned carpet, further patterned with cigarette burns and a diversity of stains. The Paradise Lounge the bar had been titled in a moment of hyperbole by the grandfather of the present proprietor, a sign still proclaiming as much on the door that opened from the hotel's mahogany hall. Beatrice's friend had hesitated, for the place seemed hardly promising: Keegan's Railway Hotel in a town neither of them knew. They might have driven on, but he was tired and the sun had been in his eyes. 'It's all right,' she had reassured him.

He took their glasses to the bar and had to ring a bell because the man in charge had disappeared ten minutes ago. 'Nice evening,' he said to the old woman on the barstool, and she managed to indicate agreement without moving a muscle of her carefully held head. 'We'll have the same again,' he said to the barman, who apologized for his absence, saying he'd been mending a tap.

Left on her own, Beatrice sighed a little and took off her sunglasses. There was no need for this farewell, no need to see him for the last time in his pyjamas or to sit across a table from him at dinner and at breakfast, making conversation that once had come naturally. 'A final fling,' he'd put it, and she'd thought of someone beating a cracked drum, trying to extract a sound that wasn't there any more. How could it have come to this? The Paradise Lounge of Keegan's Railway Hotel, Saturday night in a hilly provincial town, litter caught in the railings of the Christian Brothers': how *could* this be the end of what they once had had? Saying goodbye to her, he was just somebody else's husband: the lover had slipped away.

'Well, it's a terrible bloody tap we have,' the barman was saying. 'Come hell or high water, I can't get a washer into it.'

'It can be a difficult job.'

'You could come in and say that to the wife for me, sir.'

The drinks were paid for, the transaction terminated. Further gin and Martini were poured into the old woman's glass, and Beatrice watched again while like a zombie the old woman lit a cigarette.

* * *

Miss Doheny her name was: though beautiful once, she had
never married. Every Saturday evening she met the Meldrums
in the Paradise Lounge, where they spent a few hours going
through the week that had passed, exchanging gossip and com-
menting on the world. Miss Doheny was always early and would
sit up at the bar for twenty minutes on her own, having the
extra couple of drinks that, for her, were always necessary.
Before the Meldrums arrived she would make her way to a
table in a corner, for that was where Mrs Meldrum liked to be.

It wasn't usual that other people were in the bar then.
Occasionally it filled up later but at six o'clock, before her friends
arrived, she nearly always had it to herself. Francis Keegan –
the hotel's inheritor, who also acted as barman – spent a lot of
time out in the back somewhere, attending to this or that. It
didn't matter because after their initial greeting of one another,
and a few remarks about the weather, there wasn't much conversation that Miss Doheny and he had to exchange. She
enjoyed sitting up at the bar on her own, glancing at the reflections in the long mirror behind the bottles, provided the reflections were never of herself. On the other hand it was a pleasant
enough diversion, having visitors.

Miss Doheny, who had looked twice at Beatrice and once
at her companion, guessed at their wrong-doing. Tail-ends of
conversation had drifted across the lounge, no effort being made
to lower voices since more often than not the old turn out to
be deaf. They were people from Dublin whose relationship was
not that recorded in Francis Keegan's register in the hall. Without much comment, modern life permitted their sin; the light-
brown motor car parked in front of the hotel made their
self-indulgence a simple matter.

How different it had been, Miss Doheny reflected, in 1933!
Correctly she estimated that that would have been the year
when she herself was the age the dark-haired girl was now.
In 1933 adultery and divorce and light-brown motor cars had
belonged more in America and England, read about and alien
to what already was being called the Irish way of life. 'Catholic
Ireland,' Father Horan used to say. 'Decent Catholic Ireland.'
The term was vague and yet had meaning: the emergent nation,

seeking pillars on which to build itself, had plumped for holiness
and the Irish language – natural choices in the circumstances.
'A certain class of woman,' old Father Horan used to say, 'con-
stitutes an abhorrence.' The painted women of Clancy's Picture
House – sound introduced in 1936 – were creatures who carried
a terrible warning. Jezebel women, Father Horan called them,
adding that the picture house should never have been permitted
to exist. In his grave for a quarter of a century, he would hardly
have believed his senses if he'd walked into the Paradise Lounge
in Keegan's Railway Hotel to discover two adulterers, and one
of his flock who had failed to heed his castigation of painted
women. Yet for thirty-five years Miss Doheny had strolled
through the town on Saturday evenings to this same lounge,
past the statue of the 1798 rebels, down the sharp incline of
Castle Street. On Sundays she covered the same ground again,
on the way to and from Mass. Neither rain nor cold prevented
her from making the journey to the Church of the Immaculate
Conception or to the hotel, and illness did not often afflict her.
That she had become more painted as the years piled up seemed
to Miss Doheny to be natural in the circumstances.

In the Paradise Lounge she felt particularly at home. In spring
and summer the Meldrums brought plants for her, or bunches
of chives or parsley, sometimes flowers. Not because she
wished to balance the gesture with one of her own but because
it simply pleased her to do so she brought for them a pot of
jam if she had just made some, or pieces of shortbread. At
Christmas, more formally, they exchanged gifts of a different
kind. At Christmas the lounge was decorated by Francis
Keegan, as was the hall of the hotel and the dining-room.
Once a year, in April, a dance was held in the dining-room, in
connection with a local point-to-point, and it was said in the
town that Francis Keegan made enough in the bar during the
course of that long night to last him for the next twelve months.
The hotel ticked over from April to April, the Paradise Lounge
becoming quite brisk with business when an occasional function
was held in the dining-room, though never achieving the abandoned spending that distinguished the night of the point-to-
point. Commercial travellers sometimes stayed briefly, taking

pot-luck with Mrs Keegan's cooking, which at the best of times was modest in ambition and achievement. After dinner these men would sit on one of the high stools in the Paradise Lounge, conversing with Francis Keegan and drinking bottles of stout. Mrs Keegan would sometimes put in a late appearance and sip a glass of gin and water. She was a woman of slatternly appearance, with loose grey hair and slippers. Her husband complemented her in style and manner, his purplish complexion reflecting a dedication to the wares he traded in across his bar. They were an undemanding couple, charitable in their opinions, regarded as unfortunate in the town since their union had not produced children. Because of that, Keegan's Railway Hotel was nearing the end of its days as a family concern and in a sense it was fitting that that should be so, for the railway that gave it its title had been closed in 1951.

How I envy her! Miss Doheny thought. How fortunate she is to find herself in these easy times, not condemned because she loves a man! It seemed right to Miss Doheny that a real love affair was taking place in the Paradise Lounge and that no one questioned it. Francis Keegan knew perfectly well that the couple were not man and wife, the strictures of old Father Horan were as fusty by now as neglected mice droppings. The holiness that had accompanied the birth of a nation had at last begun to shed its first tight skin: liberation, Miss Doheny said to herself, marvelling over the word.

They walked about the town because it was too soon for dinner. Many shops were still open, greengrocers anxious to rid themselves of cabbage that had been limp for days and could not yet again be offered for sale after the weekend, chemists and sweetshops. Kevin Ryan, Your Best for Hi-Fi, had arranged a loudspeaker in a window above his premises: Saturday night music blared forth, punk harmonies and a tenor rendering of 'Kelly the Boy from Killanne'. All tastes were catered for.

The streets were narrow, the traffic congested. Women picked over the greengrocers' offerings, having waited until this hour because prices would be reduced. Newly shaved men slipped into the public houses, youths and girls loitered outside

Redmond's Café and on the steps of the 1798 statue. Two dogs half-heartedly fought outside the Bank of Ireland.

The visitors to the town enquired where the castle was, and then made their way up Castle Hill. 'Opposite Castle Motors,' the child they'd asked had said, and there it was: an ivy-covered ruin, more like the remains of a cowshed. Corrugated iron sealed off an archway, its torn billposters advertising Calor Gas and a rock group, Duffy's Circus and Fine Gael, and the annual point-to-point that kept Keegan's Railway Hotel going. Houses had been demolished in this deserted area, concrete replacements only just begun. The graveyard of the Protestant church was unkempt; *New Premises in Wolfe Tone Street,* said a placard in the window of Castle Motors. Litter was everywhere.

'Not exactly camera fodder,' he said with his easy laugh. 'A bloody disgrace, some of these towns are.'

'The people don't notice, I suppose.'

'They should maybe wake themselves up.'

The first time he'd seen her, he'd afterwards said, he had heard himself whispering that it was she he should have married. They'd sat together, talking over after-dinner coffee in someone else's house. He'd told her, lightly, that he was in the Irish rope business, almost making a joke of it because that was his way. A week later his car had drawn up beside her in Rathgar Road, where she'd lived since her marriage. 'I thought I recognized you,' he said, afterwards confessing that he'd looked up her husband's name in the telephone directory. 'Come in for a drink,' she invited, and of course he had. Her two children had been there, her husband had come in.

They made their way back to the town, she taking his arm as they descended the steep hill they'd climbed. A wind had gathered, cooling the evening air.

'It feels so long ago,' she said. 'The greater part of my life appears to have occurred since that day when you first came to the house.'

'I know, Bea.'

He'd seemed extraordinary and nice, and once when he'd smiled at her she'd found herself looking away. She wasn't unhappy in her marriage, only bored by the monotony of preparing food and seeing to the house and the children. She had, as well, a reluctant feeling that she wasn't appreciated, that she hadn't been properly loved for years.

'You don't regret it happened?' he said, stepping out into the street because the pavement was still crowded outside Redmond's Café.

She pitched her voice low so that he wouldn't hear her saying she wasn't sure. She didn't want to tell a lie, she wasn't certain of the truth.

He nodded, assuming her reassurance. Once, of course, he would never have let a mumbled reply slip by.

Miss Doheny had moved from the bar and was sitting at a table with the Meldrums when Beatrice and her friend returned to the Paradise Lounge after dinner. Mrs Meldrum was telling all about the visit last Sunday afternoon of her niece, Kathleen. 'Stones she's put on,' she reported, and then recalled that Kathleen's newly acquired husband had sat there for three hours hardly saying a word. Making a fortune he was, in the dry goods business, dull but good-hearted.

Miss Doheny listened. Strangely, her mind was still on the visitors who had returned to the lounge. She'd heard the girl saying that a walk about the town would be nice, and as the Meldrums had entered the lounge an hour or so ago she'd heard the man's voice in the hall and had guessed they were then on their way to the dining-room. The dinner would not have been good, for Miss Doheny had often heard complaints about the nature of Mrs Keegan's cooking. And yet the dinner, naturally, would not have mattered in the least.

Mrs Meldrum's voice continued: Kathleen's four children by her first marriage were all grown up and off her hands, she was lucky to have married so late in life into a prosperous dry goods business. Mr Meldrum inclined his head or nodded, but from time to time he would also issue a mild contradiction, setting the facts straight, regulating his wife's memory. He was a grey-haired man in a tweed jacket, very tall and thin, his face as sharp as a blade, his grey moustache well cared-for. He smoked while he drank, allowing a precise ten minutes to elapse between the end of one cigarette and the lighting of the next. Mrs Meldrum was smaller than her companions by quite some inches, round and plump, with glasses and a black hat.

The strangers were drinking Drambuie now, Miss Doheny noticed. The man made a joke, probably about the food they'd eaten; the girl smiled. It was difficult to understand why it was that they were so clearly not man and wife. There was a wistfulness in the girl's face, but the wistfulness said nothing very much. In a surprising way Miss Doheny imagined herself crossing the lounge to where they were. 'You're lucky, you know,' she heard herself saying. 'Honestly, you're lucky, child.' She glanced again in the girl's direction and for a moment caught her eye. She almost mouthed the words, but changed her mind because as much as possible she liked to keep her face in repose.

Beatrice listened to her companion's efforts to cheer the occasion up. The town and the hotel – especially the meal they'd just consumed – combined to reflect the mood that the end of the affair had already generated. They were here, Beatrice informed herself again, not really to say goodbye to one another but to commit adultery for the last time. They would enjoy it as they always had, but the enjoyment would not be the same as that inspired by the love there had been. They might not have come, they might more elegantly have said goodbye, yet their presence in a bar ridiculously named the Paradise Lounge seemed suddenly apt. The bedroom where acts of mechanical passion would take place had a dingy wallpaper, its flattened pink soap already used by someone else. Dirty weekend, Beatrice thought again, for stripped of love all that was left was the mess of deception and lies there had been, of theft and this remaining, too ordinary desire. Her sister, slowly dying in the farmhouse, had been a bitter confidante and would never forgive her now. Tonight in a provincial bedroom a manufacturer of rope would have his way with her and she would have her way with him. There would be their nakedness and their mingled sweat.

'I thought that steak would walk away,' he spiritedly was continuing now. 'Being somebody's shoe-leather.'

She suddenly felt drunk, and wanted to be drunker. She held her glass towards him. 'Let's just drink,' she said.

She caught the eye of the old woman at the other table and for a moment sensed Miss Doheny's desire to communicate with her. It puzzled her that an elderly woman whom she did not know should wish to say something, yet she strongly felt that this was so. Then Miss Doheny returned her attention to what the other old woman was saying.

When they'd finished the drinks that Beatrice's companion had just fetched they moved from the table they were at and sat on two barstools, listening to Francis Keegan telling them about the annual liveliness in the hotel on the night of the April point-to-point. Mrs Keegan appeared at his side and recalled an occasion when two crates of day-old chicks, deposited in the hall of the hotel for a couple of hours, had been released by some of the wilder spirits and how old Packy O'Brien had imagined he'd caught the d.t.'s when he saw them fluttering up the stairs. And there was the story – before Mrs Keegan's time, as she was swift to point out – when Jack Doyle and Movita had stayed in Keegan's, when just for the hell of it Jack Doyle had chased a honeymoon couple up Castle Hill, half naked from their bed. After several further drinks, Beatrice began to laugh. She felt much less forlorn now that the faces of Francis Keegan and his wife were beginning to float agreeably in her vision. When she looked at the elderly trio in the corner, the only other people in the lounge, their faces floated also.

The thin old man came to the bar for more drinks and cigarettes. He nodded and smiled at Beatrice; he remarked upon the weather. 'Mr Meldrum,' said Francis Keegan by way of introduction. 'How d'you do,' Beatrice said.

Her companion yawned and appeared to be suggesting that they should go to bed. Beatrice took no notice. She pushed her glass at Francis Keegan, reaching for her handbag and announcing that it was her round. 'A drink for everyone,' she said, aware that when she gestured towards the Keegans and the elderly trio she almost lost her balance. She giggled. 'Definitely my round,' she slurred, giggling again.

Mrs Keegan told another story, about a commercial traveller called Artie Logan who had become drunk in his room and had sent down for so many trays of tea and buttered bread that every cup and saucer in the hotel had been carried up to him. 'They said to thank you,' her husband passed on, returning from the elderly trio's table. Beatrice turned her head. All three of them were looking at her, their faces still slipping about a bit. Their glasses were raised in her direction. 'Good luck,' the old man called out.

It was then that Beatrice realized. She looked from face to face, making herself smile to acknowledge the good wishes she was being offered, the truth she sensed seeming to emerge from a blur of features and clothes and three raised glasses. She nodded, and saw the heads turn away again. It had remained unstated: the love that was there had never in any way been exposed. In this claustrophobic town, in this very lounge, there had been the endless lingering of a silent passion, startlingly different from the instant requiting of her own.

Through the muzziness of inebriation Beatrice glanced again across the bar. Behind her the Keegans were laughing, and the man she'd once so intensely loved was loudly laughing also. She heard the sound of the laughter strangely, as if it echoed from a distance, and she thought for a moment that it did not belong in the Paradise Lounge, that only the two old women and the old man belonged there. He was loved, and in silence he returned that love. His plump, bespectacled wife had never had reason to feel betrayed; no shame or guilt attached. In all the years a sister's dying had never been made use of. Nor had there been hasty afternoons in Rathgar Road, blinds drawn against neighbours who might guess, a bedroom set to rights before children came in from school. There hadn't been a single embrace.

Yet the love that had continued for so long would go on now until the grave: without even thinking, Beatrice knew that that was so. The old woman paraded for a purpose the remnants of her beauty, the man was elegant in his tweed. How lovely that was! Beatrice thought, still muzzily surveying the people at the table, the wife who had not been deceived quite contentedly chatting, the two who belonged together occupying their magic worlds.

How lovely that nothing had been destroyed: Beatrice wanted to tell someone that, but there was no one to tell. In Rathgar Road her children would be watching the television, their father sitting with them. Her sister would die before the year was finished. What cruelty there seemed to be, and more sharply now she recalled the afternoon bedroom set to rights and her sister's wasted face. She wanted to run away, to go backwards into time so that she might shake her head at her lover on the night they'd first met.

Miss Doheny passed through the darkened town, a familiar figure on a Saturday night. It had been the same as always, sitting there, close to him, the smoke drifting from the cigarette that lolled between his fingers. The girl by now would be close in a different way to the man who was somebody else's husband also. As in a film, their clothes would be scattered about the room that had been hired for love, their murmurs would break a silence. Tears ran through Miss Doheny's meticulous make-up, as often they did when she walked away from the Paradise Lounge on a Saturday night. It was difficult sometimes not to weep when she thought about the easy times that had come about in her lifetime, mocking the agony of her stifled love.

THE STRANGE DISEASE

LIAM O'FLAHERTY

LIAM O'FLAHERTY

Liam O'Flaherty was born in 1896 on Inishmore, the largest of the three Aran Islands, and educated locally and at Blackrock College, Co. Dublin. He won a scholarship to University College, Dublin, but spent only a year there before joining the Irish Guards in 1915. He fought at the Somme, was shell-shocked and discharged on medical grounds. After fighting on the Republican side in the Irish Civil War, he began to write seriously, producing fifteen novels as well as over one hundred short stories, and it is on the latter that his reputation mainly rests. He died in 1984.

AT DAWN, ON a wild October morning, a red-bearded rider came from the mountains into the seaside village of Carrig. He came looking for a priest. At the parochial house he said in a loud voice that a man in the hamlet of Prochlais was on the point of death from an unknown disease. The doctor was away, he said, and the district nurse declared that it was neither typhus nor scarlet fever nor any kind of pock known to her, and that a priest should be brought. The sick man's name was Lydon. He was a strong young man five days ago. Now he was moaning on his belly, refusing food and drink.

When the parish priest was awakened from his sleep, he growled and told his housekeeper to send the rider to the curate's house. So the curate was roused and mounted on the white mare that the rider had brought from the mountains.

'The wind'll be in yer back,' roared the man with the red beard to the curate, 'so you best go straight over Cockrae and then down over the Devil's Pass into our village. She's a good mare, only whip her on her right flank, never on her left.'

The curate galloped away on the white mare. Then the man with the red beard roused the tavern keeper. Shaking the rain out of his long beard, he stood on the floor and told everybody in a loud and furious voice that a strange disease had stricken a young man in his village; a strong young man called Lydon, who was now lying on his belly, moaning and refusing food and drink. He said it was a strange disease the man had and that the people were afraid of it.

The curate lashed his horse up the mountain road, grumbling at the unseemly hour and the rain and the storm that was cutting into his back from the sea behind. He was approaching middle age, but although he had been twenty years wandering around the wild district from parish to parish, he was still terrified of the people and considered them to be no whit more civilized than wild men of the African forests. Especially the natives of Prochlais where he was going. And this strange new disease?

'What on earth can it be now?' he thought.

The rain pattered on his black waterproof cape and on his felt hat that was slouching about his ears. He shuddered with fear, both of the fury of nature and of the strange disease he was going to encounter in the barbarous hamlet among the mountains.

When the ascending road grew steeper, the white mare broke from a gallop into that crouching trot which is peculiar to mountain horses. She moved as if dragging a heavy weight, with her hind legs spread and her neck stretched, scattering loose stones from the rough road with her scrambling hoofs. Here there were overhanging trees and the wind died down behind the shoulder of a hill. The rain fell heavier with a soft, mournful, thudding sound. Sodden leaves floated down from the tree branches and an odd bird, breaking from its shelter, fluttered on ragged wet wings farther into the woods. Streams of water, reddened by the granite soil, gurgled through the cavities of the road and splashed against the mare's white flanks and against the black coat of the priest. They passed the trees, on through a rocky gorge, past a herd's cottage and then came to a wide moor covered with heather and black bog. The sky sank low about them. The horizon became a sloping bank of sagging mist, quite close. The rain poured down aslant, driven by a furious whistling wind.

The curate was drenched to the bone. He grew furious with the strange disease that had befallen the unknown man in that weird hamlet that was an eyesore on God's earth. And why should he be dragged out at dawn, drenched with rain and frozen to the marrow by a cruel wind for this unnecessary, savage man, who had contracted a strange disease? The ghostly, desolate place became full of spooks and witch devils in his imagination. He lashed the mare furiously.

Goaded by the stinging whip, the dripping mare stretched out into a fierce gallop along the dull-sounding bog road, up a steep ascent into the narrow gullet of the Devil's Pass. Here the shaggy rocks rose frowning like macabre statues and drooping heads, in zigzag rows, and the narrow road wound among them, descending slowly, until it debouched precipitously into a gloomy valley that was walled with great round mountains. Through the rain and clouds of mist the hamlet of Prochlais became visible at the bottom of the valley, a desolate, grey place, huddled among rocks and willow trees, by the bank of a stream that wandered through marshland. The mare neighed when she saw it, and flew into a headlong pace, scarcely touching the road. The curate hung on grimly, with his hands grasping her mane and his coat about his ears.

They halted in the village street. The village people crowded around, shouting to one another. They helped the priest to dismount. He looked around at them, frowning.

He only knew them very slightly, as the priests of the parish avoided this village as much as possible. They said nothing could be done for these people. They were full of superstition, wild, untamable people, incapable of understanding the subtleties of the Christian faith, by profession sheep stealers. But as they stole sheep from one another they did not profit very much by that trade. Walled in by their mountains as in a prison, intermarriage had bred lunacy and decadence amongst them. Their houses were hovels. It was impossible to get any of them to pay their clerical dues, yet they were always begging at the parochial house.

That was the opinion held of them by the priests and in particular by the curate, who secretly loathed them and considered them entirely unnecessary human beings, although from the altar he was forced to admit that they were of value in the hereafter because of their immortal souls.

At this moment, as he stood among them, drenched to the skin and numb with the cold, still fasting, he wished that the ground would open up and swallow the wretches; especially the one who had the strange disease.

'Where is the man who has the strange disease?' he cried angrily.

The people had been babbling until he spoke. Then their joy

at seeing a stranger gave way to their fear of the strange disease that had appeared among them. They became silent. A woman came forward, curtsied and said that she was the sick man's mother. Walking sideways, through courtesy, she led the priest to an old thatched hovel, that had no window in its front wall. Smoke was coming out the doorway. Then she stepped aside, curtsied with queenly grace and begged the priest 'to honour her humble hut by blessing it with his sacred presence'. The priest entered the kitchen. She followed him. The whole village crowded around the door.

At first the curate could see nothing in the room. On the hearth there was a turf fire, which emitted an extraordinary quantity of smoke without making any blaze. The smoke did not go up the chimney, as they probably had not cleaned it for years. So that the kitchen was dense with smoke. The curate began to cough and his eyes became rheumy. That aggravated his rage.

'Have you no light?' he said.

The woman fetched a candle, stuck it into the fire and brought it forth flickering, covered with yellow ashes and melting tallow. She held the disreputable candle over her head and pointed to a corner of the room.

'There he is, Father,' she said.

The priest went to the corner and looked down. On the earthen floor there was a rough straw mattress. A young man, fully dressed, lay face downwards, on the mattress.

'Is this the sick man?' said the priest.

'Yes, Father,' said the woman.

The priest took the candle and put it on the rough chair that had been placed beside the mattress. He stooped down and touched the recumbent figure.

'Is he asleep?' he said.

'No, Father,' murmured the sick man in a mournful, but very strong voice.

'Ha,' said the priest angrily, standing up suddenly. 'You don't speak like a sick man.'

The sick man sat up and looked at the priest. His face was close to the flickering candle. It stood out, deadly pale and frenzied, with large blue eyes and thick lips. He wore a blue jersey that left his powerful neck exposed. He had a magnificent neck, rising like a pyramid to a skull that was also beautiful. His foolish features, pale and decadent, looked sacrilegious, facing such a glorious pedestal. His limbs and frame loomed large and soft in the gloom.

'Tell them to leave the room, Father,' he said in a whining voice. 'I want to speak to ye.'

'Clear out, all of you,' said the priest.

'Well?' he continued, when everybody had gone.

There was an awkward silence. The sick man was trying to say something, but although his lips moved, no sound came from them. He passed a large soft hand back and forth over his closely shorn skull irresolutely.

'Let's see,' said the curate irritably. 'What's your name?'

'Patrick Lydon, Father.'

'How old are you?'

'Twenty-two, Father.'

'Ha! And . . . have you a pain? Come on, man, speak up.'

'Uh . . . uh . . .' stammered the man. 'Father, will ye put out the candle?'

'What?'

'I'm ashamed to tell ye, Father,' cried the fellow in a loud, trembling voice. 'But if ye put out the candle it 'u'd be easier to tell ye in the dark. I'm ashamed o' me life.'

'What on earth . . . ?'

'Ah, Father . . .'

'All right, all right, I'll put it out.'

The priest quenched the candle. The sick man seized the candle with his trembling hand and took it off the chair.

'Would ye sit down, Father?' he blubbered. 'It 'u'd be easier for me to tell ye if ye were sittin' down beside me. I'm ashamed o' me life.'

'Eh?' said the priest.

He sat down.

'Go ahead now,' he said.

The man clutched the priest's knee and began to weep aloud.

'Oh! Father,' he said, 'I'm ashamed o' me life. I . . . I . . .'

'What?'

'I . . . I . . . I . . .'

'Speak, you fool. What is it?'

'I . . . I . . . I'm in lo-o-o-ve, Father.'

He threw himself on the mattress and began to moan.

'What?' gasped the priest. 'Eh? You . . . you . . . My God! I'll . . . I'll . . .'

'Don't curse me, Father,' said the man, springing up again. 'It's Nora Tierney, Father, I'm in love with, the blacksmith's wife, and I'm afraid to look at her; but her face does be beckoning to me and I can't swallow me breath. Anoint me, Father, 'cos I want to die. But don't curse me.'

The priest stood up, made a noise with his lips and then raised his hands to his face. His rage burst forth. He thought of the ride through the blinding rain and the wind, and the misery of life tending on such wretches. He rushed to the door.

'Hand me that whip,' he yelled.

They brought him the whip. The sick man began to scream.

'Don't curse me, Father,' he cried.

The priest began to lash him furiously. Then the lout jumped up and ran to the door, uttering piercing yells, which were lusty with vigorous health. He ran down the village street and vaulted a stone fence into the bog. He kept on running, yelling all the while.

'Glory be to God,' said somebody, 'he's cured. What ailed him at all?'

'Eh?' said the priest, brandishing his whip. 'Bring me my horse.'

The villagers gaped in silence, terrified, as he mounted his horse and rode away. No one dared speak to him, to inquire what had happened.

Riding slowly up the mountain road, the priest kept shuddering with cold and anger. Tears of indignation and hopeless misery came into his eyes. The hopelessness of trying to vent his anger on the idiotic villagers made him want to cry like a child.

Then at last he drew a deep breath, dilated his eyes and turned his wrath on the devil, who was the cause of the whole thing. He threatened the sagging clouds with his clenched fist and cried out aloud: 'This disgusting . . . this DEGRADING passion of love.'

ACKNOWLEDGEMENTS

For permission to reprint the stories specified we are indebted to:

Michael Coady: 'Watch Out For Paradise Lost', copyright © Michael Coady 1976. Reprinted by permission of the author.

Emma Cooke: 'Female Forms' from *Female Forms* (Poolbeg Press), copyright © Emma Cooke 1980. Reprinted by permission of the author.

Daniel Corkery: 'The Spanceled' from *A Munster Twilight* (The Talbot Press, 1916). Reprinted by permission of The Educational Company of Ireland.

Michael Curtin: 'The White House', copyright © Michael Curtin 1973. Reprinted by permission of the author.

Ita Daly: 'Aimez-Vous Colette?' from *The Lady With The Red Shoes* (Poolbeg Press), copyright © Ita Daly 1980. Reprinted by permission of the author.

Anne Devlin: 'Sam' from *The Way-Paver* (Faber and Faber), copyright © Anne Devlin 1986. Reprinted by permission of Sheil Land Associates.

Mary Dorcey: 'The Husband' from *A Noise In The Woodshed* (Onlywomen Press), copyright © Mary Dorcey 1989. Reprinted by permission of the author.

Patrick Doyle: 'The Dropper', copyright © Patrick Doyle 1986. Reprinted by permission of the author.

Anne Enright: 'Seascape' from *First Fictions: Introduction 10* (Faber and Faber), copyright © Anne Enright 1989. Reprinted by permission of the author.

Hugo Hamilton: 'The Compound Assembly of E. Richter' from *First Fictions: Introduction 10* (Faber and Faber, 1989), copy-